ERIN MAKELA

Worthy of Trust

That Word Honor
• Book 1 •

That Word Honor, Book I: Worthy of Trust © 2025 by Erin Makela. All rights reserved. No part of this book may be reproduced in any form whatsoever, by photography or xerography or by any other means, by broadcast or transmission, by translation into any kind of language, nor by recording electronically or otherwise, without permission in writing from the author, except by a reviewer, who may quote brief passages in critical articles or reviews.

This is a work of fiction. Names, characters, places, and incidents are either the products of the author's imagination or, if real, are used in a fictitious manner.

Edited by Kerry Stapley
Cover illustration by Curtis Makela
Map illustrations by Tyler Makela

ISBN 13: 978-1-64343-551-0
Library of Congress Catalog Number: 2024926143
Printed in the United States of America
First Printing: 2025
29 28 27 26 25   5 4 3 2 1

Book design and typesetting Dan Pitts

Beaver's Pond Press
526 Seventh Street West
Saint Paul, MN 55102
(952) 829-8818
www.BeaversPondPress.com

Contact Erin Makela at erinmakela.com for speaking engagements, book club discussions, and interviews.

"Our commander is a gentleman worthy of the trust reposed in him; a man, I believe, of invincible courage; a man of great prudence; ever serene; he defies the greatest danger to affect him, or difficulties to alter his temper; in fine, you will ever see him the intrepid hero, and the unruffled Christian."

—An officer under Colonel Benedict Arnold, November 21, 1775

*Dedicated to my family—
Mom, Dad, Kyle, Curtis, and Tyler—
my first reading buddies, story developers,
writing partners, and editors*

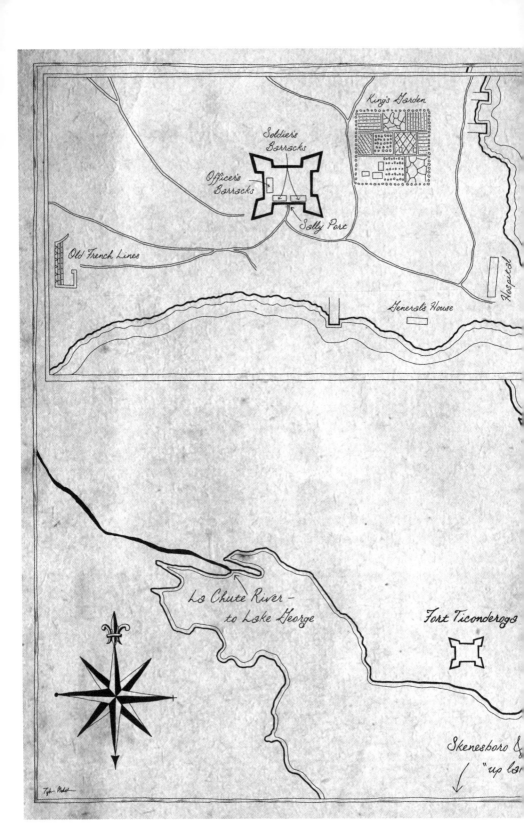

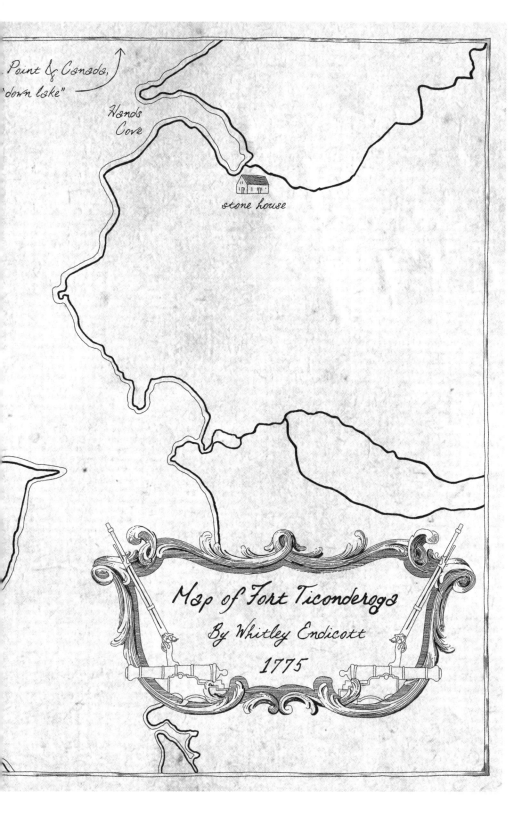

Reuni

Trois-Rivières
Battle 8 June, 177

Lac Saint-Pierre

St Lawrence River

Richelieu River

Montreal
Taken 13 Nov. 1775

Chambly
Taken 18 Oct. 1775

Saint-Jean
In siege 17 Sept-3 Nov. 1775

Ile-aux-Noix
Arrive 2 Sept. 1775

To Lk Champlain
&
Fort Ti

nte-aux-Trembles   Quebec
2 Dec, 1775   Battle 31 Dec, 1775
                   In siege 1 Jan - 6 May, 1776

Map of the American Expedition
in Canada
By Whitley Endicott
1775 - 1776

Author's Note on Terminology

Because this is a work of historical fiction, I have tried to remain true to the terminology used at the time. Through the first half of this novel, several terms are used to refer to the British Army (*Ministerial Army, Parliament's Army, Redcoats, Lobsterbacks*) since at the beginning of the conflict, the colonists saw Parliament, rather than the king, as the aggressor, and they saw themselves as British.

Indian(s) is used as opposed to the more modern *Native American(s)* or *First Nations People(s)*, and I try to remain true to the attitudes toward Native Americans that would have been held by the colonists and early Americans of the time.

Terminology for members of the LGBTQIA+ community has changed greatly since the 1700s. Instead of using offensive terms, I refrain from using any.

Falstaff: Honor pricks me on. Yea, but how if honor prick me off when I come on? How then? Can honor set to a leg? No. Or an arm? No. Or take away the grief of a wound? No. Honor hath no skill in surgery, then? No. What is honor? A word. What is in that word honor? What is that honor? Air. A trim reckoning! Who hath it? He that died a' Wednesday. Doth he feel it? No. Doth he hear it? No. 'Tis insensible, then. Yea, to the dead. But will it not live with the living? No. Why? Detraction will not suffer it. Therefore I'll none of it, honor is a mere scutcheon. and so ends my catechism.

Henry IV, Part 1
by William Shakespeare

The stranger at my fireside cannot see
The forms I see, nor hear the sounds I hear;
He but perceives what is; while unto me
All that has been is visible and clear.

"Haunted Houses"
by Henry Wadsworth Longfellow

Prologue
Boston

February 22, 1770

The February snowflakes melted on my tongue, leaving only a ghost of taste—not like fat, sweet December snowflakes, full of hope and new beginnings. Still, I smiled. I had slipped away from Zadock, my least-favorite older brother, who had been sent to fetch me from Midwife Rowe's. I'd used the narrow alleys and close-set buildings of Boston's North End to escape him, the houses and shops like friends sheltering me from his tattletale eyes. There was no way the sniveler was still looking for me in the cold, slushy streets. Surely, he had gone whining home already. I figured I had a half hour until Ma found me and dragged me home, giving me a tongue lashing the whole way.

But a half hour alone—no brothers, no sisters, no monotonous chores—was worth a lecture from Ma.

Leaning against the wall of Mr. Lillie's dry goods shop, I stretched out my tongue for the next flake, recalling what I'd learned at Midwife Rowe's. My brothers' school had been closed for the day, but if I wanted to become a midwife, I couldn't afford a day off.

Another snowflake landed on my tongue when a rumble rolled up Middle Street.

It was a sound every Bostonian knew well.

A mob.

It was self-preservation to be able to read the sounds and moods of a mob. Echoes bounced off the looming buildings, and those echoes said, *excitement.* They said, *hunger.*

I glanced at the sign hanging on Mr. Lillie's window—hand painted, and not by Mr. Lillie, for it accused him of breaking the merchants' non-importation agreement. Certain as Ma would ground me, that mob was coming for Mr. Lillie and was made up of Sons of Liberty.

Chances were, some of my brothers were among them.

I should have gone home. That would have been safe and sensible.

Instead, I stepped toward the mob, searching the motley collection of men and boys for my brothers, Winborn and Lemuel. Behind me, the shop door creaked open, and Mr. Richardson, Mr. Lillie's neighbor and a custom's officer, peeped out, cursed, and ducked back inside. The lock slammed home.

"No English goods!"

"Close the shop!"

"Oath-breaker!"

The mob chanted and waved signs; two boys dragged a cart of vegetable rot, an indication the mob meant mischief, not violence. Flanking the cart like an honor guard were my brothers and our friends Sammy Gore and Kit Seider.

Lemuel was four years older than Win and me, and he fancied himself the boss even though he was nowhere near our oldest sibling. Win was my twin, and if I had been a boy, no one would have been able to tell us apart. Hair golden brown like warm, honey-sweetened tea; eyes a little darker; upturned noses Ma called impish; mouths that naturally settled into smiles. Win waved, but Lem frowned at me. "What are you doing, Whitley? You shouldn't be here. It's dangerous. Go home."

Win coughed. If anyone shouldn't be out in a mob, it was him. If he got so much as a sniffle, he'd be ill for weeks, and I knew exactly what Ma would say if she heard him cough. But of course, Lem had given in to Win. Everyone, except Ma, let him get away with anything. "If Win can be here, so can I. Just because I'm a girl doesn't mean I can't do everything you can do."

"Can you do this?" Kit scooped up a handful of vegetable rot and threw it at the shop to the cheers of the mob.

"I can do better." I stuffed my mittens in my pocket and pretended my hand was only shaking from the cold. Grinning, Win reached into the cart, too. We were thinking the same thing. We'd never needed words to communicate.

Clutching handfuls of cold, fetid slime, we ran to Mr. Lillie's windows and smeared the rot across the frosted glass. The mob cheered us on, and I couldn't keep from flashing a giddy grin at Lem, Kit, and Sammy even as I wiped my hand clean on my apron.

But no one in the shop responded, and the mob grew bolder and louder, the echoes doubling the threat we posed. Snow and rocks hurtled toward the shop, and I tossed another handful of vegetable rot.

Cracking open the door, Mr. Richardson yelled, "Go home, all of you! Mr. Lillie's done nothing more than conduct his business! As have the men you follow—like that smuggler, John Hancock!"

We shouted him down, pelting him with snow and rot. He closed the door, but the moment we stopped throwing things, he stepped outside, shutting the shop door behind him. He stood before us, unarmed. Kit whistled, and Lem muttered, "He's a fool, but he sure has guts."

Mr. Richardson raised his hands. "Go home, all of you! Or I'll call out the regiment!"

"Informer!" someone shouted, and the mob growled, the last traces of good humor falling away. The hairs on the back of my neck prickled. I reached for Win, but he was raising his arm to throw again. Win's missile joined dozens of others, splattering Mr. Richardson's coat, hair, and face. He turned back to the shop door, but no one inside would let him in. As he faced the street once more, a chunk of ice cut across his cheek, drawing blood. Hands over his head, Mr. Richardson ran next door to his house.

"Get the Tory!" Kit screamed.

"Get him!" Win, Lem, and Sammy echoed, and I was swept along as we chased Mr. Richardson. Caught up in the frenzy, I pelted him, too, standing up against Parliament's taxes like Da and my brothers did. Standing up for our rights as English citizens.

Mr. Richardson leaned out his second-story window, shaking his musket, finger on the trigger. "By the eternal God, I will make it too hot for some of you before night!"

Unafraid, the mob screamed, bottles joining the snow, rocks, and ice. Glass shattered, and inside the house, a woman shrieked. Suddenly the danger was real, and I knew why Da and Ma forbid us from mobbing. Anger was mounting faster than the falling snow, and this wasn't fun anymore.

I grasped Win's hand. "We need to go home!"

His eyes were as wide and scared as mine. He tugged at Lem and Kit. "Let's go! "

"Not until the Tory surrenders!" Kit yelled, stepping right in front of Win and me, poised to throw a bottle.

Crack!

"I should take my sister home."

Dr. Warren shook his head. "I need to examine her as well." He instructed the men with him to carry Sammy and Kit to his surgery. Folding my hand in his, he helped me to my feet. "A girl as brave as you has the makings of a doctor."

Chapter One
April 19, 1775

Kit stared as my trembling knife hovered above the wounded militiaman.

We stood in the kitchen of Deacon Joseph Adams's Menotomy home—me, Kit, and Adams's nine-year-old son, Joel. Joel's eyes kept darting from the wounded man to me, from the knife in my hand to the blood dripping from the man's wounds onto the crisp, white sheet covering the kitchen table.

Mrs. Adams had spread the sheet as we'd carried the wounded in. "Don't want to be chopping vegetables on bloody tables when this is done," she'd said.

But the sheet looked too much like snow, and blood on snow always reminded me of—

Kit hadn't moved, his ghostly gaze still fixed on my hand. He wore the same clothes he'd died in: trousers worn thin at the knees, shirt untucked beneath his jacket, scarf trailing from his neck. Snow clung, half melted, to his dark hair. His eyes, once mischief-bright, had become a pale imitation of life.

"Doctor?" The militiaman's voice was weak and labored. *Doctor* was not an appellation I was used to. But if I were to do this, to serve the cause by treating the wounded, I would not only have to adjust to it but live up to it. "Can you save me?"

He had twelve musket-ball wounds, somehow none of them immediately fatal. They were scattered across his body—arm, shoulder, side, calf. He was a human mess of blood and lead and pain, and I wasn't sure I had the skills to save him. "What's your name?"

"Dennison. Denny."

Live up to the title. I tried to look as confident and sure as Dr. Warren always did, but I couldn't keep from rubbing my fingers over the scars on my right palm. "Well, Denny, you'll be up and about in no time."

But where to start? I'd never seen anything like this before. The people I'd treated over the last five years had been in household accidents, fistfights, or maybe a hunting accident. Most had been ill, not wounded.

Yet Denny had been luckier than most I'd seen as Dr. David Townsend and I had followed the trail of blood and bodies five miles from Lexington to Menotomy. The dead, lying in the back of Buckman Tavern, peppered with musket balls or killed as they were leaving Lexington Green; the gaping new wound in the militiaman I'd sewn up just minutes earlier; men bayoneted behind trees green with new leaves or hacked by tomahawks against fence posts. But Menotomy . . .

We'd smelled Menotomy before we saw it, not just the acrid bite of gunpowder, which fogged the entire countryside, but blood, the rich scent of it heavy in the air like the coming of a storm. By the time we'd reached the little crossroads town, the torrent of Redcoats had already wreaked its havoc and blown on toward Cambridge, leaving only bloody butchery behind.

Even in this house, where no one had died, possibly the only house in Menotomy that could make such a claim, the stench of blood and gunpowder filled my nose, mixing bewilderingly with the aroma of a meat pie cooking in the oven, a malty trace of beer, and the fresh, milky fragrance of the newborn in her cradle by the fireplace.

A babe in this place of blood and death. Dear God, why had I left Boston? What was I doing in Menotomy with a dying man on the table when I—

"What should I do?" Joel's clear, innocent voice broke through my rising panic. No longer innocent, I reminded myself. The Redcoats had looted the house while holding Joel, his mother, and his sisters at gunpoint. Then, they had set the house on fire, the flames quickly doused with home-brewed beer as soon as the soldiers left. Had Deacon Adams still been in the house, they might have killed the whole family.

But when David and I had arrived and asked to use the house as a surgery, Mrs. Adams hadn't hesitated, and both she and Joel had volunteered to assist us while the two older girls prepared dinner and took turns searching the town for more wounded.

When an injury is complicated, Dr. Warren's voice echoed from my training, *take it one element at a time.*

If I took each wound on its own, instead of the whole at once . . . Suddenly, what lay before me seemed a little less daunting.

"Tighten the tourniquets," I instructed Joel, my voice somehow steady as I pointed to the belts and strips of cloth secured above the wounds. If we were in Boston, we'd have proper screw tourniquets. Of course, if we were in Boston, I wouldn't be facing wounds like these.

As Joel tightened the knots, I adjusted the lanterns to throw as much light onto the wounds as possible. Then, I made Denny drink a large draught of rum.

"Good?" Joel asked, tugging at the last tourniquet.

"As good as any sailor," I said, borrowing a phrase from my brother Josiah. "Your mother have a spoon with a thick handle?"

While I rolled up my sleeves, he scampered across the floor, setting the cradle rocking. The baby started to fuss. On the way back with the spoon, Joel slowed the cradle and ran a finger over her cheek. He held the spoon out to me. "Here."

I fitted it between Denny's teeth, then placed Joel's hands carefully on either side of his head. "Your job is to hold his head still so he doesn't hurt himself. He's going to move, and he's going to make noise. If he starts moving too much, you'll give him more rum. Understood?"

"Yes, Doctor."

He seemed far too young to be assisting me, but I had already been working with Midwife Rowe at his age, and only a year later, I had been apprenticed to Dr. Warren. I had to trust he could do this because there wasn't anyone else.

"I'll make this as quick and painless as I can, Denny." Using my forceps, I dug out the first musket ball, and it plonked on the bare boards by my feet. Denny groaned and twitched, but he held tight to the edges of the table, doing his best not to move. Another fragment out, and I shoved my sleeves above my elbows. Stupid things wouldn't stay, and they were already blood soaked. They fell again as I moved to the next wound, and I huffed in frustration.

"Here." Joel rolled my sleeves and secured them with lengths of cloth we hadn't used as tourniquets.

"Thanks." I dug into the next wound, lying across Denny's knees to keep him still. Kit still stood at the foot of the table, my fingers tingling under his stare. These injuries were so like those which had killed him, it was impossible not to think of that day—the snow, the shouting, the gunshot, Kit's blood warm between my freezing fingers.

"Whit, are you done?" David called from the dining room. "I need you."

I blinked out of my memories. "I have a few wounds yet to close."

"I can close them," Mrs. Adams said, entering from the garden. "I've been sewing clothes for long enough. At least the stitches will be straight."

Stitching skin wasn't the same as sewing a seam, but she would discover that for herself soon enough. I handed her the needle and joined David. He had been Dr. Warren's apprentice when I first began my apprenticeship, and we had worked together often, though he had started his own practice in '73. "What do you need me to do?"

"Stitch up the bayonet wounds while I work on his jaw." Half of the man's jaw had been shot away, and he had enough bayonet wounds to make a sieve of his body. One wound at a time, I reminded myself, and began.

By the time we finished, the smell of meat pie had become torture as I hadn't eaten since leaving Boston at dawn. Both our patients still lived, and as long as they were alive in the morning and the wounds hadn't soured, they had a good chance of surviving. The Adams's girls had returned with only a few men suffering minor wounds, which were quickly tended. I stretched the stiffness from my muscles, only then realizing Kit was gone.

Where, I wondered—not for the first time—did Kit go when I couldn't see him? Was there some land of ghosts beyond human sight? Did he return home to see his family? And why did he keep returning to me?

"You'll stay the night," Mrs. Adams declared from the kitchen doorway.

"Thank you," David said.

"You two best wash. There's a pump outside. And I'll lay out some of my husband's clothes. Your shirts are probably beyond saving." She glanced at the tables where our patients still lay. "As soon as you're decent, we'll eat in the parlor. Will you need anything else?" She gave me an odd look, but I was too tired to interpret it.

"Just a place to sleep. Come, Whit. Let's clean up."

In the spring twilight, birds called, insects buzzed, and bats began their nightly feed. The clouds of gunpowder earlier obscuring the town had dissipated, giving way to a sunset of soft pinks, purples, and golds. It was hard to believe this peaceful village had been a battleground only hours before.

"You go first, David." I settled on the steps, rubbing the scars across my palm. Sometime during the last few hours, my hands had stopped shaking. I wiped off what blood I could before taking a tattered scrap of paper from my pocket.

Boston
15 April 1775

Dear Whit,

We must all to the wars.

Your brother,
Win

Henry IV, Part 1, act 2, scene 4. Win knew I'd recognize the Shakespeare reference, but this was the only clue he'd left that he, Lem, Da, and—I'd discovered after visiting his shop—our friend Henry Knox had snuck out of Boston to join the militias. When I saw Win again, I'd give him a piece of my mind. How dare he—how dare they all—put themselves at risk without bidding me goodbye or offering to take me with them? Then I remembered all I'd seen that day, and fear gripped me again. Had they fought at Lexington or Concord or—God forbid—Menotomy? Did they lie injured somewhere?

I would know if Win were hurt or . . . dead. I could always sense when he was going to fall ill, which happened often because of his weak lungs, a legacy of our early and difficult birth. A birth neither of us should have survived.

But the others, had they survived the day?

We had passed by so many dead on the road, and we hadn't checked each one. What if one of them had been—

"Your turn, Whit."

I started, crushing Win's note. David frowned, but I hurried to the pump before he asked. My fears, however, weren't so easy to leave behind. My hand was shaking too hard to work the pump, and tears blurred my eyes.

The memories struck faster than musket balls—everything I'd seen during the day: the wounded, the dying, the fixed faces of the dead.

I dropped to my knees, retching, but there was nothing in my stomach but bile, which burned my throat and made my tears come faster.

"Whitley, what's taking so lo—Oh."

I spat and wiped my mouth. "I'm fine. Really. It just all caught me and—"

David's hand settled on my shoulder. "No need to explain. Today was . . . a lot."

I remembered how he had thrown up outside Menotomy's tavern earlier, and I felt less embarrassed.

"Take your time. Come inside once you're cleaned up."

I remained where I was for a few minutes, breathing in the rapidly cooling night air, letting the evening sounds of crickets and birds soothe my soul. When I was shivering more from cold than my own thoughts, I washed, letting the freezing water drown the last of the memories. Maybe with dry clothes, food, and some sleep, what we'd lived through wouldn't seem so terrible.

David and Mrs. Adams were talking just inside the door, but when she saw me, Mrs. Adams broke off the conversation. "Clothes are upstairs. First door on the right. Shall I be making up one bed or two?"

Her words stole the breath from my lungs.

She knew.

She knew I was a young woman, not a young man, and she assumed . . . "No! No, we're not—he's—Dr. Townsend is more of a brother. Truly." The heat coming from my face could have warmed the room.

"Yes, uh, Whitley's right. We're siblings. If not by blood, then . . ." David rubbed his hand across his face. If my cheeks were as red as his, Mrs. Adams would never believe us. Many girls considered David handsome with his dark brown-copper hair, strong cheekbones, and easy smile, but we had been like siblings too long for David and me to be anything else. Then he said, "We can share a room."

I couldn't have heard him correctly. "What?"

Mrs. Adams's eyebrows rose, deepening the disapproval aimed at David. She stepped closer to me, mother-like.

In all the years we'd worked together, we had never shared a room. I'd lived at my parents' house during the early years of my apprenticeship, and when I had moved into Dr. Warren's, I'd shared a room first with his daughters and later with Miss Mercy Scollay, his fiancée.

"Whit, if you plan on staying with the militias beyond today—"

"I do." The words were out before I had time to give them any thought, my quick reaction born of a lifetime of fighting against what I was told I couldn't do. Did I truly want to do this? To face more bodies invaded by lead?

But could I say no? If I did, I was a coward, running from the field of battle. I would let myself down, and worse, I would let Dr. Warren down. He had trained us to not only save lives but support the cause. How could I do less? I thought of Kit, how his ghostly eyes would judge me. This was my best chance to do something in his memory. But still, it was with more surety than I felt that I said, "Of course I plan to stay."

"Well, then, I assure you, you'll be expected to share smaller quarters with more men than me. Isn't it better to adjust now?"

He had a point. The only male I'd ever shared a room with was Win. If Da's stories about the French War were to be believed, quarters would become crowded quickly. Realizing David posed no threat to me, Mrs. Adams watched our back and forth, bemused.

"Could we have one room with two mattresses?" I asked.

"One can be taken from the girls' room."

"I'll move it," David said, disappearing up the stairs. "You shouldn't be lifting so much this soon after the birth."

Mrs. Adams turned a Ma-worthy look on me. "Young lady, we need to talk."

Chapter Two
April 19, 1775

Arms folded, Mrs. Adams's glare pinned me in place. "I don't approve of what you're doing, Miss Endicott—I wouldn't let my Mary follow a man to war, and you can't be much older than she is. But—" She took a breath, posture relaxing a fraction. "I'm not your mother. However, I am a fellow woman, and we protect our own."

"Truly, Mrs. Adams," I said, taking her hand, "I'm not chasing a man. I've known David since I was ten and he seventeen. There's nothing romantic between us. I only want to save lives."

"That wouldn't matter to some men."

"It does to this one."

"You would know him best, I suppose." She brought our joined hands up. "No man would take my hand like that. You're set on this, are you?" I wasn't completely certain, but I nodded. "Well then, if you don't appear and act more like a man, they'll spot you for certain. Go change. After supper, we'll work on your disguise."

David was in the midst of changing when I entered the room. I averted my gaze, face flushing. Though I'd seen men as patients and was no stranger to male anatomy, I thought of them as wounds or illnesses, not . . .

"You can't do that," David said, tying up his trousers. "No blushing or turning away. You'll have to find a way to look at us, or at least see us, without embarrassment."

I tried to find a way to undress myself without revealing too much. "I don't want to be a man. I only want to treat our wounded."

"To do one, you have to become the other."

"That's not fair. I've apprenticed for five years, and Dr. Warren says I'm as good as any doctor he's trained, but I still can't practice on my own because I'm a woman. It's—" I deflated like a punctured bladder. "It's just not fair."

"I know." David squeezed my shoulder like Josiah would have. It didn't fix anything, but it made me feel a little better.

During the meal that followed, the older Adams girls kept casting glances at David and me from under their lashes, something he ignored and I blushed at. Joel was nearly falling asleep in his plate, and Mrs. Adams wasn't much better. Her pallor worried me.

Once the meal was finished, the dishes done, and our patients settled more comfortably in the parlor, Mrs. Adams took me to the kitchen and cut my hair to shoulder length.

It'll grow back, I told myself with each snip of the scissors. If you change your mind, it'll grow back soon enough, and you can hide it under a mobcap until it does.

"A shame," Mrs. Adams said, holding up the hair she'd severed. "You have beautiful hair. Mind if I sell it to the wigmaker? There's many who'd pay a pretty penny for a head of hair like this."

"Consider it payment for your help."

I started to stand, but she pushed me back into the chair. "We're not done yet, Whitley Endicott."

She found cloth to bind me flat, a waistcoat to further disguise my figure, and men's underdrawers. "These should make it easier during your time of the month." Then she held out a cravat. "It won't be your doctoring that gives you away or your voice—thank the Lord it's on the lower end—it'll be your anatomy. You'll want to wear a cravat or scarf at all times. And wear it high, like this." She wound the cravat around my Adam's-apple-less throat and almost up to my chin. "It'll be uncomfortable, like the bindings, and you'll be overly warm in the summer, but this should keep you safer."

My black jacket and trousers would complete my ensemble once they were washed. Bloodstains hardly showed on the dark fabric. No wonder black was the doctors' color.

I took Mrs. Adams's hand again, subtly feeling the pulse at her wrist. It fluttered too fast. "Thank you, Mrs. Adams, for everything. Tomorrow, though, you must rest. You've pushed yourself too hard too soon after giving birth."

"Rest? With the house in this state? And the town—"

"You have capable daughters, and Joel can do anything he sets his mind to. He proved that today. Your heart is beating too fast, and you're pale and clammy—you cannot tell me you're not in pain. You must rest tomorrow, for the sake of little Ann if not for yourself. I've seen women push themselves too hard too soon with disastrous results."

I didn't say the women had been prostitutes, whom Dr. Warren had treated as part of his charity work. He believed slowing the spread of disease among the women would, in turn, slow its spread through the city, and I had helped him with that work for the last four years. Without us, those women would have no doctor checking on them. I worried how they would fare without our ministrations. Women, I had learned, were often in need of the most care and received the least.

"Very well. You are the doctor."

"Perhaps I could examine you now? Make sure everything is as it should be." I doubted a doctor had helped with the delivery. I doubted Menotomy had a doctor. And since this wasn't her first child, she might not have even sent for a midwife. "I apprenticed with a midwife before Dr. Warren."

"Dr. Warren? He trained you?" Mrs. Adams led the way to her room, leaning heavily on the banister and pausing on each stair.

"You know Dr. Warren?"

"Everyone in Massachusetts Colony knows who Dr. Warren is. They printed both his Bloody Massacre orations in all the papers. His last speech, it seems, was prophetic." She lay back on the bed with a groan and, as I examined her, began to recite, "If 'it appears that the only way to safety is through fields of blood, I know you will not turn your faces from your foes, but will, undauntedly, press forward, until tyranny is trodden under foot, and you have fixed your adored goddess Liberty on the American throne.'"

Dr. Warren had given that speech over a month ago, and it still gave me shivers—and not just because of the words. Delivering the speech in Old South Meeting House with Redcoat officers in attendance, Dr. Warren had dramatically worn a toga, and the ill-timed return of a regiment had nearly started a battle outside the meeting house doors. When I heard Dr. Warren's words, I was back in Old South, huddled with his children and Miss Scollay, waiting for shots to ring out.

The shooting had begun at last.

I thought about his words, "I know you will not turn your faces from your foes, but will, undauntedly, press forward . . ." It was as though he were offering me a challenge. But I still wasn't sure it was a challenge I could accept.

"Everything looks fine, Mrs. Adams, but here's a list of ingredients for a tea to aid in your recovery. I don't have any with me, but they should be available at any apothecary. Send one of your daughters for them. You must rest."

"Thank you, Miss—Dr. Endicott. It is a welcome change to have a woman examine me."

It wasn't the first time I'd heard that sentiment, and I hoped, someday, to serve as a doctor to all the women in Boston. Compared with the other work I'd done since reaching Lexington that morning, I was much more comfortable with doctoring like this.

David was already asleep on the mattress on the floor. Exhausted as I was, I couldn't sleep. I wanted to blame it on the sound of David's slightly wheezy breathing disturbing the room's silence, but the horrors I'd earlier pushed from my mind—cowering on the floor of Buckman Tavern as the Ministerial Army returned to Lexington, cannonballs and musket balls flying overhead and glass raining down; the house in Menotomy with blood so deep it rippled as David and I walked through it searching for survivors; and the tavern David wouldn't let me enter—haunted the dark behind my eyelids. My imagination filled the night with the dead, mutilated in the worst ways.

I sat up, breathing deep to slow my racing heart and mind. We had indeed trodden through fields of blood, and I doubted there would be less blood or fewer wounds in the battles to come. So, if I were truly going to doctor during this war, I had to find a way to adjust.

Counting sheep had never helped me fall asleep; it was too easy to start counting patients. Telling myself stories worked better. I took my favorites, often Shakespeare, and made myself a character, rewriting parts of the story as I drifted to sleep. Most of the Shakespeare I loved, though, was too bloody after what I'd seen. Instead, I found myself thinking of Joel Adams and how simple and safe life had seemed when Win and I were his age, playing with our friends in the snow.

Chapter Three
April 20, 1775

Fwump. *A snowball splatted against the side of my head, trickling cold inside my collar.*

I scooped my own handful of snow and launched it at Kit and Sammy while Zadock pouted behind a snowbank. I ducked behind another bank, grinning at Win.

"It's not fair," Zadock whined. "They didn't give any warning."

"Shut up, Zad."

"Come out, cowards!" Kit yelled.

Win and I exchanged looks, all our strategy decided wordlessly. He glanced at Zadock, and I rolled my eyes. We didn't need him.

Hands full of snow, we rushed their position. First one, then the other, we launched our missiles, a continuous barrage. Leaping their bank, Win tackled Kit while I stuffed snow down the back of Sammy's shirt.

"Uncle!" Sammy cried. "Uncle!"

"Say we win," Win demanded.

"You win," Kit said.

"Say girls are better."

"Never!" yelled Sammy.

I was about to stuff more snow down his shirt when a voice said, "What's going on here?"

Josiah and Lem loomed above us, and although Josiah wore a serious expression, his eyes twinkled.

"We're winning," Win said.

"Are you? Well, I think Lem and I can take you all."

Before we could mount a defense, Lem and Josiah were on us. Josiah lifted me and, ignoring my protests, plunged me face-first into the snow. I would have surrendered if only I could have stopped giggling.

I woke, an ache for my brothers lodged in my throat, and I wondered again where they were and if they were alive. Josiah was at sea, but that had never been a guarantee of safety. Seventeen-year-old Zadock, sniveler that he was, would never join the militia, and I hadn't seen my oldest brother, Ben, since he married and moved to Marblehead half a lifetime ago. But Win and Lem . . . I could only hope to find them.

David and I set off after checking on our patients, both of whom still lived. Cambridge was only three miles away, and judging from the smoke smudging the sky, the militias were encamped there.

Remnants of the previous day's fighting lined our way, out of place in the bright morning sunlight. There were deep ruts in the road from gun carriages, blood-stained grass, musket balls lodged in tree trunks, and paper from cartridges caught among the roots. I tried not to look at what the crows were picking apart.

"Did you sleep at all last night?" David asked. "I heard you tossing and turning."

"Sorry. I didn't know I was keeping you up. You looked sound asleep."

"Just because my eyes were closed doesn't mean I slept. I saw the same things you did yesterday. No one could sleep easily after that."

"Why . . . why didn't you say something? I thought—"

"Thought after throwing up outside that tavern I didn't keep reliving what we'd seen? I wish I could say that was true, but I felt sick over it all night. Still do. Just didn't want to talk about it. Some things are better left unuttered."

It would have been nice to know I hadn't been alone last night. Win or Josiah would have understood, and another swoop of worry rolled through my stomach.

"Stop that," David said a few minutes later.

I halted. "Stop what?"

"Fidgeting with your cuffs, pulling on your trousers, tugging on your cravat—nice touch, by the way. You can't look uncomfortable in your clothes if you're going to pass."

"But I am uncomfortable. This cravat is choking me, and all these layers are making me sweat. My legs feel trapped, and the seams rub against the insides of my legs—don't you laugh, David Townsend! I'd like to see you adjust to wearing petticoats and stays."

"Maybe next war." He knocked my hand away from my cravat. "So, do we need to find a new name to go with your new outfit?"

"What?"

"Your name—if you're going to pose as a man, are you going to keep Whitley, or do we need to find you a new name? Personally, I like Comfort—good name for a doctor. Or Enterprise, Albigence, Theophilus."

"I weep for your children."

David laughed. I had never liked my name. Ma had used old family surnames for Winborn and me. But Whitley was mine, and I was already changing enough. "Whitley does as good for a boy as a girl."

"Good. I don't think I could remember to call you something else. Unless it was Theophilus . . ."

I swatted at him. He ducked, laughing, and I couldn't keep from joining in. It felt like the first time I'd laughed in ages. For a moment, it could almost have been a normal spring morning. Then we reached the first lines of militia, and the illusion disappeared.

Militiamen were cobbling together shelters far beyond Cambridge's limits and were happy to stop their work and inform us of all that had happened the day before. After being chased out of Concord, Parliament's Army had retreated all the way to Boston where their ships' cannons protected them. Militiamen were still streaming in from all corners of Massachusetts, some starting to arrive from other colonies. Boston was nearly encircled, and Cambridge had become the de facto Patriot military center.

We found Dr. Warren just inside Cambridge proper, and he threw his arms wide at the sight of us. "Dr. Townsend, Dr. Endicott—how good to see you both!"

Dr. Joseph Warren was only thirty-three, but he was the head of Boston's Patriot operations. He served on more committees than he had time for while still running his practice, which was why he always had at least two apprentices, currently myself and William Eustis, who had remained in Boston. One look at Dr. Warren, and it was easy to see why the Patriot leaders had chosen him to be the face of the cause instead of, say, Mr. Samuel Adams, whose clothes were always on the verge of falling apart. Even after fighting all day, Dr. Warren's clothes were pristine and accented with a green silk cravat. His clean-shaven face and sandy-blond hair made him appear younger than he was, but his blue-gray eyes lent his face gravitas. A new graze creased the skin near his right temple.

"What happened there, sir?"

He lightly touched a finger to the spot, a remembrance of fear lighting his eyes, but he covered it quickly with a smile and a laugh. "Just a scratch. A musket ball at Menotomy thought to kill me but only took a pin and a lock of hair. Left me this scratch as a reminder to duck."

"What!" I went cold. Dr. Warren had been a breath away from being one of our patients, or worse. I seized his sleeve. "Sir, I promised Miss Scollay you wouldn't do anything to get yourself killed. How can I—"

"Miss—Dr. Endicott, I'm fine." He patted my hand in a fatherly way. "Mercy never should have asked that of you. She knows I don't intend to stay behind the lines." Miss Mercy Scollay, his fiancée, currently had charge of Dr. Warren's children in Worcester. In the past year and a half, she had become family, not just to Dr. Warren and the children, but to me, closer than my three true sisters. Dr. Warren shook away my fears, smiling again. "Come. I'll show you the hospital and introduce you to its director, Dr. Church. The house we're using was owned by Tories—the Vassal family—until they fled to Boston."

"Dr. Church is head of the hospital?" David asked, swerving around a huddle of militiamen. "Not you?"

"With the Provincial Congress, Committee of Correspondence, and Committee of Safety, I don't have time to run the hospital. Besides, when it comes to battle, we'll need leaders on the field, not behind the lines."

"Whit!" The voice was high with hope and disbelief, but I would have recognized it anywhere. "Whitley!" Win slammed into me, arms enclosing me like barrel hoops, and I squeezed him tightly in return.

"Win! Are Lem and Da—"

"Fine. Da's arm was grazed by a musket ball, but he's fine."

A knot of worry in my shoulders loosened. "After what I saw yesterday, I feared . . ."

Win paled. With his dislike of blood, the previous day would have been a true test of his mettle. He changed the subject. "What about Ma?"

"Fine when I saw her last, though not happy about so many of us going to war and leaving her with Zad." Zadock thought himself above the rest of us and would never risk himself in battle, especially since he didn't agree with our politics. Our two sisters still at home, Abigail and Sarah, were also Loyalists and were being courted by two Redcoat officers. I wondered if their sweethearts had fought and whether they had survived. For the first time in years, I felt a twinge of sympathy for my sisters.

"Have you seen Henry at all?" I couldn't help but ask. Henry Knox was a good friend, as well as the first man I'd been smitten with even though he was ten years my senior.

Win shook his head, not quite meeting my eyes. "Too hard to find anyone among all these people. It's a miracle I ran into you. Are you—" Win tugged at his right earlobe, a sure sign he was thinking hard about what he wanted to say next.

"I'll be fine, Win." I resisted the urge to twitch my trousers. "No one's looking for me to be anything other than I am."

"Well, that makes two of us, then." Win's smile was less than convincing. He needn't have bothered since he didn't have to pretend with me. His secret was one that didn't show, but if it were discovered, he risked worse punishment than I did. I linked my pinkie with his, our secret signal of support and love.

"Dr. Endicott!" Dr. Warren called.

"You'd better go. Find us later. Da's building our shelter near the Roxbury men. Ask around. You'll find us. I'll tell Da you're here." With one last press of our pinkies, we parted.

The hospital was a long, three-story house with white trim, black shutters, and more windows than I would want to wash every week. Its furnishings had been crammed into the smallest ground-floor room, replaced by cots filled with wounded men. The scents of tobacco and perfume lingered, but I was sure by week's end they would be only memories.

"Dr. Church!" Dr. Warren called, but it was Johnny who clattered down the stairs. He was about my age and had worked at one of Boston's newspapers. He had brought news of General Gage's plans to take Concord to Dr. Warren's two nights ago. "Ah, Johnny. Helping out while you wait?"

"Yes, sir." Johnny rubbed his maimed hand. "You said tonight, right?"

"Yes, I'll fix your hand this evening. Now have you seen—Ah, Dr. Church." Dr. Benjamin Church was heavyset and round-faced with thick brows. His mouth was too small for his face, which gave him a perpetually sour expression. "These are Dr. David Townsend and Dr. Whitley Endicott.

Both trained under me."

Dr. Church frowned at me. "Isn't he a little young?"

"Perhaps, but Dr. Endicott has apprenticed with me for five years. You'd be hard-pressed to find anyone with more skill." I flushed, flustered, glad Dr. Warren hadn't been in Menotomy to see me panic. "I leave them to you. Committee of Safety has a noon meeting. Johnny, I'll see you tonight."

Dr. Church's squinty eyes followed Dr. Warren all the way out. With a huff, he turned to us. "Well, Doctors, there's work to do. Plenty of men still staggering in wounded. And you." He rounded on Johnny. "Keep cutting bandages if you're going to hang about underfoot. If you can't be useful, return to your militia regiment."

"Yes, sir," Johnny said but rolled his eyes as soon as the doctor's back was turned. I stifled a giggle, and Johnny winked at me.

"Come on, *Doctor* Endicott," David said, emphasizing my new title. "You heard Dr. Church; there're wounded to tend."

Swallowing my trepidation, I followed him upstairs.

Chapter Four
April 20, 1775

It was nearly dark before Dr. Church dismissed us, and I wasted no time escaping the hospital, intent on finding Da and my brothers.

Among the bustle of evacuating townsfolk, incoming militiamen, and mounted couriers, I saw several new ghosts. I spun away, setting my eyes on the town ahead. Who were these ghosts? Why were they following me? Kit, at least, had been a friend, and I had theories about why he continued to haunt me, but these men?

I had another reason for keeping my distance. Touching them was dangerous as I had learned with Kit long ago. The last time—the only time—I had touched Kit, he had been able to possess me. I had been trapped in my own mind, and when Kit had left my body, the pain from his wounds had remained. I had felt every one of those eleven swan-shot pellets.

I had felt what it was to die.

David had witnessed Kit releasing me from his possession, and for a few days he, Dr. Warren, and my parents had watched me for signs of madness, whispering plans to send me to Dr. Warren's family home in Roxbury if I worsened. But Kit had disappeared for weeks, and we had been careful not to touch again.

Most frustrating, though, was that during the possession I hadn't learned how to free myself from Kit or Kit from me. When I'd asked, all Kit had been able to say was "Let go—"

But let go of what? Five years later, I still didn't know.

Kit hadn't meant me any harm, but I didn't know these new ghosts, and I didn't want to risk them possessing me when an accusation of madness could lead to the discovery of who I really was.

So, I burrowed into the militia-clogged streets, trying to avoid gutters already filling with trash and questionable liquids. I shook a page of newspaper off my foot and fought the urge to look behind me to see if the ghosts followed. Around me, men called back and forth, laughter drifting on the air with the scents of dozens of different suppers cooking. Fish was frying somewhere, and someone else's meal was burning. With so many men passing me, brushing against me, looking at me, it was all I could do not to cross my arms over my chest, lower my eyes, and shrink down to avoid their notice or scrutiny. But it was like David had said with the clothes; I couldn't do that.

Dry mouthed, I met the eyes of every man I passed, nodding or tipping my hat. None of them called me out or even looked at me sideways. My confidence in my disguise grew, and I walked taller and even ventured a smile or two.

But when I reached the Roxbury encampment, I slowed. Like the other huts I'd passed, these were constructed of anything and everything—boards, sailcloth, bricks, turf, and stones. Most were only half built, and it didn't look as if they'd withstand an April shower, let alone a nor'easter. Da's skills as a joiner, however, had been put to good use, and the hut he and my brothers sat in front of looked like a mansion among hovels.

I rubbed the scars on my palm. What would Da say when he saw me? If Win had told him I was in Cambridge, he'd had time to plan his speech. He'd never been harsh with any of us before, but his youngest daughter had never run away to war before either.

Da's back was to me, but both Win and Lem saw me. Lem shook his head, but he grinned as he carried on dishing up stew. Win frowned, confused by my hesitation. I tipped my head at Da, and understanding bloomed in Win's eyes. A twitch of his head said I had nothing to worry about. But that didn't make my next step forward any easier.

"Hello, Da."

Da turned, his beard hiding his expression, as it always did, but his eyes held warmth, not anger or reproach. He studied me for a few moments, and I wondered if, like me, he was searching for any hurts. I noted the bandage on his arm and the way he kept absently rubbing his bad leg. He sighed. "Whitley. Always where you shouldn't be. Where did you get those clothes?"

"Dr. Warren." I braced myself for Da to chastise me and send me back to Boston, half hoping he would. If he sent me back, it wouldn't be cowardice. I could take up my place as Midwife Rowe's assistant again. It wouldn't be what I really wanted to do, but it would be safer, and I'd never see another musket-ball wound. Da's second sigh ended in a chuckle. "Of course he did. Well, you'd best sit, Whitley, and eat before the food goes cold."

"You . . . you aren't sending me home?"

"No." Da's gaze swept over the three of us. He stretched his right leg, the one injured during the French War, toward the fire. "Someday, when the three of you have children, you'll understand. You hope never to see your children marching off to war. Especially after you've survived one. You hope you will have fought enough for your children to live in peace." His gaze lingered on each of us as if memorizing our faces. "But when you have two children fighting just to live from the moment they're born, children who overcame all odds, you know they'll never avoid a battle when they can charge headlong into one."

"That's the two of you for certain," Lem said with a laugh, helping himself to more stew, always trying to fill his bottomless stomach.

Win met my eyes. We'd heard the story of our birth often enough. Born more than a month before our time during a blizzard in January 1760, Win was small and sickly from the moment he drew breath, and I'd had the cord wrapped around my neck. Midwife Rowe had saved us both that morning.

Da continued, "Winborn, Whitley, you were born to fight. You've survived so much that should have killed you—the blizzard the night of your birth, the fire that swept the North End after, smallpox that spring, influenza that autumn." Silently, I added the day of Kit's death. Had he not stood in front of us, that shot would have hit Win and me. "This war would have to work hard to kill you, so send you home? If I thought it would do any good, I'd send you all home, but one way or another, this war will drag you in. It's who you are. Can't pass up a fight and won't accept a loss either."

It was true. We'd been fighting since day one, and both of us still fought silent battles daily. I had to decide if this one was worth the risks or if I should return to the safer path that led to Midwife Rowe's.

"You're welcome to stay the night, Whitley," Da said.

"No. I need to return to the hospital. David will worry."

"Townsend? Good man. Few others I would trust your safety to."

"He's almost more protective than my brothers."

Win bumped his shoulder against mine, and Lem ruffled my hair before he turned in. Da stood to follow him. "Da . . ."

He paused. I wanted to ask, but I didn't want Da to think less of me. Win pressed his shoulder more firmly against mine, encouraging me.

"Do you dream, Da? About the war?" I rubbed my palm as I continued, "What I saw yesterday . . . I hardly slept last night, and if I stay . . ."

Da stared down at the pattern of shifting embers. When he broke the silence, his voice was hushed and weary with old pain. "The things I saw in the last war still haunt me on bad nights. Our souls were made for peace but the body for war. The scars on the soul—those sights we've now all seen—are not easily healed. Those memories will always be with you, but you can work to soften them. Before I sleep, I remember all the good things I have in my life—your mother, you children, the simple joys of every day. Doesn't always keep the dreams at bay, but it helps me fall asleep."

I'd never heard Da talk like that before. He'd stood at this same crossroads, and he'd had more to lose—Ma, my older brothers and sisters, and Lem newly born—yet he'd chosen to fight. And knowing the risks, he had stepped forward to do it again. I had always loved Da, of course, but it had been Dr. Warren I'd looked up to for the last five years. In that moment, though, I had never been prouder to call myself Zeph Endicott's daughter, and I only hoped I could live up to his example of strength and commitment.

Without another word to either of us, Da kissed the tops of our heads and went into the hut.

Win tapped my knee, and we turned to face each other. Looking at him was almost like looking at myself, but little differences were starting to show. The firelight revealed the fair fuzz of a mustache coming in. Another problem I was going to have to solve if my male disguise was going to be believable.

"What is it, Whit?" His voice was quiet and wouldn't carry beyond the glow of our fire. "It almost seemed like . . . like you wanted Da to send you home."

We didn't lie to each other, Win and I. We didn't immediately tell each other everything, but when one of us asked, the other always told the truth. "I thought I did, but after what Da just said . . . He believes in me. In us."

"And despite all, he's here." He took a length of rope from his pocket and began knotting and unknotting it. Something Josiah had taught him to keep him from fidgeting so much.

"I don't know if I can do this kind of doctoring," I confessed.

"What do you mean?"

I added some water to the empty stewpot and set it to heat. "You know what you saw yesterday? I saw those same men, but I was trying to put them back together—undo the damage of bayonet and ball and tomahawk while they groaned and cried, and all the while . . ." I stopped myself before I mentioned Kit. I had never told Win about Kit's haunting, and to explain it would be too much after the last few days. I scraped the spoon around the pot, loosening the stuck-on bits. "I've never seen such horrible injuries—nothing in Dr. Warren's surgery prepared me for this. I was adequate yesterday, but I . . . I panicked. What happens when I face a wound that's beyond my capabilities? It's not just myself I'd be failing. Men's lives are at stake. Our cause is at stake."

"What would you do if you went home?"

"Midwife Rowe has always said she'd take me on again."

Win looked up from the complex knot he was weaving. "And that would be enough for you?" When I didn't answer, he said, "It's not enough for me anymore—helping Da in his shop in the winters, on the Warren farm in the summers. Someday, I want to own my own farm and settle down with . . . Well, I don't want to live alone, anyway. But to have that, we have to win our rights. If I went home now, I'd regret it forever. And so would you. You're a good doctor, Whit, and you're only going to get better until you're the best in the colonies, and they'll have to accept you."

My laugh was disbelieving. "Boston accepting a female doctor?"

"Either that or they'll burn you as a witch."

I flung a ladle of scummy water at him even though I knew he was teasing. If the people of Boston were going to label me a witch, it wouldn't be because of my doctoring. Another good reason to keep the ghosts haunting me secret. Win sat beside me tying knots until I finished scrubbing the pot. "Thanks, Win."

"I know you'll be there for me when I need you. That's how we work, right?"

I linked my pinkie with his. "Always."

Chapter Five
April 20, 1775

I didn't go straight back to the hospital. I needed a few minutes to think without anyone or anything to distract me. Since there were no sentries, there was no one to stop me from walking to the edge of the encampment. Beyond the light of the last fire, I stopped and stared out over Back Bay to the lighted windows of Boston. There was the deeper shadow of Old North's steeple, from which Robert Newman had hung two lanterns just days prior. I hoped General Gage hadn't caught him. From Old North, I traced my way through the candles of the North End to home.

It would be easy to return. In the morning, exchange my trousers for skirts and talk my way past the Lobsterbacks guarding the Neck, and I could be home by evening, working with Midwife Rowe by the next morning.

Safe. Still helping people, but never allowed to perform surgery or diagnose an illness or serve anyone but women in childbirth. The words of Dr. Warren's Massacre oration returned to me: "I know you will not turn your faces from your foes, but will, undauntedly, press forward, until tyranny is trodden underfoot . . ." I could not claim I was undaunted—I was as far from undaunted as it was possible to be—but Win was right. If I turned away, I would regret it forever. I had to press forward. It was what Da and Dr. Warren expected, and I couldn't let them down.

Da had said our bodies were made for war. Mine wasn't, not yet, but I would hone my skills and knowledge until I could handle anything this war threw at me.

For one moment more, though, I could be Miss Whitley Endicott. Say goodbye to Boston properly. I untied my cravat and stuffed it in my pocket, rubbing at my throat. It had only been one day, but my cravat and my bindings itched. Tucking my tricorn under my arm, I loosened my hair tie and combed my fingers through my strangely short locks.

"Goodbye, Ma, Midwife Rowe, and Boston. I'll return someday, and maybe Win will be right, and you'll accept me then. Maybe—"

Out of the corner of my eye, something moved. I spun, hand reaching under my coat for the pistols I'd carried from Boston, but I'd left them at the hospital. A gun wouldn't have helped me, though, for it wasn't a living man who approached but a ghost.

I recognized him. He'd died in Lexington, not in the first battle—if it could be called a battle and not just murder—he'd died when the Redcoats retreated and passed through Lexington a second time. He'd been wounded in the first assault, and I'd patched up his shoulder wound in Buckman Tavern. Then he'd gone out and died not an hour later. The guilt of it filled me, and I took a step back. "Don't—"

"What have we here?" A man appeared out of the night behind me. He wasn't terribly big or strong, but he was bigger and stronger than me, and his smile made goosebumps break out across my body. I backed a step closer to the ghost, who was the lesser danger. The militiaman's smile glinted, and he prowled closer. "Looks like a girl playing dress-up in her brother's clothes. Or her sweetheart's. Do you have a sweetheart? No? I can be your sweetheart."

Dr. Warren had made sure all his apprentices could handle a firearm. I'd thought it stupid at the time, but if I only had a pistol . . . All I could do was back away, and, dropping my hat, I raised my fists.

He laughed.

Before I could swing, the ghost stepped into me. I absorbed him, like a bandage soaking up blood. Cold swallowed me as though I'd been plunged into the Charles River. Then he was there, in my mind, and my inner self was thrust aside, buffeted by a storm of whispers and memories not my own. Sounds and images too fast to follow swirled in a vortex around me, holding me in place. I could still see, hear, and feel the world, but I had no control over my body.

My inner self screamed, pushing against the waves of him crashing against me. For a breath they paused, and one word came clear. *Trust.*

I stopped fighting him just as he swung my fist at the militiaman's stomach.

The impact shuddered through my arm, from my nails biting into my palm to my shoulder socket. I felt the give of his body—a new sensation because I didn't know how to fight. The only time I'd ever fought anyone had been when I attacked Zad on the night of Kit's death, and that hadn't been a proper fight but more a grief-fueled drubbing.

But the ghost knew how, for as soon as my first blow landed, he was swinging my other fist. We struck the man's face, my hand stinging, his stubble scrapping against my knuckles. He was still doubled up when we struck again. A hit to his kidneys followed by a kick right between the legs.

He toppled to the ground, not enough hands to hold his hurts.

"Now you know to keep your hands to yourself," the ghost growled, his much deeper voice rumbling up my throat and out of my mouth. We bent to pick up my hat. With movements borne of habit, he tied my cravat, pulled my hair back—I winced at the too-sharp tug—and jammed the hat on my head. Leaving my would-be attacker still groaning on the ground, we strode back through the encampment and Cambridge to the hospital.

And I mean strode—like a man does, so different from how I normally walked. I focused on remembering the cadence of my steps, the swing of my arms, how my whole body moved through the world with unfeigned confidence, claiming the space I inhabited.

When we reached the hospital, he didn't enter the front door, but took us around the back and leaned my body against the wall as if he knew what would happen to me when he left. I was already bracing myself for it, but I couldn't let him leave yet.

"Wait," I said, forcing my inner voice through the storm holding me captive, that one word sapping the strength of my inner self. "Name?"

Again, his voice from my mouth. "Jedediah Munroe."

"Thank you, Jedediah."

He touched my right shoulder, the shoulder in which he had been wounded. The wound I'd dressed. "I pay my debts. Do you?"

I was struck dumb. How could he know—? That didn't matter. This was my opportunity to learn the answer of how to free myself from these hauntings. The answer Kit hadn't been able to give. "How—"

But in a rush of cold, Jedediah left my body.

Pain struck like a musket ball. Like two: one to my right shoulder and the other to my chest. Jedediah's wounds visited upon me. My head screamed with pain; the human brain wasn't made to hold two consciousnesses. Teeth clenched, hands over my mouth to hold back my cries, I slid down the rough siding, reliving the agony of Jedediah's death.

Unable to hold back any longer, I opened my mouth. One moan escaped before I vomited. I fought to remain conscious, digging my fingers into the thawing ground, but the pain overwhelmed me, and the world disappeared.

I must not have been out for long because the sky was no darker or lighter, and no one had found me. I spat out the taste of vomit, but another taste lingered—that of hot iron. I could smell it, too, and knew this, like the bone-deep ache pulsing through me, was a remnant of Jedediah. With Kit, I'd been left with the taste of syllabubs, his favorite sweet treat, and it had taken days to fade. Perhaps Jedediah had been a blacksmith to leave me with such a taste.

He was nowhere to be seen, and if this followed the same pattern as Kit's possession, it would be weeks before I saw him again.

I spat once more and, after testing the steadiness of my limbs, used the support of the hospital wall to stand.

"'And thou, O wall, O sweet, O lovely wall,' do not let me fall." An involuntary huff sobbed out at my Shakespearean misquotation. If Win had been there, he would have rolled his eyes and said something about how I would be quoting Shakespeare as the world ended. I wished for Win, but the wall would have to do.

Leaning against the trusty wall, I staggered to the back door, which opened into the kitchen. After a little searching, I found some cider, though it did little to wash the conflicting tastes from my mouth. I found mint to chew, which was a little more helpful.

I was about to drag myself to bed when a scream of pain ricocheted down from one of the floors above. I hesitated only a moment before hauling myself up to the second floor and the room at the end.

A man thrashed on the table, his right leg a mess of blood, bone, and torn skin. Below the knee, his leg was mangled beyond repair. Dr. Church, Johnny, and Dr. Warren held his upper body down while David tried to hold the good leg and amputate the other. Dr. Warren's face was pinched and pale. A clear sign of one of his headaches.

"Whitley," David snapped. "Make him swallow some rum."

As terrible as the soldier's leg looked, I was no stranger to amputations, having faced several at Dr. Warren's, usually due to badly broken bones. I quickly scrubbed the dirt from my hands and fought to shove my own pain to the back of my mind. If Dr. Warren could assist while in pain, I could, too. I poured a generous dose of rum, though the smell mixed with that of blood, sweat, and bowels nauseated me, and stirred in laudanum. Prying his mouth open, I tipped the liquid in, then forced his mouth shut and plugged his nose with my other hand. He fought but finally swallowed. As the fight drained out of him, I lay all my weight across his thighs. "What happened?"

"Shot yesterday," David grunted. "Just arrived. Everyone, brace!"

I pressed harder and closed my eyes against the *grish-grish* of the saw through bone. No matter how many amputations I'd seen, assisted with, or performed, the sound still set my teeth on edge.

The man went limp as the pain pushed him unconscious, and I relaxed my hold just a little.

"Johnny, the irons," David barked. Johnny didn't hesitate to draw the irons from the fire even though it was a burn that had maimed his hand.

"Hold steady," David said. I held hard as David pressed the hot iron against the stump. The man screamed back to consciousness, sobbing and pleading. We all pushed down, fighting the bucking of his body. His hip bone caught me in the shoulder, and I gasped, new pain layering atop that which Jedediah had left me.

"One more." David applied the second iron. The roast-pork smell of burning flesh filled the room, and I clenched my teeth against the urge to vomit. The man passed out again.

"There, I can handle the rest on my own," David said. "Thank you, everyone. I'll sit up with him tonight."

Even though the amputation had been successful, the man only had a slim chance of survival. I sensed Kit hovering in the corner, but I followed David's eyes to Dr. Warren, who leaned against the table, arms locked to keep himself upright.

As much as I ached, I was still in better shape than Dr. Warren. I tugged one of his arms over my shoulders, stiffening my knees. "Let's find you a bed, sir. Johnny, can you get his other side?"

Between the two of us, we maneuvered Dr. Warren to an empty room. Johnny scurried off to fetch chamomile tea, white wine, and Dover's Powder—a pain-relieving mixture of opium, saltpeter, ipecac, tartar, and licorice—while I helped Dr. Warren into bed.

"No," he said weakly. "I promised the boy his hand—" A sharp gasp cut through his words.

"Johnny can wait one more day." I dampened a cloth and laid it over his eyes and forehead. "You're in no condition to—"

"You can. We've done it before."

Several years ago, a hunting accident had nearly severed two fingers from Henry Knox's left hand, and Dr. Warren, suffering from one of his headaches, had guided me through the amputation. The first amputation I'd performed.

I hadn't been recently possessed when we'd taken Henry's fingers, but I knew if I didn't do this, Dr. Warren would, headache or not. I lifted my hand. Steady. And the desire to vomit had faded. "Fine, but only if you lie there, still and silent, until we're ready."

"Yes, Doctor."

Johnny returned. I had a cup of tea while Dr. Warren drank the mixture of white wine and Dover's Powder. Then he gestured to Johnny. "Now your hand."

"I can wait another day or two, sir."

"Let the medicine work a little," I said.

Dr. Warren waved a hand at both of us. "You've waited long enough, Johnny. Dr. Endicott is just as capable as I am."

That was the second time Dr. Warren had complimented me since I'd arrived in Cambridge, and warmth filled me. It wasn't that he never gave praise, but his compliments had to be earned. I wasn't sure I had earned these.

Johnny and I sat knee to knee, and, rolling my sore shoulder, I held out my hand for his. "Burned, right?"

"Yes. Molten silver."

I winced. The skin of his thumb was melted across his palm, and a couple fingers were webbed together.

"Is there any muscle damage?" Dr. Warren asked. The cloth still lay over his eyes, but he didn't need to see to know what I was doing.

"I don't think so. The burns were deep, and the scars are deep as well, but I think with exercise, the muscle will be fine."

"Should be a simple operation, then."

Johnny bit his lip, not looking at either of us. I tapped his hand until he met my eyes. "It won't be pretty when it's done, and the surgery will hurt. I'll have to use a hot knife to cut through the scar tissue. You sure you want this?"

Johnny's eyes were wide and his jaw tight, but he nodded.

"What'll you do once you have full use of your hand?"

"Fight. My . . . my friend died yesterday. Left me his musket."

"I'm sorry."

He wiped at his eyes, cleared his throat, and tried to look older. "I'm going to fight for him and for our cause."

Johnny and I were the same age, yet he had no doubt about what he had to do. I wished I felt the same surety. Win, Da, and Dr. Warren believed in me. Perhaps it was time I started believing in myself.

I gathered the instruments I needed and set a knife to heat. I exchanged the cloth on Dr. Warren's forehead for a new one.

"Ready?" he whispered.

"Yes."

"Then just listen to my voice."

As I cut Johnny's thumb free, I couldn't help but remember how Dr. Warren's pain-tight voice had walked me through Henry's surgery—removing the fingers, cutting down the jagged bit of remaining bone, sewing the wound closed. I'd been so nervous then, but the surgery had been a success.

I stitched Johnny's skin closed and bandaged his hand. "Let me or Dr. Townsend check it in a few days."

"I will. Thank you. Thank you both." Johnny left, but I didn't move. I was just as likely to get rest in this chair as I was in the room David and I were sharing. I poured tea for Dr. Warren and myself.

"You look as worn as I feel, Dr. Endicott," Dr. Warren said.

"It's been a busy two days, and I'm not feeling very well tonight."

"Yet you still helped with an amputation and Johnny's hand." He smiled. "You're ready."

"Sir?"

"You don't need me anymore, or didn't you notice I stopped giving you instructions partway through the surgery?"

"I . . ." I hadn't. I'd heard Dr. Warren's voice throughout. I hadn't realized it had only been in my mind.

"David told me about the wounded yesterday. He said you faced them without fear and knew how to treat each even though you'd never seen their like before."

That wasn't true in the slightest. I'd been filled with fear and panic. Had David really not seen it? Had I seemed as calm and competent as he had?

I wanted to correct Dr. Warren, but what if he decided I wasn't capable? What if he sent me back to Boston just when I had decided to stay? Would he feel the last five years training me had been wasted?

"This war will spread, Whitley," he continued before I could decide what to say. "We'll need doctors to spread with it. Good doctors. Doctors who see a wound and know what to do without question or hesitation. You are such a doctor. If we need you elsewhere, will you go?"

"I . . . Sir, you should be resting, not worrying about—"

He half sat up, the blue-gray depths of his eyes burning with the same intensity that had united the Patriots of Boston. "I will rest easier once you've answered my question. If we need you, will you go?"

"I . . ." I didn't want to leave him, David, or Win, but Dr. Warren hadn't trained me to put myself first. Despite my own misgivings, he trusted my judgment and abilities. I couldn't let him down. "If I'm needed elsewhere, I will go. Of course, I will."

"Good." He settled back and laid another cloth over his eyes. "Now, if you could mix me another draft, I think I might be able to sleep."

Once he was asleep, I went to my own bed. David was still with our patient, so I had the room to myself. Sleeping was no easier, but for a different reason. What had I just agreed to?

Chapter Six
April 21 – May 1, 1775

As routines developed and my mind became occupied with the mundane minutiae of daily life during a siege—scrounging enough food and clothes for our ragtag forces, finding time to practice with my pistols, trying to choose which book from the Vassals' collection to read before bed—the nightmares faded, though never truly went away. I saw flashes of Kit everywhere, sometimes with another ghost or two I didn't recognize— men I must have treated at Lexington or Menotomy who hadn't survived. Jedediah didn't return, but I was certain he would. The ghosts never stayed long. A glimpse while I walked through Cambridge, another while I checked Johnny's hand, again when we buried the man whose leg we'd amputated. I felt a bit like Hamlet, but he'd had only one ghost to contend with, and his, at least, told him why he was being haunted. The more I thought about it—and I had plenty of time to think—the more I was certain I knew why they were haunting me.

I owed them.

As Da had reminded me, Win and I shouldn't have survived this long. Ma claimed we were born under a lucky star, but there was no luck about our survival. This world gave nothing for free—everything had to be earned, bought, and paid for, as I'd seen again and again growing up in Boston. Win and I owed far more than most. We owed Midwife Rowe, who'd ensured we survived our birth. We owed Kit, who'd been standing in front of us when Mr. Richardson fired.

And those debts couldn't be repaid with goods or money. They were life debts, which could only be repaid with life. I hoped I'd paid my debt to Midwife Rowe after working with her for several years, but Kit . . . The only way I could think to pay that debt was to save the lives of others. I figured I would know my debt was paid in full when he no longer haunted me.

More ghosts meant my debt had increased, and why shouldn't it, when we'd lost nearly a hundred men? And debts didn't pay themselves, so as men poured into Cambridge from Massachusetts, the Maine Province,

Connecticut, and Rhode Island, I doctored. Aside from treating minor wounds and dealing with diseases, my time was spent trying to convince the nearly twenty thousand militiamen to dig and use latrine pits a safe distance from sleeping and cooking areas, and to keep the water and themselves clean.

It may have been easier to keep the men clean and healthy if Dr. Church had shown more interest in running the hospital. Instead, he attended Committee of Safety meetings and was found in the hospital infrequently.

While most of the new militia arrivals settled in quietly, one man did not. He was a Connecticut man, a merchant of some reputation, and the captain of New Haven's Second Company of Foot. They alarmed us upon their arrival, for they wore scarlet uniform coats with buff facings above white breeches, white stockings, and black leggings—uniforms too close for comfort to those of the Redcoats. In the two days following their arrival, their captain was everywhere, acquainting himself with everyone and everything. Like Dr. Warren, he appeared to need neither rest nor sleep, and no one could match his energy and endurance.

His name was Benedict Arnold.

Dr. Warren and I were discussing latrines in the Committee of Safety's meeting room when Captain Arnold entered.

"Dr. Warren, I have a venture to propose. Everyone tells me you're the man to see."

The captain was short but built sturdy as a ship. Only the strongest gale could capsize him. With black hair shading gray eyes set in a handsome face, he cut a striking figure, but it was the confidence and determination he emitted that drew attention.

Dr. Warren's glance at me was apologetic, but I waved him off. I wanted to hear what Captain Arnold had to say.

"Three days in camp and a plan already?" Dr. Warren asked.

"It's a plan I've had in mind since leaving New Haven. A plan to obtain cannon for our siege—maybe enough to drive the Ministerial Army out of Boston."

"Cannon?" Dr. Warren straightened. "How? Where? How many?"

"Fort Ticonderoga." Captain Arnold outlined a plan to capture the old and severely underdefended fort on the shores of Lake Champlain in the wilds of New York. According to him, the fort boasted more than sixty cannons and a garrison of less than fifty men. "If we time our attack right, a small force could take and hold the fort."

Dr. Warren paced, lips pursed and fingers tapping against his chin, the same habit he'd displayed when writing his Massacre orations and the Suffolk Resolves. "We must think beyond Boston because General Gage and the generals coming to reinforce him soon will. We have them trapped by land, but they can escape by sea. If they march a force from Canada down through New York Colony, they will cut us off from any support the southern and middle colonies might provide. Fort Ticonderoga could be the key to preventing that outcome."

"So, you support my plan?"

"I do, but the Provincial Congress must approve it. You'll need a higher rank than captain, as well as men, supplies, funds, and a doctor. I will present your plan to Congress this afternoon."

"I await your word."

"Don't wait. Start organizing now. Your plan will be approved. I'll make sure of it." Dr. Warren smiled. "And Dr. Endicott here will accompany you."

Chapter Seven
May 1-3, 1775

I'd half hoped Dr. Warren had forgotten our conversation from the night of his headache. The other half of me stood up straighter under Captain Arnold's frowning assessment. "Is he even old enough to be a doctor?"

"I would trust Dr. Endicott with my life." He said it with such sincerity that I knew he was speaking the truth, not just empty words for Captain Arnold's benefit. Though his words filled me with pride, I felt unworthy of his trust. How could he trust me when I wasn't sure I trusted myself?

But Dr. Warren's trust was enough for Captain Arnold, who nodded sharply. "I'll start preparing immediately." With a salute, Captain Arnold left.

"We need more men like him. Men who think, not just fight." Dr. Warren sat at the table and pulled a piece of paper to him. "You will go, will you not, Dr. Endicott?"

"I didn't expect to be sent away so soon," I hedged.

"Nor did I expect to be sending you. But if Captain Arnold is correct in his assessment and his attack is successful, Fort Ticonderoga could be extremely important to have in our hands. During the French War, both sides thought it was the key to the continent."

"I know. My father fought in the Battle of Fort Carillon in '58."

Dr. Warren nodded, surely having heard the story from Da himself since they were both Masons and involved in the North End Caucus. "I want someone I know and trust with Captain Arnold. Either you or David. I would send you both, but there will be a battle here sooner or later, and I fear we'll have more need of doctors here than at Fort Ticonderoga."

"Another battle? Here?"

"The Ministerial Army in Boston will not wish to leave April's losses unanswered. As soon as reinforcements arrive, I'm certain they will attack."

My mouth dried out at the thought of a planned battle, not spontaneous as those on April 19 had been. A planned battle would mean cannons and mortars, not just muskets, tomahawks, and the two small cannons General Percy's reinforcements had brought with them. That, in turn, would mean more crushed and severed limbs, more amputations. The best chance for a patient's survival was if a limb came off quickly and cleanly, which required strength. David was stronger and more experienced than I was. The wounded would benefit if he stayed in Cambridge.

There was, however, the promise I had made Miss Scollay.

"I'll go, but for Miss Scollay's sake, for your children's sake, please don't take any more risks. We need leaders, and you're the best we have. If we lose you—"

"You won't lose me."

"You almost died in Menotomy!"

He touched the scar near his temple. "I did what needed to be done, Whitley. If we are not willing to take risks, if we do not charge forward bravely, then the fist of tyranny will close around us once more, and this time there will be no way to free ourselves. We have one chance to win our freedom, and we'll lose that chance if we wait for others to act. Do you understand?"

I did, but I wanted to return to a Boston with Dr. Warren living in it, and not only because without him my medical career would be over. He was family.

"Here." Dr. Warren held out a letter. "This certifies that you have completed five years of apprenticeship with me and are now, officially, Dr. Endicott."

"Thank you, sir. This means . . . thank you."

"You've earned it, Doctor. Now, while you're with Captain Arnold, you will of course provide treatment for any wounded, but you will also send me accurate information about the fort and situation."

"Won't Captain Arnold send reports?"

"Yes, but I don't know him. Besides, he's a Connecticut man. I know you. I trust you. You won't exaggerate or inflate your deeds to finagle a better position for yourself."

The enormity of the trust he was placing in me tightened my throat. I swallowed several times before I managed, "I'll do my best, sir."

"Thank you, Whitley. Move into the Oliver House with Captain Arnold's men and be ready to leave at any time."

As I was packing, David's voice interrupted. "What's all this, then?"

"I'm leaving."

"What, back to Boston? I thought—"

"No, to New York." I explained Captain Arnold's plan and what Dr. Warren had asked me to do.

"New York? But war hasn't even been declared yet—"

"Which is what makes this whole venture beyond foolish." Dr. Church glowered at us from the doorway, mouth pinched. "This could still be resolved without further bloodshed, for the events of the nineteenth could be construed as defense of our own property. Intentionally spreading this conflict is folly."

David and I exchanged glances. There was no way to reverse time and return to the way life was before. Dr. Church was living under a delusion to think that possible.

"And you are to participate in this folly, Dr. Endicott?"

"I've been ordered to by Dr. Warren, sir." I waited for him to countermand the order—as head of the hospital, he probably had the right—but he only sniffed and grumbled under his breath as he left.

"Well, that was . . . odd."

"He's a strange fellow," David agreed. "Do you have everything you need? Do you need any help carrying your things?"

"I don't have that much." An extra shirt, underdrawers, and bindings; my apron, instruments, and book of medical recipes; my pistols. "If I can't haul it across town, I'll never make it to Fort Ticonderoga."

"Make sure you say farewell before you leave Cambridge."

"Of course." I hugged him then, though, for who knew who else would be watching when the time came to depart. "You'll write, won't you?"

"Faithfully."

"Can you try to keep Dr. Warren from doing anything too . . . anything where he might get himself killed? I promised Miss Scollay I would try, but if I'm not here . . ."

"I'll do my best, but you know what he intends. So does Miss Scollay." I nodded, and he hugged me once more. "I'll watch out for your family, too."

"Thank you, David." I wasn't half as worried about Da and my brothers. Although I knew they would be in danger during any battle, I knew none of them would take foolish risks. Dr. Warren might.

Shouldering my pack, I wished it were weighed down with my books, especially my Shakespeare, but they remained at Dr. Warren's.

Captain Arnold and his men were billeted in the house of the former lieutenant governor, Andrew Oliver. It also served as a secondary hospital. It was further down the road to Watertown than any other house in use and was crowded with Connecticut men who looked at me with distrust. Unlike the main hospital, the trappings of the Oliver House had not been shunted into a closet. Fine rugs still adorned the floors, and paintings hung on the walls. In the study Captain Arnold had claimed for himself, a silver tea set rested on an end table and a decanter of fine wine waited on the desk among expensive pens, a silver inkwell, and smooth, creamy paper. I was used to fine things; Dr. Warren had expensive tastes. But these struck me as wrong. Dr. Warren had bought his possessions; these were . . . stolen.

I found a corner of the house to claim as my own. With no immediate duties, I wrote a quick note to William Eustis, who remained in charge of Dr. Warren's practice in Boston, asking for *Anatomy*, *The Diseases Incident to Armies*, and my Shakespeare to be sent to Fort Ticonderoga as soon as he could find a way to sneak them out of the city. I also asked him to tell Ma that Da, Lem, Win, and I were alive and well. I was certain Dr. Warren could find a way to slip the letter into Boston. Hoping to see my father and brothers that evening, I started back into Cambridge to the house of Mr. Benjamin Wadsworth, where the Committee of Safety, including Dr. Warren, had taken up residence. The house stood at the edge of Harvard Yard, surrounded by a hodgepodge of shelters. Luck was with me, for I caught Dr. Warren exiting.

"Have you already settled into the Oliver House? That was quick work."

"I had little to pack, sir. Instruments, pistol, and clothing."

"You wish for more to carry? Not the usual soldier's complaint, I'm sure."

"It's just . . . my books."

Dr. Warren laughed. "Of course you're missing what most schoolboys join the army to avoid! I'm sending a letter to William. I can include a request for him to send your books."

"Truly?"

"Yes, truly. If you didn't have your heart set on being a doctor, you would have made an excellent scholar."

When he made comments like that, I believed Dr. Warren forgot I was a young woman and had no more right to be a scholar than to be a doctor. With thanks, I handed him my letter and went to tell Da my news.

"Fort Ticonderoga?" Da massaged his bad leg. "That's where I was wounded. We fought all day, throwing ourselves at the French lines again and again, but they wouldn't break. We could see it in the distance, above the smoke, the fort we just couldn't reach. Fort Carillon it was then." Da stared at the flames, but he was seeing something else. What ghosts haunted him? A stick snapped in the fire, and Da started, shaking away whatever had filled his mind. "I would have thought taking Fort Ticonderoga impossible without a full army."

"According to Captain Arnold, it's vastly underdefended and in disrepair. He thinks it can be taken easily and quickly."

"Humph. Beware the overconfidence of officers, Whitley. If it will bring them honor and promotion, they think anything is possible."

Dr. Warren had said nearly the same thing. All I truly knew about war came from Shakespeare's plays, the few stories Da told, and my experiences in Lexington and Menotomy. How was I supposed to know if or when Captain Arnold was risking too much? I should have read some of those military books Henry Knox was so fond of.

"I'm coming with you," Win declared.

My heart lifted at the thought, but . . . "Win, I can't just make Captain Arnold take you."

"You won't have to. I'll convince him. I can't sit here waiting for this siege to end." He put another knot in his rope, undoing it just as quickly. He'd never been able to sit or hold still for long. "And they want to make me a drummer! They said I'm not tall enough to soldier, but I'm at least five foot five—I meet the height requirements!" I was certain he had demonstrated his ability to load and fire a musket because the indignation on his face was close to outrage. "Can I go, Da? Can I ask him?"

"If he'll have you, you can go. I'd rather the two of you were together, watching out for each other."

"Thanks!" Win was off before anyone could stop him.

Da shook his head, but he was half smiling as he wrapped me in a hug, his sawdust scent enveloping me in memories of days sitting in his shop, of laughter and love. "Look after your brother, Whitley."

"I will, Da. Be careful with your leg."

"No need to worry. Sturdy as an oak, me. You worry about yourself and your brother. Godspeed, Whitley, and good luck."

"Thank you, Da." I held him a moment longer, biting my lip and blinking fast.

I was about to enter the Oliver House when Win ran out. "Whit! He agreed to take me!"

Then he was off again, probably already on some errand for the captain, who didn't seem like the kind of man who would waste time nor reject a willing volunteer.

I helped with the organizing and packing, not only medical equipment and ingredients but two hundred pounds of gunpowder, two thousand pounds of lead, and one thousand flints. I was relieved to see that none of the Oliver's fine things were coming with us. Maybe Captain Arnold had just been borrowing them after all.

Dr. Warren and Captain Arnold were together constantly, two kindred spirits. Their heads often bent over a map or letter, plotting future endeavors in fervent whispers.

Win ran messages for the captain, flying in and out of the room we shared with a few minorly injured men.

"Whit." He slid to a halt as he entered the room, breathing hard. "Dr. Warren says the Provincial Congress will approve the plan tomorrow. They're promoting Arnold to colonel, and he says we'll leave as soon as they sign the paper. I'm to deliver this for him." He started for the door, then stopped. "Oh, I saw Henry Knox." He twisted a loose string at his cuff. "He's with the artillerists."

"Did you tell him I was here?"

"No. Didn't get close enough to talk. Too hard without . . . Well, it's always just easier when you're there." He held up Colonel Arnold's message. "Better deliver this."

"Win—" But he was already gone. I understood his wish to avoid Henry given how he'd once felt, despite the fact Henry didn't know. After our sisters, Sarah and Abigail, had told Henry I liked him, I'd avoided him for a week, but I eventually overcame my embarrassment, and we remained friends. Henry's was one of the few friendships I had, and I valued it all the more because he was the only one besides Win who enjoyed reading Shakespeare with me. Already it seemed like a lifetime ago that we'd been sitting in his shop nibbling our lunch between lines of *Henry V*.

Early the next morning, I made my way to the artillery camp and found the artillerists at breakfast near a few old cannons, not nearly enough to drive the Ministerial Army out of Boston.

"Winborn Endicott!" Henry exclaimed. "Have you come to join the artillery?"

"It's Whitley, actually. Hard to tell twin brothers apart, I know," I said before he gave me away. "How are you, Henry?"

"Well," he said, voice slow as he reconciled my appearance with the girl he'd known in Boston. "So, you haven't come to join the artillery?"

"No, I'll stick with doctoring." We wandered away from the others. "I never read any of those military books you enjoyed so much, so I'll leave the fighting to you."

"All my reading will finally be useful. I'll just be glad you're around to patch me up in case of any accidents." He waggled his left hand, which was wrapped, as always, in a black handkerchief to disguise his missing fingers.

He joked about it, but it was all too easy to remember his fear and pain and my own fear of doing something wrong. But it had turned out all right in the end. "I'm afraid you'll have to rely on another doctor. I'm leaving later this morning. Accompanying Colonel Arnold to Fort Ticonderoga."

Henry leaned against a cannon. "You'll be safe?"

He wasn't asking about the dangers of war. "Henry, you've known me for years and even you mistook me for my brother. With my clothes, limited bathing opportunities, and by lowering my voice a bit, I'll be fine. It'll be like bringing *Twelfth Night* or *As You Like It* to life."

Henry laughed. "You're more like Queen Margaret, fierce and taking charge."

I wondered if he would still believe that if I told him about my nightmares. "Speaking of fierce women, did Lucy escape Boston?"

Lucy had married Henry last June, despite her father's objections—he and the rest of her family were staunch Tories—but Henry couldn't have found a better match.

"She slipped out with me. Sewed my sword into the lining of her cloak. She's staying with friends in Cambridge."

"Good. Well, I just wanted to wish you luck, Henry, and say farewell in case—just in case."

He nodded, his levity melting away. "I'm glad to know we have doctors like you on hand, Whitley. Keep yourself safe."

"You, too, Henry. I'll see you at war's end. With all your current limbs and digits."

"I wouldn't dare injure myself if you're not here. Good luck, Whitley. Until we meet again."

By the time I reached the Oliver House, the mission to Fort Ticonderoga had been approved, and within the hour we were ready to leave. Dr. Warren and David saw us off.

Dr. Warren pulled me away from the others. "Whitley, I want you to be especially solicitous of Colonel Arnold's health."

"Of course, sir, but why?"

"That man could decide the fate of this war. He has ideas, plans," Dr. Warren's features were suffused with hope. "He has a genius for war. Keep him alive, Dr. Endicott."

So quickly had Dr. Warren been converted from skeptic to true supporter. "And your other instructions, sir? Am I still to send reports?"

"Of course. Just because I like the man— maybe because I like him— doesn't mean he won't try to use our friendship to his advantage. So, keep him alive and keep him honest."

"I'll do my best, sir." Although how I was to do that, I didn't know.

"I don't doubt it. When this is over, we'll return to Boston and run the practice together."

"I look forward to it, sir."

David embraced me, slapping my back, like men did. We pulled apart, avoiding eye contact for a blink or two. I couldn't think of anything to say.

David held out his hand. "Until the war brings us together again, Whit."

"Until then, David."

"Here." David boosted me up into my saddle, just as he had the morning we'd fled Boston. I threw a leg over, clutching the saddle, so I didn't topple over the other side. The horse turned her gaze on me, deep brown eyes skeptical about my capabilities. I tried to find a comfortable way to sit, but it proved no more possible than it had been on April 19. Grinning, David handed me the reins. "Hold on tight."

"Forward!" Colonel Arnold cried. My horse sprang to obey the command, and I clenched my legs, hands, and every other muscle, trying to keep my seat as we galloped west.

Chapter Eight
May 3-9, 1775

If it had been in his power, Colonel Arnold would have ridden night and day to reach Fort Ticonderoga. To my relief, the horses, both those we rode and those pulling the wagons, could not go so long without rest. The only time I'd ever ridden was from Charles Town to Lexington, only about fifteen miles, so the three days it took us to reach Williamstown at the very edge of Massachusetts were days of torture. Thank God the weather held, or there would have been no end to my misery. I only had the barest notion of how to control the horse and lived in terror of being thrown or falling off. My thighs were chafed raw, and every muscle knotted from the effort of staying in the saddle. I'd seen plenty of horse-related injuries in my work with Dr. Warren, so I knew how dangerous riding could be.

As often as I could, I rode in one of the wagons to give myself a reprieve, though bouncing over rutted roads on bare boards could hardly be considered comfortable, especially with the saddle sores I had developed. A ride in the wagon, however, did nothing to relieve the chafing under my shirt or my itchy neck, and it meant breathing all the dust kicked up by the other horses, too. Travel, I decided, was overrated.

Win fared better since he had ridden often during his summers working on the Warren farm, but even he was in pain by the third day. Stubborn as my brother was, he refused to ride in the wagon. He was determined not to show any weakness to the colonel. Colonel Arnold took no notice of our pain, and I began to see what both Da and Dr. Warren had worried about. If the colonel's goal overrode all else, he could be dangerous to the health and morale of those who followed him.

By the time we reached the Williamstown tavern, I was ready for a hot meal, a bed, and, if it could be managed, a bath. The bath would be tricky, but I would find a way to make it happen. Colonel Arnold's and Win's horses were already tied to the hitching post. I half fell out of my saddle, catching myself against my horse's flank. She snorted and shifted away.

I had almost reached the tavern door when Colonel Arnold burst out, followed by a hobbling Win.

"Connecticut commanded some backwoodsman—Allen—to take the fort, and the Regulars are moving south to reinforce it! There's not a moment to be lost! Those of you here to recruit, start drumming up men and send them on as they sign. Wagons, follow as quickly as you are able. You Endicotts, ride with me."

"Where are you headed, sir?" British-born Captain Eleazer Oswald, the handsome officer in charge of recruitment, asked.

"Bennington."

Colonel Arnold put spurs to his horse before Win and I were mounted. Win helped me into my saddle before leaping into his own. All we could do was point our horses after the colonel and give them their head. Darkness fell, swift and complete, as we rode through the New Hampshire Grants, only the thin road beneath our horses' hooves hinting that this land was inhabited.

It was only fifteen miles to Bennington, thank God. Had it been any further, we wouldn't have made it. Deep spring mud sucked at our horses' hooves, and I gave up holding the reins and just clung to my horse's mane, something she did not appreciate. All three horses were lathered and blowing when Colonel Arnold wheeled to a halt before the Catamount Tavern. He leapt from his saddle, straightened his uniform—he still wore the red coat of his foot guards—and adjusted the hang of his sword and pistols. Orders in hand, he strode into the Catamount, Win and I staggering behind.

The moment we entered, the room stilled. Nearly twenty men in fringed-buckskin hunting shirts held drinks, their muskets stacked near to hand, every eye fixed on Colonel Arnold.

Colonel Arnold in his very red uniform.

Drinks crashed to the floor. Men lunged for their guns. I pulled Win down behind a chair, collapsing as my exhausted legs gave way. Clicks of cocking muskets echoed through the tavern.

Colonel Arnold stood firm. Sweeping his steel-hard eyes across the room, he spoke in a voice that could halt a nor'easter. "I am Colonel Benedict Arnold, lately of New Haven and commissioned by the Massachusetts Provincial Congress to take Fort Ticonderoga. Here are my orders. Where is Colonel Ethan Allen?"

For a moment, silence. Then, laughter erupted from the frontiersmen. Guns lowered and drinking resumed as they pointed at Colonel Arnold, hooting. Several imitated him, to the growing hilarity of their comrades. Others danced on the tables.

These were the men Connecticut had sent to capture a fort? They acted no better than drunkards. Colonel Arnold had caused me to think better of Connecticut men, but these men sent my opinion plummeting. The colonel remained motionless though his face had gone as red as his coat.

The longer Colonel Arnold stood still and silent, the quieter the men grew until there was not a sound in the room but the crackling fire. They sat, throats bobbing, as they eyed the colonel. He let the silence stretch, making eye contact with each man, and they were unable to hold his gaze.

My heart hammered, and I couldn't breathe, but a slow smile spread across Win's face.

"I have orders." Colonel Arnold's voice was as low and threatening as distant thunder. "These orders give me charge of any expedition to Fort Ticonderoga. I ask again, where is Colonel Allen?"

"Let me see those orders," one of the backwoodsmen demanded. Colonel Arnold handed them over, then rested his hands on sword and pistol. I prayed he did nothing rash. My pistols were out with my horse, so I would be useless in a fight, and if one began, I doubted we would make it out alive. If by some miracle we did, we wouldn't make it far. All the medical supplies were with the wagons.

"They're official," the frontiersman said. "Colonel Commandant Allen and several of our Green Mountain Boys have already left for Fort Ti. They're sure to raise a thousand men. Where are your Massachusetts men?"

"Following hard behind. We'll need a meal and beds for the night—the best you have of both. And we'll need horses in the morning. Ours will go no further."

Obeying the authority in Colonel Arnold's voice, the men cleared a table and brought food. While Colonel Arnold chose new horses, Win and I were shown to a room.

"One room?" I whispered. "For the three of us? And there's only one bed. What if Colonel Arnold notices?"

"He won't. We can sleep on the floor."

A night on a hard floor after riding all day sounded awful, but sharing a bed with Colonel Arnold, even if Win slept between us, sounded worse. Sleeping arrangements covered only half of my worries. I couldn't remove my waistcoat or loosen my bindings. If I took off my cravat, I would have to ensure I woke before the colonel to put it back on, and I realized, in a way I hadn't when sharing a room with David, that this would be my life.

Colonel Arnold made no comment about the sleeping arrangements and didn't ask why I was wearing my cravat, waistcoat, and jacket to sleep. I wasn't even sure he noticed. His self-centeredness grated on me, but Win saw only the hero in Arnold.

"Wasn't he brilliant?" Win enthused in a whisper once the candle was out and Colonel Arnold was snoring. "The way he stared them down. Next time, Whit, don't pull me out of the way. If I'm going to serve Colonel Arnold, I need to be just as fearless as he is."

I snorted softly. "As crazy as he is."

"Crazy brilliant."

I knew it was pointless to say more. The way Win had doggedly stayed in the saddle for three days told me all I needed to know. Win believed wholeheartedly in Colonel Arnold. The colonel was bold and fearless, yes, but I wasn't convinced he had anyone's best interests at heart apart from his own.

We were off before daybreak, a breakfast of biscuits in hand. I'd slept only in snatches, fearful my sleeping self would give me away, and my fatigue combined with my chaffed legs and saddle sores made every mile a torment. At the same unrelenting pace we'd maintained since Cambridge, we crossed the New Hampshire Grants, that lawless land claimed by both New Hampshire and New York that was, if newspaper reports were accurate, attempting to become an independent colony.

Outside Shoreham on Lake Champlain, a stone house stood just above Hand's Cove, and there we found Colonel Allen at a council of war.

I bit back a groan as I dismounted. My underdrawers stuck to my thighs, and not just with sweat. I was certain a few of my saddle sores had burst, and my skin had rubbed raw enough to bleed. I needed a bath, bandages, and salve. My muscles throbbed, even my hands and arms ached from trying to control the horse. A bath and a full day of uninterrupted sleep, and maybe I would start to feel human again. I took two hobbling, bowlegged steps away from my horse, looked up from the ground, and stopped, the awe of the place breaking over me.

The gray sky hovered low, hiding the tops of the mountains, making them appear even taller. Their rounded forms were cloaked in the vibrant yellowy-green of spring, made even brighter by the gray, glowering skies. Wisps of cloud rose from them like smoke. Across the lake, the fort stood surrounded by mountains. They loomed behind it and were reflected in the still lake waters below. For at least a mile to either side, no trees grew, only low scrub. Lake Champlain stretched as far north and south as I could see. I had never imagined a lake so large. It was more like the ocean than any lake I'd ever seen.

"Whit!" Snapping my mouth closed, I shambled after Win and Colonel Arnold, who were headed straight for Colonel Allen.

He was a large man, with a nose that ended bulbously, dark hair and eyes, and a prominent chin. All in all, it was a face made more for action than for thought. He wore a green uniform coat, and the brass buttons caught what daylight remained. About 150 Green Mountain Boys watched our approach, muskets at the ready.

For the third time in as many days, Colonel Arnold introduced himself and presented his orders. There was some grumbling when he said Massachusetts had commissioned him. Unfriendly eyes assessed us while Colonel Allen read. When he finished, he handed the orders to the man standing next to him.

"Official orders for certain," he told Colonel Allen. "I recognize the signatures well enough."

"Another set of orders?" a third man asked, and I was surprised I recognized him. He had frequented Henry Knox's bookshop, and Henry had even sold his book—*Concise Natural History*. Bernard Romans was near sixty and had left Boston for Connecticut years ago. "This fort has too many claimants. Come on, lads. We'll make ourselves useful elsewhere."

A dozen or so men followed Mr. Romans, heading south. The man who had confirmed Colonel Arnold's orders snorted. "Good riddance to Captain Romans. He was more trouble than he was worth."

"And who are you, sir?" Colonel Arnold asked.

"Colonel James Easton of Pittsfield, Massachusetts. Some of these men are mine. We agreed to join Colonel Allen and his boys in this venture."

Colonel Easton's thin lips hung crookedly in a sneer, and there was something sly in his pale eyes. He gave me the same feeling I got from women in Boston who would bring you tea, chat all friendly, then turn around and gossip about you all over town.

"Massachusetts?" Colonel Arnold said. "Then you fall under my command."

"We're militia," a nondescript man at Colonel Easton's elbow said. "We're only answerable to the officers we elect."

"John," Colonel Easton murmured, but others voiced their agreement.

"I'll only serve under the officers I elected!" one shouted. He lay down his musket and walked away.

"Same for me!"

"Me, too!"

Colonel Easton smirked, and Colonel Allen shrugged an apology, but his eyes glinted a little too much for sincerity.

"The fort won't fall without my aid," Colonel Arnold declared. "I know the fort's layout, have a plan—"

"Based on what?" Colonel Allen interrupted. "Your years as a merchant? Trading and keeping accounts has prepared you so well for combat?" The men laughed, and Colonel Arnold's teeth creaked as he ground them together. Colonel Allen puffed out his chest. "I've been leading the Boys in the backwoods for five years. Nothing a merchant can teach me."

I couldn't believe what I was hearing. The enemy was just across the lake with reinforcements supposedly on the way, and these men were squabbling like children. In Boston, the leaders of the cause had been united. Yes, they had disagreed, even argued, but they had never tried to one-up each other. The cause had always come first, not the individual.

How would we ever win this war if our officers were more concerned with their own self-importance than with winning?

"Damn you," Colonel Arnold growled. "What if we shared command?"

My opinion of the colonel rose a little. At least he was willing to compromise for the sake of the mission.

"Share?" Colonel Allen asked like he was tasting the word for the first time. "I was here first. With men. And boats to carry us across the lake."

"My men are coming, and I have the gunpowder and other supplies you'll need to hold the fort if these rumors of reinforcements are true. I've also a doctor to care for any wounded. Finally, I have the only official orders to take this fort. Unless you're hiding yours somewhere?"

Colonel Allen hesitated. It was clear he didn't want to risk reinforcements arriving either. "My men won't follow you."

"You lead your Boys; I'll lead the Massachusetts men."

"Pittsfield follows Colonel Allen," Colonel Easton said, snake quick.

Colonel Arnold glared at Easton. Colonel Allen chuckled. "That leaves you a bit short, Arnold."

"My men will be here, Allen."

Colonel Allen searched mockingly for Colonel Arnold's men. I didn't need more time to know I didn't like or trust Colonel Allen.

"It's agreed, then," Colonel Allen said. "I'll even lend you a blunderbuss for the attack. You won't make it very far with just those pistols."

"Thank you." Colonel Arnold stuck the blunderbuss through his belt. "Mr. Endicott, ride back toward Massachusetts and hurry along any troops you find. We attack before dawn."

Win saluted and, wincing, mounted once more. Colonel Arnold didn't notice Win's pain. All his focus was on the fort across Lake Champlain.

Chapter Nine
May 9-15, 1775

The colonels retired to the stone house to plan. The moment the door closed, I slung a saddlebag over my shoulder and hobbled into the woods. A creek flowed down to the cove, and I followed it until I was sure no one would accidentally stumble upon me while relieving themselves. Still, I secreted myself behind some bushes before I stripped off my travel-stained clothes.

I nearly put my teeth through my lip as I peeled the underdrawers from my thighs. I buried those in my pack—there'd be plenty of time to wash them after we took the fort. I undid my bindings as well, wincing at the sight of my irritated skin.

I washed quickly in the freezing creek, just enough to clean off any blood or fluid from ruptured blisters, certainly not the bath I longed for. Then I rubbed a salve made from nettles into my chafed skin and applied lard to help moisturize. Clean and in slightly less pain, I bundled myself into my costume once more and returned to the cove.

The men were spread out on the grass, finding what comfort they could. Despite my exhaustion, I couldn't sleep, partly because I was in too much pain, partly because of the scenery. The clouds moving across the mountains were mesmerizing and kept me from thinking that in just a few hours, I would again face battle injuries. I knew when I closed my eyes, my memories of Menotomy would become nightmares once more. I rubbed my thumb across the old scars on my palm.

"Here."

I was startled to find one of the men holding out a waterskin, the same man who had declared the Pittsfield men were militia—John. To my surprise, he sat down. He was at least ten or fifteen years older than me, and his face and features were bland and hard to read. I was good at reading people—I had to be because patients rarely told the whole truth. So, to meet someone whose expression and thoughts I couldn't parse unnerved me.

He offered a hand and a smile I didn't quite trust. "John Brown of Pittsfield."

"Dr. Whitley Endicott of Boston."

"Doctor?" I waited for a comment about my youth, but he said, "Boston? How'd you come to be following a Connecticut man?"

"Not who I expected to be following. If I had my choice, I'd still be taking orders from Dr. Warren in Cambridge." I explained Colonel Arnold's arrival at camp and his conversation with Dr. Warren. "I trust Dr. Warren's judgment. If he thinks Colonel Arnold is the man for the job, I have to believe he's right."

"Even if you're not sure about the colonel yet," John said, reading into what I didn't say. I didn't like that he could read me when I couldn't read him. "I have my own doubts about Colonel Allen."

"Why follow him, then?"

"He's fearless, and there are worse men to follow. That fort will fall tonight—he's made up his mind about it, so that's what will happen. After that . . ." John shrugged. "We should rest. It'll be a long night."

We crouched among the trees surrounding Hand's Cove. Rain pattered down, and the men—about 230—had corked their muskets and covered their flints and flashpans in hopes their guns would stay dry enough to fire when needed.

Win huddled next to me. He had returned with about fifty Massachusetts men as night fell. A shiver coursed through him. He tried to hide it by shifting positions, but he couldn't fool me. He shouldn't have been out in such weather, not with his propensity for illness. I touched his arm. He twitched away, suppressing a cough in the crook of his elbow.

We should have crossed the lake hours ago.

Colonel Allen had sent twenty men down to Skenesboro to fetch the schooner *Katherine* and several bateaux. They should have returned by one o'clock.

It was nearly three.

Nearer the shore, Colonels Arnold and Allen argued in whispers, hissing like wind in the reeds.

"There!" one of the Green Mountain Boys called and was instantly shushed. A flat-bottomed bateau approached. Only one.

"Where are the rest?" This time it was Colonel Arnold who was audible.

Colonel Allen made no answer.

"We've no time to wait any longer," Colonel Arnold said. "As many men as we can get across before dawn. Colonel Easton, stay here to organize the men. Half Allen's, half mine, each time."

Colonel Easton began to protest, but at Colonel Allen's nod, he subsided. John Brown boarded first since he was to serve as our guide into the fort.

"Endicotts," Colonel Arnold said, "to me."

I stood, muscles protesting. Win tried to stand and gasped as his muscles knotted from the combination of riding and cold. His gasp dissolved into another cough, and I cursed the slowness of Colonel Allen's men as I pulled Win to his feet. We waded into the shallows and climbed aboard. One of the crew was apologizing to Colonel Allen.

"Couldn't get the riggin' right on the schooner."

Colonel Arnold pulled the man close, sniffed, and shoved him away in disgust. "You're drunk." He rounded on Colonel Allen. "Drunkenness will not be tolerated, Colonel."

Again, Colonel Allen said nothing.

Eyes flashing like lightning-gilded clouds, Colonel Arnold marched to the bow. Colonel Allen stayed in the stern.

When the bateau was full, holding about forty men, we pushed off. The lake, stirred up by wind and rain, waved into whitecaps, which sloshed into the low-riding bateau. For every two strokes forward, the lake pushed us back one. The distance across hadn't seemed so great from the shore, but it felt like miles. When we landed and jumped into the shallows, I couldn't feel my feet. I thought of our brother Josiah, a sailor by trade, and I wondered what enjoyment he took from a life of wet and cold.

No one dared make a sound since we were within spitting distance of the eastern redoubt. Win swallowed back cough after cough, shoulders shaking with the effort. I pressed close to him, trying to share what little warmth I had as we waited for the bateau to make a second crossing. Once the second load of men landed, Colonel Arnold signaled to John Brown.

"Sir, the rest of the men," Brown began, but Colonel Arnold cut him off, not waiting for Colonel Allen to weigh in.

"We're out of time. The rain is halting and the sun rising, Mr. Brown. We attack now, or we give up our hope of surprise."

Brown gave in. "We'll go around to the back—there'll only be one guard on duty. Our route will also take us by the collapsed eastern wall. Some men can enter over the rubble."

We formed up behind the colonels. Win positioned himself directly behind Colonel Arnold. I stayed at the back of the column. Unlike Dr. Warren, I had no desire to be where wounds were made.

We crept along the shoreline, directly below the fort and out of any sentry's sightlines. Brown led us uphill, and we came even with the pile of rubble and trash, which had once been the east wall. The garrison indeed felt safe to have let the fort fall into such disrepair.

Some men scaled the remnants of the wall. Colonels Arnold and Allen drew their blunderbusses and pistols and charged around the corner to the sally port. By the time I reached it, trampled wickets were all that remained of the sentry post. The gate hung wide open.

Inside, Massachusetts men rushed the barracks and herded the garrison out, stripping them of their weapons. Green Mountain Boys rounded up sobbing women and children, keeping them separate from their men. As one of the men exited the barracks, he broke free of the Massachusetts men, bayonet in hand, and charged toward the women and children. He slashed one of the Boys on the arm before a few Massachusetts men wrangled him into submission and confiscated his bayonet.

The colonels and Win raced up the stairs. Win trained his musket on a soldier—a lieutenant by his coat. Colonel Allen pounded on a door, bellowing, "Come out, you old rat!" while Colonel Arnold tried to calm him.

The door opened.

Colonel Allen, thrown off balance, stumbled forward. Arnold pushed him out of the way and then said loud enough for all to hear, "Captain, I am Colonel Benedict Arnold, commissioned by the Massachusetts Provincial Congress to take and hold this fort for the defense of these colonies. My men hold the fort. Surrender and all shall be spared."

The captain took a moment to survey the scene: his men unarmed and surrounded, the women and children petrified, his lieutenant held in place at the end of Win's musket. Without a word, he surrendered his sword and pistols to Colonel Arnold.

Fort Ticonderoga had fallen in less than a half hour with only one minor injury and not a man killed.

But our troubles had only begun.

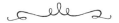

My relief at the lack of wounded was soon tempered by the situation in the fort. Fort Ticonderoga was little better than a ruin. The eastern side, which the French had blown up before abandoning the fort in '59, was beyond repair, and the two stone barracks, one for the officers and one for the soldiers, were tenuous structures at best. The outer, wooden defensive walls were badly in need of repair, and stores of everything were limited. Cannons sat precariously on half-rotten carriages or were buried under trash and rubble.

There was only a garrison of forty-two officers and soldiers of the 26th Regiment of Foot and twenty-four women and children in the fort. Colonel Arnold confined the prisoners to the soldiers' barracks until they could be sent down to Albany. He also commandeered the two storerooms in the officers' barracks for the gunpowder and other supplies arriving from Cambridge. He allowed me to use part of one storeroom for my stillroom, surgery, and quarters until something better could be devised. He claimed Captain Delaplace's quarters, leaving Lieutenant Feltham's for Colonel Allen. But Allen preferred to camp out in the open with his men, who quickly cobbled together shelters for themselves. Colonel Easton had been dispatched by Colonel Allen to deliver news of the fort's capture to the Continental Congress although Colonel Arnold had sent his own reports to Massachusetts and Philadelphia. In his report to Massachusetts, he included a request for more men and money to pay them, as well as additional funds for repairs and provisions. Mr. Brown took a few others and left to spy out the enemy defenses further north and into Canada, something he had apparently done before. Perhaps his history of spying was why I couldn't tell what he was thinking.

Medical supplies were very limited, which was distressing given the number of old and ill soldiers-turned-prisoners, but I was pleasantly surprised to find the large and unfortunately named King's Garden just to the northeast of the walls. Not only were there rows of vegetables, but there was also a large plot of medicinal herbs. It wasn't much, but it was better than nothing.

Kit appeared as I transformed my corner of the storage room into a temporary surgery. He hadn't shown himself since Cambridge, and my dismay at seeing him was matched by the bleak expression on Kit's face. I'd hoped I was beyond his reach—weren't ghosts supposed to haunt places, not people?—or that something I'd done had paid my debt to him. He didn't trail me but settled beside Win's bed. After our night in the rain and cold, several men had developed coughs, but Win's was the worst. I scrounged enough ingredients to make a batch of throat lozenges, an onion poultice for Win's chest, and a decoction of linseed, licorice, raisins, sugar, rum, and vinegar. I also gathered chamomile to dry and make into tea.

"You're not to leave this bed until you stop coughing," I ordered Win. Or until Kit leaves, I added silently. I didn't know if the ghosts served as harbingers, but the fact that Kit hadn't appeared until Win was ill did nothing to allay my unease.

"But, Whit—"

"No buts. You don't want this cold to develop into pleurisy or something worse. Besides, there's nothing for you to do at the moment. You won't be any use to Colonel Arnold if you don't get better."

After the fort's fall, the rest of the Green Mountain Boys were ferried over, and Colonel Allen's men once more outnumbered Colonel Arnold's. As word of the fall spread, more frontiersmen arrived until there were nearly four hundred men nominally under Colonel Allen's control.

It didn't take them long to find a cellar full of rum and liquor. Luckily, I'd snatched a few bottles of rum and wine for my medicines before they emptied the cellar, became roaring drunk, and broke free of what little control Allen had. I was in the barracks treating ill prisoners when they burst in. Hooting and whooping, the scoundrels snatched the prisoners' possessions and threatened the helpless men, women, and children. One of the bullies shoved an ill child to the ground. A child I had just treated.

"What do you think you're doing?" I demanded.

A slow, drunken blink preceded a wash of anger and indignation. In a motion far too swift for someone so drunk, he leveled a pistol at my head. "Stay out of it, Doctor, 'cause there's no one who'll be able to put you back together again."

I realized I knew how to load and aim a pistol, how to clean one, and how to repair the damage done by one, but I didn't know how to keep one from being fired in the first place. Why, I wondered a little wildly, had Win and Dr. Warren skipped that lesson?

Another man picked up a woman's sewing table.

"No! No, please! That was my mother's!" She clutched at his sleeve. He swatted her away, striking her face. Wailing, her hand against her cheek, she trailed him and the rest of the Boys out. The man holding me at gunpoint shoved the pistol closer, and I flinched back. With a laugh, he lowered the gun and followed the others. I pressed my nails into my scarred palm to keep from sobbing with relief. But the danger wasn't past until those men were under control.

On the parade ground, the woman clung to Colonel Arnold's arm, begging for the return of her table. Colonel Arnold faced Colonel Allen, the Boys menacing behind him. I crept around the Boys to Colonel Arnold's side as he attempted to restore order.

"This is unacceptable, Allen! These are not military stores but personal effects of our prisoners. Prisoners of war! As such, they must be accorded a certain level of dignity. This is not how soldiers behave, and if you cannot control your men—"

Colonel Allen cocked his blunderbuss and pushed the muzzle against Colonel Arnold's forehead. I froze, mouth going as dry as if the weapon were again pointed at me. The woman, still clinging to Colonel Arnold, fell silent.

"My men aren't soldiers, and last I heard, no war has been declared. My men hold this fort, and we have no need of a jumped-up little frog like you. Surrender your command, Arnold, or you'll surrender your life."

Complete silence.

No one stepped forward to aid Colonel Arnold. In truth, there were too few of us. The good-looking Captain Oswald, who had only arrived this morning, had been sent straight back to Cambridge with Colonel Arnold's report and my own. Most of the other Massachusetts men were employed repairing the walls and the General's House down on the point, building their own shelters, or digging out the cannons at Fort Ti and at the remnants of Fort Amherst, which stood ten or so miles north at Crown Point. Unlike the Boys, Colonel Arnold made sure his men were sober and industrious. Another mark in Colonel Arnold's favor.

Despite the muzzle against his skull, Colonel Arnold did not shrink or wilt. With contemptuous deliberation, he drew out his orders. "You may take my orders now, Allen, but mark me. I shall win them back soon enough and more besides. Then you'll be taking orders of a different kind."

With a smirk, Allen plucked the paper from his hand. Only then did he lower his gun. His men cheered a loud "Huzzah!" and returned to their plundering and drinking. With a signal to me and the few Massachusetts men present, Colonel Arnold retreated to his quarters.

Unlike his quarters in Cambridge, there was nothing fine or expensive, just a desk, bed, and clothes chest. A soldier's quarters. Perhaps what I had seen in Cambridge had just been Colonel Arnold adjusting from the life of a merchant to that of a soldier.

The moment the door closed, Colonel Arnold began barking orders. "I want the prisoners secured. Tomorrow, they shall be taken down to Albany. Once Allen's men pass out, as they surely will, retrieve the looted property. Set off before the Boys wake. Dr. Endicott, you are not to treat any wounds got by drunkenness or stupidity. We do not have medical supplies to waste on such. Understood?"

"Yes, sir." I thought more highly of Colonel Arnold at that moment than I had yet.

The colonel barricaded himself in his quarters. Since my own quarters were on the ground floor and more accessible to drunken Green Mountain Boys, I barred my door and made sure my pistols were close at hand.

Kit and Win watched me. "What happened?"

"Allen threatened Colonel Arnold. Prisoners are to be moved to Albany."

"What? I could help!"

"No." I felt his forehead. Still warm. I eyed Kit, but his face gave nothing away. "You're not well enough. Besides, it'll be safer in here. Allen will not be happy when he wakes and finds the prisoners gone."

There was much coming and going from Colonel Arnold's room over the next few days. Captain Seth Warner of the Green Mountain Boys had taken men to secure Crown Point but started sending his communications to Colonel Arnold instead of Allen. Word reached us that Captain Romans had secured Fort George at the southern tip of Lake George. Colonel Arnold made a full inspection of Fort Ti and continued to direct Massachusetts men as they arrived.

On our fourth day at the fort, I woke to find Kit gone and Win well enough to leave his bed. His fever had been the worst on our second night, and I had woken hourly to listen to Win's breathing. I'd dreaded hearing wheezing or crackling or, worse, a rough, heavy grating like sandpaper scratching against itself. But his fever had broken, and his lungs remained clear. I'd kept him in bed an extra day just to be sure.

"If I have to lie here and tie one more knot, I'll use it to strangle you," Win said. "There aren't even any books to read. At least if we had your Shakespeare, we could read *The Merry Wives of Windsor*."

"You know I prefer the histories. And Dr. Warren asked William to send my books as soon as he could." I felt his forehead one more time. Cool to the touch. "Fine. You can leave bed, but don't do anything taxing and—"

"Use the lozenges. I know the drill, Whit."

Later that afternoon, some of Captain Romans's men delivered the schooner *Katherine* from Skenesboro.

The next morning, Colonel Arnold knocked on my door. "I'm leaving, and I need a doctor to accompany me. I wouldn't say no to another soldier either."

Win's puppy-dog eyes begged me. "Please, Whit. I'm fine."

I wanted to escape Fort Ti and Allen's men as much as Win wanted action. "Bring extra lozenges and tea," I told Win. Only then did I think to ask, "Where are we going?"

"To capture a ship."

Chapter Ten
May 15-19, 1775

By the time I'd gathered my pistols, some of my dwindling medical supplies, and shot and powder from the storeroom, the *Katherine* had been rechristened *Liberty,* and Colonel Arnold had nearly finished arming her with four carriage guns and six swivels. She also carried a week's worth of provisions. The two bateaux accompanying us were armed with bow guns and swivels. Win stood at Colonel Arnold's side.

"Ready for an adventure, Dr. Endicott?" Colonel Arnold was in better spirits already.

I held up my pistols and medical chest. "I'm prepared, sir."

Colonel Arnold eyed the pistols. "You know how to use those?"

"Yes, sir. Dr. Warren was adamant I and my fellow apprentices be able to defend ourselves and any patients under our care."

"So, your aim has improved?" Win asked quietly. I pulled a face at him when Colonel Arnold's wasn't looking. Win had taught me how to shoot one summer at the Warren farm, and my first attempts had been less than satisfactory. But I had improved in the last two years.

"Dr. Warren only ever rises in my esteem," Colonel Arnold said. "Perhaps we can find you some more medical supplies at St-Jean."

"Fort St-Jean?" The fort was in Canadian territory on the Richelieu River. Trepidation filled me at the thought of spreading the war beyond the American colonies. What would Dr. Warren say?

"I thought we were capturing a ship, sir," Win said, his voice uncertain for the first time.

"Yes, the *Betsy*. Mr. Brown returned with a report. If luck and God are with us, we'll be able to strip the fort as well as capture the ship."

"But, sir, I thought the orders were to hold Fort Ti, not provoke the Regulars at a Canadian fort."

"You don't know much military strategy, do you, Dr. Endicott?" The question wasn't asked in a condescending way, but as if he had just realized those around him didn't have the same vision he did. "If you plan on serving through this war, Doctor, familiarize yourself with the strategies involved. Consider our position. If the Regulars are going to retake this fort, troops will come from Fort St-Jean. Weakening that fort will strengthen our hold on Fort Ti. Dr. Warren knew of my plan to . . . explore options for St-Jean."

What he said made sense, but I had no way to verify if Dr. Warren knew. Not that I or anyone could stop Colonel Arnold from doing what he had set his mind to.

"Sir?" a soldier called. "We're ready."

"Excellent. Cast off!"

I looked to Win, who shrugged. Whatever misgivings we had, it was too late. Our course was set.

Though I'd grown up in Boston with a merchant captain for an uncle and a sailor for a brother, until recently, I had never been aboard a ship, and my first experience on Lake Champlain had not made me excited to take to the water again. But the *Liberty* was larger than the bateau, and I hoped that meant we would remain drier. As we drifted away from the dock, I could hardly tell we were moving, but then the wind caught the sails and snapped them full. We flew down the lake, leaving tension-filled Fort Ti behind. It was a glorious feeling.

Lake Champlain, I was told, flowed north, so although we sailed north toward Canada, we were, in fact, sailing down the lake. I thought it was ridiculously confusing, but, as I learned over the next few days, most sailing terms were.

Thankfully, I wasn't cursed with seasickness—a good thing, since doctoring took place belowdecks where each wave could be acutely felt. My surgery would be the captain's quarters, located in the stern, which also served as storage for the small arms, gunpowder, and shot. It would be a tight fit if the need for surgery arose. I eyed the room with apprehension and tried to imagine tending wounds like those at Menotomy while the floor pitched and rolled beneath my feet. I prayed our foray to St-Jean would be as bloodless as our capture of Fort Ti.

The fresh air was exactly what Win needed, and I was willing to put aside my doubts about this mission for his health. Cheeks glowing with excitement, not fever, he shimmied up a mast as soon as we cast off.

Unfortunately, no sooner had we set out than the wind died. I glanced back at Fort Ti. "Um, sir?"

Colonel Allen had loaded four bateaux with men and was rowing after us. Becalmed as we were, we watched as they closed, then passed us.

"See you in Canada!" Colonel Allen called, throwing a mock salute.

"Damn him! Damn that man!" Colonel Arnold cursed Allen for a good five minutes, as creative with his oaths as any sailor. With a clear effort, he calmed himself, pulled his memorandum book from his pocket, and muttered as he wrote, "Oars."

We hardly moved an inch all day and watched as Colonel Allen and his little fleet grew more distant. With nothing to do, Win fidgeted. I found him a piece of rope, which he immediately started knotting and unknotting. "No wonder Josiah said I could never be a sailor. This is too small a space. Not enough room to, to—how long before the wind returns, do you think?"

It *was* a small space and filled with men. I double-checked that all the buttons on my waistcoat and jacket were secure and that my cravat was high enough. Relieving myself would be a problem. The privy, or *head* as they called it on a ship, was simply two holes cut into boards on the lower deck in the bow. I would have to be creative with the use of my shirt, which hung down nearly to my knees, and feign intestinal distress so no one would think it amiss that I was always sitting.

When the wind didn't return, Colonel Arnold used the time to instruct the crew in sailing and firing the cannons, as most of the men, like Win, were new to both. With no wounded to care for, I joined the sailing lessons. There was no telling when such skills would be useful.

To everyone's relief, the morning brought a fresh wind, and we covered thirty-five miles, anchoring, at Mr. Brown's direction, at Split Rock Mountain. The mountain towered over us, and I could hardly keep my eyes from it or from scouring the more distant mountains on either side of the lake, which narrowed at Split Rock, bringing the peaks even closer. Before arriving at Fort Ti, the steeple of Old North was the tallest thing I'd ever seen, and my mind couldn't encompass the height and wonder of the mountains which made the steeple seem no larger than the meanest fishing hut. If I climbed to the top of any one of the peaks, I'd be able to gather handfuls of stars.

The following day, we made sixty-five miles, passing Colonel Allen and leaving him and his men far behind. We anchored at Point au Fer, within sight of the Canadian shore.

Colonel Arnold sent Mr. Brown out to scout once more. "If the report is favorable, we attack tomorrow."

But the wind again betrayed us and was nowhere to be found in the morning. Brown returned and reported that while the *Betsy* sat at her wharf lightly guarded, St-Jean expected reinforcements. After another round of cursing, Colonel Arnold proclaimed, "We'll take the bateaux and row there tonight!"

He was leaving fifteen men behind to guard the *Liberty*, and I was to be one of them.

"I need my doctor safe and whole. Not wounded and useless to me."

"I can fight, sir, and you said we might be able to obtain medical supplies. I should be there to secure my own supplies, to ensure what is taken is indeed what we need."

"I apprenticed with an apothecary, Dr. Endicott. I think I can be trusted to secure what is needed."

"I don't doubt it, sir, but you don't need to worry about medical supplies when there's a ship to take. If I'm there, you don't have to divide your attention."

Colonel Arnold considered me shrewdly. "Perhaps you understand more strategy than I thought. You will stay to the rear of the attacking party."

"Of course, sir."

"And your doctor's hands won't be spared the rowing."

As evening fell, thirty-five of us loaded into two bateaux. The oars rubbed my hands raw, and the spray coated my freezing fingers, making the oars slip and the rubbing worse. In whispers, Colonel Arnold steered us around rocks. The moon and stars wheeled above, and we rowed faster so as not to be caught visible in enemy territory when dawn broke.

The sky was graying as we pulled ashore a half mile from Fort St-Jean. Colonel Arnold sent Brown up to the fort again. The rest of us stretched the cold and stiffness from our muscles and checked our guns. My pistol was heavy and cold against my new blisters, and I prayed I wouldn't have to use it.

"You'll be fine," Win whispered. "You're my twin, and I fight well, so it only follows you should, too, right?"

"I don't think that's how it works."

Brown returned. "They've no idea we're here. No defenders on the walls even."

Colonel Arnold grinned. "Back to the boats, boys."

We covered the half mile in minutes and ran the bateaux aground one hundred yards from the barracks. As we jumped out onto the marshy ground, mosquitoes and midges swarmed us. Foul-smelling mud sucked at and coated our boots. We weren't yet all ashore when a dozen half-dressed soldiers charged out of the barracks. At the sight of them rushing us, bayonets fixed, panic pumped through my veins. I fumbled to draw my pistol, but my hands were slick with river water and sweat, and the pistol slipped from my grasp. I managed to catch it before it landed in the mud. But then I just stared at it, my mind blank.

"Charge!" cried Colonel Arnold. The surety and authority in his voice steadied my hands, and my mind latched on to the simple instruction: charge. I hurled myself forward with the others, carried along on a tide of excitement and fear. We outnumbered the Redcoats, and they quickly realized it. They slid to a stop and, tripping over each other, scrambled back into the barracks.

"You men, keep them in the barracks!" Colonel Arnold commanded, sweeping his arm at a small group of us. "The rest of you, follow me!"

Three of us guarded the barracks' front door while three others went to watch the other exit.

From the wharf, a cheer rose. The *Betsy* and the fort were ours.

Colonel Arnold returned and motioned us to stand aside. He entered but came out only a few minutes later. "They say reinforcements are expected this morning. Move the prisoners onto the ship, then strip the fort of all food and military supplies. No looting! Any man caught looting personal effects will be whipped."

The thirteen prisoners didn't protest when we took their weapons. Aside from the men who had charged us, there had been a few others guarding the ship and two who had never even made it out of their bunks. We escorted them to the *Betsy*, where the sloop's captain was pleading with Colonel Arnold. "Please, sir, those are my private funds, not monies of the Crown."

Colonel Arnold stared at the money in his hands. I made my way to Win's side and asked, "How much is it?"

"One hundred sixty pounds."

I let out a whistle. I knew how badly the colonel needed money, and such a sum could do much for us. But if it truly was personal property, we could have no claim to it without being considered looters. Colonel Arnold had upheld that rule at Fort Ti, but with so much at stake—

"Keep it." Colonel Arnold handed the money back to the captain. "It is yours and shall remain so."

Win elbowed me, and I nodded. Maybe Win had been right about Colonel Arnold all along. He was certainly rising in my esteem. Leaving Win to help guard the prisoners, I went to the hospital.

I almost wept seeing the fully stocked shelves. Linen bandages, thread for sutures, surgical instruments, opium, ready-made medicines, and ingredients to make more. Enough, in our present state, to sustain Fort Ti for months.

At the docks, Colonel Arnold loaded five bateaux as well as the *Betsy*. Crates of medical supplies joined pounds of shot and powder, food and rum. There were five additional bateaux we couldn't crew, so we holed and sunk them. Colonel Arnold observed the scene, as satisfied as a canary-fed cat. "Colonel Allen wouldn't have done half so well, would he, Dr. Endicott? Probably would have shot someone."

"I'm sure—"

"I should still have command of Fort Ticonderoga, and I will regain it, Dr. Endicott." Colonel Arnold stared south, a hungry light in his eyes. "And I will make Fort Ti the most formidable fort we hold."

Within two hours, anything useful had been stowed or destroyed, and our fleet of eight cast off.

"This ship is rechristened the *Enterprise*," Colonel Arnold proclaimed, pouring a little wine on the *Betsy's* boards. "May her name be a sign that our own enterprises shall succeed. Set the sails!"

We ran upriver to the open lake, flying before a fair wind. We raised the *Liberty* an hour and a half later, and she joined our cavalcade. I stood in the bow of the *Enterprise*, sun warming my face. Movement ahead caught my eye.

"Sir? There's something in the water."

"The Île La Motte?" Colonel Arnold peered through the spyglass. He barked a laugh, the first I'd ever heard from him. "I do believe it's Colonel Allen and his Boys. I must say, they do have spirit. Luff the sails! The least we can do is give them something to eat."

Colonel Allen and his Boys had rowed for four days with no food and little sleep, and they cheered when they saw us. We all drank several toasts to Congress with rum from the stores at St-Jean. Hearing the fort was, at least when we had left it, undefended, Colonel Allen determined to take and hold it. Colonel Arnold tried to dissuade him, but nothing would change Allen's mind. Still chuckling, Colonel Arnold watched the four bateaux row off.

"Make for Fort Ti, lads. We're for home."

Chapter Eleven
May 21 – June 17, 1775

Handsome Captain Oswald returned from Massachusetts with three men from the Connecticut Provincial Congress to inspect the fort and their men. They praised Colonel Arnold and the meticulous notes and records he kept and frowned at Colonel Allen, who had returned from St-Jean with his tail between his legs. Allen had been losing men daily—they were not cut out for sentry or fatigue duty—and while Colonel Arnold's force had grown to nearly four hundred, Colonel Allen had less than one hundred men. Just days after the Connecticut committee left, Allen returned command of Fort Ti, Fort Amherst, and Lake Champlain to a triumphant Colonel Arnold.

Colonel Arnold made Win one of his aides, so when he set off on the *Enterprise* to make notes on the lake, Win accompanied him. I forced my brother to take lozenges, tea, and a camphor rub. He rolled his eyes. "Quit mothering me, Whit. You're worse than Ma."

I folded my arms and gave him my best Ma impression. He held up his hands in surrender and took extra lozenges.

With Colonel Arnold absent, Captains Warner and Romans took charge of repairs, building cabins for the men, and digging out cannons. I requested a hospital. "I'll even help."

Both gave me incredulous looks. "You, Doctor?"

"My father is a joiner, or was before the war. I know the basics of cutting wood and building."

I was soon put to work, and I was glad to have something to do. There were few injuries, most incurred while repairing the fort, but not much illness, not even smallpox. The men hadn't been inoculated, but I couldn't inoculate without a fresh case. There were a few cases of chronic malaria, one of which was Colonel Arnold's. He'd caught the disease years ago in the West Indies, and it flared up often. He also suffered from gout, but neither gout nor malaria slowed him.

"I can see why Dr. Warren trusts you, Dr. Endicott," Colonel Arnold said as I prepared an infusion of cinchona for his malaria. We were in my newly completed hospital, though it hardly deserved the name. It was a single long room with a table for surgery or making medicines, several rough beds, and a fireplace. The building sat on the edge of the lake near the General's House. I missed Dr. Warren's large, orderly, and far-less-drafty surgery.

I couldn't see anything I'd done for Colonel Arnold that made me trustworthy, especially when I was lying to him daily about who, exactly, I was. "Why, sir?"

"Most doctors over-prognosticate and bleed you every chance they get. Not you. You're direct and keep it simple. Easier to trust a man who doesn't overcompensate or sugarcoat."

"Thank you, sir."

"Your brother and I are headed up to Crown Point to make contact with some of the Indians and convince the local population to support our cause. I'll send him back next week for more of this."

Win returned midday on June 17. I had the colonel's medicine ready, but Win had been given permission to stay the night. We spent the afternoon working on my shooting with both musket and pistol. Win shook his head at my musketry.

"Stick to pistols, Whit, and you'll be fine."

"I hope I won't have to use either, but I'm glad I'm prepared."

"Prepared?" Win grinned. "You'd have a better chance if I was there to cover you."

"Because you'd love to sit behind the lines on the off chance the wounded are attacked?" I reloaded and took aim. I couldn't afford to be less than excellent if I might someday have to defend my patients.

We joined one of the Massachusetts regiments for dinner at their cookfire. Someone had caught fish and made an excellent chowder. Without the local fish and game, we would have been starving, for hardly any food supplies had arrived since we took the fort. In Boston, I'd always had enough to eat. Even with seven of us kids at home and taxes, Ma and Da had made sure we were never hungry. Since leaving Cambridge, there had hardly been a day when I went to bed full. The only positive, if constant hunger had a positive, was that the weight loss helped my disguise as there wasn't as much of me that needed binding.

Still, I wasn't about to pass up a good meal to maintain my disguise. I mopped the edge of my bowl with a heel of bread. The back of my neck tingled as though I were being watched. I looked up, bread and bowl falling from my fingers.

"Whit, are you all right?" Win asked.

Dr. Warren's ghost stood between two unsuspecting Massachusetts men.

His white breeches were streaked with dirt and blood, as was his white waistcoat. His satin one. The silver lacing was unmistakable. He wore his wig, which hid most of the scar at his temple. The edge of his Bible peeked from his waistcoat pocket. His entire wardrobe was impractical for battle, but with a pistol and sword at his belt and a musket across his back, there was nowhere else he could have died.

"No. No, no, no, no."

"Whit?" Win touched my arm, and I leapt up like a startled rabbit. I fled through the twilight, stumbling over uneven ground, but I kept my feet until I reached the hospital. Back against the door, I slid to the floor, fist shoved into my mouth in a vain attempt to silence my heaving sobs. I bit down and squeezed my eyes shut, but I couldn't stop the sounds or the tears. He couldn't be dead. Oh, God, he couldn't be dead.

Yet I had seen his ghost.

How could he be dead if I could still feel the warmth of his hands as they covered mine, frozen and sticky with blood, the night Kit died? How could he be dead if I could still smell the herbs and tinctures he taught me to use? If I could hear the passion in his voice as he delivered the Massacre oration? Could see the despair in his eyes the night his wife died? How could he be gone from the world before we'd achieved our goal?

Dr. Warren's ghost stood in the center of the room, the only thing visible in the darkness.

"Whit, are you all right?" Win called through the door.

I wiped my face, but there was nothing I could do to erase the signs of tears or the teeth marks on my hand. As soon as Win entered, he lit a candle, worry filling his face as he took in my appearance. I rubbed at the scars on my palm, avoiding his eyes. Win ran his thumb over the teeth marks on my knuckles, marks that would bruise before morning.

"What happened, Whit? What's wrong?"

"What did you tell the others?" I asked, stalling.

"I didn't have to tell them anything. One said you must have the quickstep, and another said if you did have dysentery, you'd gone the wrong way for the privies. A third suggested you had a magic cure, and they told me if you did, I was to force you to share it immediately."

A whisper of a laugh escaped. "They think if I had a magic cure, I wouldn't have already shared it? At the moment, I'm sure the reek of our privies alone would keep the Redcoats away."

"So, what is it, Whit? You don't run away and cry for no reason."

"I see him," I whispered. "Standing behind you. I see him as clearly as I see you."

Win glanced behind, the creases in his brow deepening. "See who, Whitley?"

I closed my eyes. "Dr. Warren's ghost."

"What?"

"I see Dr. Warren's ghost, Win. Standing just behind you."

Win spun around, searching every inch of the room. "There's—I see nothing, Whit."

"He's there, Win, blood spattered, powder staining his hands and face. Dressed like he was going to meeting, not battle, wearing his white satin waistcoat with the silver lacing—a ridiculous choice for battle, so maybe they were ambushed or—"

Win was toying with his earlobe and his expression—for the first time in my life, I was sorry I always knew what Win was thinking.

"You . . . you don't believe me, do you?"

"Whit, ghosts are something out of Uncle Abiel's or Josiah's superstitious sea stories or last century's witch trials, or Shakespeare. I—"

"It *is* like Shakespeare. 'There are more things in heaven and earth, Horatio, than are dreamt of in your philosophy.' When have you ever known me to lie, Win? To have flights of fancy?"

He shook his head. "You're the most reasonable person I know, Whit, which is why this sounds like m—"

"I am not mad! How can I prove he's here if you won't believe what I see?"

He was silent a moment and then nodded decisively. "By touch. Aren't the spaces ghosts occupy supposed to be colder than the surrounding air? If I walk through the space he's in—"

"No!" I dragged Win back before he could touch Dr. Warren, the doctor backing out of Win's reach. "Don't! If you touch him, he could possess you."

Win looked from me to where he guessed Dr. Warren might be, emotions tumbling across his face like autumn leaves. He touched my hand, still clamped around his arm. "You're shaking. Here."

He guided me to the table and made me sit. Brought me a cup of wine.

"This is for making medicines."

"This *is* medicine tonight. Drink." He sat across from me, the candle between us. Belief and disbelief warred on his face like light and shadow, changing with every flicker of the candle. He waited until I had drunk half the glass before he said, "You said this ghost could possess me. Has that happened to you? Has this thing hurt you? Does it mean us harm?"

"No! Dr. Warren would never hurt me or you." The ghost moved closer, sorrow and apology on his face, and I knew he was recalling the same events I was—when he had thought me touched by madness after Kit's possession. I said more quietly, "But it does hurt to be possessed."

Win shoved to his feet, hands splayed on the table, fury flaring in his eyes. "It *has* hurt you? I'll—"

"Win, it wasn't Dr. Warren's ghost. It was two others." I didn't want to say Kit's name, not yet. "And the second time—"

"How do you know it wasn't this ghost? Aside from appearance, how do you know that's really Dr. Warren and not some demon?"

"Because when they possess me, I can see their memories."

Fury melted into shock into uncertainty. Win lowered himself back into his chair. "Explain everything."

I took another sip of wine, nervous to begin. Once I told him, there was no going back. And if he didn't believe me . . . If he didn't believe me, I was afraid I would lose faith in myself. "It all started with Kit." The day of his funeral. His ghost standing in the middle of the street beside his own coffin.

"Kit?" The name trembled from Win's mouth.

"Yes."

"You've seen Kit—Kit's ghost—and you didn't tell me? Why?"

"Because this is going so well now?" He dropped his eyes. "Besides, what good would it have done for you to know I saw—*see*—Kit every time someone's life is in danger?"

"But you'll tell me now?"

"You'll listen to everything? Really listen?"

"I will."

So, I told him everything from the day of Kit's funeral to Dr. Warren's appearance at the fire. The candle burned down; Win lit another and poured us each more wine. When I finished, Win sat silently, tipping his cup back and forth with one hand, the other rubbing at his earlobe. Dr. Warren's ghost stood at my shoulder, and I was glad to have him supporting me still.

"Win?" I whispered at last.

He blinked. "I can't not believe you. You wouldn't make something like this up, but I . . . I need time to process it all."

"I understand." And I did. It had taken me months to reconcile myself to Kit's presence. But I had hoped Win would believe me and support me without question as I did him.

But then, that hadn't happened overnight, either.

"Do you want me to stay tonight?" Win asked.

"No, I—" It hit me anew. Dr. Warren, the man who had been like a second father to me, was dead. He was dead, and nothing would ever truly be right again. "I want to be alone." Against my will, my voice wobbled. "Please, Win."

"If you're sure."

I nodded, not trusting myself to speak again.

"All right. I'll check on you in the morning before I leave." He linked his pinkie with mine. "Good night, Whit."

I blocked the door with the table, so no one else could disturb me. Then I laid my head on the table and let myself weep. This time, I didn't try to silence my sobs but let my grief overtake me.

The candle guttered, and the flame choked out. Head throbbing with heartache, I wobbled to my bed and curled up like a child. Dr. Warren sat in the chair watching me. Watching over me as he had for the last five years. Guilt twined around my heart, squeezing more tears from my eyes.

"It's my fault," I whispered. "I should have stayed in Cambridge. I promised Miss Scollay I would. If I had been there, I could have—"

But I wasn't the only one who had made a promise. I glared at the ghost. "You weren't supposed to die. You promised you would live! We were supposed to run the practice together. You can't! You can't be dead."

He looked at me with such compassion, regret, and guilt that my anger melted. I had known war would take from me, I'd known that since I was ten years old, but the loss didn't hurt any less, nor did it become easier to bear.

Dr. Warren reached for me, hand stopping short of my cheek, lips parted as though he would speak, and words surfaced in my memory.

Remember me.

They weren't his words, but those of Shakespeare's ghost of King Hamlet. Dr. Warren would be forever in my memory, but remembering someone was more than thinking about them, as I had learned from Kit's death. Remembering was in how you lived. If I were going to honor Dr. Warren's memory, I had to be the doctor he believed I was.

I couldn't find my own words to explain this to the ghost, but I had long ago memorized Hamlet's response to his father. "'Remember thee? Ay, thou poor ghost, while memory holds a seat in this distracted globe.'"

Dr. Warren faded, but like Hamlet, I knew I hadn't seen the last of him.

Chapter Twelve
June 18-24, 1775

I wanted everything from the night before to have been nothing more than a bad dream, but my head was stuffy from crying, and the bruises on my hand were certainly not imagined. The worst part was not knowing what had happened to Dr. Warren. If he'd died just before his ghost appeared, it would take at least a week for news to arrive. It was possible, though, that his death had been several days ago. Kit hadn't appeared until the day of his funeral. If the battle or ambush or whatever had killed Dr. Warren were days old, it was possible news could arrive sooner. Writing David was futile, for by the time he replied, some kind of news would have already reached us. All I could do was act as naturally as possible and wonder wide-eyed in the darkness each night. When I did sleep, my nightmares, which had largely faded, returned, featuring not only the wounded and dead but Dr. Warren as well.

On June 23, a trio of Massachusetts Provincial Congressmen passed through Fort Ti in search of Colonel Arnold. They made a quick tour of the fort and the growing encampment. I was weeding in the King's Garden when Colonel Easton led them past me.

"It's really due to Colonel Allen the fort was taken," Colonel Easton was saying, his voice slick as whale oil. "I was just behind him when we stormed the gates. Arnold was quite raving, probably drunk, nearly shot Captain Delaplace when—"

"That's a lie, sir!" I jumped to my feet, and the four men started, flinching at the dirt flying from the weeds in my hand. This was what Dr. Warren had feared—men twisting the truth to advance their own agendas. I didn't always agree with Colonel Arnold, but Dr. Warren had trusted him, and in some way, by defending Colonel Arnold, I was defending Dr. Warren. "I was here that night, Colonel Easton, while you were still across the lake. You came over on the third crossing, I believe, while the attack occurred after the second."

Colonel Easton scowled.

"And you are?" one of the Congressmen asked.

"Dr. Whitley Endicott of Boston, sir. I was an apprentice to Dr. Warren for five years and helped care for the wounded after Lexington and Concord. I arrived with Colonel Arnold, sent by Dr. Warren himself."

"And how have you found Colonel Arnold's deportment?"

I decided not to mention his impulsiveness or single-mindedness, which sometimes led him to disregard the health or feelings of others. I couldn't let them reinstate Allen as commander or give command to Colonel Easton. "Honorable, courageous, and industrious, sir. It's due to him we have control of the forts and the lake and struck a blow against the Regulars at St-Jean. He has worked to find and free the cannons from the rubble so they might be sent to Cambridge to be put to use there. I said as much in my reports to Dr. Warren." I had mentioned the doctor three times, and none of the men had said anything about him. But there was a chance they knew something. "Any news from Cambridge?"

"Men continue to arrive. No action."

"When did you leave?"

"The fourteenth."

Dr. Warren's ghost hadn't appeared until the seventeenth. A battle must have occurred in the intervening days. A battle these politicians didn't know about.

The next morning, a haggard courier arrived at the hospital door.

"I have two letters for Dr. Whitley Endicott."

I swallowed. This had to be it. After a week of waiting, I would find out what had happened to Dr. Warren. "That's me. What news from Cambridge?"

"There was a terrible battle on Bunker Hill nearly a week ago. The Bloodybacks won the day, but we made them pay for it. Where can I find Colonel Arnold and the congressmen?"

Bunker Hill. Where Dr. Warren had died. The letters shook in my hands. I recognized the handwriting on the bloodstained papers—David's on one, Dr. Warren's on the other.

"Doctor?"

I blinked. "I'm sorry. What?"

"General Arnold and the congressmen?"

"Out near Crown Point aboard the *Enterprise*, I believe."

Tipping his hat, the courier left.

For a long moment, I stared at the letters—smears of dried blood and black ink on cream paper. Not opening them wouldn't change what they said, but these were Dr. Warren's last words to me, perhaps the last words he had ever written. Though I had known for days he was dead, I needed more time even if it was just a few minutes more. I broke the seal on David's first.

Cambridge
19 June 1775

Dear Whitley,

I would have waited another day to send this, but the courier is leaving, and this news must reach you.

Two days past, we had a battle on Breed's Hill in Charles Town to forestall an attack on our own positions. We have suffered nearly three hundred wounded and over one hundred dead or taken prisoner, but the Regulars suffered worse losses. Someone estimated they lost nearly a thousand men to death or injury.

Dr. Warren has not yet returned. It is hoped he is among the prisoners, but we have received no communication from Boston.

I fear he is dead. He would never let himself be taken alive.

He had been suffering one of his headaches. I hadn't expected to see him, but when the call to arms came, so did Dr. Warren. He walked with me and William (who arrived just days ago) from Cambridge to Charles Town. I tried to convince him to return to Cambridge or to stay with us to tend the wounded, but he was determined to be in the midst of battle. I tried my best, Whitley, believe me.

There are rumors. Some swear they saw him escape the hill. Some say they saw him taken. And some, some rumors are too terrible to repeat. I only pray they aren't true.

I have not yet found your father or brother.

I shall write again as soon as I have news.

Please write so I know you are well.

Yours,
David

    I wished I could tell David the rumors of Dr. Warren's escape or capture were only rumors, but because this letter was already five days old, he probably knew that. I wondered what rumors David had been afraid to repeat. I wondered if I really wanted to know how Dr. Warren had died.
    Setting David's letter aside, I drew another deep, slow breath before opening Dr. Warren's.

Watertown
17 June 1775

Dear Dr. Endicott,

Midnight has just passed, and I am to leave for Cambridge as soon as I finish these letters. I know you and my dear Mercy would order me to sleep, but I cannot. The Ministerial Army may soon attack Charles Town, and I intend to be there when they do.

After my narrow escape at Menotomy, I cannot deny going into battle is a risk, but I cannot sit behind the lines while other men risk their lives for my freedom—our freedom. I would rather die up to my knees in blood defending our liberties than safe and old in my bed. When liberty is the prize, who would shun the warfare? Who would stoop to waste a coward's thought on life? There is no sacrifice too great, no conflict too severe.

I know you promised Mercy to keep me from harm. I release you from that promise. It was unfair of her to ask it of you when she knew my intentions always were to be where wounds are made, not healed. I have written her and absolved you of your duty.

If these are indeed to be my last words to you, I urge you to continue practicing—during the war and after. Seek formal training in Europe. Both Italy and Germany have graduated female doctors. You are intelligent and talented, and we will need doctors like you in our new country.

I also urge you to remain with Colonel Arnold for he, like me, seeks to be where the action is, and it will not be long, I am sure, before he needs your services.

I am out of time and must ride. I trust Providence and the Almighty, who saw me safely through Menotomy, shall also see me through what is to come. I will see you again in Boston when this war is ended, and we can call ourselves, at last, free Americans.

Your Humble Servant,
Dr. Joseph Warren

Tears ran down my face. I wiped them away before they fell and smudged the ink. Dr. Warren's ghost stood beside me, solemnly watching.

"I'll do it," I told him. "I'll be the doctor you trained me to be. I'll serve through the war and earn my degree after. I won't let you down, sir."

A knock. The hospital had grown dark and, lighting a candle, I wondered how long I'd sat there as the light faded around me. Colonel Arnold stood at the door and behind him, Win.

"Sir?" I didn't dare say more as my voice wasn't even steady for that one word.

"You've heard news of the battle." Colonel Arnold's voice wasn't steady either.

"And Dr. Warren's death."

Win reached for my hand, heedless of Colonel Arnold's presence, and at that moment, I didn't care if taking my brother's hand exposed me. I needed Win, and he was there for me. I wrapped my pinkie tightly around his.

"Another loss. Dear God." Colonel Arnold wiped a hand over his face and cleared his throat. "I have been relieved of my command. Colonel Hinman will take charge of Fort Ticonderoga and the Lake Champlain region."

I couldn't have heard him correctly. "What? But, sir—"

"I have also learned my wife—" Colonel Arnold's words choked off. He swallowed and failed twice more to speak. At last, he managed, "My wife has died."

Another loss, indeed. "I'm so sorry, sir."

Colonel Arnold forged ahead. "I have disbanded my regiment. Those who have not reenlisted in Colonel Easton's company are headed south. I leave in the morning for my home before I return to Cambridge. I hope, since my contributions here have not been properly valued, I may be of more use there. Your brother is coming with me."

I heard the offer he didn't voice. I glanced at the table where Dr. Warren's letter lay. Where Dr. Warren still stood.

Serve, he'd said.

Remain with Arnold, he'd said.

Remaining with Colonel Arnold seemed the most logical choice. I knew him, how he worked, and if some of his habits and tendencies irked me, at least I knew him and knew Dr. Warren trusted him. I didn't know Colonel Hinman. He was a New Yorker, but I'd had no interactions with him. If he was more observant than Arnold, he might spot me for what I truly was.

Besides, staying meant I lost Win.

But what if Colonel Arnold decided to stay at home? He did have three young sons to care for. I would be stuck in Connecticut with no connections. Even if Win and I made it back to Cambridge without Arnold, I didn't have Dr. Warren to vouch for me this time, and sour-faced Dr. Church didn't like me. With him in charge of the hospital, Dr. Warren's letter might not be enough to gain me a position. David would support me, and William Eustis would, too, but they didn't have Dr. Warren's stature.

I could find myself back in Boston with Ma and Midwife Rowe before the end of July. My part in this war would be over, and then I would have failed to follow both of Dr. Warren's directives.

And I would lose the opportunity to pay my debt to Kit, Jedediah, and Dr. Warren.

I rubbed my scarred palm. Was I ready to return to the last place I'd seen Dr. Warren alive?

I looked to my ghostly mentor. His gaze swept the hospital—the drafty walls, uneven cots, neat stacks of bandages, and carefully labeled medicines. He set his hand on the table and nodded.

This post was mine, the men of Fort Ti my responsibility. As much as I hated to part from Win, I needed to stay.

I lifted my chin and met Colonel Arnold's eyes. "As much as I would like to accompany you, sir, my place must be here. This is where I'm needed."

Chapter Thirteen
June 24 – July 17, 1775

Win and I curled up on my bed as we had when we were little, both our heads on one pillow, nearly nose-to-nose. The candle on the bedside table cast the only light. There were none ill enough or injured so badly they needed to stay in the hospital, so we had privacy. Outside, the ceaseless sound of waves washed against the shore and in the far distance a wolf howled. Fort Ticonderoga slept.

Whenever Win and I had been separated before, we'd known when we would see each other again. Every spring, he'd gone to Roxbury and Dr. Warren's family farm, but we'd see each other when he came in for market or when Dr. Warren gave me a week to spend with him. After harvest, he'd return to Boston for the winter. But when he left Fort Ti in the morning, there was no telling when I'd see him again, and there was too much to say in one night.

"I'm sorry about Dr. Warren, Whit. I had hoped you were wrong about what you'd seen. About his ghost. I'm sorry I didn't believe you, and I'm sorry he's gone."

"Thank you. I—did I show you the letter?" He sat, leaning against the wall to see better. I read over his shoulder. "It's almost like he knew. Despite his words at the end, he—"

Tears closed my throat, and Win pulled me against his shoulder. For a moment, neither of us said anything, just grieved for a good man gone too soon. Win held up the letter. "That's what you'll do when this is over? Go to Europe?"

I nodded, still not sure I could speak.

Win touched Dr. Warren's signature. "What do they look like? I know you told me what Dr. Warren was wearing, but—"

Growing up, we'd heard plenty of ghost stories from Josiah and Uncle Abiel, for sailors love a good ghost story. I could only imagine the images in Win's head.

"I'm sorry. If it's too soon—"

"It's all right. It's a relief, really, to talk about this with someone."

"You should have told me long ago."

At the angle we were sitting, he couldn't see my expression. "We all hold our secrets close, and—"

"And it's hard to find the words."

I linked my pinkie with his. But since I'd given myself permission to speak at last, it wasn't so hard to find the words. "They, the ghosts, they look just as they did in the moments before they died. No wounds. Kit is—every time I see him, snow is still melting in his hair." My voice hitched, and Win swallowed hard. I pressed my cheek against his shoulder. "They aren't frightening or threatening; even when they've possessed me, I don't think they meant to frighten or hurt me. When they're out in the world, they can't speak."

"You keep saying *they*. There're more than just Kit, Dr. Warren, and the one who saved you?"

"Jedediah. I see Kit the most, but there are men from Lexington and Menotomy. I don't even know all their names."

Win was silent for a little while. "So, they look just like me or . . . or Colonel Arnold?"

My stomach tightened when Win compared himself to a ghost, and I hoped his words didn't tempt fate.

"Whit?"

"Yes, they're like the living, but—" How to describe them? They weren't transparent exactly. My eyes fell on the candle flame. "When you blow out a candle, have you ever kept staring at the place where the flame was?"

"You still see the flame."

"They're like that first moment after the flame is gone. You can still see the color, and they glow just a little around the edges, but you know they're not really there." I clutched Win's hand, pulling away enough to see his face. "Promise me I'll never see you like that, Win."

"I promise, Whit. I'll stay alive and safe." He set the letter on the table and wrapped an arm around my shoulder. "Why you? Why can you see them?"

"I don't know. I think it's because I owe them a debt. A life debt."

"Hmmm. You don't think it's—"

"What?"

"That it has to do with our birth? You almost died. If Midwife Rowe hadn't loosened the cord in time and hadn't breathed into you—"

I shuddered. Having felt the chill and pain of death, I didn't like remembering how close I'd come without ever having the chance to live. "Maybe, but then why don't you see them? You came just as close to death as I. And why do they keep coming back? Following me all the way here? There has to be more to it. A purpose behind their hauntings."

"Whatever it is, I'm sure you'll figure it out. You have all the wit, after all."

"And you the winning good looks."

"Exactly."

I fell asleep with Win's pinkie caught around mine, smiling, and wishing this feeling would last beyond the dawn.

I bid Win and Colonel Arnold farewell and returned to what had become my normal routine at Fort Ti, mixing medicines and inspecting the men and their quarters. The only change was learning to do everyday tasks beneath the weight of my grief. At times, I felt like it was a millstone tied to my ankles, and I had to fight to drag myself through each moment. Yet other times, my grief was a fog, blanketing my mind and making me forget what I was doing or where I was. Then again, it could be a knife or a storm or a dance. If it had only felt like one thing, it would have been easier to live with, easier to adjust to. But the only thing I could do was take each day and each change in my grief as it came and live with it the best I could.

I wrote Miss Scollay and told her to contact me if she ever needed anything. Writing eased my grief a little, though I wished I could do more for her and the children.

It didn't take me long to miss Colonel Arnold's industry and control. Colonel Hinman had no interest in enforcing regulations, like digging latrine pits properly or keeping the men and their bedding clean. Many of the men who had arrived in the last weeks had never had smallpox, nor had they been inoculated against it. When it had been just a few, I hadn't worried too much, but more men meant an outbreak would quickly become an epidemic. I hoped for and feared a new case in equal measure.

One smallpox case meant I could begin inoculations, but if I didn't catch it immediately, the disease would sweep through Fort Ti with the speed and devastation of a fire.

News trickled in. Letters from David confirmed Dr. Warren's death, though he said nothing about how exactly the doctor had died. He informed me Da and Lem were alive and with the army besieging Boston. George Washington, a Virginian, had been appointed commander-in-chief of the Army of the United Colonies by the Continental Congress. General Philip Schuyler was given command of the Northern Army at Fort Ti, which, under Colonel Hinman, had become little more than 1,300 men gambling, drinking, and arguing.

I continued writing reports though no one had asked me to, and I sent them to General Schuyler in Albany. I hoped he would send a more competent man than Hinman to command.

The days passed hot and dry, leaving us in a drought, so I added watering the garden to my list of daily tasks. Hauling buckets of water up from the lake strengthened my arms and legs, as it was an uphill scramble from the lake to the garden. So much time outside darkened my skin and gave my face a masculine, ruddy complexion. Using ashes, I shaded my jawline, and I felt at last my disguise was complete—hot, itchy, and uncomfortable as it was.

Keeping the garden alive, however, was important for more than just concealing my identity. We needed the vegetables growing there, for we had already picked the countryside clean, and there wasn't game to be found for miles. The drought only made food scarcer. We still weren't receiving supplies with any regularity from Albany, so Colonel Hinman cut rations. We tightened our belts, and I tightened the bindings around my chest. If I kept losing weight, I wouldn't need to bind myself at all.

At the beginning of July, a knock at my door interrupted my routine. "You have a visitor, Doctor."

"A visitor?" It couldn't be Win—he wouldn't have needed an escort—but I couldn't think of anyone else who would visit me.

My brother Zadock entered.

"Zad! What are you doing here? You—have you come to join the army?" Out of all my brothers, Zadock was the last one I'd ever expected to see in a military encampment or expected to visit me. He was my least-favorite brother, mostly because he'd spent a good portion of his life telling tales on the rest of us.

He sneered. "Hardly." The word dripped with condescension. "Have you seen these soldiers? Little better than animals, and you're living here among them. You're lucky I don't tell them what you are, Whitley."

Zadock was seventeen, but he hadn't changed much from the holier-than-thou snitch I'd grown up with.

"Then why are you here, Zad?"

"That doctor you worked with—you know, Eustis. He came by the house months ago with your books. Said you'd asked for them to be brought to you. Heard he wriggled out of Boston and joined your traitorous friends in Cambridge. *I* left Boston legally with a pass obtained by Abigail's Sergeant Hughes. Both she and Sarah are being courted by soldiers."

"I'm well aware." My sisters—Sarah, age twenty, and Abigail, eighteen—had been stepping out with Regulars for the last year. Only one of the many reasons the three of us didn't get on. I wanted to say more, but the possibility of getting my books kept me silent and eyeing the large satchel hanging against Zad's hip. If I said the wrong word, the weasel would happily leave with them.

"I only came because Ma made a deal with me—I bring you books and find out about Winborn, and I can attend Harvard in the fall. They've relocated to Concord until the riffraff clear out. So," he peered behind me, "where is Winborn? He isn't ill? Nothing happened to him, did it?"

Zad's one redeeming quality: he cared about Win. The whole family had a soft spot for my twin, but in Zad, it was surprising.

"Win went south with Colonel Arnold. He was fine when I saw him last. He's probably back in Cambridge by now."

Zad covered his relief with another sneer. "Well, I don't want to stay in this place any longer than I have to." He made a show of opening the satchel. "Here you go."

He held out my books: *Anatomy*, *The Diseases Incident to Armies*, and my Shakespeare. *Diseases* might help me convince Colonel Hinman to dig latrines properly, but I was most glad to see the Shakespeare. I had purchased it from Henry Knox's bookshop and had read the plays with him nearly every day for years. I was careful not to take the books too eagerly. I wouldn't put it past Zad to stuff them back in his bag and leave just to spite me. "Thank you, Zad."

"Well. It's a long ride and—"

"Wait, what news?" I couldn't believe he'd leave without telling me how everyone was. "Any word from Josiah?"

"None. The rest of us are well, though Ma fears Sarah and Abigail will marry their soldiers before long. You should come home, Whitley. If Abigail and Sarah marry and I leave for Harvard, Ma will be alone. You should come home and be a proper daughter." His eyes narrowed, taking me in. His scrutiny made me aware I was wearing the same clothes I'd left Cambridge in, and neither they nor I had been washed in some time though I changed my underdrawers, cravat, and bindings nightly. "If you're even capable of being one."

It took everything in me not to smack him with my books. I set them carefully on the table to remove the temptation. "I'm not coming home, Zad. I'm needed here."

"Needed?" He snorted. "By these wild men? Spending so much time treating prostitutes all those years must have rubbed off, since there's nothing these men could need you for except to warm their beds and—"

I slapped his face so hard he staggered against the door. He pressed his hand to his cheek. "You—you hit me!"

"And I'll do it again. I've beaten you up before, and I have no problem with a repeat performance." The last time I'd trounced Zad had been the night of Kit's death. "Da isn't here to save you this time, so if you'd like to leave without any more bruises, I suggest you get out. Now."

A pious expression of condemnation painted his face every shade of ugly. "It'll only be a matter of time before you're discovered. What'll you do then? What do you think they'll do to you?"

I charged him. He whipped the door open and sprinted toward the landing. If only the fear he'd raised could go with him. Someday, who I was would be revealed. It was inevitable. And I had no delusions that my masquerading as a male would be treated as lightly as it was in Shakespeare's plays. I shoved away thoughts of how I might be punished. Think about that, and I would be as useless as Zad thought me, and I couldn't let the little toad be right.

Chapter Fourteen
July 18 – August 14, 1775

The answer to my prayers for a new commanding officer arrived on July 18 in the form of Major General Philip Schuyler. Colonel Hinman and I waited at the landing for his bateau. Even on the rocking boat, General Schuyler, in a blue uniform coat and buff breeches, stood straight-backed and steady, which made him appear even taller than he was, and he was not a short man. He was slender, his ruddy face dominated by a sharp beak of a nose. His eyes, the same dark brown as his hair, also held something of a predatory bird, piercing us across yards of water.

The general stepped ashore, and only then did I realize he hadn't arrived alone. Such was his commanding presence. A few paces behind ambled a spindly man in the typical black suit of a doctor.

"Welcome to Fort Ticonderoga, General Schuyler." Colonel Hinman saluted.

"Colonel Hinman, I presume. Where are your men?"

"About their duties, sir."

General Schuyler frowned. "They should be ready for inspection—my inspection." His eyes fell on me. "And you are?"

I straightened, hoping my disguise would hold under his piercing gaze. "Dr. Whitley Endicott, sir."

"Ah, the one who's been sending reports." General Schuyler threw another frown at Colonel Hinman, who in turn shot me a look of intense dislike. "Call out your troops, Colonel. I want to see what we have to work with. Where are your fifes and drums?"

The general limped toward the fort, his limp caused in part by gout, I assessed, and Colonel Hinman scurried after. I was about to join them when the doctor stopped me. "A moment, Dr. Endicott. I'm Dr. Samuel Stringer, head of the Northern Medical Department and serving as General Schuyler's personal physician during this trip. Will you show me your facilities?"

The sound of fifes and drums playing "The Troop" drifted down from the parade ground as we walked toward the hospital. "It's good to see another doctor, sir." A few other surgeons had arrived with their regiments, but most—though older than me—had less practical experience. "I've been here since the fort was taken. Dr. Warren, under whom I apprenticed, sent me north with Colonel Arnold."

I turned to explain more, but Dr. Stringer was no longer beside me. He had fallen behind, hands linked behind his back as he gazed around at the scenery.

"Sir?"

"Hmm? Oh, yes, Dr. Warren—a good man and a terrible loss to the cause. Let's see what you've been doing since May."

I showed him the hospital and introduced him to the other surgeons, though I was the only one staying in the hospital since I wasn't assigned a regiment. Throughout the tour, he kept absentmindedly staring off or falling behind, seemingly unconcerned if he missed pieces of what I said.

"You've done well, considering." He nodded, smiling insipidly. "But it won't do for the future, especially since we're expecting quite a few more men to arrive soon."

"We are? For what reason, sir?"

He chuckled to himself. "Of course, you won't have heard yet. We're to take Canada from Ministerial control. You must be assigned to a regiment because, as of now, there's not to be a general hospital or general hospital staff. Which regiments are in need of surgeons?"

"I—here, sir." I handed him a copy of the troop returns we used to determine how many effective men we had and where new cook pits, latrines, and encampments were to be placed. While he read through them, I tried to wrap my mind around the idea of invading Canada. Only three months ago, we had been at peace, and our army was so new the men didn't have uniforms. Yet, we were to bring Canada into this conflict. "When are we to leave for Canada, sir?"

"As soon as we gather enough men and supplies." He looked up from the returns, peering at me as if trying to remember something. "You're a Massachusetts man, yes? Why don't we assign you to the Pittsfield regiment?"

I managed not to make a face. I hadn't seen Colonel Easton in weeks, thank goodness, and though I still didn't quite trust him, I got on tolerably well with John Brown. It helped that he was often absent, spying on the

Regulars. But it was too easy to remember how the Pittsfield men had joined with the Green Mountain Boys in disorderly behavior after the fort fell. At least it wasn't Hinman's regiment. With the knowledge that I had been sending reports to General Schuyler, Colonel Hinman certainly wasn't going to warm to me. "That will work, sir."

"Very good. I'll see what I can do about getting you more medical supplies before you leave."

"Thank you, sir, more supplies will be helpful, but I feel the real problem will be smallpox. Most of the men haven't had it, and they haven't been inoculated. All it will take is one ill man—"

"Don't fret yourself, Dr. Endicott. As long as the men are kept active, clean, and have plenty of fresh air, we have nothing to fear from smallpox. Now, as you are ranking surgeon—"

"Ranking surgeon? Sir, I'm only fifteen and—"

"And from what the other surgeons said, you have experience with battlefield wounds and five years' training—under Dr. Warren, no less. For now, you are the ranking surgeon. As such, you will be responsible for examining any men who arrive, keeping supplies in order, and sending reports and requests. And you'll be responsible for General Schuyler's health when I return to my duties in Albany. I'll do my best to find a more experienced surgeon to aid you, but I'm sure you will have no problems. I'll also send you another set of blacks." He straightened my coat's lapels. "Yours are a little faded and worn. We can't have our ranking surgeon looking like a beggar."

I was overwhelmed. Most of what Dr. Stringer had outlined was no more than I'd already been doing, but with it being official, it was somehow more daunting. Dr. Warren had trained me to run my own practice, but this ... I hoped Dr. Warren's ghost would appear and whisper confidence to me, but the hospital remained empty.

Dr. Stringer returned to Albany two days later, but General Schuyler settled into the General's House on the point and stayed to transform our soldiers into an army. He kept up continuous correspondence with points south, organized the northward flow of men and supplies, set up contacts among the Indians, and sent John Brown north again to obtain intelligence. Although General Schuyler was often beset by illnesses, he, like Colonel Arnold, was not slowed by them. In fact, it was hard to imagine a more active or dedicated officer. Gout in his right foot was his most consistent problem, but he wouldn't allow the pain of it to keep him from the training yard, standing when he often should have been sitting, and walking far too much. But every time I urged him to rest lest his condition worsen, he argued he had no time and too much to do.

The rest of us were hardly less active. Regiments arrived almost continuously from all the northern colonies. Mid-August, the 2nd New York Regiment of the Continental Army arrived under the command of Colonel Goose Van Schaick.

"Good to see you again, Goose," the general said, shifting his weight off his right foot. He was a little pallid and a sheen of sweat glistened on his forehead, not just from the heat of the day, I was certain. I would have to check on him later.

"And you, Philip." Colonel Van Schaick surveyed the fort. "I must say, the fort isn't quite how I imagined it."

As they chatted, I signaled to John Wood, the competent but inexperienced and, therefore, nervous surgeon from Colonel Waterbury's regiment. We began inspecting the new arrivals.

"How many of you have had smallpox or have been inoculated against it?" I asked.

Only a few raised their hands. I bit back a sigh of dismay and frustration. More fodder for a future epidemic.

A soldier in the middle of the ranks caught my eye. He shifted from foot to foot, fingers drumming a nervous tattoo on his musket. The burly man to his right gave him a half-confused, half-worried look. The nervous one wouldn't meet his eyes or mine. When his gaze accidently brushed mine, he dropped his eyes to the ground and went still as a rabbit under a hawk's glare.

I examined his companion first. "Name?"

"Paul Kilgare." He stood still and relaxed as I poked and prodded. His arms, shoulders, and chest were more than brawny, and the right side a little more heavily muscled than the left. Little white scars flecked his hands and face, and he reminded me of my brief encounter with the ghost of Jedediah. I asked, "Blacksmith?"

"Yes. How'd you know?"

"With your build, it was either printer or blacksmith, and the burn scars gave you away." I stepped back. "You're the picture of health, Private Kilgare."

He nudged his nervous comrade, his easy smile doing little to relax the young man. "See, Remy? Nothing to it."

Remy attempted a smile, but it fled when I stepped in front of him. His fair hair had been terribly cut, and it straggled out of the tail he'd tied it in. He was slender though he stood in a way that made him appear to take up more space than he actually did. His face was freshly sunburned under the smears of dirt along cheeks and chin, and there were bags under his blue eyes. I was fairly certain, but when he flinched away from my fingers probing his glands, I knew for sure. I'd also felt enough male throats in the last month to know where an Adam's apple should be.

"Name?"

"Remember Alden." The voice was low and raspy, like that of an old man who'd smoked all his life, not a teenaged boy.

"Mmm. Your glands are swollen. I want to give you a more thorough examination. Wait over there, please."

Remember mouthed at me silently for a few moments before his whole body slumped in defeat. He stepped outside the ranks to join the others who merited a second examination.

"Doctor?" Private Kilgare looked from me to Remember, worry crinkling his brow and sharpening his friendly, dark eyes. "He'll be all right, won't he?"

"I'm sure he will, Private Kilgare."

"It's just," he leaned closer and lowered his voice, "I think he lied about his age so he could fight instead of drum and—"

"Don't worry, Private. I won't spoil his chance at fighting because of his age. As long as he's healthy, he'll join you at your encampment." While Colonel Van Schaick gave orders to the others, I led the handful of men to the hospital. "Leave your muskets outside, please."

The men lined up, and I wasn't surprised to see Remember at the end, fingers twisting in knots. I examined the other men quickly, prescribing a white bark infusion for a fever, a purgative for a man suffering from diarrhea, and chamomile tea and lozenges for another with a headache and an inflamed throat. At last, Remember was the only one left in the hospital. He wouldn't come any closer. "Doctor, I assure you. I'm not ill. I'm just—"

"A woman."

Remember froze. Too late, she forced a laugh. "A woman?" The two words squeaked high, and she coughed, lowered her pitch, and rasped out, "Doctor, that's ridiculous."

I performed my best Ma impersonation. "You're saying after five years' apprenticeship and three months examining and treating men, I can't recognize a woman?"

Everything within her collapsed. Tears brimmed, and she dashed them away. "Please, I can't go home." She had dropped the pretense of a male voice, and I understood why she'd affected the rasp because her voice was naturally pitched higher than mine. "My parents—"

I held up a hand, and she gulped back her next words. She clearly couldn't tell I, too, was a woman. A little of the fear of discovery I'd been carrying eased. If another woman didn't recognize me for what I was, chances were men wouldn't either. I almost blurted out who and what I was, but I stopped myself. Just because she was a woman didn't make her trustworthy. My sisters Abigail and Sarah had made sure I learned that lesson well.

"Sit," I said. I gave her some space while I prepared a pot of tea. Since my stores of chamomile were running low, I used lemon balm for its relaxing qualities. Remember perched on the edge of her chair like a bird poised for flight. I poured her a cup. "There's a little honey if you'd like. Not too much, though. I need it for making medicines."

She didn't even touch the cup. "What are you going to do?"

"At the moment? Drink my tea and listen to your story while I make my decision."

"Decision? So, you aren't going to tell Colonel Van Schaick?"

"I haven't decided what I'm going to do yet."

"And you aren't going to . . .? You don't want anything from me?"

I didn't understand what she meant until her gaze darted to my bed. "No!" I cleared my throat, lowering the pitch of my own voice. "I mean, unless you're injured or ill, I won't touch you. I take my oath to do no harm very seriously. I can prop the door open if you wish."

It was her turn to exclaim, "No! I—I don't want anyone to overhear."

"Well, then. Let's start with your true name and age."

"Rebekah Bradt. I'm seventeen."

She struck me as younger, but perhaps that was just her fear and nerves. "How long have you been passing as a man?"

"A little more than a week, but for the first three days, I was on my own. Didn't want to risk joining one of the regiments forming up near home, Newburgh, down south of Poughkeepsie."

I shrugged. "I'm a Massachusetts man."

"Well, it took me three days walking the Post Road to reach Albany, where Colonel van Schaick was taking on men."

"So now the real questions. Why are you here? Why do you want to fight?"

At last, she drank her tea, then made a face at it, perhaps wishing it had been something stronger. She stared into the dregs as though she might read her fate in them, and she told her tale. "My parents are staunch Tories, always have been. Growing up, I didn't care much about politics, but my older brother Alden did, and his views began to differ from those of our parents. After the massacre in Boston, I started paying more attention, and Alden began arguing with Mother and Father. When Boston and New York City destroyed their tea, Alden took all our tea from the house and burned it.

"Father almost kicked him out then, but Mother stopped him. They didn't speak much after that. Alden talked about leaving, but he had nowhere to go. Our aunts and uncles were just as loyal to the king as Mother and Father were. Alden shared everything with me—his views, the newspapers Father had forbidden, his hopes and dreams for our colony's future. I came to believe as Alden did: we need a voice in Parliament."

She stopped, and I recognized on her face an expression I had lately felt so often on my own: grief and the pain of remembrance. I knew I didn't want to hear the rest of her story, for it couldn't have a happy ending if she had joined the army, but I also knew I needed to hear it, probably as much as she needed to tell someone.

I fetched the last of my wine—I couldn't risk using what rum I had—and poured her a cup. When I turned around, Dr. Warren stood beside her. He gave no sign of whether I should trust her or not, of whether he was there to protect or warn me or was just there because I sensed grief in her tale.

Setting the wine before her, I took my seat once more. As gently as I could, I asked, "What happened to your brother? Why isn't he here with you?"

She glared at the wine for a moment and then downed it in one swallow. For the first time since she'd started her story, she met my eyes. "When he heard about Lexington and Concord, Alden decided to join the army in Cambridge. I wanted to go with him, not to fight, but to look after him. Support the cause by supporting him. But he didn't want me to go. Too dangerous, he said. And someone had to stay home to look after our parents. So, he left, and I stayed behind. Alden died at Bunker Hill."

Remember swallowed hard, and I resisted the urge to reach for her hand. I offered her a handkerchief instead. She took it but only crumpled it in her fist. My own grief rose, echoing her own. Had her brother and Dr. Warren fought together? Died together? I blinked back my tears as I looked at Dr. Warren standing next to her, his expression sorrowful. He looked at her, then me, and nodded. He thought I could trust her. I had never doubted him before and wasn't about to start now.

Remember breathed deep and squared her shoulders. "I couldn't remain at home after that. I wanted to honor Alden, to do what he would have done. So, I took my brother's name for my surname, dressed in a set of his old clothes, and stole my father's musket." She leaned forward on her forearms, a pleading desperation in her blue eyes. "I have to fight. For Alden. Please, don't tell Colonel Van Schaick."

"I never said I'd tell anyone. I said I had a decision to make." I was stalling. Although I knew I was going to tell her, I was nervous. Since Mrs. Adams had knotted my cravat around my neck, I had been a man. But the moment I told her, a near stranger would know I was truly Miss Endicott, not Dr. Endicott. However, I couldn't deny the kinship I felt, the bond of our loss, of being women in a man's world, and if someone didn't help her, she would be discovered before the week was out. Dr. Warren nodded again, resolving my wavering thoughts.

"Decide what?"

"Whether or not to tell you the truth. You see—" I untied my cravat and loosed my hair. "I'm a woman, too."

"What?" Her eyes were jumping all over me: face, chest, hands, throat.

"I can strip down if that would reassure you."

Her eyes went even wider. "No! No, but how? Who are you?"

"Whitley Endicott. Dr. Endicott now, though I prefer my friends call me Whit. I'm sorry I frightened you, but I had to be sure I could trust you before I revealed myself. As for how, I can help you with that. It's a good thing I was the doctor to examine you. I don't think your disguise would have held much longer. Your fellow soldiers were already becoming suspicious."

"What? Who?"

"The big fellow who stood next to you. Blacksmith. Thought you lied about your age."

"Paul? He's been nice. Helpful. A friend."

"If he spends enough time around you and we don't fix your disguise, it'll only be a matter of time before he realizes it isn't age you lied about."

"But how do we—what do I have to do? I thought once I was here—" Tears were brimming in her eyes, eyes underscored with dark bags. I recalled my journey to Fort Ti with Colonel Arnold and my sleepless nights. "When's the last time you slept?"

Remember laugh-sobbed, a little desperately, and pushed a hand through her hair, pulling more uneven strands loose. "I hardly dared close my eyes on the march up. Too much fear. We camped wherever darkness caught us and slept in our clothes, but still. "

"Take a nap now. You can stay here a day or two, and I can teach you all I know about being a man."

"Why? Why are you helping me? You could have just let me be discovered. It would probably be safer for you if you were the only disguised woman here. Why help me?"

"When I first decided to be part of this war, another woman helped me. She said we women protect our own. And you're not the only one to have lost someone at Bunker Hill."

"You lost someone? Who? Will you tell me? You know my story. It's only fair."

"Then we'll need more tea." We went through a whole pot as I told her, as concisely as I could and with no mention of ghosts, the story of how I had ended up at Fort Ti.

"You knew Dr. Warren, worked with him." She shook her head. "Alden idolized him, read his Massacre orations and Suffolk Resolves repeatedly. Perhaps we were fated to be together, Dr. Endicott."

"Whitley or Whit, please."

"Whitley."

"Better. Now, why don't you get some sleep?"

Tucked up in one of the spare cots, she was asleep before I left to inspect the new encampment. As soon as he saw me, Private Paul Kilgare approached. "How's Remy?"

"Remy?"

"Less of a mouthful than Remember."

I couldn't argue with that. "He's fine, Private. A little fever and some swelling in his throat, but nothing medicine and a few days' rest won't cure."

"Good. Thank you, Doctor."

"Friends, are you? Or relatives?" I asked even though I knew the answer. I wanted to get a better feel for who he was.

"No. Didn't meet him until I joined up. He just seemed a little lost, needed someone to watch out for him."

He reminded me a bit of David, and I decided I liked Private Kilgare. "I'll be sure to tell Private Alden you asked after him. He'll rejoin your regiment in a couple days."

That night, lying in our separate beds in the darkness, the muggy night air serving as a blanket, I was reminded of the last months I'd lived at Dr. Warren's, when Miss Scollay and I had shared a bedchamber. The lavender scent she preferred surrounding us, her body warm next to mine in the large bed. Though she was eleven years older than me, we had often whispered to each other in the darkness, our secrets safe in the night between us. I hadn't realized how much I'd missed those conversations, the company of another woman.

I shifted, my dried-grass-filled mattress rustling under me and releasing the faint scent of past peaceful summers. "Remy?"

"Hmm?"

"Do you find men's clothes as uncomfortable as I first did?"

A giggle quickly stifled. "Yes! The way the trousers rub!"

I grinned. "And they're so warm."

"I thought petticoats, stays, and a dress stifling, but at least my skirts breathed."

"Just wait until we find you a waistcoat and cravat. In this August heat, they're torture."

"I do like the boots, though. So much more comfortable than heeled shoes."

"I've only ever worn boots. In my work with Dr. Warren, fancy shoes never made sense."

"Lucky. They pinched at my toes and rubbed against my heels. Of course, my boots have given me blisters in different places. Who knew the top of your toes could blister?"

"I can tend those in the morning."

"Thanks." For a few moments, our breathing was the only sound. Then Remy asked, "Whitley?"

"Hmm?"

"Do you really think I can pass myself off as a man?"

"You've made it this far. With my help and the two of us to cover for each other, we'll be the best men this army has ever seen."

Chapter Fifteen
August 15 – September 6, 1775

The day after Remy's regiment arrived, Captain Eleazer Oswald, Colonel Arnold's dashing aide-de-camp, returned to Fort Ticonderoga with a letter for General Schuyler. When I heard Oswald was in camp, I made my way to the General's House. There was nothing grand about the house, but with its private bedroom (furnished with a real bed and down mattress), a study, a kitchen, and a dining room, it was far more luxurious than anything else at Fort Ti.

"Good to see you again, Captain Oswald." Like the rest of us, he was thinner than he had been when we'd first set out from Cambridge, but he was still clean shaven and as handsome as I remembered.

"And you, Dr. Endicott. I've a letter for you from your brother."

"You've seen him? How is he? Is he still with Colonel Arnold?"

Captain Oswald ticked off the answers on his fingers. "I have, he's well, and we both are. We're going with him to Canada."

"Colonel Arnold's for Canada? He and Win are coming here?" If I were reunited with Colonel Arnold, then I would be able to follow the second of Dr. Warren's directives: stay with Arnold.

"No." Captain Oswald leaned closer and lowered his voice. "We're headed for Quebec City by a back route through the Maine Province. Very secret."

"Captain!" General Schuyler stumped out of the study. He was pale and sweat trickled down from his hairline. He winced at every step. He tried to hide it, but I noted the twitch in his jaw and the corner of his eye. His gout was playing up again. He shouldn't be at Fort Ti with all the stress that came from commanding an army. He should be home in Albany, resting and recovering.

Captain Oswald straightened, and I stepped back.

"Tell General Washington I give my wholehearted approval. Tell Colonel Arnold I will see him in Quebec."

My heart lifted. The colonel and Win weren't coming to Fort Ti, but it sounded like we would join them in Canada.

"I will, sir." Captain Oswald took the dispatches, then held out a hand to me. "Until we meet in Canada, Dr. Endicott."

"Until Canada. Give my brother my best."

"What can I do for you, Doctor?" General Schuyler asked.

"Nothing, sir. I came only to speak to Captain Oswald, but, sir, you aren't well. You push yourself too hard. You should return to Albany."

"You know I can't do that. At least not until General Montgomery arrives, which should be tomorrow."

"General Montgomery, sir?"

"Yes. He served in this region and Canada under Amherst and Abercromby during the French War. He's coming to lead the army in Canada and should take some of the workload off my shoulders. I can rest after he arrives."

"But, sir—"

"Dr. Endicott, I promise to stay inside for the rest of the day and do all my work sitting. Will that satisfy you?"

It didn't, but I doubted any argument I made would change his mind. "May I at least look at your foot, sir?"

"As long as I can work while you do it." In his study, he propped his foot on a stool and began answering correspondence. I eased off his boot and stocking, and he hissed. The first joint of his right big toe and both sides of his ankle were swollen and an angry red. He grunted as I carefully probed each tender spot. "Well, Doctor?"

"If you remain at your desk and keep your foot elevated, you may work. I'll send some tea to reduce your fever and something for the pain."

"A compromise. If only all New Englanders would be so obliging." With a wave of the letter in his hand, he dismissed me. Grumbling about the stubbornness of generals, I made my way back to the hospital.

Once I'd sent tea and medicine to the general, Remy and I worked on her disguise. I had given her the spare waistcoat and cravat Dr. Stringer had sent from Albany with the new suit of blacks. I had also showed her how fine-ground ashes were better than dirt to give the impression of a beard coming in and gave her a lesson in shaving.

"If you play the barber, no one wonders who shaves you. Besides, we let them see you shaving me and me shaving you once or twice, and they'll stop thinking about it."

"Mother always shaved Father and Alden." She held the straight razor out nervously. "Where did you learn to shave a man?"

"I'm a doctor. I have to know how to use every kind of blade. Actually, my ma taught all us girls. Said it was a skill we'd need to keep a husband."

"Never thinking you'd use it to play a man." Remy scratched at her side, under her breasts. "Does this binding ever stop itching?"

"I'll let you know. But it helps if you change it often. I use bandages and wash them every couple of days." I gestured to the strips of linen hanging before the hearth. "No one even suspects what I use them for. It also helps to rub some lard into your skin each night and each morning. Keeps your skin from chaffing as badly."

She wrinkled her nose. "Lard? Doesn't that smell?"

"Because everyone else here smells like roses?" We both laughed. The fort reeked of stale sweat and loose bowels; a little lard would hardly be noticed.

At a knock on the door, we both froze, laughter dying. Had our laughter carried beyond the walls? How feminine had it sounded? Wide-eyed, Remy looked ready to bolt. I gestured for her to stay calm. The worst thing would be to panic. I took the razor from her and pointed to her bed. She was supposed to be ill, after all. Despite the day's warmth, she pulled the tattered edge of the blanket up to her chin. I set the razor on the table and went to the door, my hand slick on the latch.

Paul Kilgare paced outside. "Doctor! I came to check on Remy. How is he?"

I swallowed back my sigh of relief. He didn't seem suspicious at all. "He's just fine." I raised my voice so Remy was sure to hear. "You can come in, Private Kilgare. He's not contagious. A visitor for you, Remy."

Clearing her throat, she reverted to the slightly raspy voice she affected as a male. "Paul, what are you doing here?"

"Just wanted to check that you were all right. I promised to help you with your shooting."

"Tomorrow," I said. "I want to keep an eye on him for one more night. You're welcome to stay for our midday meal if you wish."

"Thank you."

"I'll go find us some food," I said. Remy shot me a fearful look, but she had to return to acting like a man. We both did, and the sooner the better.

"I'll be back as soon as I can."

When I returned, the large young man was teaching Remy the card game Brag.

"You can deal me in after we eat," I said.

"You play?" Remy asked.

"We're not so uptight in Boston that we don't play cards, but I learned Brag after I joined up. I can only read for so long, and cards have been the entertainment of choice."

"It works better with more people," Paul said.

"At least we can teach Remy the basics."

When Paul left an hour later, it was clear Brag wasn't Remy's game.

"You just need to bluff better."

"You mean lie." She lay back on her cot. "If I can't lie about cards, how can I lie about myself?"

"Well, it's a good thing we adjusted your disguise before Paul showed up. He didn't suspect a thing. You did well. The real test will be when you rejoin your regiment tomorrow and stand inspection in front of General Montgomery."

Drums and fifes called us to assemble when General Richard Montgomery arrived midmorning. The regiments lined up in much better order than even a month ago, muskets shouldered and backs straight. I stood to the side with the other surgeons, my eyes on the generals. General Schuyler looked no better than yesterday, but he stood steady, a proper officer and an excellent example for his men.

General Montgomery was tall and, to my surprise, bald. Of greater surprise, he wore no wig to disguise his baldness. His prominent nose drew one's gaze down from his hazel eyes, sharp enough to cut and too keen to miss anything. His face was pockmarked, a good sign in my book. In his blue and buff uniform coat, he cut quite the figure among our mismatched and ragged troops.

"From now until we sail for Canada," General Montgomery said, an Irish accent flavoring his speech, "you will drill daily, and each regiment will have fatigue duty as well. You will look and act like the soldiers you are. We are fighting for our rights and homes, and the Ministerial troops will fall before us. Canada will be ours!"

The men lifted a cheer. He dismissed all but us doctors. We thrust our shoulders back and lifted our chins as he approached, General Schuyler at his side, trying to hide his uneven gait. General Montgomery's eyes swept over us, a slight frown drawing brows and mouth down. "I understand you have a hospital here. Who has charge of it?"

"I have, sir. Dr. Whitley Endicott, Boston, Massachusetts."

His frown deepened, and I knew it was because of my youth. But the other surgeons were hardly much older. The oldest was only twenty-one. Under his keen gaze, I felt my disguise being picked apart piece by piece, but I refrained from licking my lips or tugging on my clothes. Confidence was what I needed to portray. If I believed myself to be Dr. Endicott, he would believe it.

"Give me a report, Dr. Endicott."

This was my chance to prove myself. I straightened until my spine protested and met those cutting eyes. "We have little in the way of ready-made medicines, sir, most of our ingredients coming from the King's Garden below the fort. The supplies we captured at Fort St-Jean in June are nearly gone, and we do not have enough bandages or opium to see us through a battle. Two of our surgeons have no instruments. All this has been reported to Dr. Stringer in Albany, along with requests for more supplies. As for the men, conditions here are greatly improved since General Schuyler arrived last month to enforce adherence to my repeated orders for proper spacing and digging of latrine pits. The men suffer from a number of minor ailments—fevers, diarrhea, and some malaria." I took a breath and pushed forward. "Our greatest danger, though, is from smallpox. Hardly any of the men have had it, nor have they been inoculated. If even a handful of cases appear, smallpox will sweep through our troops like an all-consuming fire."

Time and again, I had seen the effects of smallpox in the streets of Boston: the red quarantine flags hanging from the houses; houses being smoked clean; the dead wrapped in tarred sheets, nailed in coffins, and a town crier walking before them so we knew to stay hidden in our homes. Inoculation hospitals with rooms full of men, women, and children whimpering in pain, surrounded by the stench of excrement and the sour odor of illness. With how closely our men were quartered, I could only imagine the devastating effects the disease would have.

General Montgomery looked impressed, but he only said, "For now, don't let the smallpox worry you. God willing, we will take Montreal and

Quebec before winter sets in, and we'll have ample space for our army to spread out, preventing an epidemic. Write Dr. Stringer again with another request for supplies. Dismissed."

I wrote Dr. Stringer immediately, and General Schuyler carried the letter with him when he left for his home in Saratoga the next morning, promising to return soon, though for the sake of his health, I hoped he continued to his Albany home and remained there.

The next ten days were a flurry of arrivals, fortifying, and packing. Each night, I drew my meager rations, still largely supplemented by what little the men were able to forage, from the Pittsfield cookfire. Then I sought out Remy. More often than not, Paul Kilgare joined us. Both were exhausted from constant drilling and building the fortifications of Fort Ti. General Montgomery was determined the fort would survive an attack should the worst happen, and we had to fall back. Paul had been put to work making entrenching tools, repairing weapons, and making nails for the fort and the boats being built down in Skenesboro.

"I don't think I've ever had so many blisters." Remy stared mournfully at her hands. "If we do need to fight, I don't know how I'll hold or fire my musket."

"The blisters will callus over soon," I assured her. Even so, I drained them and lightly bandaged her hands.

"And we'll find time to practice your shooting tomorrow," Paul said, running a soot-stained hand through his dark hair.

"I'll join you," I said. "It's been too long since I practiced."

"I didn't know you could shoot," Remy said.

"Dr. Warren insisted. I'm better with pistols, but if we're going into battle, I'd like to feel more confident with a musket."

We managed to practice during our midday meal for the next couple days, but then we ran out of time. On August 27, General Montgomery announced we would leave for Canada in the morning, despite General Schuyler's continued absence. What tents we had were struck, and everything was loaded onto waiting bateaux and galleys. My surgical chest was too cumbersome if we were continually moving across Canada, so I packed my instruments in a satchel. I also packed the extra black coat Dr. Stringer had sent, wishing he'd sent more of the promised supplies. I added *The Diseases Incident to Armies* and my recipe book but had to leave my

Shakespeare and *Anatomy* behind. I wrapped them in a scrap of treated canvas, pinned a note on top, and secured them in the fort's storeroom.

The next morning, the first part of our 1,700-man army sailed for Canada. Remy stood next to me at the gunwale of the *Enterprise*, her grip white-knuckled around the rail. As I had in the spring, I gawked at the scenery: trees and mountains heavy with the dark greens of summer. I didn't think I could ever tire of such beauty growing around us, reflecting in the lake below.

"Do you think we'll fight today?" Remy asked in a whisper.

I laughed. "Canada is over a hundred miles from here, and Fort St-Jean is beyond that. You have a few days at least."

She grinned, embarrassed. "It's not that I'm afraid. I mean, I am, but, what if I can't fight? What if I turn and run because—" She lowered her voice further. "Because I shouldn't be here to begin with?"

Her words could have been my own and brought me back to that fateful February night.

We stepped out of the snow and into the warmth of Dr. Warren's surgery. The men carrying Kit and Sammy laid them gently on two long tables. Josiah held me back, and we stood uncertain beside the door.

"David!" Dr. Warren called, and a young man entered from a back room. "See to Miss Endicott's hand and then the boy with the injured legs."

"Sammy," I said, and Josiah's hands tightened on my shoulders. Dr. Warren's eyes met mine, assessing but still reassuring. "Sammy," he repeated. "I will tend to—"

"Kit."

"Kit. Mr. Endicott, why don't you fetch your parents? I promise your sister will be safe in our care."

Josiah left with a promise to return soon, and David cleaned the blood from my hands, then tended and bandaged the cut across my palm. With a pat on my head, he left me sitting by the fire and went to Sammy. One slow step at a time, I drew near the tables.

My makeshift tourniquets on Sammy's legs had been replaced with real ones—a thick cloth strap with a brass screw contraption to tighten or loosen its hold. David plucked out the swan shot, piece by piece. He noticed me but didn't send me back to my seat even though his eyebrows rose.

"Will Sammy be all right?"

"He will. Someone did a good job tying tourniquets."

My proud smile slipped as I turned to Kit.

Midwife Rowe had always busied me outside the birthing room during difficult births. Even so, I was no stranger to blood or people's insides, but the sight of Kit's stomach and chest torn open, blood running down his sides, onto the table, and dripping to the floor, froze me. I backed away and then stumbled as I fled outside. I stopped two steps from the door, trembling, crying, and ashamed.

"Miss Endicott?" Dr. Warren's voice was gentle, which only made my tears come faster. "Are you well?"

"I thought I was brave because I work with Midwife Rowe and never have to leave the room, and I can do anything my brothers do, even tonight in the mob, but—I'm not brave because I'm a girl."

Dr. Warren knelt in the snow before me. "Being a girl doesn't make you a coward."

"I ran away from Kit. My friend. When he needs me."

Dr. Warren took my hands, his sticky with Kit's blood. I lifted my eyes to his, and I knew what he was about to say would change my life.

"Being afraid doesn't make you a coward," I told Remy, echoing what Dr. Warren had told me all those years ago. "A coward wouldn't be here. A coward wouldn't share their fears. They would just go on pretending until they couldn't anymore. You—we—can do anything the rest of them can do. A few differences in anatomy doesn't change our ability. And you can bet there are others like us out there fighting in this war. You'll stand and fight, Remy. I know you will."

"How do you know?"

"Because I've done it." I had followed Dr. Warren back into his surgery that night and held Kit's hand until my parents had come. Less than two weeks later, I had stood in the surgery again, helping to tend the victims of the Bloody Massacre.

"I just worry Alden is watching, and I'll disappoint him."

I, too, was afraid to disappoint, and I knew Dr. Warren was watching me. But Remy didn't need the burden of my fears as well. "You won't."

We unloaded at Crown Point, and the boats went back for more men and supplies. But then the traitorous winds trapped us at Crown Point for the next two days.

I hadn't been to the Point before and was dismayed at the condition of what remained of Fort Amherst. Earthworks circled the ruins, but little of the actual fort still stood—only the barracks, which were largely roofless. Even less stood of the older French fort. We camped on the parade ground of Fort Amherst and waited for the winds to blow in our favor.

We set out again on August 31, reaching Île La Motte on September 2, where we set up a temporary camp. General Schuyler joined us two days later with the remainder of the army but without Dr. Stringer, who remained at the general hospital in Albany. With General Schuyler's arrival, our numbers reached nearly two thousand. Almost as soon as General Schuyler arrived, we moved camp to Île aux Noix.

Île aux Noix was a narrow strip of land about a mile long and maybe half as wide, set in the middle of the Richelieu River. It was muddy and beset with mosquitoes, rats, and snakes—no fit place for an army encampment. To my dismay, the generals intended to use the island as a hospital and staging area from which to send the ill back to Fort Ti and the able-bodied on to our lines in Canada.

"Sirs, I must protest," I said. The two generals sat at a small table in General Montgomery's tent studying maps of Fort St-Jean. General Schuyler's foot was propped up on a cot, and General Montgomery had removed his hat, bald head gleaming in the lantern light. "This island is no place for ill men. It's no place for well men, either. It's crawling with vermin, and the mosquitoes are as thick as wool blankets. If we stay here much longer, many of our effective men will fall ill. Keeping already ill men here will spell certain death for many."

"We understand your concern, Dr. Endicott," General Montgomery said, but he didn't raise his eyes from the map he was studying. His thumb moved absently over a large pockmark on his cheekbone. "As soon as St-Jean falls, we will abandon Île aux Noix."

"And the ill men will be moved quickly from the isle to Fort Ti, then on to the hospital at Fort George," General Schuyler added, wiping sweat from his brow.

I frowned. "Sir, are you sure you should be with the army? Your malaria—"

"Is under control, Dr. Endicott." His hawk-like eyes pierced me, and I snapped my mouth shut.

"The doctors will remain on Île aux Noix until we establish ourselves at St-Jean," General Montgomery continued. "We'll leave a fatigue detail on the island to dig latrines and crew the bateaux."

I thought of St-Jean as I had last seen it: the swampy ground and undefended walls. I doubted they were still undefended. I studied General Schuyler, his pasty skin shiny with sweat, the bags of sleeplessness under his eyes, and the slight rasp of his breathing. This was not a man who should be in the field. I opened my mouth to entreat him once more, but he said, "Dismissed, Dr. Endicott."

Major John Brown and Ethan Allen waited outside for their briefing with the generals. Since Colonel Easton was still down south, Brown had been promoted and led the regiment I was attached to, but I had hardly seen him since he and the former commander of the Green Mountain Boys had been spying and scouting for General Schuyler. I ignored Allen and he me, but Major Brown, unreadable eyes always assessing, said, "I take it that didn't go your way."

"Does anyone listen to a doctor before they're too ill to do otherwise? Are you bound for enemy territory again?"

"Most likely. Anything to get off this island."

I snorted my agreement. "Good luck, Major."

The following morning, orders were given for the men to assemble, and I bid farewell to Remy. "Stay down when they start firing. The next time I see you, I don't want it to be because you're wounded."

"I wish you were coming with me, Whit."

I beamed my most confident expression. "I'll be there before you know it. Just stick with Paul, and you'll be all right."

As they loaded into bateaux and pushed off for Fort St-Jean, my ghosts appeared, and a shiver of foreboding ran through me.

Chapter Sixteen
September 6-16, 1775

A rumble as of distant thunder reached us, but the sound was nothing natural. It wasn't our cannons because we had so few and no trained artillery unit to fire them. Everyone on Île aux Noix, ill and well alike, watched the shore, as if by peering hard enough, we could see through the trees to the battle.

Eleven wounded men from Colonel Waterbury's regiment returned in late afternoon. Dr. Wood's eyes widened as the boat drew near. "I was at Bunker Hill, but I only treated minor wounds. A couple of Massachusetts doctors took the worst wounded."

David and William—it had to be. If I were to live up to Dr. Warren's training, I could do no less than they had. "I saw wounds like this after Lexington and Concord. You and I will take the worst wounded and let your surgeon's mates take the least severe ones. I'll take the most serious wounds if that will help."

"Thank you, Dr. Endicott."

We laid the wounded on makeshift surgery tables in our driest tents. Eight were privates, and Kit, Jedediah, and Dr. Warren hovered by the three most grievously injured. Two had belly wounds and the other a head wound. There was little chance any of the three would live.

I stood next to the man who was to be my patient. My hands hovered above his wounded stomach, but I couldn't seem to uncurl them from the fists they had formed. Dr. Warren stood across the table from me. When I met his reassuring eyes, he nodded. He still believed in me. I stretched my fingers and picked up the forceps.

Like Dr. Warren had once taught me, I took the wound a bit at a time, and before I quite knew it, the private's wounds were closed, and I hadn't panicked once. Tears pricked at my eyes, but tears of relief. I bit the inside of my cheek and looked up at Dr. Warren, who nodded once more.

Thank you, I mouthed and turned to the next patient.

After the privates were treated, we saw to the three officers—a thigh, a shoulder, and a hand. The hand was the trickiest, so I took him.

A musket ball, or a piece of one, had ripped through his left hand between his pinky and ring finger, tearing muscles and ligaments and shattering bones. I was reminded of Henry Knox and the hunting accident that had taken two of his fingers. These fingers I could save, and if I kept the wound from turning, he would keep the hand. Even if everything went well, though, he would still likely lose the use of his last two fingers. "What's your name?"

"Lieutenant Bezaleel Brown. How bad is it?"

"Not as bad as it looks or feels. Here." I handed him a glass of rum with a few grains of opium mixed in. We didn't have much opium, so we had to use it sparingly. I kept him talking as I worked. "What's happening out there?"

"It's all swamp. No idea how we're going to stage an attack in that. There's nowhere to mount guns. We were the advance and ran into a party of Indians." He winced as I packed and bandaged the wound. "Don't know what happened after that. Will I be able to use the hand?"

"Probably not the last two fingers, but the rest of the hand should be functional. Get some rest, Lieutenant."

I didn't follow my own advice. I sat between the beds of the three privates, Dr. Warren and Kit standing vigil beside me. Jedediah and a few other ghosts haunted the edges of the tent. There was nothing I could do for the wounded but listen to their whimpers and moans and watch the ever-slower rise and fall of their chests. One by one, their breathing faltered and stopped.

The first casualties of our push to Quebec, and I didn't even know their names.

I stared down at the peaceful face of the wounded man whose stomach wounds I had stitched. Who, despite my best efforts, had still died. This time, I couldn't hold back the tears. I had known when he came in there was little chance he'd survive, and I had done all within my power to save him—I knew that—but I still hated that I had failed. And I was sure it was only a matter of time before his ghost appeared.

"That was James Shaw," said a voice at my shoulder. Lieutenant Brown, his hand cradled against his chest. "He was in my company, and that was—"

"I don't want to know their names!" It came out louder and more forcefully than I had intended, drawing stares from everyone in the tent. I swallowed, my face heating, and I didn't look up until I felt more in control. "I'm sorry, Lieutenant. I just—I can't know all their names. I already carry the weight of their deaths. I can't carry the weight of their lives as well. I'm sorry."

I fled, but there was no escape from my ghosts or from the returning army, who brought with them more dead and wounded. Within days, we were overrun with ill men: fluxes, diarrhea, and malaria flare-ups. Our sick tents were full. As the sun set and mosquitoes rose in buzzing clouds, General Schuyler sought me out. His face was lined in pain and exhaustion, and on the marshy, uneven ground, he couldn't hide his hobbling. But he held up a hand before I could comment on his health. "How many ill, Doctor?"

"About six hundred. Plus the eight wounded and three dead of their wounds from a few days ago."

"Six hundred," he whispered. "We'll have to fortify the isle and wait for reinforcements."

"Fortify the Isle of Noise?" That was one of the nicknames the men had given the island on account of the constant hum of mosquitoes. "Sir—"

"We don't have another choice, Doctor. Unless we retreat, and I'll not leave Colonel Arnold alone in Canada. So, until artillery and reinforcements arrive, we fortify."

"But you don't have to fortify the island yourself, sir. You must rest. Stay in your tent and send orders through your aides. If your two aides aren't enough, I know another New York soldier who could help. Please, sir, we can't have you growing too ill to be of use."

To my surprise, he didn't argue. "Send me your friend, and make sure the latrine pits and cookfires are properly placed and dug."

I found Remy at one of the New York cookfires. She smiled tiredly at me. "I made it back without a scratch."

Words like that tempted fate, and I rubbed my palm. "Well, I hope you're not too comfortable. I got you a job."

"A job? I was hoping for sleep."

"It'll keep you off latrine digging duty."

"Take it!" Paul pushed Remy toward me. "Quick, before one of us takes it instead!"

So, the fortification of Île aux Noix began. While General Schuyler wouldn't confine himself to his tent, his aides, Remy, and I kept him more sedentary than he'd been before.

The drought that had plagued us all summer broke, drenching us daily as we attempted to raise the walls of our defenses. The wet weather meant more illnesses, and I kept a constant watch for any signs of camp fever and smallpox. If they made an appearance on this island, there would be no stopping them, and no way to quarantine the ill. I never thought I'd be happy to only see fluxes, dysentery, and colds.

Each night, exhaustion pulled me down onto my slowly moldering mattress in the tent I shared with the other surgeons, the funk of rot and wet cloth thick in the air. But sleep didn't always come as worries clamored for attention, nightmares startled me awake, and my ghosts broke the darkness, glowing faintly.

We slept in our clothes, so there was little chance of accidentally revealing my sex, but sharing quarters meant I could no longer remove my bindings nightly. Under the cover of my damp, rat-nibbled blanket, I tried to rub lard into my irritated skin and change one stiff, grubby set of bindings for fresh ones while the others slept. I tried to complete my ministrations quietly, for the fear of waking one of the others with my rustling haunted me almost as constantly as my ghosts. But no one woke, and I remained undiscovered.

It was also while we were on the Isle of Noise that my monthly bleeding stopped. I had missed my time in August, but when I missed again in September, I breathed a little sigh of relief. Knowing I couldn't be pregnant, I deduced it was what I had sometimes seen with Midwife Rowe in some of her poorest patients. When the body didn't have enough nourishment, the monthly bleeding stopped. Enough of our men had had the bloody flux that I'd had a ready-made excuse if anyone noticed, but I was relieved to have one less way to be discovered.

On the morning of September 12, I was writing yet another plea to Dr. Stringer for medicines, tents, and blankets when Remy shouldered in, rain dripping from the tent flap and off her tricorn. "Whit, come quickly. It's General Schuyler."

The general lay on his cot under several blankets, and I sent Remy straight out again. "Bring General Montgomery. But go slow. We don't want to start a panic."

"Right."

I let the tent flap fall closed behind me. Without the rain-fresh air flowing in, the lip-pursing stench of illness was all too evident. I blinked, adjusting to the smell and the lantern light. "How do you feel, sir?"

"If I were well, Doctor, I wouldn't be in this damn bed!" He inhaled and regained his composure. "Apologies. It seems I should have listened to you earlier."

I hummed a reply as I felt his clammy forehead. His eyes were a little glassy and his breathing labored. I tugged his feet free of the blankets and pulled off his socks. His ankles above both feet were swollen and red, and his right toe was not only enlarged and bright red but blistered.

"Your other joints?" I ransacked the tent for something to elevate his feet, settling on his portable writing desk which I padded with a blanket.

"Achy. Rheumatism, most like, and my malaria."

"You're not to leave this bed today or tomorrow. I'll see what I can concoct to give you some relief."

I hoped I sounded more positive than I felt. Our supplies were almost exhausted, and though some cannons and gunpowder had arrived, no medicinal supplies had. I cursed Dr. Stringer and his slowness.

The tent flap stirred, and I glimpsed General Montgomery. I ducked out and led the general a few steps away, cold water and muck oozing through my boots.

"How is he?" General Montgomery asked.

"Ill. Severely. He's not to leave his bed. Any planning will have to take place in his tent, and his feet must remain elevated."

I hesitated, and General Montgomery took the opening. "What is it?"

"Illness weakens a body, and I'm worried he may contract a more serious disease if he remains with us. We have no medicines, so if he worsens . . ." I shrugged helplessly.

General Montgomery swore. "We cannot do this without him. He cannot die."

I agreed. I didn't need another ghost, another reminder of my failure, another impossible debt to repay. But I didn't understand why General Montgomery was upset. A general who couldn't leave his bed was of little use.

Seeing my confusion, General Montgomery explained, "He has the connections, the influence with those who will send men, money, and munitions. He also has contacts among the Indian tribes and has worked to ensure they remain neutral or join our side in this war. If we lose General Schuyler, we lose Canada."

"Then you must convince him to go south, sir, for his good as well as ours. He won't listen to me, but he might listen to you."

"I'll do my best. And I will try not to tire him."

I did what I could for General Schuyler with teas, ointments, and tonics, but what he needed most was comfortable rest, dry warmth, and good plain food, none of which were available on Île aux Noix. He remained in bed for two days, then rallied, so, of course, he left his bed against my orders, but by evening, he was forced to return, in worse condition than before. As rain poured down for the fourth straight day, General Schuyler finally agreed to go south with others too ill to fight.

As if to assure General Schuyler he had made the right decision, reinforcements arrived as his bateau pushed off. Colonel Seth Warner, the man who had replaced Ethan Allen as commander of the Green Mountain Boys, brought 170 men, and some of Colonel Bedel's New Hampshire Rangers arrived, though without their colonel.

"More weren't far behind," one of the Rangers told General Montgomery as they squelched ashore in a light drizzle.

"Then we waste no time," General Montgomery declared. "We leave for St-Jean today."

Chapter Seventeen
October 15-17, 1775

Chill drops of rain found the gap between shirt and skin, trickling down my spine as I paused at the edge of the siege camp south of Fort St-Jean. The only reason I was warm at all was Portia, the brown mare beneath me. After carrying me all day from one encampment to the next in our siege lines around St-Jean, her head was low, mane bedraggled, and steam rose from her flanks. She was a placid, sweet-tempered horse. "Perfect," Remy had said, "for a beginning rider."

When we'd begun our invasion a month ago, most of the doctors had remained on Île aux Noix, but General Montgomery had brought me to the mainland. He'd positioned our men all around the fort spread over a good ten or so miles.

"To check on the health of the men at each encampment, you'll need a horse," General Montgomery had said. "A few just arrived from Fort Ti. Choose one."

The first few days, reacclimating to riding had been painful, but Remy, who had ridden often at home, gave me a few lessons to improve my seat. I hadn't fallen off yet, and a month on, I felt quite comfortable on Portia's back.

The wind picked up, spattering the rain a little harder against my face. Portia snorted, the sound muffled through the cloth plugs in my ears, and she lifted a hoof, white fetlock stained a muddy brown. The open ground stretched around us, flat and barren but for the fort and our encampments. I missed the clatter of skeletal branches on the wind, the bright warmth of autumn leaves in the gray, wet world. If I closed my eyes, I could picture Boston: the flame-topped trees, the houses snuggled against each other, my family.

Portia danced, tossing her head, wet strands of mane slapping against my hands. I sighed. "All right. Let's go, girl."

I urged her into the siege camp we called home. Once I'd secured Portia at the horse lines, rubbed her down, and fed her, I slogged through the mud toward my tent. I cleared my throat, trying to loosen the tickle that had lodged there in the last few days, and the sound echoed through my earplugs which muffled the *throom* of our cannons.

General Montgomery had wasted no time setting up a siege and putting our small, limited cannons to use. Reinforcements continued to arrive from Connecticut, Massachusetts, and New York. These included Captain John Lamb's artillery company, which had prompted General Montgomery to build a new battery on the east bank of the river, finished the previous day, with two twelve-pounders and two four-pounders. They had been firing ceaselessly since.

In addition, the Kahnawake, one of the Canadian Indian tribes, and the Six Nations of the Iroquois had promised to remain neutral, an agreement in which General Schuyler had played a role. With the threat from the Indians reduced and the addition of Colonel James Livingston's Canadian unit, we began to hope the siege might end at last—an outcome that couldn't come soon enough.

Aside from the weather making everyone miserable—we'd already had several hard frosts, and it was only a matter of time before it snowed—conditions in the siege camps were wearing on what little morale we had left. Our tents scarcely kept out the seemingly constant rain, and every scrap of cloth we had was continually damp. Many of the men's feet were covered in rashes, and the skin on some of them appeared to be rotting away. Dry skin and dry footwear were the only answer, and both were hard to come by. When men weren't on duty, I suggested they go barefoot.

Food, as always, was in short supply, and the lateness of the season meant there was little to be gleaned from the land. Hunting was a cold, wet prospect, and the Canadian farms within a day's walk had been stripped of anything useful. We had captured a convoy of food meant for St-Jean early on, but those supplies were gone. Men deserted, some heading south for their homes, but a few crossed the lines and sought refuge in Fort St-Jean.

The last factor sapping morale was the constant squabbling between men from different colonies. The New Yorkers didn't get along with anyone, and there was much grumbling from my own New Englanders about General Montgomery. General Montgomery's only solution was to separate men into camps by which colony they were from in the hopes of keeping infighting to a minimum. The only things that would improve the soldiers' opinions of the general, however, would be three good meals a day and victory.

Only two incidents had broken the boredom and misery of the siege since General Schuyler sailed south. The first had nearly been devastating, the second merely frustrating. On September 22, while General Montgomery was walking the lines, a cannonball had passed right between his legs, slicing the tails from his coat and knocking him off his feet. He hadn't been injured, but it had been such a near thing, I was loath to let him go so close to the action again. If he died, we'd have no one to lead us.

Then, only three days later, Ethan Allen had led an ill-conceived attempt to capture Montreal, which resulted instead in the capture of him and his men. When Major Brown brought the report, I hadn't been surprised; impulsivity was part of who Allen was. General Montgomery had cursed Allen although I thought the general was more upset about losing the men than he was about losing Allen.

I entered my tent to find Remy waiting on my cot. Even though I was a Massachusetts doctor, my tent was pitched among the New Yorkers who were encamped near headquarters and our main sick tents. Since the New Yorkers were the one group that didn't complain too loudly about General Montgomery's leadership, he kept them close.

Remy wasn't in the artillery unit, so she didn't have much to do beyond fatigue duty. I was kept busy with a stream of minor injuries and continuous illnesses. Those too ill to remain on duty were sent back to Île aux Noix and our doctors there. By my calculations, we had already sent 250 ill men back to the Isle of Noise. I was very glad to be on the mainland.

"Whit," Remy began as I removed the plugs from my ears. The tent walls did nothing to deaden the sound of the cannons, but I could hardly hear Remy with the plugs in. "There are women here!"

"The camp followers?" I shrugged out of my wet coat, shivered, wrapped a slightly-less-damp blanket around myself, and eased off my boots and stockings before curling up next to her on my dank mattress. "They've been arriving for a while now."

Some of the women were wives of our soldiers, determined to care for their men. Others were unattached women, American and Canadian, who had come to offer their varied services to the army.

"But do you know what they're doing? I went into my tent and found—" Remy's face flared red.

Realizing what she must have seen, I bit back a laugh. I wasn't the least bit surprised, but it seemed the possibility had never occurred to Remy. "It wasn't Paul, was it?"

"No!" Her blush deepened, and I grinned. "What? Why are you smiling like that?"

"Just waiting for you to confess."

"Confess?"

"Your feelings for Paul."

She jumped up, hands pressed to her cheeks. "Is it that obvious?"

"Only when you blush at the mention of his name or go on and on about what he said or a joke he made or . . ."

"Shut up!" She swatted me with my wet coat, and I laughed as I fended her off. She collapsed beside me. "Do you think he's noticed?"

"I think he would have said something if he had, but you need to be careful, Rem. You're passing as a man. You're not supposed to fall in love with one."

I thought of Win, and my heart reached for him. I hadn't had any sense of him in weeks, but for the dryness in my throat, a familiar symptom I experienced when Win was ill, which only made me worry more. Where was he? How was he? We'd heard nothing of Colonel Arnold's army although they should have already reached Quebec, and no word had come from General Schuyler as to their fate.

"I know, I know," Remy moaned, burying her face in her hands. "I didn't mean for it to happen! He's just so nice and goes out of his way to help me, and his smile . . ."

"Ugh, enough! I don't need the sappy rundown." I laughed as she shoved me. More seriously, I asked, "You don't share a tent, do you?"

"No! Oh, Whit, what am I going to do?"

"You're going to act as naturally as possible and pretend he's your brother."

She crossed her arms and froze me with a withering stare. "Have you ever been in love, Whit?"

Henry Knox flashed into my mind. His easy smile, his kindness, his enthusiasm for the written word. "Let's call it infatuation. He was far older than me and already had a fiancée. I knew it was hopeless from the start."

"And how did pretending he was your brother work?"

"Point taken. Well then, keep in mind that if anyone discovers your feelings, you'll be drummed out of camp. Of course, that's assuming your fellow soldiers don't take punishment into their own hands before the matter can be brought before General Montgomery. Which would reveal you're a woman, which would get you drummed out anyway."

"You're so helpful, Whit."

"I try." I shoved my feet back into my cold, clammy stockings and boots and picked up my coat.

"Where are you going?"

"If the camp followers have, ahem, gone to work, I need to examine and start treating them. We have enough diseases to be dealing with. We certainly don't need more."

"What about my problem?"

"Well, you have two choices. One, confess to Paul, hope he feels the same way after he gets over the shock of you being a woman, and leave the army to live happily ever after. Or two, keep acting as a man, and do your best to hide how you feel."

"I can't leave. We haven't even fought yet! I have to fight in at least one battle. That's the whole reason I joined."

"Then, I guess you're stuck with option two." She groaned and fell back on the mattress. I patted her foot where it hung off the cot. "You're welcome to come here anytime, Rem. I'll listen and give you a place to hide. And I'll keep reminding you what'll happen if you're discovered."

"So helpful. I can't wait until you meet someone you like."

"Not going to happen, Rem. Who's going to fall for a girl determined to work in a man's profession?" I cut myself off before I said, "And one who is haunted by ghosts." She didn't know about them and didn't need to. I gave her a tight smile. "It's just not in the cards for me, Rem."

She humphed. "We'll see."

I left, shaking my head. I might have once dreamed of the kind of romance I'd seen between Dr. Warren and Miss Scollay or the deep love I'd witnessed between my own parents or Henry and Lucy, but the path I'd chosen made that next to impossible.

Chapter Eighteen
October 18 – November 3, 1775

The siege dragged on with cold and cannon fire. On October 18, Colonel Livingston led 350 men to capture Fort Chambly, which lay between St-Jean and Montreal, and sent back much needed gunpowder. When word reached us of Chambly's fall, the camp echoed with huzzahs, and General Montgomery ordered a new battery built on the north side of St-Jean.

After we took Chambly, we thought St-Jean would capitulate, for the fort was cut off from supplies and reinforcements. A Redcoat deserter reported the garrison was running out of food. Judging by the way the man's ribs stood out, St-Jean was more desperate for food than we were.

My own stomach ached. At first, I feared I was falling ill and checked myself for fever regularly and waited for the inevitable sprints to the latrine pits to begin. But after two days, I determined it wasn't illness. Still, my stomach ached with a persistent hollowness, no matter what or how much I ate. Paired with my increasingly sore throat, I began to worry.

"Something's wrong," I told Remy. She was avoiding Paul and a card game in his tent. "There's this empty feeling in my stomach and a scratch in my throat. It's been there for days. I think something's wrong with Win."

"Your twin? You're sure it's not something else? Worry, fatigue?"

I shook my head. "I've always been able to feel when he's ill—if he has a cough, my throat aches, much like it does now. We've still no word from Colonel Arnold."

"After Alden left home, I felt awful, achy and unable to settle down to anything. I was certain every twinge I had was a premonition that Alden was wounded. But when word came he had—" Remy swallowed hard, blinking rapidly. I took her hand, and she held tight. "I never would have guessed he'd died."

Since my sympathetic symptoms had started, Kit had been following me about, Dr. Warren and the other ghosts appearing only when someone was terribly ill and death was near. I glanced at Kit, who watched me almost anxiously, lip caught between his ghostly teeth. "I'd know if he were dead."

Whether it was my expression or the conviction in my voice, Remy didn't argue. I leaned against her shoulder. "I just wish I knew what was wrong with him."

"I'm sure you'll hear from him soon."

"Remy?" At Paul's voice, we sprang apart. I threw myself onto the spare cot and opened *The Diseases Incident to Armies,* the damp and cold doing my poor book no favors. Paul stuck his head inside. "We have sentry duty. Ready?"

"For another long, cold night? Why not?" With a quick smile at me, Remy shouldered her musket, leaving me alone with my worries.

On November 1, the northern battery was completed, and at ten o'clock in the morning, all our cannons began firing in concert. Even with cloth stuffed in my ears, my head rang with the constant thunder of the guns. The very air shook, and the earth shuddered as each ball and shell hit. The already gray sky darkened further as gunpowder, like fog, blanketed our camps. Since we were taking no return fire, I wasn't needed, and I spent the day huddled in my tent, hands over my ears.

With sunset, the cannons fell silent, though the ringing in my ears continued for hours after.

General Montgomery sought me out, powder staining his hands and uniform. "Dr. Endicott, I need you to choose a prisoner to deliver my terms of surrender to the fort."

Opening and closing my mouth in an attempt to clear my ears, I followed the general to the makeshift prison. I chose Mr. La Coste, a healthy Loyalist who had been captured just days ago by Colonel Warner. He was sent to the fort with a flag of parley and a letter of terms.

"Wait with me for a response, Doctor. If the commanding officer agrees to surrender, formal negotiations will begin tomorrow, and I want a doctor present as an assurance of peaceful intentions." His eyes flickered over me. "Have you a clean set of clothes?"

"A coat and shirt, sir."

"It'll do. You'll sleep on the *Enterprise* tonight." General Montgomery kept his quarters on the schooner in an attempt to keep his papers dry. That a ship was the driest place we had told just how poor conditions in camp were.

Less than an hour later, Mr. La Coste returned. "Major Preston says he will respond formally in the morning. He'll send an officer to negotiate."

General Montgomery frowned. I could almost hear his thoughts: the major wouldn't come himself? But there wasn't anything he could do about it.

There was only one cabin on the *Enterprise*, but there was plenty of space below in the crew's quarters, for the only men aboard were those standing sentry. I would be alone. There was a cookstove and plenty of dry space. The temptation was too much.

Once I secured the hatches, I heated water on the stove. While the water warmed, I strung a few lengths of rope across the crew's quarters. When the first pot of water was hot, I poured it into a bucket, set another pot to heat, and after double-checking the hatches were latched, stripped off my filthy clothing. Crouched over the bucket, I scrubbed my clothes. The shirt was so thin in places it practically disintegrated. The jacket, waistcoat, underdrawers, and trousers held up better. I tipped the first bucket of filthy water down the head and used a second to wash my boots, bindings, cravat, and stockings.

Clothes dripping from my makeshift clotheslines, I used two more buckets to wash myself. It was as close to a proper bath as I'd had since leaving Boston. At Fort Ti, I'd scrubbed in the creek that first day and washed quickly in the hospital regularly, but this felt more secure by far. I winced as the soap stung the rashy, dry skin where my bindings had chaffed. Most of the skin had hardened and almost calloused from months of mistreatment, but there were enough raw patches to leech a little of my enjoyment away.

I used one of the blankets, a dry one that was only slightly mouse-nibbled, as a towel while I contemplated my clean clothes. I had a new white cotton shirt and black coat, courtesy of Dr. Stringer, for I'd been saving them, as well as clean underdrawers and fresh bandages for bindings. But the thought of trussing myself up like a turkey again made my shoulders slump. Surely, I could let my body breathe for one night. Alone and with the hatches latched, I would be safe. Pulling on only my new shirt—the very newness was like silk against my skin—I flopped into a hammock, drew two fresh blankets over myself, and slept dry for the first time since leaving Crown Point.

Warm, dry, and comfortable, I didn't wake when I should have. I didn't wake when one of the hatches opened and clapped against the deck. I didn't wake when General Montgomery's steps descended. I only woke when the general bellowed, "Dr. Endicott!"

I tipped right out of the hammock, blankets falling after me. I sprawled on the deck, hair loose, wearing nothing but my shirt, the blankets draped over me the only things keeping me from immediate discovery.

General Montgomery glared down his prominent nose at me, those hazel eyes piercing like hot knives. It was only because I was paralyzed by fear that I didn't clutch at the neck of my shirt and give myself away. "Having a nice, lazy morning, Doctor?"

"No, sir. I'm sorry, sir." Judging by the light coming down through the hatch, it was only just daybreak. "I didn't mean to oversleep, sir. It's just been so long since I've been dry and warm."

He held up a hand, and I swallowed my foolish, rambling words. "You do intend to join us up top?"

"Yes, sir. Just as soon as I'm dressed."

When I didn't move, the frown lines on his forehead deepened. "Well, hop to it."

"Yes, sir." Oh, God, he didn't mean to leave until he saw me up and getting ready. If I kept my back to him, I should be able to pull this off. From the back, men and women didn't look so different, especially with the shirt hanging down to my knees. Grabbing my clean underdrawers, I stood, blankets falling away, and hastily put my back to the general. Only then did I see Kit and Dr. Warren behind me. Kit looked ready to pounce, and Dr. Warren held his musket at the ready, both of them willing to protect me. But no one could protect me from my own stupid mistakes. Holding my breath, I drew the underdrawers on. One leg, then the other.

"Be quick about it, Doctor. I shall see you topside." His footsteps retreated, climbed the companionway, then walked the deck above.

I finally dared breathe, and I slapped my hands over my mouth before I vomited across the deck. I ran to the head and heaved, bile burning my throat and my nose streaming. Never, never, never again would I take a risk so foolish! How could I have been so stupid? Nowhere was safe, no matter how secure it felt. I had to remember that.

I took three deep breaths to compose myself—I couldn't spare time for more—then dressed both carefully and quickly, grimacing at my still-damp clothing. But damp was nothing compared with discovery, I told myself as

I knotted my cravat. Better a little uncomfortable than drummed out of the army.

Hair up, tricorn secure, covered from chin to wrists to ankles, I took a final deep breath, and climbed above.

The first thing my eye fell on was the hatch. The latch could be set and opened from the topside as well as below. I'd been a fool not to consider that.

The sun was just breaking free of the horizon, dying the river golden and glistening off the dew that had collected on every surface of the *Enterprise*. My breath fogged the silent morning air, and I shivered. No cannon fire disturbed the morning.

It was November 2, and we should have already reached Quebec. Winter was coming, and we still had a long way to go.

"Glad you could join us, Dr. Endicott," General Montgomery said from where he stood at the portside rail. "Our guest should be arriving any moment."

There was a hail from shore. At an answering call from our sentries, a boat pushed off, carrying a blindfolded, red-coated British officer.

I blinked. For the first time I was aware of, I had separated myself from those we faced. They were British, and we were . . . not. Maybe we never had been, at least not in the eyes of the king, Parliament, or their army. We were Americans, and the officer being rowed toward us was British. It might not be a large difference, but in that moment, the distinction seemed important.

"You'll examine the emissary when he boards and record his condition," General Montgomery instructed me. "I do not want Major Preston making any false accusations about the treatment of his officer."

"Yes, sir."

The officer was hauled up, and his blindfold was removed. He was young and handsome with hair of black silk, dark eyes, high cheekbones, a narrow face, and perfectly arched brows. He wore the red coat with dark blue facings and gold lacing of the Royal English Fusiliers and carried his distinctive bearskin-covered hat under his arm. He moved with light steps, like a dancer.

He was, by far, the most handsome man I had ever seen.

I heard Remy's laughter in my mind, and I was glad she couldn't see me goggling at this officer.

General Montgomery cleared his throat, brows lowering further, and I hurried to perform the examination. The officer smiled, his eyes meeting mine—eyes deep enough to drown in. There was a canniness there, too, and I was certain that as soon as he had me helpless in those depths, he would pry every secret from me. Having so narrowly escaped discovery below, I had no desire to be parsed apart by this handsome enemy. I quickly averted my gaze and hoped any redness in my face would be put down to cold. "If you could extend your arms, sir."

He stretched out his hand and took mine, shaking it. "Lieutenant John André, at your service, Doctor."

This wasn't protocol at all. Could he feel that my hand was too small, too delicate to be male? Did he notice that the hairs at my wrist, on the back of my hand, on my knuckles weren't dark or thick enough?

He frowned, and my heart stopped. He turned my hand over and ran a finger over the scars on my palm. "What happened here?"

Shivering, I snatched my hand back. "An unfortunate accident when I was a child. Could you hold both your arms out from your sides, please?"

"Of course." Another smile as he obliged. "I was chosen, Doctor, because I have not yet fallen ill, so I hope you find nothing amiss. Though I must admit, I may be a little thin. We've been on reduced rations for some time."

I could hardly believe he was joking at a time like this, and I wondered if he was using humor to hide his nerves or for a more devious purpose. My own nerves were on full display; I couldn't stop my hands from shaking. But his charming smile said he was completely at ease. Finished with my examination, I stepped back.

"What's the diagnosis, Doctor?"

I forced myself to meet his eyes and smile. "You're in perfect health."

"Let's hope you can say the same when negotiations are complete." He winked and then stepped around me and bowed to General Montgomery. "Lieutenant John André, quartermaster, to formally negotiate the peaceful surrender of Fort St-Jean."

"Welcome to the *Enterprise,* Lieutenant. Come into my cabin, and we shall discuss."

I caught myself watching Lieutenant André as he followed General

Montgomery. I snapped my eyes back to writing my report, very glad Remy wasn't aboard.

They didn't talk long before Lieutenant André was rowed back to shore. General Montgomery glared after him, face red beneath his pockmarks.

"Is it over, sir?"

"No. Major Preston's terms were completely unacceptable. The lieutenant will return."

And he did, back and forth several times. At one point, Mr. Despins, another Loyalist prisoner, was sent back with the lieutenant. As the day wore on, General Montgomery grew more frustrated until, in late afternoon, he yelled, "You tell Preston if he does not surrender, I will commence bombardment immediately and continue until there is nothing left of the fort! Anyone left alive shall be considered prisoners of war without the honors of war!"

His threat erased Lieutenant André's smile. The lieutenant's trip to and from the fort was his quickest yet, and he didn't even let General Montgomery lead him into his cabin before he said, "Major Preston agrees, sir. St-Jean is yours. He will surrender tomorrow morning at eight o'clock."

"Inform the major that is acceptable. Doctor, a final examination."

"Still hale?" Lieutenant André asked when I stepped back.

"Try to eat a couple good meals," I said without thinking.

He barked a laugh. "I shall inform my jailers that feeding me well is doctor's orders."

With a final salute, Lieutenant André was rowed back to shore, and I took my first easy breath in hours.

The next morning, as we accepted the formal surrender and added the British cannons and stores to our own, we discovered six of our men who had deserted. At the sight of them, General Montgomery's eyes hardened like musket balls.

"Take them into custody and have them brought to the yard. Doctor, we will need you."

"Me, sir? Do you need me to examine the prisoners?"

"A less happy duty. Deserters must be executed. As our ranking doctor, we need you to confirm their deaths."

For a moment, it was like the cannon had begun firing again because I couldn't hear anything clearly, only odd echoes. "What?"

"You must confirm the deaths of the deserters."

I hadn't misheard. I felt lightheaded. If I was to confirm their deaths, I would have to witness their execution. General Montgomery steadied me. "Will you be all right, Doctor? I realize you're young for this."

"I'll be fine, sir. Just not what I was expecting."

"I'd like to say it will get easier," he sighed, "but I'd be lying."

The deserters lined up in the yard. A company of Continentals loaded their muskets.

Remy's company.

All were pale and most were trembling. Remy's eyes locked on mine, full of panic. There was nothing I could do to stop this for either of us.

I stood beside General Montgomery as he pronounced the charges. I kept my eyes on Remy.

"Ready," General Montgomery said. I wondered how his voice could be so calm when the muskets being leveled visibly shook. "Aim." We'd been working on Remy's aim. The deserters were close enough she might actually hit one. "Fire!"

Crack-crack-crack-crack!

The deserters crumpled to the ground. When the smoke cleared, Kit, Dr. Warren, and my other ghosts stood behind the bodies. The ten yards of open ground I had to cross felt like a mile. There was no good place to look between the ghosts, the dead, and the living. Each deserter had been struck multiple times. I hoped they would not join my cohort of ghosts.

"They're dead, sir," I said, relieved to turn my back on the dead and the ghosts alike.

"Then it's done." The general raised his voice, "Let this be a warning to all who would desert! Those who are to remain as the garrison, dig graves. Everyone else, we march in ten minutes."

That night, Remy came to my tent. She was still shaking.

"Rum?" I offered her a glass.

"Isn't this for the wounded?"

"It is, but I think we need it today."

She emptied the glass with a gasp and watering eyes. When I offered the bottle, she held out her glass for a refill. She drank the second draught more slowly.

"That wasn't what I was expecting to do when I ran off to war. In battle,

I imagine at least, you wouldn't really know if you killed someone or not. But today—"

"I've only ever seen the aftermath of battle, but I was in a mob once where people were shot." I rubbed my palm and tried to push away the memories. "That was terrible, but today was worse because I knew it was coming, that I'd have to watch them die, and I wouldn't be saving anyone."

Sleep would not come easily with these new horrors in my head, so I poured us each one more measure before closing the bottle. We couldn't afford to be hungover. I raised my glass.

"To hoping there are no more days like today."

Chapter Nineteen
November 4 – December 1, 1775

We pushed on to Montreal, but the city did not capitulate immediately, and, with much grumbling, we again settled into a siege. My stomach was still hollow, my throat achy, and Kit was everywhere as if he, too, could sense the danger Win was in. Something had gone wrong with Colonel Arnold's expedition, I was certain. I rubbed at my palm and tried to avoid Kit's ghost. I feared the next time I saw him, Win's ghost would be at his side.

"Letter for Dr. Endicott!"

My hopes fell as quickly as they had risen. The letter wasn't from Win. It was from David.

Cambridge
20 October 1775

Dear Whit,

I hope you are well, or as well as can be in the wilds of Canada. I continue serving in Cambridge where the siege goes on. We had some excitement when it was discovered Dr. Church has, for some time (perhaps as long as a year) been sending intelligence to the enemy in Boston. His fate has not yet been decided, but he is imprisoned.

Your brother, Lemuel, came to see me yesterday with news of your brother Josiah. He has taken a berth on one of General Washington's new schooners, the Lee.

His Excellency is determined to harry and distress the enemy's shipping using armed schooners to capture supplies. Josiah sends word he is well and eager to engage with the enemy.

At least some of us shall see action. Not that I wish for wounded, but sitting here day after day doing nothing is maddening.

I am sure you know Win is on his way to join you. Perhaps you have already been reunited.

Write soon.

Yours,
David

I dashed off a quick note to David, but Dr. Church weighed on my mind long afterward. He had been one of the Patriot leaders for years. He had given one of the Massacre Day orations, had been a delegate to the Provincial Congress, and was a member of the Committee of Safety. How had his double dealing gone unnoticed? What signs had we missed? If someone so entrenched in our leadership could be a traitor, could anyone truly be trusted?

To everyone's relief, Governor Carleton surrendered Montreal on November 13, but when we entered the city, he was nowhere to be found. Somehow, he had slipped through the lines and escaped to Quebec.

But overshadowing the disappointment of the escaped governor was the relief of new uniforms and clothes. Most of us had been wearing the same clothing since leaving Fort Ti, and much of it was mere rags, insufficient for winter. Uniforms, including red, fur-trimmed cloth caps; underjackets with corduroy sleeves; and white, hooded overcoats, were distributed from the British stores.

Montreal stretched along almost two miles of the west bank of the St. Lawrence River; a ditch and wall protected the landward side of the city. Just outside this wall, three suburbs had grown up, one to the south, one to the north, and one to the northwest. It was the first city I'd been in since leaving Boston, and the city girl in me breathed a sigh of relief to be sheltered by buildings once more. Our regiments encamped in the public storehouses and citadel barracks on the north end of the city. I set up in an abandoned apothecary, and General Montgomery claimed Château Ramezay, just a few blocks south of the citadel barracks, for his headquarters.

In celebration of taking the city, the men looted the town, suburbs, and countryside, against General Montgomery's orders. Only a few officers attempted to stop them. Most looted alongside their men. Remembering the chaos caused by Colonel Allen's men after the fall of Fort Ticonderoga, I didn't leave my new quarters without my pistols loaded and ready.

As I picked my way across the city on our second morning, searching for more medical supplies, a whoop followed by a cry of pain echoed from a nearby street. Drawing one of my pistols, I approached. What I saw stopped me in my tracks.

The door to a house in the middle of the street hung off its hinges, broken shards of pottery and splintered chairs strewn across the street like scattershot. One of our soldiers, a Pittsfield man, sat against the wall, a silver tea set hugged to his side and a bottle of wine at his lips.

A second Pittsfield man stumbled out of the house, arms laden with pillows, sheets, and quilts. "There's a whole cellar of cheese and preserves and dried meats! Get off your drunken arse, and help me!"

The first man threw his empty wine bottle at the other, and it shattered against the cobblestones.

A whimper drew my attention to the other side of the house, where an elderly couple, Catholics if the wooden crucifix the woman clutched in one hand was any indication, huddled against the neighboring house. Her husband had his arm around her shoulders, and she pressed her free hand against her throat. Both stared at the man holding them at knifepoint.

"Major Brown! What are you doing?" I demanded.

He turned, a silver locket swinging from a silver chain in his left hand. Looking more closely at the woman's neck, I saw the red burn the chain had left when Major Brown tore it away.

Major Brown didn't look sorry in the least. "These people," he said, gesturing with his knife, which made the couple shrink back even further, "refused to renounce the king or their idolatrous religion. We're only showing them what happens to those who oppose us."

Although I had never gotten on with that snake Colonel Easton, Major Brown and I had managed a cordial relationship even if he made me uneasy. This, however, not only went against General Montgomery's direct orders, but threatened to turn the local population against us, a population we needed on our side if we were to succeed in Canada. "Major Brown, General Montgomery ordered no looting. You and your men must return these things to the house, apologize to the owners, and pay for what you have destroyed."

Major Brown's eyes narrowed. "They are *Catholics*, Dr. Endicott. Surely you, as a good Massachusetts man, understand the threat their religion poses. Their very existence here proves Parliament is no longer acting in the interest of its citizens, good Protestants that we are! After fighting against the French threat in the last war, are you as willing as Parliament to let that threat flourish here? Don't tell me you're going to side with a former British officer who mismanaged two sieges, especially one who settled in New York."

His words woke warring feelings of shame and indignation. I had heard plenty in Boston rail against the Quebec Act, which had been passed at the same time as the Boston Port Act in 1774, both in retaliation for the tea we had destroyed the previous December. The Quebec Act had given the French Canadians the right to practice their Catholic religion and live as they had prior to the French War. Of course, it was a religion of idolatry and excess, and I didn't want it to exist in our colonies any more than I wanted Parliament to keep passing acts against us. I also didn't like being lumped together with General Montgomery. As New Yorkers went, he wasn't bad, but Brown made it sound as though I wasn't loyal to Massachusetts or the cause. Didn't all I had given up, all I had lost, my very presence, prove my commitment?

The elderly couple shivered and cowered closer together, the fear in their eyes recalling memories of mobs, burning effigies, and tarring and feathering. If we started with looting, where would it end? General Montgomery was right: if Parliament had given them freedom of religion, we could not afford to do less. The cause was bigger than Massachusetts, bigger, even, than how one worshipped God. I lifted my chin and met Major Brown's eyes. "Orders must be followed, Major. Return those things to the house at once."

One of the soldiers laughed. "And you're going to make us, Doctor?"

I knew what they saw: skinny, twig-armed, beardless, dwarfed by my new overcoat. I raised my pistol and drew my second. I aimed one at the laughing soldier and the other at Major Brown. "Either you return their things, or I shoot."

"Dr. Endicott, we're your countrymen! Fellow soldiers!"

"You're a doctor," the soldier sputtered. "You can't shoot us."

I held steady. I had never shot anyone or any living thing before, but this close, I wouldn't miss. I cocked the pistols. "So, it's a good thing I'll be able to put you back together again. Return their things. Now."

The soldiers looked to Major Brown, who wavered and finally dropped his eyes. "Return their things."

I holstered my pistols and aided in setting the house to rights. I pressed some of the money General Montgomery had given me for medical supplies into the woman's shaking hand. Major Brown didn't say a word to me, his lips a thin line, but the rest of his face was as unreadable as ever.

The next morning, Remy burst into my quarters. "Is it true? Did you hold our men at gunpoint yesterday? It's all over town!"

I sipped my tea—real tea, a luxury of capturing so many English goods. We hadn't had real East India tea in Boston since the Tea Act passed in '73. Aside from the superior taste, it did much to ease the phantom tickle in my throat. I took another sip before setting the mug aside. "They were looting, and General Montgomery's orders were clear."

"As they are now. He wants to see you."

"What? General Montgomery?"

Remy nodded.

"Damn." I pulled on my coat and shoved my pistols through my belt.

"Do you really think it's a good idea to bring those?"

"I'm not going into the streets unarmed when others are breaking orders and I'm the one being called to account. Coming?"

With a groan, Remy followed, musket held crosswise in front of her.

It was a short walk from my apothecary to the imposing Château Ramezay. Built of brownish-gray stone with an extensive garden behind, the château boasted six chimneys and a round tower on one end. Each window was covered with brilliant red shutters. The rooms inside were just as grand with wooden paneling, fine rugs warming polished wooden floors, and glittering chandeliers, their light reflected in mirrors as tall as me.

"I'll wait outside," Remy said.

"Thanks a lot." Wiping my boots at the door, I wound my way through the halls to the general's door and rapped against it.

"Enter."

"Dr. Endicott reporting, sir."

He sat at a large desk, the window behind him throwing brilliant morning light across the surface and around the room. A fire burned in the hearth, and a glass of dark wine or port sat at the general's elbow. He set aside his papers but didn't gesture for me to sit. He rubbed the large pockmark on his cheekbone as he considered me. Then, leaning forward, he said, "Dr. Endicott, Major Brown has leveled a serious charge against you. He said you threatened to shoot him and two of his men."

"I did, sir, but they were breaking orders and looting the house of a Catholic couple. I ordered them to return the possessions, but Major Brown refused, saying the couple would not forswear the king or their religion, which gave him the right to loot. I only drew my pistols to uphold your orders, sir, and protect our relationship with the locals."

General Montgomery frowned but settled back in his chair, hands folded over his stomach. "And I was going to promote the major to colonel. I will look into the matter further. Thank you for upholding my orders, Doctor. If you face the same situation again, though, I hope you can do so without drawing on our own men."

"I hope I won't have to defend your orders again, sir."

"As do I." He straightened once more and tapped a paper. "This morning, I received word from Colonel Arnold. He and his men have arrived outside Quebec and are in need of reinforcements. It is my understanding you came to Fort Ticonderoga with the colonel."

"Yes, sir." It took all my self-control not to ask about Win even though I knew Colonel Arnold's letter wouldn't have mentioned him.

"Tell me, how did you find him as a commander?"

"Very determined, sir, sometimes to the exclusion of all else. Honorable, as he has the same aversion to looting as yourself, and he treated all our prisoners with respect. He followed his orders but also took opportunities when they arose. He can be touchy about his own honor and cannot abide slights."

"A gentleman, then. Good. We leave for Quebec as soon as can be arranged. Inspect the men and determine which are too ill to go on. Pack as many of the medical supplies as can be moved."

"Yes, sir." Just days away. Win was just days away. Soon, I would know.

"Oh, and Dr. Endicott."

"Yes, sir?"

"There was a letter for you amid Colonel Arnold's correspondence. From a Winborn Endicott." He held out the letter.

I forced myself not to immediately rip it open. "My twin brother. Thank you, sir."

I sent Remy to the company commanders with instructions to have their troops ready for review that afternoon. Then I set the women I'd recruited from the camp followers to packing medical supplies. Only then did I read Win's letter.

Outside Quebec
November 1775

Dear Whitley,
God must indeed love Colonel Arnold, for despite all adversity, we have reached Quebec alive.

Our march through the Maine wilderness was grueling. Our boats leaked and were too heavy by far for easy portaging. Captain Enos of Connecticut and his men abandoned us, running back to Cambridge and taking with them much needed supplies. They are, each and every one, cowards. I know every man here, upon seeing Captain Enos or any of his men, would challenge them to a duel.

The last week of our march, we went with little to no food. But through the brave, never-flagging leadership of our good colonel, we reached Canada and were welcomed warmly by the inhabitants though I have yet to acquaint my cheeks and chin with a razor. If we were seen together now, I doubt any could tell we are twins.

We are in desperate need of reinforcements and supplies. Colonel Allan Maclean, who commands Quebec under Governor Carleton, has 2,500 soldiers, militia, and marines defending the city. I know not what influence you have over General Montgomery, but stress our need for men, arms, and food.

I hope with every breath to see you marching over the horizon.

Your Dearest Brother,
Win

The hollowness in my stomach was explained. I'd been feeling Win starve. I pressed my hands flat against my desk to stop their shaking. He was alive, and we were going to his aid.

Word spread quickly that we were marching to Quebec instead of wintering safely in Montreal. With true winter only a blink away, moving deeper into Canada sounded like madness to many of the men.

Instead of risking a winter in the frozen north, many deserted. By the time we weeded out the ill and left behind a garrison under General David Wooster, we marched for Quebec with only three hundred men to reinforce Colonel Arnold.

Chapter Twenty
December 2, 1775

It was cold enough to split stone when we arrived at Pointe-aux-Trembles amid fast-falling snow. Without enough men to attack Quebec on his own, Colonel Arnold had fallen back to this town twenty miles south on the St. Lawrence River. Pointe-aux-Trembles was small, not even a town really, just a few houses, St. Nicholas Church, and a nunnery. All the buildings were sturdily built of stone and provided good shelter from the wind and cold. While General Montgomery and Colonel Arnold discussed our next move in the kitchen of the farmhouse they had claimed for headquarters, I settled Portia, dumped my scant belongings in the room I was to share with Colonel Arnold's surgeon, and went in search of Win.

Most men were bearded and so thin they disappeared when turned sideways. Their clothes were rags, and they were none too clean. I would have to speak to General Montgomery about issuing an order for general hygiene and see about dispensing new uniforms; we still had plenty from the British stores in Montreal.

"Dr. Endicott!" A man waved. It wasn't until he stood directly in front of me that I recognized him.

"Captain Oswald!" The young aide-de-camp looked haggard and hard-used, far too thin, and bearded, not nearly as handsome as I remembered him. "You hardly look as you did at Fort Ti."

"It's the beard." He patted his new facial hair. "And the weight loss. It was not an easy journey from Cambridge."

"Win hinted as much in his letter. Do you know where I can find him?"

"He should be at headquarters. He and I remain the colonel's aides."

"I was just there, but if he's as changed as you, I can see how I missed him."

As we walked back, Captain Oswald told me more about the march up the Kennebec River. Between incorrect maps and lost or damaged supplies, it was indeed a miracle they had survived at all. Besides the desertion of Captain Enos's company, another fifty men had either died or deserted, and diseases such as smallpox and dysentery were spreading quicker than gossip. Of the thousand-some who had left Cambridge, only six hundred arrived in Canada.

At the mention of smallpox, my insides twisted. That was the last thing we needed. I had to convince General Montgomery and Colonel Arnold to quarantine the men. We needed to inoculate before the disease spread further.

"It would have been better if you'd brought more men," Captain Oswald said. I started to explain, but I saw Win on the steps of headquarters, scanning each passing face. Half-laughing, half-crying, I threw my arms around him. I felt his ribs and spine press into my better-fleshed body. His scrawl of a beard rasped against my cheek. We would need to get rid of that right away. Part of my safety when Win and I were together depended on us looking alike. When I pulled away, though, I realized something else had changed.

"You've grown."

"Six months apart, and that's the first thing you say to me?" His voice had deepened, too. Another problem. I would have to start speaking in a little lower register.

"Only you would be stubborn enough to grow while starving." There was a third difference besides the height and the beard, but I couldn't put my finger on it. "I'm glad to see you alive. Captain Oswald was telling me more about your trek up the Kennebec."

Win frowned at Captain Oswald. He started to say something, but a cough cut him off. It was a dry, deep cough, an old cough which could easily develop into something worse.

"Win—"

"I'm fine," he choked out. "Just—"

"Don't say it's just a cough. You know it's always more than a cough with you." I tugged him inside the farmhouse and lowered my voice so as not to disturb General Montgomery and Colonel Arnold. "Where's your room?"

He pointed upstairs. "I'm sharing with Eleazer. He never should have said anything."

"I knew something was wrong before Captain Oswald said anything, so don't go giving him grief for telling me what you went through. I felt it. A hollowness in my stomach and a scratch in my throat. Don't lie to me, and don't try to shield me, Win."

He suppressed another cough. "I should know better than to hide anything from you." The door to my room opened, and I pulled up short as a man I'd never seen before emerged, a journal under his arm. Win gestured to him. "Dr. Isaac Senter, may I introduce my brother, Dr. Whitley Endicott? I may have inherited the winning good looks, but he got all the wit."

I shook my head at the old joke, but Dr. Senter chuckled and held out a hand with ink-stained fingers. "A pleasure to meet you, Dr. Endicott. Having another medical man here is a relief."

"The feeling is mutual, sir." The other doctors who had come north with General Montgomery had been left behind at St-Jean or Montreal or returned to Fort Ti with those too ill to serve. At the same time, Dr. Senter made me nervous, especially since we were sharing a room. As a doctor, he knew male anatomy and would know that mine was not. I couldn't make any more mistakes like those I'd made on the *Enterprise*.

"I was just repacking my things," Dr. Senter said. "Colonel Arnold plans to return to Quebec now that you lot have arrived. Attack before enlistments expire or more men desert."

So not sharing a room for long. But I frowned. "Surely with the smallpox we should wait."

"I've already spoken with Colonel Arnold about the smallpox problem. He told me I would have to wait until we returned to Quebec to begin quarantines."

Win coughed. Dr. Senter and I studied him with concern.

"Endicott, that cough—"

"I was just about to treat my brother. And find him a meal and a shave."

"Shave first."

"Medicine first." I nudged Win to his room. I gave him a handful of lozenges before I braved the kitchen for some hot water. General Montgomery and Colonel Arnold barely noticed me as I crept to the large pot hanging over the fire.

"We must send a letter to General Schuyler requesting more men and supplies," General Montgomery said, thumb absently smoothing that same pockmark.

"And hard coin," Colonel Arnold said. He, too, was changed by the hardships of the march north. He was thinner, and his facial bones were more stark, but his eyes were made of the same steel I remembered. "I am nearly out of specie, and the Canadians I've met have been reluctant to accept Congressional script."

I slipped out with my hot water and returned to Win's room. Out of money already? We truly needed to take the city quickly.

Win grimaced when I made him drink my concoction. "Couldn't you add any honey? All I can taste is vinegar."

"Out of honey at the moment, and it's a little hard to come by during winter in Canada. Now sit back, and let's get rid of that beard."

While I shaved him, tea steeped, perfuming the room with chamomile and mint. Win sighed when he took a sip. "This tastes so much better."

"And you should have a cup before bed, and another dose of the cough medicine as well."

"I know, Whit. I've done this often enough. And you'll have a rub or poultice for me, too, both if you can manage it."

It struck me then what was different. Despite being ill and more than half-starved, Win was happy. Happy in a way I couldn't remember him being in years. I'd only ever seen him this happy on the Warren farm. He glowed. His mouth continually twitched up, his voice was light, and his eyes were bright, and not with fever either.

"You're too thin to be so happy. What happened?"

"God, I've missed you, Whit." He began pacing, hands running through his hair, pulling it loose from its tie. "One look at me, and you've discovered all my secrets. No hiding anything from you. Not that I want to. I've wanted to tell someone since—I'm rambling, aren't I?" He dropped down beside me, hands clasped as he tried to hold in his excitement. "I've met someone."

"Not you, too," I said before remembering Win's someone would not be a camp follower but, like Remy's Paul, a fellow soldier.

Win's eyebrows rose. "Me, too?"

"Long story. I'll explain later. Please tell me you don't share the same tent."

"Uh," he toyed with his earlobe, "there weren't really tents on the trek up."

I groaned. This was worse than Remy. "Win, if he finds out, you'll—"

"He already knows."

I blinked. And again. If he knew, then he and Win had talked, at the very least. Heat rushed through me at the thought of what else they might have done, and I banished those thoughts quickly, focusing on the problem. Others could have seen or overheard.

Win took my hands. "Don't worry. We were discreet. No one suspects. I want you to meet him. Will you eat with us tonight?"

"Win, it's dangerous. If anyone even wonders—"

"There'll be others eating with us. We know the consequences. Please, Whit. I—if I don't even have you on my side . . ."

That hadn't been what I meant at all. I linked my pinkie with his and raised our joined hands. "You have my support, Win. Always. Of course I'll meet him."

The cookfire belonged to a company of riflemen under the command of Captain Daniel Morgan. They wore hunting shirts belted at the waist and gaited trousers, which strapped under their boots and buttoned down over them. Large round hats, some of them with the brim pinned up on one side, completed the uniform. Knives and tomahawks hung from every belt, and their Pennsylvania long rifles leaned against nearby trees.

"Everyone," Win announced when we stepped into the firelight, "this is my twin, Dr. Whitley Endicott."

I tried not to look nervous as every set of eyes fixed on me. Without the beard, Win and I looked more like twins, but he was still several inches taller and his voice deeper.

"Doctor, huh? He must have gotten the brains."

"But not the good looks. Whit, everybody. The smart-ass there is George Morison. That's John Joseph Henry; he just turned sixteen in November. Beat us to it by two months." Win went on naming another ten men before he said, "And George Lee rounds us out."

I knew from the way Win said his name George Lee was the one. He was taller than Win, a year or two older, and, like all of them, too thin. The weight loss was all the more obvious on George because he was broad shouldered. Not as broad as Paul, but certainly well built. He had red-gold hair, made more so by the firelight, and snow-pale skin, which probably burned horribly in the summer. Freckles spattered his cheeks and nose. His eyes glinted a merry, summer blue, but he didn't seem given to smiling. His handshake was firm, fingers and palm callused. That was puzzling. His manner and bearing suggested a wealthy upbringing. I'd treated enough of the well-to-do in Boston to recognize them. But they didn't have workmen's hands, nor were they often found among backwoodsmen like these. He was nothing like Henry Knox, who Win had once liked, and he wasn't as handsome as Oswald, who Win had doubtless spent much time with. I wondered what had drawn my brother to him. A riddle to be sure.

Dinner passed in a swirl of conversation, jokes, and laughter. They all ate three or four helpings, and I was reminded this was probably only their second or third proper meal since October. Win and George paid no special attention to each other, but I knew Win. He was aware of George's every move. As for George, he blinked every time Win coughed, but he didn't look at my brother once. Maybe my fears of their discovery had been misplaced.

While the conversation whirled about, George sat in his own pocket of silence. He didn't join in the jokes or teasing. He was also set apart by his manners. While the rest shoveled food down as fast as fingers could move, George ate with a decorum the others, even Win, lacked. Another line of the riddle. Win, though not a Virginian or a rifleman, fit in better than George because Win's demeanor was open and easy, all smiles and laughter.

When Win finished eating, he began twisting and tearing up sticks and bits of grass and tossing them into the fire. I had noted the length of rope looped through his belt earlier. It was good to know some things never changed.

When they had exhausted tales of their adventures north, the conversation veered to the one thing on almost every man's mind.

"Did you see? There are women here," said one.

"Going to take advantage of that," said another. He nudged George. "What about you, Lee? Going to find a woman when we reach Quebec tomorrow?"

George said nothing, only stared at the fire, face stiff and red. Even I knew a lie, joke, or redirection of the conversation would have been a good strategy, but George didn't seem to recognize this.

"Nah, not Lord George," said the first. "He's got a fancy lady waiting back home."

"Ah, once you've tasted fine food, you can't go back to common fare!"

"What would you know about fine food?"

The men laughed. Win was taut as a tourniquet beside me, shredding the sticks into smaller and smaller pieces even though he smiled. George didn't move a muscle.

"What about you, Win?"

Win's hands stilled. "I must defer to my brother's knowledge before I do any sampling."

All the men turned to me.

I cleared my throat and remembered to use a deeper voice. "I have examined the women of the profession among the camp followers, and I have to recommend keeping your distance unless you wish to come away with more discomfort than when you arrived."

The men groaned, and Win shrugged. "I'm afraid I must decline the invitation."

"And I must return to headquarters," I said. "You coming, Win?"

He swallowed back a cough. "I'll stay a little longer."

I frowned, but before I could say anything, George said, "I'll walk with you, Doctor."

It was a strangely gentlemanly gesture from one man to another, and the others noticed. Realizing his mistake, he stammered, "I-I acquired a rash on the march north. Perhaps you could examine it."

"Of course. Win, don't stay too long. I'll have a poultice and tea waiting for you."

Win rolled his eyes. "Never have a doctor in the family, men. They're worse than mothers."

I kicked a chunk of snow at him, and the others laughed as George and I walked away. Once we were far enough from the fire, I said, "There isn't really a rash, is there?"

"No."

"Let's walk a bit further then." I took us on a meandering route between the tents and the outer sentries. I waited until we were well away from all others before I spoke again. "I'm very glad to meet you, George. I've never seen Win this happy."

"When he told me his twin sister knew and understood, I didn't believe him." George cast a questioning glance up and down my body. "I didn't expect you."

I chuckled. "I'd be dressed differently if it were possible. I'm only here to doctor."

"Well, I hope I won't need your services."

"I hope none of you do, but I'd be a fool to hold too hard to that hope."

George didn't answer, eyes carefully averted from mine. He hadn't once made eye contact with me all night, and his expression was more than a little wary. I thought of my warnings to Remy and Win and couldn't help but say, "You'll be careful? The both of you? I don't want to see either of you in my surgery because—"

"I know what's at stake, Doctor." His face closed off even more. "I know what will happen if we're caught better than your brother or you. You cannot think just because of who we love, we have no sense."

"No," I said slowly, taken aback by the vehemence in his voice. "But I know sometimes love outweighs sense."

George's anger worried me. He was as defensive as a cornered cat. Clearly, he had some experience with the cruelty of the world toward men like himself. But his clenched jaw told me he would say no more, and I was half-afraid to ask.

When we reached headquarters, George asked, "He will live, won't he? The cough . . ."

"Won't kill him. I've been keeping my brother alive for years, George. I'm not about to stop now or let a measly cough take him."

George nodded solemnly. "Very good. Well, good night, Doctor."

"George, wait." He paused, half turned from me. "Please, call me Whit or at least Whitley. I don't pretend to know what you face, but I've always been there for Win. Always and no matter what. He cares about you, which makes you as good as family. If you need someone to talk to, or anything, you can come to me."

Surprise flashed across his face before he dropped his mask back in place. "I'm sure I shall need no such aid."

George disappeared into the darkness, shoulders hunched against the world. How, I wondered, had Win broken through that forbidding exterior?

Chapter Twenty-One
December 3, 1775

We were on the road to Quebec early the next morning. I walked with Win and George, snow crunching under our feet, and the chill air making our noses drip. Despite the cold, Colonel Arnold's men were in better spirits, for they were dressed in the warm British uniforms from Montreal.

We walked a bit behind the rest of the riflemen, and Portia trailed on a lead behind me, just as content to carry our gear as she had been carrying me.

"Portia?" Win said when he heard her name. "I mean, of course Shakespeare, but don't you think someone will recognize the reference and wonder why you chose *that* Shakespearean character's name?"

In *The Merchant of Venice*, Portia had disguised herself as a doctor of the law, not medicine, to rescue her fiancé's best friend from death. "And just how many Shakespeare devotees do you think are among us? Anyone who's heard me call her by name thinks I named her after my sweetheart. As if any woman wants a horse named after her."

George listened to our exchange without comment. It was, I decided, the perfect opportunity to try unravel the riddle that was George Lee. "Where are you from, George?"

He started, as if surprised I'd spoken to him, and it took him a moment to answer. "Outside Richmond, Virginia. My family owns a plantation."

He closed off again. That was half the riddle solved, and the nickname the others had given him—*Lord George*—made sense, but that didn't explain how he'd ended up as a rifleman in Canada. I switched Portia's lead to my other hand. "So. You have a big family? Lots of brothers and sisters? Win and I are the youngest of nine. Lots of siblings keep things interesting."

"And ensure you get away with quite a bit of mischief," Win added with a wink.

"No, I've just a younger brother and a younger sister."

I waited for him to go on. I was certain Win had already told him at length about our family. But George said no more.

I tried again. "So, you'll inherit the plantation one day? A lot of responsibility, I would think. You must have a plan for the place."

"I won't inherit." His tone made it clear the conversation was over. The flicker of a frown across Win's face told me he didn't know any more than what George had already said. I was at a loss for where to take the conversation next, but Win came to the rescue. "George helped me keep my promise to you, Whit."

George's face settled into what I was coming to believe was his usual solemn expression, though I thought I caught a flash of relief in his eyes.

"Which promise?"

"The one about not dying. George saved my life."

The cold I felt had nothing to do with the weather. Just how close to death had Win come? How close had I come to losing another person I loved? Not only loved, but the person who was my other half. I could have arrived at Pointe-aux-Trembles and found that Win had perished. Portia bumped her nose against my shoulder, and I stroked it, calming myself. I kept my tone light and voice steady. "How did George manage that?"

"On the way up the Kennebec, we stumbled into a swamp. We had abandoned the boats days before, traveling on foot, carrying everything we had left. The water was freezing. We had only flour cakes to eat, didn't know where the rest of the army was, and had no idea how far from Canada and salvation we might be. We were wading blindly through the swamp when I hit a drop-off. One moment I was waist deep, the next I was gulping down muck, my feet kicking for something, anything." Win shuddered, fear reigniting in his eyes. "Then a hand grasped mine and pulled me back to the land of the living. We were able to start a small, very smokey fire that didn't do much to warm us, so we, ah, well, we kept each other warm until morning." Win was all kinds of red, George too, and I was sure my face matched theirs. Win rubbed his ear. "In the morning, my clothes were still damp, so George lent me his jacket."

"Anyone else would have done the same," George muttered, then, realizing how that could be interpreted, hurried to add. "Pulled you out of the water, I mean."

"And given me their jacket?"

"It wasn't that dry."

"Drier than anything I had."

I grinned at their banter. "Well, I'm truly grateful, George. Someone's got to watch out for my witless brother when I'm not around."

"Hey!"

"What? You're always saying I have all the wit and you the good looks."

George's lips twitched up, as close to a smile as I had seen from him yet.

Win moved on to a topic he could, apparently, expound on for hours: Colonel Arnold. He had nothing but praise for the colonel, and George nodded his agreement with every statement. To them, Colonel Arnold was a paragon of a soldier, as fearless as Henry V, a very god of war. He could do no wrong and didn't know the meaning of the word *failure*.

They weren't alone in their hero worship. Arnold's men cheered whenever he rode by. Unlike the men who had come with us from Fort Ti, the Kennebec men looked and acted like a seasoned, battle-tried army. Though the foe they'd faced hadn't been human, it had tempered them.

"You know, Whit, you're not the only woman in this army anymore," Win said.

"I haven't been the only woman for some time."

"I didn't mean the camp followers."

"Neither did I." Win frowned at me, but I didn't elaborate.

"He means them," George said, jutting his chin ahead.

My eyes fell on the young Indian woman riding next to Lieutenant Aaron Burr, one of General Montgomery's new aides, though he had come up the Kennebec with Colonel Arnold. Rumor moved faster than armies, so I had already heard several stories about the pair, most of which left the realm of reality far behind, but all of which contained the grain that gestated the rumors: Burr and Jacatacqua were intimate.

"You don't consider her a camp follower? I know she helped guide you north, but I don't think she intends to fight."

Win followed my gaze. "No, not her." He pointed a bit to the right. "The two there. With the other riflemen."

With the blanket rolls, powder horns, canteens, and shot bags hanging slantwise across their bodies, it was hard to distinguish one rifleman from another. But the longer I stared, the more apparent it became. Two women in skirts marched among them, one of whom carried a rifle. How had I not noticed them before?

"Both followed their husbands," Win said. "Mrs. Suzannah Grier is the one without the rifle. Waded through the swamp that almost swallowed me carrying her husband's gear above her head. And Mrs. Jemima Warner. Her husband died on the march. She sat with him until he passed, then took up his rifle and marched twenty miles to catch up with us. Colonel Arnold won't send them back. Said they earned the right to fight with us."

"Because he can't afford to lose any soldier, man or woman." I knew what Win was saying. I was just as valuable, perhaps more so, to the army, and it wouldn't matter if I did my doctoring as a man or a woman. "But what happens when this campaign is over? When the war moves on or more regiments arrive to hold what we've gained? You think when they're not desperate, they'll let the women stay on? They'll let a fifteen-year-old girl with no formal medical education keep doctoring? No, Win, I'll stay as I am."

Win shrugged and let the subject drop. But I kept thinking about Mrs. Grier, Mrs. Warner, Remy, and all the possibilities these other women offered.

Chapter Twenty-Two
December 3, 1775

The city of Quebec sat on a spear of land which pierced the St. Lawrence River. Though not nearly as island-like as Boston, Quebec was still well protected by water. On the river side, steep cliffs rose, lifting the city up, and making the Upper City attainable only by scaling the cliffs or going through the Lower City. A wall, studded with cannon, protected the landward side. When the river froze, however, Quebec would be slightly more vulnerable from the rear.

Our army encamped on the snow-covered Plains of Abraham and in the outskirts of St. Roch and St. Jean, neighborhoods outside Quebec's walls. Colonel Arnold took Menut's Tavern in St. Roch as his headquarters, and General Montgomery took command at Holland House.

"There's a hospital already established," Colonel Arnold explained to General Montgomery, Dr. Senter, and me as we rode from Holland House across the Plains of Abraham. We aimed for a large stone building and windmill situated on the edge of the Charles River about a mile from Quebec's walls and a half mile from St. Roch's gate.

"It's simply called Hôpital-Général, or General Hospital," Colonel Arnold said. "Run by nuns as a home for the indigent, elderly, and infirm of Quebec. Ideally supplied and located for our own hospital."

"Do they support our cause?" General Montgomery asked.

Colonel Arnold hesitated. "They seem to have been treated well by the English, perhaps even given funds, so they're not thrilled with our presence. I assured them we will not interfere with their religious observances and only request their medical, not spiritual, aid."

General Montgomery hummed in satisfaction. Dr. Senter leaned close and spoke only loud enough for me to hear. "I don't know about you, but I'll be happy for any help they can give. I never finished my apprenticeship."

I stared at him for a moment. "How old are you?"

"Twenty-two. I was nearly finished with my apprenticeship, but this march north was a bit of a baptism by fire."

"You weren't at Bunker Hill?" Even Dr. Wood had been at Bunker Hill.

He shook his head, and my stomach sank. No battle experience. I had assumed he'd been at Bunker Hill and seen wounds like we were going to see when we attacked Quebec.

"It'll be nice to work with others who have some battle experience," he continued, "though I'd feel easier if they weren't *so* Catholic."

I was still trying to process that he had less experience than me. I hadn't even thought about how we were headed for a Catholic church. While I wasn't too bothered by the thought of the Catholic French Canadians practicing their religion in their homes and churches at a distance from me, living among those who had dedicated their lives to that religion made my neck tighten. I imagined the place bedecked with idols, and I wasn't far from the mark.

The General Hospital consisted of a collection of buildings: an old monastery, a prelate, the hospital, an apothecary, the Notre-Dame-des-Anges Chapel, and a bakery. The mill, where the nuns ground their own flour, stood apart. Though the exteriors were all stone, dark wood clothed the interiors. Every niche was occupied by painted statues of saints, and little dishes of holy water were nailed next to each door. Crucifixes and religious paintings dotted the walls. Most disturbing was the interior of the chapel. The front was dominated by an ornate gilded altarpiece. And some of the windows contained colored glass. I shuddered at the idolatry and waste, suddenly homesick for the pure, whitewashed walls of Brattle Street Meeting House. I turned my back on the garishness and resolved not to set foot in the chapel again.

Father Superior de Rigauville and Mother Marie-Catherine met us at the doors of the hospital. Both wore the black robes of their order and crucifixes around their necks. Each had a second crucifix hanging at their waist from a beaded chain. Glasses perched on Father de Rigauville's long, thin nose. Everything about him was long and thin but not weak. He held himself straight-backed as any general. Mother Marie-Catherine, shorter and rounded, was just as steady.

"You return, Colonel Arnold." Father de Rigauville's voice was just as thin as the rest of him, and his French accent gave an unaccustomed shape to his words.

"As I said I would," Colonel Arnold replied with a slight bow. "May I present General Montgomery and our doctors, Whitley Endicott and Isaac Senter."

Mother Marie-Catherine's eyes lingered on Dr. Senter and me. I fought the urge to look away.

"We are perfectly able to care for any wounded without outside help," Father de Rigauville said. "As we did at the Battle of the Plains of Abraham in '59. We care for all sick and wounded, no matter their native land or religion."

"For which we are grateful, Father," General Montgomery said. "But surely the Lord would not want you to reject two pairs of willing hands. Besides, both these men are surgeons, accustomed to the more serious wounds inflicted in battle."

I winced at the lie and hoped no one noticed, but Mother Marie-Catherine's eyes were on me again. Eyes narrowed in suspicion.

Father de Rigauville sighed. "Very well. They may stay. But no soldiers unless they are ill or wounded. I will not have the sisters or our patients molested."

"Of course." General Montgomery turned to us. "We'll take your horses back to the lines, make sure they're cared for."

I dismounted and reluctantly handed Portia's reins to Colonel Arnold. She gave me a baleful look, and I wished I could keep the friendly mare closer, but the sisters had no stables. I scratched under her chin. "I'll see you soon, girl."

With our horses in tow, General Montgomery and Colonel Arnold saluted and rode back to headquarters, leaving us in a silent staring contest with the Father and Mother of the Hôpital-Général de Quebec.

Chapter Twenty-Three
December 3-4, 1775

Snow drifted down, dusting the black robes of our hosts and our own black coats. My toes were numb, but I refused to let my discomfort show. Dr. Senter seemed unaffected by the cold. Legacy of the Kennebec, I was sure.

"Come," Mother Marie-Catherine said at last. "I will show you the hôpital. Père, if you could inform the sisters of our visitors?"

Inclining his head, Father de Rigauville disappeared into the monastery.

The hospital was more austere than the rest of the building, though crucifixes hung above every bed. There were beds for fifty patients, and the hospital was well stocked with clean linens and surgical instruments. Since they had their own apothecary and sisters trained to make medicines, I found myself in the best-supplied medical facility I'd seen since leaving Dr. Warren's house on Hanover Street.

Mother Marie-Catherine showed us to guest rooms in the old monastery. *Rooms* was too generous a word, for they were no different from the cells of the nuns. Each contained a bed with better linens than we'd had at Fort Ti, a washstand, a bedside table holding a candle and a prayer book, and a chest for clothes and linen. No fireplace. It would be a chilly winter in this room. On account of the size, Dr. Senter and I each had our own room, so I had no cause to complain.

"Breakfast is at five, dinner at one, and supper at five in the refectory. You may join us for prayer and worship if you wish, but otherwise, you will restrict yourselves to these rooms, the refectory, the apothecary, and the hôpital." With a swish of her robes, Mother Marie-Catherine left.

"Pray we capture Quebec quickly," Dr. Senter said. "I doubt the good Mother and Father will tolerate our presence long."

The bells rang out again, calling the sisters to another set of prayers. Shivering under my thin sheet and blanket, I held my pillow hard over my ears, but the tolling was still audible. I didn't think I could abide living like this.

Abandoning any attempts at sleep, I dressed and went to the apothecary. A fire burned in the grate, but I felt winter through the walls and heard it blowing across the plains. The room might be strange, but the work was the same, and I found the herbs I needed. Measuring and chopping, straining and drying calmed me. The smells of the apothecary were as familiar as the work—sharp and bitter, made more so by the cold. Although Dr. Warren's ghost was nowhere to be seen, I felt his presence. I could almost hear his voice giving me instructions.

"Trouble sleeping?"

I jumped. Mother Marie-Catherine stood in the doorway. I willed my heart back to its normal pace. "Not used to all the bells. In Boston, the bells only ring at six, noon, and nine. And to toll deaths after the morning bell."

Mother Marie-Catherine examined what I'd made. "It is an ajustement, but order and regulation can bring calm to the most turbulent life or mind."

I made a noncommittal noise and reached for the mortar and pestle.

Mother Marie-Catherine's hand closed around my wrist. I pulled back instinctively, but she didn't let go. As soon as I pulled back, I knew I'd made a mistake. A man in the same situation would not have reacted as I had.

She saw me recognize my mistake and released me. "Why?" she asked. "Why do you hide under l'apparence de l'homme? Protection? Shame? Determination to be part of the blood and death to come?"

"To save lives," I said. To pay my debts, I thought. And debts don't pay themselves.

"You could do that as une femme." She gestured to herself.

I shook my head. "Not as a doctor, only as a nurse or a midwife. You heard General Montgomery. He wants Dr. Senter and myself here for our surgical skills. Though the general may have overstated our experience with battle wounds."

"With both of you so young, I did not think you could have much experience with such wounds."

"But I *am* skilled, and I've seen more than Dr. Senter has. If I wore my own guise, I wouldn't be able to help, and people would die."

Mother Marie-Catherine considered this. "I do not doubt you. Les femmes have always had the same capabilities as men, the same strengths, the same faiblesses. Look at our own Jeanne d'Arc or Queen Elizabeth of the Anglais. You might be as strong or as great as either of them. But there is a difference between them and you."

She eyed me, waiting for me to ask. I held out as long as I could. "And what difference is that?"

"They did not hide themselves, but faced the world as les femmes, proving they were equal to any man and better than most. Bonne nuit, Dr. Endicott."

She moved to leave, but I stopped her. "You won't tell, will you?"

Mother Marie-Catherine's expression softened, and she patted my hand. "Ma fille, I have been a confessor for many years. I will not start betraying that office now."

I had, it seemed, no choice but to trust her.

Chapter Twenty-Four
December 4-5, 1775

Despite my misgivings about living among the nuns, there was something comforting about being surrounded by so many women after months with men. A tension I hadn't known I carried, which had tightened my shoulders and stiffened my neck, leaked away over the following days. It was like when Miss Scollay had insisted I spend time with the ladies of Boston. I hadn't realized how much I needed female company until I joined them. This hospital, filled with women, was a place I belonged despite our differences in language and religion. Dr. Senter didn't notice a difference in me, too preoccupied with keeping his journal, but I felt the eyes of the nuns on me, and I knew they knew without Mother Marie-Catherine saying a word.

About a half mile behind the hospital, we set up a quarantine house for those taken ill with smallpox, but we didn't have the doctors to staff it or enforce quarantine. We also needed to start inoculating, but with battle on the horizon, neither General Montgomery nor Colonel Arnold wanted any more men ineffective due to illness. Inoculations would have to wait until after we had taken the city.

If smallpox had been the only disease we faced, we might have stood a chance, but men staggered into the hospital suffering from dysentery, pneumonia, and pleurisy, as well as cases of frostbite. Win was not the only one for whom I brewed teas and made poultices and camphor rubs. We also recommended rest, warmth, and hearty meals, but these were in short supply.

On our first full day at the hospital, Mother Marie-Catherine sought me out. "There is a patient you should see."

"What's wrong with him?" I asked, not looking up from the dried herbs I was crushing.

"Not un homme. Une femme. She has sought us out because she wishes to be treated by a woman. She should know you can treat her if we cannot."

I stopped. "Mother, I have a male identity to protect."

"If we cannot trust our sisters, whom can we trust?" She took me by the arm like a child and brought me to the small room where another nun waited with Jacatacqua. Her black hair was braided neatly atop her head, and she wore a deerskin dress over leggings. Jacatacqua considered me with dark eyes.

"Sister Marie-Therese?" Mother Marie-Catherine said.

"Oui, Mère Supérieure?"

"Dr. Endicott will assist." Sister Marie-Therese bowed her head and left. Mother Marie-Catherine directed her next words to Jacatacqua. "The doctor can be trusted."

I pulled the leather tie from my hair and untied my cravat. Jacatacqua inclined her head. "She can stay."

She was pregnant, so at least one of the rumors about her and Lieutenant Burr was true.

"If you are still here when your time comes," Mother Marie-Catherine said, "we will deliver the baby at the hôpital or in Quebec."

Jacatacqua nodded and looked at me.

"If we leave and you come with us, I can deliver the child. I've assisted with many births."

"Good." Jacatacqua started toward the door. "I will bring the others to meet you, Dr. Endicott."

When Mrs. Jemima Warner and Mrs. Suzannah Grier arrived, I sent a runner to find Remy.

"You're truly a woman?" Suzannah asked. She was in her midtwenties and stood nearly six feet tall. Her expression was a little severe, but her hazel eyes softened whenever they fell on Jemima. I didn't have to be in their company long to sense the sisterly bond between them.

"I am both a woman and a doctor."

"We wouldn't have come if Jacatacqua hadn't told us about you," Jemima said. She was seventeen, like Remy, but it was clear Jemima was cut from tougher cloth than my friend. Her dark eyes were harder, more world-wise, and she carried more wiry muscle. "I'm sure the nuns know what they're doing, but a woman doctor—that's an opportunity not to be missed."

They were in surprisingly good health after what they had endured. No signs of dysentery, smallpox, or the cough that plagued Win.

I met Remy at the door. "I have a few people I'd like you to meet, if you want."

"Who? Nuns?"

"No, the women who made the Kennebec march."

"Truly? They're here?"

When I showed Remy into the refectory, Suzannah and Jemima were taking tea with Jacatacqua. They fell silent the moment we entered, smiles falling away and shoulders tensing.

"Who is this, Doctor?" Suzannah asked.

"Allow me to introduce Remember Alden, or, when she's not disguising herself as a soldier, Rebekah Bradt. Remy, these are Jemima Warner, Suzannah Grier, and Jacatacqua of the Abenaki."

"I've already heard about your march up the Kennebec," Remy gushed. "I can hardly believe you survived that."

"Sit," Suzannah said. "Tell us your story."

"It's not much of a story," Remy began, but I interrupted, "That's a lie. Tell them."

When Remy finished her story, Jemima said, "You're no less impressive than we are. Joining the army alone, living among the men as one of them. Not to mention taking part in two sieges."

Remy ducked her head, and Jacatacqua shook hers. "We are human—man or woman should make no difference to what we can and cannot do."

"To women," Suzannah said, raising her cup of tea. "And what we can accomplish."

It didn't matter that we were from different colonies or had different experiences. Within minutes, we were sharing and laughing. As relaxed as I felt living among women again, something changed when I had a group of women to talk to. And not just any women, but women like those I had known in Boston, women who were willing to work and fight for the cause.

"What are you smiling about, Dr. Endicott?" Jemima asked.

"Just, in Boston, a group of like-minded women met each week. Though it was ostensibly a sewing circle, we wrote and discussed articles, made saltpeter, developed ideas to pass on to the men, and supported each other. I didn't realize how much I missed them. Missed this."

"I never had anything like that in Pennsylvania," Suzannah said, and Jemima shook her head.

"Me neither," Remy said. But Jacatacqua met my eyes, and I knew whatever differences separated us, we understood each other.

"A week is too long between meetings," Jemima said. "Especially for you two, pretending to be men all the time. I think we should gather every day."

Jacatacqua nodded. "Here. The nuns will guard your secrets."

"Yes," Remy said, and I agreed.

"What is happening here?" Mother Marie-Catherine stood in the doorway. "Dr. Endicott, I thought we made it clear that none of les militaires were to enter unless they are wounded."

Remy, face flaming, jumped up, stammering, "I'm sorry. I didn't mean to—"

I gripped Remy's arm before she could flee. "Mother, like me, Remy is not what she appears."

Mother Marie-Catherine's eyes swept over all of us. "Un corps de femmes," she murmured then nodded. "You are welcome here. Doctor, might I have your assistance?"

"Of course."

The door had barely closed behind us when she asked, "How many of you are there?"

"Remy's the last of us. As far as I know."

Mother Marie-Catherine shook her head. "Any more and I shall begin to wonder if there are any men in your army. Wouldn't that be a sight to see—the Anglais beaten by an army of les femmes!"

That night, Jemima practically carried Remy back to the hospital. Rem was reeling pickled, so drunk she couldn't stand. I knew Mother Marie-Catherine would throw us all out if she discovered Remy in this state.

I led them down to the bakery. It would be warm at least. "What happened?"

"I don't know. One of the men in her company, a large, muscled man—Paul, I think—was holding her hair as she threw up. Said she said something about her brother. I told him I'd bring Remy to you."

I lit a few lanterns. Along with the glow from the banked fire, they made the bakery bright enough. Large ovens stood along one wall, paddles leaning next to them. Every table and chair, and even the floor itself, was dusted with flour. The comforting scent of warm bread embraced us. Jemima puddled Remy into a chair, and I poured her a mug of coffee. "Here, Rem. Drink this."

"No, no more. 'M not feelin' so good."

"It's coffee, Rem."

"Just let it sit, Whit." Jemima pulled up chairs for us, and I poured us each a mug.

Remy's head tipped back, and what little consciousness she'd retained fled. Jemima studied her, face drawn and somehow—perhaps it was the candlelight—thinner than it had been before. I was reminded suddenly that Jemima was not so much older than me, which was hard to remember since she had already been married and widowed.

"Grief strikes at the oddest of times," Jemima mused, twisting her cup around but still watching Remy. "I'll be doing something simple—washing a pair of trousers, preparing a meal—and be struck anew by the realization that James is dead. It'll freeze me in my tracks quicker than this Canadian wind."

"Bandaging a wound, mixing medicines, gazing up into a snow-filled sky. That's when I remember. Takes everything in me not to cry." Jemima tilted her head in question. "My mentor, Dr. Joseph Warren, died at Bunker Hill. He was like a second father to me."

I cleared my throat, trying to disguise the crack in my voice, but Jemima heard and took my hand. "War is no place for mourning, is it? The only time to cry is at night when you're alone in your bedroll, and even then—"

"You don't want the man in the next cot or room to hear."

"James didn't want me to come, not to Cambridge and definitely not here. But Suzannah and I swore we wouldn't be left behind. Once James realized I was determined to follow him, he taught me how to shoot. I'll never forget the look on his face the day I outshot him." Jemima chuckled, but her mirth quickly faded. "Now I fear to go home without him."

"I fear returning to Boston. What street or building won't remind me of Dr. Warren?" As a memory surfaced, I smiled. "Last March, he gave the annual Bloody Massacre oration in a toga."

We traded memories, tears, and laughter as the night waned. Remy groaned, eyes fluttering, and began to lean.

"Get her outside!" I hauled one of Remy's arms over my shoulder, and Jemima grabbed the other. We just made it out before she vomited. I held her hair as she heaved and heaved again. At last, she sat back. Jemima handed her a cloth to wipe her face. Remy looked from one of us to the other.

"Whit? Jemima? Where's Paul?"

"You drank too much, and he let me bring you to the doctor. Got you away before you could spill any secrets."

"You were talking about your brother, Rem."

Remy took a shaky breath and ran a hand through her hair. She dug out a tie and secured it in a tail once more. "It's Alden's birthday today. Well, yesterday now. I just—it just overwhelmed me."

For a little while, none of us said a thing. Then Remy shivered, and I pulled her to her feet.

"Let's get you back to your quarters." We tidied the bakery, put out the lights, and kicked snow over Remy's vomit. She staggered a bit as we walked but was able to hold herself upright.

Campfires still burned across the plains. As we neared one, Paul hurried toward us. "Is Remy all right?"

"I'm fine, Paul." Her words only slurred a little. "Just too much drink."

"He needs sleep," I said. "Maybe a bit extra in the morning if that can be managed."

Paul clapped a hand to Remy's shoulder, causing her to sway. "He'll be taken care of. Thank you, Mrs. Warner, Dr. Endicott."

With murmurs of good night, we went our separate ways, pushing our grief back below the surface.

Chapter Twenty-Five
December 5, 1775

General Montgomery and Colonel Arnold were scheming, Win reported when he rode around the camp with me early the next morning. I'd barely slept, but I was willing to sacrifice sleep to spend time with Win.

His cough sounded better. It helped that he slept in Menut's Tavern and was eating regular meals, even if those meals were smaller than they should have been. He noticed my appraisal, rolled his eyes, and tucked his scarf tighter around his throat. "Happy?"

"Are you drinking the tea nightly, wearing a poultice to bed, and using the camphor rub during the day?"

"Yes, yes, and yes. Can't you smell it on me? I know better than to disobey you, Whit."

"Good. Now, you were saying, about Montgomery's and Arnold's plan?"

"They're planning an attack before enlistments expire if Governor Carleton doesn't surrender first."

"That doesn't give them much time." Enlistments expired at the end of the month. "How do they mean to force Quebec's surrender?"

"Offer them terms."

I stared at Win. The British behind Quebec's walls outnumbered us, some speculated by as many as three to one. Governor Carleton had no reason to surrender. All they need do was wait until spring when the St. Lawrence opened and reinforcements arrived from England unless they didn't have the stores necessary to last five months.

Later that morning, General Montgomery rode toward the walls under a white flag. Hidden among the houses and buildings of St. Roch and St. Jean, Captain Morgan's riflemen crouched, ready to protect the general should the flag of truce be ignored.

I stood among the officers, Colonel Arnold at our head. Jacatacqua, the only other woman present, watched from beside Lieutenant Burr. Colonel Arnold was stone-still, his expression unreadable and his eyes fixed on General Montgomery. The colonel was a man of action, and I wondered how much convincing it had taken to get him to agree to offer terms of surrender and then to allow Montgomery to ride into danger instead of him.

General Montgomery came within musket shot of the walls. He paused.

I held my breath.

No movement from Quebec's walls.

He started forward once more. A collective release of breath fogged the air around us.

Crack! Crack! Crack-crack! Crack!

A volley of musket fire flashed down from the walls. General Montgomery dropped the flag, wheeled his horse, and galloped back as Captain Morgan's men returned fire.

For a fleeting second, Colonel Arnold smiled. His expression was neutral by the time General Montgomery reined in. Dr. Senter and I stepped forward, but the general waved us off.

"I'm unharmed." He dismounted and watched the fire exchange between Captain Morgan's men and Quebec's defenders. "We must try again."

Colonel Arnold said nothing, but when his eyes lighted on them, the rest of the officers protested, Burr louder than the rest. "Sir, it's death to go out there! They obviously won't honor any flag, so it's impossible to give them our terms. We have no recourse but to fight!"

The other officers voiced their approval. Colonel Arnold remained silent but nodded.

"From what I've seen, you are not men to give up after failure," Jacatacqua said, laying a placating hand on Lieutenant Burr's arm. "There may be a way. You simply have to see the problem from a different angle."

Jacatacqua glanced at me, but I couldn't read her mind. Then her eyes slid to Jemima and Suzannah, marching back from St. Roch with the rest of Captain Morgan's company, and I began to have an inkling.

"What's your idea?" Colonel Arnold asked. I was surprised he was willing to listen to a woman's plan, but Jacatacqua had helped them up the Kennebec, so perhaps he held her in higher esteem than most.

"Give me an hour," Jacatacqua said. "Dr. Endicott, can you find me a room to use at the hospital?"

A quarter of an hour later, we gathered in my too-small room: Suzannah, Jemima, Jacatacqua, and me. I felt I was only there because I had provided the room, for if Jacatacqua's plan was what I suspected, I would be of no use.

"They will not fire on a woman," Jacatacqua said. "For the English, it would be dishonorable."

"As long as there can be no mistake she is a woman," I said. None of us looked unmistakably like women. Jemima and Suzannah both wore skirts, but after weeks of marching and living wild, even I hadn't realized they were women at first. I wondered if I should have sent for Remy, but, like me, she didn't look like a woman and had a male identity to protect.

"Find me a gown, and I'll do it," Jemima said.

"Jem—" Suzannah began, but Jemima cut her off.

"I'm willing to risk it, Suzi. I don't have anything left to lose. You still have a husband to care for, Jacatacqua has a baby on the way, and Whit's skills will be needed if they don't surrender. If we're going to try, it has to be me." She met our eyes, and one by one, we nodded. "Someone find me a proper gown."

As the nuns prepared a bath, Jacatacqua presented her plan to General Montgomery and Colonel Arnold, while Suzannah, Colonel Morgan's men, and I hunted for a gown. We found one in a well-to-do house in St. Roch. It was all silk and lace, the emerald green of the countryside in summer. Luckily, the gown fit, but the shoes we'd found were too small.

"I can wear my boots. No one will be looking at my feet."

Minutes later, Jemima stood before the officers, elegant in the green gown. Colonel Arnold's brow creased. "Are you certain about this?"

"I am. My husband was willing to risk his life for the cause and gave it on the march here. I serve in his stead, and I am just as willing."

"Very well." Colonel Arnold handed her a new white flag. General Montgomery gave her the letter with the terms of surrender.

Jemima wore no cloak so there would be no mistaking her for anything but a well-dressed woman. She refused the horse Colonel Arnold offered, so the men on Quebec's walls would have plenty of time to see her for what she was. Flag in one hand and terms in the other, Mrs. Jemima Warner faced the walls of Quebec.

Colonel Morgan's men were once again spread among the houses of St. Roch and St. Jean. Jemima slogged through the shin-deep snow alone.

She reached musket range and stopped. We were nearly a half mile away, yet I saw her square her shoulders before she walked on.

Ten paces.

Twenty. Not a shot fired though men stood on the walls.

At last, Jemima reached the gates. They swung slowly open, and she entered. With a thud, the gates closed.

We waited. The gates remained shut with Jemima trapped behind them.

"Dear God," Colonel Arnold murmured. "We've sent her to her death."

Chapter Twenty-Six
December 5-10, 1775

Afternoon slid into evening, and still Jemima was not released. Frozen from fingertips to toe tips, we returned to our quarters for the night. Jacatacqua and Suzannah's husband, Sergeant Joseph Grier, had to pull Suzannah away.

The next morning, Suzannah stood again at her post wrapped more warmly, hot tea in hand and eyes fixed on the gates of Quebec. Remy stood vigil with her, afraid of what Suzannah might do if she were left alone.

I stood with Suzannah the following day. Every two hours, I forced her to change stockings and drink a mug of coffee or tea. Win wanted to watch with us, but I forbid him from standing in the cold for so long. He was just starting to improve; I didn't need him to worsen. He contented himself by bringing us food and drink.

I had just returned to the hospital from my vigil with Suzannah and was sitting down to a late supper, thanks to kind-hearted Sister Marie-Therese, when Mother Marie-Catherine entered the refectory. "I'm sorry, ma fille, but your brother is at the door."

Sighing, I left my steaming soup. "What is it, Win?"

"Colonel Arnold. His malaria is flaring up."

"And he couldn't bother Dr. Senter for once? No, I know," I said as Win opened his mouth. "He trusts me."

I knew I should be grateful for Colonel Arnold's trust, but after standing in the cold wind all day, I just wanted a warm meal and bed. Still, I fetched the cinchona bark infusion and a feverfew tea, benefits of a fully stocked apothecary. Thankfully, Win had brought Portia along with his own horse. She nickered when she smelled me, and I gave her a bit of dried apple and scratched between her ears. "Hey, girl. Next time I have to stand in the cold, I'll bring you with me."

I hoped the British released Jemima before my turn came around again. Win coughed, and I eyed my twin. He didn't need to be out in this cold any longer. I mounted up, and Win led the way to Menut's Tavern.

I hadn't yet been to Arnold's headquarters, and I stopped just inside the door. The dark beams of the ceiling absorbed the light from the few candles and made the room feel smaller. The rushes on the floor hadn't been changed since before Colonel Arnold claimed the tavern, releasing the fusty odor of stale ale and the fug of old tobacco smoke with each step. A few tables were still scattered about the room, but lining the walls were stacks of goods: bolts of cloth, sets of silver and china dishes, chests of clothes, and casks of tobacco, molasses, and wine.

"What is all this?"

"Goods Colonel Arnold has collected from the houses in St. Roch and St. Jean. He hopes to use them to barter with the locals or sell them to support the army through the winter," Win said matter-of-factly as if he weren't describing looting and profiteering. Win continued, "Sleeping quarters are upstairs, but Colonel Arnold is probably in his study. He's set up in the tavern's private room."

Win led me through the main room, around the bar, and into what had once been a private dining and meeting room.

There were no dirty rushes on the floor, just a fine, thick rug of rich reds and blacks deeper than the night sky. A fire crackled in the fireplace and tapestries hung on the walls, holding in the warmth. The room's one window was shuttered against night's chill. A shelf of books stood against one wall, and two lanterns burned brightly on the singe table, scattered with maps, letters, and ledgers. The tang of ink gall and the comforting smell of leather hung in the air, reminding me for a moment of Henry Knox's bookshop.

Arnold sat behind the table, not any ordinary tavern chair for him but a plush crimson armchair. He raised his eyes from the map he was studying, sweat dewing his forehead. "Ah, Dr. Endicott, thank you for coming so quickly."

"Of course, sir." I set both the infusion and the tea sachets on the table. I performed a quick examination, but aside from being too thin and not getting enough sleep, there was nothing else ailing the colonel.

He frowned when I didn't leave. "Was there something else, Doctor?"

"What is all this?" I gestured not only at the creature comforts decking his study but toward the stacks in the main room.

"Goods collected from Loyalist houses to be used to support the Army of the Northern Department."

"But how is this any different from looting? I thought—I *told* General Montgomery you were against looting."

"And I am. I would never take the possessions of those who support us or those who are our prisoners. These things were taken from the abandoned houses of our enemies."

"How do you know they're our enemies?"

"If they were on our side, they would not now be hiding behind Quebec's walls. What do you think the British are doing to Patriot houses in Boston? Do you think they're posting guards at the doors? No, they, too, are claiming the spoils of war. Here, it's a matter of survival. We must eat. We must clothe our troops. Unless Congress sends more specie, this may be the only way we survive."

I thought about what Colonel Arnold had said all the way back to the hospital. I understood the need to feed and clothe our army, but Colonel Arnold's method made me uncomfortable. I said as much to Win when I handed him Portia's reins.

"Wait till you're starving, Whit. Then we can debate the morals of taking the leavings of our enemies."

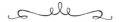

The British did not release Jemima the next morning, and Suzannah returned to her post, Jacatacqua by her side.

Suzannah's husband took the next day, and Remy began again on the fifth morning.

While we waited to hear Jemima's fate, we prepared for battle. General Montgomery and Colonel Arnold included Dr. Senter and me in their councils, so we knew when to prepare for wounded. Through these councils, I became more familiar with military strategy and with the other officers. Major Brown, Colonel Livingston, and Colonel Warner I already knew, but I came to understand how much contempt—it bordered on hatred—Captain Daniel Morgan carried for the British, and how eager Captains Henry Dearborn and John Lamb were to prove themselves. General Montgomery and Colonel Arnold could not have asked for officers more determined to succeed. How we were to succeed was another question entirely. It was clear the British were not interested in surrender, so plan after plan was proposed, and each was scrapped in turn.

Cannons were moved to St. Roch and St. Jean so their shot could reach the enemy's walls, not that they were large enough guns to do real damage. With Captain Lamb's artillery regiment short of men due to illness, Remy was temporarily assigned to an artillery crew as a swabber. Reconnaissance teams scoured the countryside for Canadians willing to join us and to scrounge what foodstuffs could be found. Others crossed the river to assess any weaknesses Quebec might have.

Dr. Senter and I prepared as well. With the nuns, we scrubbed the floors and washed linens. I cut bandages. Dr. Senter sharpened knives and saws.

I was folding a set of sheets when I heard the distant *rat-a-tat-tat* of drums. Dr. Senter and I met in the corridor.

"Is the attack beginning?" I asked.

"Without informing us? They wouldn't."

We stared at each other for a moment, then ran for our coats.

Outside, a crowd had gathered where five days ago we had watched Jemima walk into Quebec. Captain Morgan's and Captain Lamb's men stood ready at their positions.

Quebec's gates opened, and the drumming grew louder. Drummers in dark jackets with red facings emerged forming a double line on either side of the gate. It was only then I recognized "The Rogue's March."

General Montgomery frowned. "They're drumming someone out."

I squinted at the gate. To be drummed out meant they were not only rejected from the army, but were banished from British territories forever.

Marching to the cadence, head high and emerald skirts dragging through the snow, came Jemima.

Captain Morgan's men froze in the act of raising their rifles. Instead, they raised a cheer. Jemima had been given a cloak, but she wore the same gown, grimed with five days' worth of dirt. Behind her marched a train of men and a few women, civilians by their dress.

When Jemima was only fifty yards away, Suzannah ran out and gathered her into a hug. Jemima sagged against Suzannah momentarily then straightened and, arm linked with Suzannah's, finished her march. She halted directly in front of General Montgomery and saluted.

"Sir, Governor Carleton refused to read your terms. He tore them to pieces and burned them in front of me. He questioned me several times over the course of the last five days and attempted to convince me to turn my coat. When it became clear I would not aid him, he offered an ultimatum to our supporters in Quebec—either swear their allegiance to King George III or be drummed out of the city." Jemima gestured behind her. "They chose to leave."

A couple hundred Canadians had chosen exile and our cause rather than safety behind Quebec's walls. They carried nothing but the clothes on their backs and pitiful armfuls of possessions. As the officers sorted through the exiled Canadians, Suzannah and I led Jemima to the hospital. Upon seeing Jemima, a flock of nuns descended and carried her away to be bathed. Three-quarters of an hour later, Mother Marie-Catherine came to find me.

"Not me?" Suzannah asked. We were in the refectory, mugs of cooling and untouched tea cradled in our hands.

Mother Marie-Catherine shook her head. "She asked for the doctor first."

Jemima was dressed in her old clothes, the silk gown nowhere to be seen. She looked just as worn as the night we'd grieved together, but there was determination in her eyes and the set of her jaw.

"Are you injured, Jemima?"

"No. Governor Carleton was mostly courteous and treated me well. Most of his officers wished it were otherwise. I was kept locked in one of the governor's own rooms for my safety, though if those men had tried anything—" She flexed her fingers. Shaking her head, she straightened. "I want you to give me a full examination."

"Why?"

"Because I'm going to convince Captain Morgan to allow me to fight. I have valuable information. I know the layout of the city and how many men Carleton has. I will fight, not just haul wounded from the field."

A Joan of Arc indeed. "Very well. Let's get started."

Jemima Warner was as close to perfectly healthy as one could be. Once I assured her I'd help her make her case to Captain Morgan, Jemima spoke with Suzannah before we went in search of the captain.

We found him at Menut's Tavern in Colonel Arnold's study, pouring over maps of St. Roch, St. Jean, and Quebec. He was a bear of a man, at least six feet tall, with dark hair and cheeks in need of a razor. He wore a rifleman's hunting shirt like his men, and no additional uniform to set him above them. He was straightforward, blunt in his speech and manner, but still approachable, and of all the officers under our generals, I liked him and Captain Dearborn the most.

Jemima snapped a salute. "Captain Morgan, I come with a request, sir, and intelligence of the enemy."

He eyed me before asking, "A request, Mrs. Warner?"

"I want to fight when battle comes, sir. Not be relegated to hospital duty."

"She is perfectly fit and able, sir," I said. "More fit than some of the men I've examined."

"I've earned this chance, Captain. I can shoot as well as any man and have risked just as much as they have."

Captain Morgan held up a hand, beard twitching in a smile. "You don't need to argue your case with me, Warner. I'll gladly have you fight with us. Now, what is this intelligence?"

"Quebec is not as well defended as we thought. Fifteen hundred men, perhaps a hundred or so more. Too few to effectively man the whole wall and river approach. I can show you where the troops and lookouts are positioned."

Captain Morgan watched as she pointed to locations on the Quebec map. "This is very helpful, Private Warner. Be ready to move out at a moment's notice. Dismissed."

Jemima squeezed my hand. She had gotten her wish, and we were headed for battle.

Chapter Twenty-Seven
December 11-12, 1775

Captain Morgan granted Suzannah the same opportunity to fight, but she declined.

"I'm perfectly happy carrying and fetching, cooking and mending, hauling wounded and running messages," she said over breakfast the next morning. "At least now you're official, Jemima. Do you think they'll pay you?"

Jemima snorted, and Remy shook her head. "They haven't paid us yet, so I wouldn't count on it."

"Even if they did pay you, you couldn't spend it," I said. "The paper Continentals are worthless. The specie from Congress, Massachusetts, and General Washington is long gone. Win says Colonel Arnold is using his own funds and credit to feed, clothe, and arm us, and it's bankrupting him. He hopes to supplement with goods seized from Loyalist homes, but who is there to buy such goods? Win says every letter sent south—to Schuyler or Washington or Congress—contains a plea for specie, not Continentals."

"Then we'd better take Quebec before their credit runs out," Jemima said. "I don't fancy spending the winter here naked and starving."

That night, I was just starting to undo my cravat and bindings when there was a pounding on my door.

"Whit!" Remy's voice was terror high. I stuffed myself back together and unlocked the door.

Remy, white as a shroud, seized my arm. "Whit, you—come! Now! Jemima, she—"

Every muscle clenched. Behind Remy stood my entire cadre of ghosts, urgency in every expression.

I grabbed my coat, swept instruments and bandages into a bag, and ran, leaving Remy in my room. Kit and Dr. Warren kept pace with me, other ghosts trailing. Whatever drew the ghosts to me—my birth or my guilt or my debts to them—they seemed to appear most often and in the largest numbers when death was near. I swiped falling snow from my eyes and pushed away my fear. I would hold onto hope as long as I could.

Jemima had been assigned to Remy's gun crew in Sainte-Foy. Governor Carleton must have decided to answer our fire with some of his own.

Flames spread through St. Roch and St. Jean, devouring houses with a hungry roar. Cannons screamed death, and flashes from the walls exposed the defenders' positions. Our guns struggled to reply.

I slipped, tripped, and slid across the unevenly frozen ground. I couldn't lose another friend. A wail rose over the battle din. Faster, I told myself. Faster.

Near a destroyed cannon emplacement, the wooden barricade burned. A few wounded were being helped toward the hospital. One man was clearly dead. The wailing came from a group huddled around what could only be another body.

"No! No, Jemima!"

"Mrs. Grier, Suzannah, please," Captain Lamb tried to pull Suzannah away, but she was as tall as he was, and strong. Grief lent her greater strength, just as fear was leeching mine. I knew I didn't want to see what was making Suzannah sound and act like that, but I had no choice. I pushed through the soldiers.

Jemima lay there, Suzannah clutching at her. Most of Jemima's head was missing. And what was left—

I made it a few paces away before dropping to all fours and vomiting. Too late, too late. I'd never even had a chance, and Jemima, I didn't need to see her again. The mangled remains of her face were imprinted in my memory: jagged shards of bone splintering through skin; teeth, muscle, brain, blood bright against the snow. I vomited again. These were the sights that nightmares were made of, and I knew they would revisit me.

"Doctor, are you all right?" Captain Lamb asked.

I'd thought the aftermath of Lexington and Menotomy had prepared me for anything I might witness during war. But this was the first time since Kit died that the body lying in front of me belonged to someone I knew. Belonged to a friend. Only days ago, we'd shared our grief. Just that morning we had laughed over breakfast.

"Doctor?"

I wiped my mouth on my sleeve. "I'm fine. It was just a shock, seeing her like that."

"For all of us." Captain Lamb's hands shook as he pulled me to my feet. There was no sign of Jemima's ghost. Perhaps her ghost wouldn't appear. After all, what debt did I owe her? Though most of my ghosts were gathered near Jemima's body, Dr. Warren stood by Suzannah, who wept in her husband's arms. She sagged, her knees unable to support her. Dr. Warren eyed me expectantly.

"Our duty does not end when a patient dies," he had told me after the Bloody Massacre when four men lay dead at the back of the surgery. "We must make sure the body is prepared and give comfort to those left behind."

I was the one who would have to do that, despite my own grief and the tears freezing to my face. "Bring her body to the hospital."

"What about—" Colonel Lamb gestured to the fragments of Jemima scattered across the snow.

"No, just the—"

He nodded, saving me from having to complete the sentence. He ordered several men to carry Jemima. One of the soldiers draped his coat over her, covering the terrible damage.

"I'm not leaving her!" Suzannah cried.

Sergeant Grier tried to hold her back. "Suzannah, please."

"It's fine," I said. "She can come with me."

I slid a shoulder under Suzannah's arm, and together we trudged to the hospital. Just yesterday we had walked this same path supporting Jemima. As Boston had been tainted by Dr. Warren's death, I knew everywhere I went in our encampment would echo with memories of Jemima. Whether her ghost haunted me or not, she would never be far from my thoughts.

I brought Suzannah to my room while the soldiers laid the body out in the preparation room behind the surgery. Remy still sat on my bed, pale and dry-eyed in shock. I settled Suzannah next to her and went to wake Dr. Senter and Mother Marie-Catherine.

"Dr. Endicott, are you well?" Dr. Senter asked when he opened his door, journal and pen in hand.

"What?"

He gestured to my face. It was still numb from cold. I touched my cheeks. They were damp with tears, and fresh tears still fell.

"What happened?"

"Jemima Warner. She's dead." I saw her again, lying in pieces on the snow. My gorge rose, and I clenched my teeth, swallowing hard.

"What? How?" He paled, shock filling his eyes. I had forgotten he knew her from the march north. "I should see—"

"No!" He jumped at my sharpness. "Sorry. You don't want to see her like this. She was assisting one of the gun crews, and a cannonball . . ." I closed my eyes, trying to banish the sight of her. "A cannonball struck her in the head."

Dr. Senter somehow grew paler and staggered, leaning against his door for support, pen and journal falling to the floor. I couldn't steady him when I was hardly steady myself.

"No one should see that if they don't have to. I need your help, though. There are a few others injured, and I don't know how much use I'll be right now." I held out a shaking hand. "And Mrs. Grier is distraught. She witnessed Jemima's death. She's in my room, and . . ."

"Of course, Whitley. I'll see to the wounded." He took a few breaths and gathered the things he'd dropped. "If we don't support each other, we won't be strong enough to support our patients."

It sounded like something Dr. Warren might have said. He was right. We had to be strong for those who would soon be coming in wounded and frightened from battle. "Thank you, Isaac."

Mother Marie-Catherine was next. When I explained what had happened, she said, "Father Superior de Rigauville and I will perform a funeral service for her."

"Not a Catholic one?"

Mother Marie-Catherine lay a hand on my head. "We will make it acceptable to you, ma fille. I will wake some of the sisters to prepare the body. You and Madam Grier should not have to do that."

"Thank you, Mother."

I returned to my room, to Remy and Suzannah. Although the rest of my ghosts had vanished, Dr. Warren stood next to the bed as though he had been watching over Suzannah and Remy until I returned. Upon my entrance, he placed his hand over his heart, bowed his head, and faded away.

On my bed, Suzannah leaned against Remy, and both were crying. Neither were in any shape to go elsewhere. I pulled off their boots and made them lie down. I stripped down to my shirt and underdrawers, knowing Mother Marie-Catherine would stop anyone from reaching my room, and curled up with them, pulling the blankets over us all. The bed was far too narrow, and we were pressed together like spoons in a drawer. But there was comfort in the closeness, the warmth of the living to banish cold thoughts of death and loss.

Still, my heart ached and cracked for a world without Jemima in it. Her laughter, her strength, her friendship, only alive in memories now. She would never return home to Pennsylvania, never remarry or have children. She wouldn't grow old on the farm next to Suzannah and Joseph Grier. She would never fight for the cause that had meant so much to her. Another life, like Kit's, Dr. Warren's, and Jedediah's, had ended far too soon.

Jemima's service was held at midmorning. I entered the chapel for the first time since that first day. Somehow, in that place, the sounds of cannon fire were muted, almost silenced. I paused, trying to put a name to the feeling surrounding me. Soft as the first flakes of winter, it brushed against my soul and settled my mind.

Peace.

I couldn't recall the last time I'd felt anything close to peace. And that I should find it in a Catholic church, of all places.

Suzannah and Joseph sat together in the first pew, and Remy and I took the one just behind. Others filed in: Jacatacqua, Dr. Senter, Colonel Arnold, and Captain Morgan's entire company, except those on duty. Win slipped in next to me, linking his pinkie with mine, and George sat next to him.

Father de Rigauville began the service, his usually thin voice fuller, stronger, filling the chapel with his rolling Latin. I expected to feel angry or upset at the unfamiliar words, but the peace only grew deeper. My eyes wandered around the sanctuary to the morning light, falling like a rainbow through the stained glass. The service and light washed over me, a work of art, like one of Mr. John Singleton Copley's paintings, and tears filled my eyes, awed that there could be such beauty in the world amidst war and sorrow.

She stood amid the light. Her gaze was full of sorrow as it fell on Suzannah, then she turned her ghostly eyes on me.

What did I owe her? I owed Kit my life, I owed Dr. Warren my career, my skills, but Jemima? She'd been my friend. Her death hadn't been my fault, and she hadn't given her life for me, so why had she returned to haunt me?

After the service, Win found some rum and poured it out for Suzannah, Sergeant Grier, Jacatacqua, Remy, George, and me, but he turned to me for the toast. Suzannah was in no condition to speak. Jemima's eyes were still on me as if waiting for me to figure out why she was there. As if I could forget what she—

And then I knew what I owed her. Her and those who had died in the Bloody Massacre and at Lexington, Concord, Menotomy, at Fort St-Jean. I owed them my gratitude, and I owed them remembrance.

They had died so we might live, so our cause and country might live. And unless someone remembered them and told their story, their lives and sacrifices would be lost forever.

Remember me. The words of King Hamlet's ghost echoed again in my mind. Memory was the least I could give.

I lifted my glass. "To Jemima Warner. A brave woman who loved her husband and her country and gave her life in her country's service. May she never be forgotten."

Chapter Twenty-Eight
December 13-31, 1775

In the days following Jemima's death, Suzannah's sorrow twisted into determination, and she asked Captain Morgan for the opportunity to fight. She was not the shot Jemima had been, but Captain Morgan didn't deny her even though Suzannah's husband objected. But he hadn't married Suzannah because she was weak and submissive, and he soon relented. Just as I served to honor Dr. Warren and Remy fought for her brother, Suzannah would fight in Jemima's name.

Rumor spread and soon proved true: we would attack on the next stormy night. Enlistments were fast running out, and the choice was either attack or watch our army drain away south. I didn't like the idea of Win being out in a storm, but he had mostly recovered from his cough, and I had no reason except selfish ones to keep him back, which he would never accept. Twice storms and darkness descended, and the men were called out, but neither time did the attack move forward. Both nights, the only weapons fired were our cannons in the futile hope Quebec's walls would weaken.

The second time the men were called out was the night of December 25, and the southern soldiers were none too happy to be standing in the dark and cold instead of sitting by their fires drinking and singing jolly songs. We from New England didn't celebrate Christmas, transplanted pagan holiday that it was, but we were no happier to be standing in the middle of a storm.

One of our cannons exploded, either from cold or mismanaged loading, and the wounded were brought to the hospital. None of the wounds were too serious, the most difficult being a piece of cannon embedded in a man's shoulder. My ghosts didn't even appear. Dr. Senter took the shoulder wound while I saw to the rest of the minor cuts and one broken arm. I was just finishing up the last of them when Win crashed in, George's arm across his shoulder.

"Whit! George's been hit!"

"Where? With what? I thought the battle wasn't moving forward."

"When the cannon exploded," Win said. "He didn't come here. He went back to his quarters—"

"I'm fine," George said, but his voice was thin.

"A piece of the cannon went through his side from back to front. There's lots of blood."

"I'll take him." Win was babbling and would give both himself and George away if I let him keep talking. George's hunting shirt was blood all down the left side, and Win was almost as pale as George. I gestured to the table my patient had just vacated. "Get him up."

"I'll be fine," George said again through clenched teeth. "Just cauterize it, and I'll—"

"Not a chance." I reached for George's side, but he pushed my hand away with more strength than I had anticipated. "George, I have to examine it."

Pain rippled across his face, and his knuckles went white, but he didn't make a sound. At last he nodded. "Not here. Not where others can see. And," he glanced at Win, "he doesn't come."

"What?" Win's whisper was outraged. "I'm not leaving you, you great, stupid—"

"You're not—"

"If you don't want to draw attention, we need to move somewhere else. Now." I held up a finger as George began to protest. "My brother and I are very stubborn, Private Lee. This is not a fight you're going to win. Mother Marie-Catherine." The nun stopped. "I need a private room in which to treat this man."

"Right here, Dr. Endicott."

The room was small, containing only an operating table and two chairs. I gestured George to the table and laid out my instruments. At a glare from George, Win backed away, but he didn't leave the room. George's grip around himself tightened as I approached.

"George, I have to examine it. You'll bleed to death if I don't. We are not the enemy. You're safe with us." I didn't know what he was afraid of, but I knew fear when I saw it. The eyes meeting mine were not those of a strong, seventeen-year-old man but those of a much younger, frightened boy.

"I don't know if I—"

"George," I set my fingers lightly over his. "You saved my brother's life. Let me save yours. Please."

Slowly, George removed his hand and closed his eyes.

I cut his shirt away. The wound wasn't too bad, but it was bleeding stubbornly. Most of the metal had gone straight through, but a piece was still lodged inside. I would remove that—

Win gasped.

He stared at George's back. George pressed his hands against the table, every muscle rigid. His head tipped forward, and tears slipped down his cheeks.

My hands froze. George didn't show emotion, and he certainly didn't cry. If whatever he had been hiding, whatever Win saw, was terrible enough to make him cry, I wasn't sure I wanted to look. But I had to know.

George's back was crisscrossed with thick lines of scars. A belt, I thought. A belt wielded with significant force and plied again and again.

"George, what—" Win started, but I cut him off.

"Not now, Win. Right now, I need to close this wound." George's back was horrible, but those wounds had healed long ago. At least the flesh had. His side had to be the focus. "George, I need you to lie on your right side. Win, stay out of the way."

George did as I ordered, fists tight and eyes wide as he tried to halt his tears. Win pulled up a chair and took George's hand.

"Go away, Win," George whispered, trying to pull free, but Win only pried George's fingers apart and slid his between them. "Never."

Following the path of the wound, I cut George's side open wider so I could remove the piece of cannon lodged inside. All the while, I tried to keep from jumping to conclusions about George's back, each scenario worse than the last.

I cleaned out the wound, making sure no smaller pieces of metal had escaped my notice. George winced at my probing, but he didn't make a sound.

"I need your hands, Win. Hold the edges of the wound together, like this, while I sew it closed. Good. Just like that."

Win's skin took on a greenish hue as George's blood coated his fingers. His eyes flickered to the scars on George's back, and he took a steadying breath, focusing on the ceiling.

"I can finish the rest on my own, Win. Wash your hands."

Once he did, he laced his fingers with George's again.

"My father," George said. He shuddered, as if there were cold deep inside, and I stopped sewing until he stilled himself. I kept my stitches small and steady as he continued. "He caught me kissing—it was stupid, where anyone could see us. He took his belt, and I thought he was going to beat me to death. Maybe he should have." A protest was on Win's lips, but George's thumb moved over the back of Win's hand, and my brother stilled. I tied off my suture and found myself staring into George's eyes. "See, Doctor, I know exactly what we're facing."

"I never doubted you, George, though I wish I could have." I couldn't imagine Da beating Win, no matter what he was caught doing. "You can sit up now, George."

I wrapped his middle with bandages.

"No one can know," George said.

"No one will," Win promised.

"No one will know. I'll find you a shirt. You have a few minutes together."

My hand was on the doorknob when George said, "Doctor. Thank you."

He wasn't looking at me but staring at Win's hands clasped around his own, his face once more an expressionless mask.

"Of course," I said.

I was on my way back with a shirt when Mother Marie-Catherine stopped me. "How is the patient?"

I hesitated only a moment. "Well, the wound to his flesh will heal."

"Some wounds are deeper than skin and muscle. Perhaps he should stay here a night or two. This place can do much to heal what doctors cannot see."

I remembered the peace I'd felt in the chapel, but still I hesitated. Mother Marie-Catherine touched my arm. "When will you trust us, ma fille? A difference in religion does not mean we wish you harm, physical or spiritual. And the ward is empty but for tonight's shoulder patient."

"Thank you, Mother. I must ask, though, that I be the only one to treat Private Lee. I fear if anyone else tries, even Dr. Senter, he might try to harm them or himself."

"Je comprends, Dr. Endicott."

We moved George to the ward. He was too tired to protest much, and I convinced Win to return to his own quarters. "I'll stay with him."

"Thanks, Whit." A quick pinkie link. "I'll be back tomorrow."

I made myself comfortable in a chair at George's side. His eyes were only half open when he asked, "Don't you need to sleep?"

"Didn't you know, George? Doctors never sleep. They train it out of us during our apprenticeship."

"You don't have to stay. I'm used to being on my own."

His words made my heart ache, and I wanted to take his hand, but I sensed George would not welcome the touch, especially where others could see. "I promised Win. I don't want to find out what he'd do if I broke my promise. You're not alone anymore."

For a moment, I thought he was going to say something. Instead, he closed his eyes, turned his face away, and was soon asleep.

Win came every day, and some others from the rifle company visited, too. George's wound was healing well, but it had not healed enough when General Montgomery called Dr. Senter and me to Holland House early on December 31.

"That means we'll attack," George said. "You must let me join the others."

"I have to make sure you heal, George. And you don't know for sure that's what this council means."

"When has the general called you and Dr. Senter to council and not intended to attack? I must fight!"

Too well I remembered Jedediah in Lexington, who had left my care only to end up dead minutes later. George would not come to the same end. "There will be other opportunities to fight. You go out there now, you'll reopen that wound."

"It's fine. I can fight! I have to fight! I have to prove I'm just as able as the rest of them!"

"Prove? Prove to whom?"

George clamped his mouth shut and ground his teeth, clearly regretting how much he'd already said. "It doesn't matter who. I must be out there."

"Private Lee, I don't have time to argue this now! Just wait here, and we can discuss what happens next when I return. Please?"

George glowered, his hands clenched around his blankets.

"Whitley!" Dr. Senter called from the door.

I exhaled in frustration. "If not for me, then for Win. I'll be back as soon as I can."

George didn't answer, but I couldn't keep Dr. Senter waiting. Muttering under my breath, I rode with Dr. Senter to Holland House. The house's high peaks pierced the low, gray sky, and I could almost imagine them tearing through the clouds, releasing the snow dusting our shoulders and faces. A storm was coming, and that meant we would indeed attack.

General Montgomery confirmed this as soon as we were all gathered around the council table. "Enlistments expire at midnight. If we do not attack tonight, we must be prepared to sit in siege until either our reinforcements or theirs arrive. I fear if we wait, what little momentum we have will disappear with our men. It is my intention to attack tonight. What say you?"

"Ayes," chorused from around the table.

General Montgomery's eyes held something that looked like relief. He turned to Dr. Senter and me. "How many able men do we have?"

Dr. Senter took a last glance through the records he'd brought with. "About eight hundred."

General Montgomery's jaw tightened, and he bent over the map spread across the table, thumb worrying the pockmark on his cheekbone. Colonel Arnold joined the general and murmured in his ear. General Montgomery nodded, and they both straightened.

"There will be two main attacks and two feints. Colonel Livingston, you will lead your Canadian regiment in one feint toward St. Jean's Gate. Major Brown, you shall lead the second feint toward the St. Louis Gate." Major Brown, who had been denied his promotion after the looting incident in Montreal, frowned but nodded. "Colonel Arnold will lead his men past Intendant's Palace and down Dog Lane to Lower Town where his column shall rendezvous with mine. I shall lead my men along Cape Diamond and into Lower Town. You famine-proof Kennebec men will go with Colonel Arnold."

"And the artillery, sir?" asked Captain Lamb.

"I want some cannon support when we enter Upper Town. But you only take your original men. Any temporary artillery men will be needed in their own regiments. Follow Colonel Arnold. I will have the Fort Ti men under my command. Any questions?"

No one spoke.

"Very well. Since so many of our men wear British uniforms, they are all to attach a sprig of hemlock and a paper with the words *liberty or death* to their hats. The men are to gather after nightfall but should be at the ready from this point on. Two red rockets shall signal the start of the attack. Any of the camp followers who can be organized should help bring the wounded to the hospital. Go, ready your men."

Dr. Senter and I went to the camp followers to find volunteers. It wasn't easy to convince most women to venture toward gunfire in a snowstorm in the dark to find wounded, but a surprising number volunteered. These were not the wives of lords or wealthy merchants or generals but the wives of frontiersmen, who were used to shouldering the burden of survival alongside their husbands.

By the time I returned to the hospital, it was late afternoon. I went straight to George's bed, but he was gone.

"Mother Marie-Catherine, have you seen Private Lee?"

"Not since this morning. He left?"

"Yes. I have to find him."

"His fate is out of your hands, ma fille. He has made his decision, and you are needed here. More lives than his depend on you now."

"But—" I couldn't tell her Win would kill me if George died in this battle. I couldn't tell her George was going into this battle for the wrong reasons.

She patted my cheek. "Come, we need your help."

I hated it, but Mother Marie-Catherine was right. There was much to do, and George had made his choice.

We cleaned; cut bandages; prepared rum, laudanum, and other medicines; sharpened blades; filled lanterns; and laid out our instruments. Then we went to the doorway to wait and watch. Somewhere behind the clouds, the sun set, and the sky darkened. The men, mere shadows against the greater darkness, gathered in their regiments and waited.

Snow fell fast and heavy, and a bitter wind slapped snow in my face as I peered toward Quebec, wondering which shadow was Win or Remy or George or Suzannah. The snow I breathed in tasted like metal and gunpowder and death. One by one, my ghosts materialized around me: Jemima on my left, Kit and Jedediah in front of me, Dr. Warren on my right. I wished he were with me in the flesh, not only in spirit. I could only hope my skills were, as he had believed, equal to the task ahead.

Chapter Twenty-Nine
December 31, 1775 – January 1, 1776

We waited in the doorway of the hospital as the night passed and the storm worsened. Still the attack didn't begin. Midnight passed. I thought of the soldiers in *Henry V* waiting through the long night to fight the battle of Agincourt. A battle they had won though the odds were against them. Just as the odds were against us. I shifted from foot to foot, arms crossed, arms down, arms crossed.

"I'm nervous, too," Dr. Senter said quietly.

"I'm not nervous exactly." I tried to explain, "I've just never waited for a battle to begin. At Lexington, I arrived after the first shots had been fired and just followed the wounded. I didn't have time to worry or panic. The sieges weren't truly battles, only waiting. Now, I just keep imagining worse and worse wounds."

"And I worry I won't be able to save the wounded," Dr. Senter finished my unspoken thought. Somehow, it made me feel better to know he had the same doubts and worries.

"We'll do this together," Dr. Senter said. "Together, we'll be strong enough for them."

"Together."

Two red rockets exploded high in the sky, visible even through the driving snow. A minute later, a cacophony of bells rose from behind Quebec's walls, making the hair on the back of my neck stand up. Their clamor carried foreboding. The nuns crossed themselves.

"I guess the waiting is over," Dr. Senter said.

"There will be waiting yet," Mother Marie-Catherine said. "The first wounded will be those who are not so badly injured, those who can reach us under their own power, or those lucky few your camp followers find. The worst wounded will arrive at battle's end. Come, let us be sure we are ready."

We went inside as gunfire pierced the night.

I could almost ignore my ghosts as I operated. Kit watched my every move, and Dr. Warren stayed at my elbow. At times, he reached out as if to assist, careful not to touch me or the wounded. Jedediah and a few other ghosts gathered by those with the worst injuries, but Mother Marie-Catherine had been correct: most of the men who'd staggered in so far had only minor wounds.

Just after dawn, all my ghosts swiveled toward the door, heads up and eyes intent, like sentries on alert.

The door blew open, the cold air bringing the sound of gunfire and the pungent burn of gunpowder. Win and Reverend Spring staggered in carrying Colonel Arnold. My relief at seeing Win alive was quickly swept away by worry for the colonel. His left leg was bloody from the knee down.

"Dr. Senter!" I called.

He looked up from the shoulder he was working on and swore. "See how bad it is. I'll be there as soon as I can."

"Help me get him on the table," I ordered. Colonel Arnold cried out when we jarred his leg, but he hung onto consciousness.

Reverend Spring immediately went back out into the storm, but Win grabbed my arm. "It's not going to plan. If they break us, get out of here. If they discover you're a woman—"

I yanked my arm away. "I'm not abandoning my patients, Win."

"Where's George? He'll make sure you—"

"He left against orders. He's somewhere out there." Win blanched, and my heart went out to him, but Colonel Arnold's leg took precedence. "I have work to do, Win. Either help or get out of the way."

He twined his pinkie with mine. "Be safe, Whit."

"You, too."

Before I even touched Colonel Arnold's leg, his hand shot out and seized my collar. I choked as he dragged me close. He propped himself up, pistol gripped in his hand. "You won't take my leg!"

"I haven't even examined it."

"You will not take my leg! You will do whatever must be done to save it! Swear!"

"I must at least—"

"Swear!"

He shoved himself to sitting and shook the pistol in my face. His grip on my shirt tightened, and I feared it would rip, exposing me in every way. "I swear, Colonel. We'll save your leg. Please, put the pistol down."

"I keep the pistol!"

"Only if you promise not to shoot Dr. Senter or myself, and you drink this rum."

He considered a moment before grunting agreement. Breathing hard, he fell back against the table, biting back a cry of pain. Without complaint, he let me tip a generous portion of rum laced with laudanum down his throat.

My hands shook as I straightened my shirt. I had just promised to do what might prove impossible: save his leg. I prayed it was not as bad as the blood suggested and joined Dr. Warren, who had already begun his examination.

When I pulled off Colonel Arnold's boot, blood poured out, splattering my apron and boots. He bit back a groan, and his hand tightened around his pistol. Dear Lord, don't let him touch the trigger, I prayed. I cut away his stocking and trouser leg. No bones had broken the skin, a very good sign. Dr. Warren held a finger above Arnold's leg at the musket ball's entry point just below the knee. I placed my own fingers on Arnold's leg, beneath Dr. Warren's, and together we traced the path of the musket ball. By some miracle, it had missed hitting both the tibia and the thinner, outer fibula. Colonel Arnold sucked in a breath as my fingers gently probed, but he didn't cry out. The bones shifted, fractured but not completely broken. I found the musket ball, or what was left of it. It must have ricocheted off something before striking Arnold and lodging in the gastrocnemius muscle just where it narrowed to the Achilles tendon. Bits of Greek myths floated through my mind, and I shook them away. Unlike Achilles, this wound would not prove fatal.

"How does it look, Dr. Endicott?" Dr. Senter asked over my shoulder.

"The bones are fractured, not broken, and the fragment of ball should be fairly easy to remove." I met Colonel Arnold's eyes. "You will never walk the same again, sir, but you can keep the leg."

"And I will walk." He let his head fall back and relaxed his grip on the pistol. I snatched it and put it out of his reach.

He started to protest, but I cut him off. "You can have it back when we're done. Neither of us will operate while you have a gun in your hand. Now, drink this."

As I forced him to drink more rum, Dr. Senter asked, "You can handle this, then?"

"Yes. Yes, I can." And for the first time while facing a battle wound, I believed what I said. As Dr. Warren pointed to which instruments I should use and nodded his approval, I extracted the remains of the ball, stitched both the entrance and extraction wounds, and was just starting to splint the leg when the door slammed open again.

Paul careened in, Remy in his arms. "Help! Remy's been hit!"

"Dr. Senter, can you finish Colonel Arnold? I have to check him."

Dr. Senter took the splints, and I went to Paul, trailed by Kit and Dr. Warren. "Where's he hit?"

"Shoulder and side."

"Lay him down." Remy cried out as her shoulder bumped against the table, which was still bloody from the last patient. Remy's eyes flew open with a gasp, and she sank her teeth into her lip. Paul took her good hand. Remy's panic-filled eyes found me. "Whit! Whit, I—"

"Shh, it's all right, Rem. I'm going to fix you up, and Paul's going to help."

Her gaze shifted to him. She bit her lip again and nodded.

"Sister Marie-Therese, assist me. Give him a dram of rum with laudanum and be ready with more." Remy swallowed the rum and slipped into semiconsciousness. I glanced at Paul, his hand tight around Remy's. "Paul, you should go back to the battle."

"I know the truth," he whispered. "About Remy. Known for some time he isn't a he."

Distantly, I wondered when he'd figured it out, but there'd be time for that later. "Then you be ready with the rum. Sister Marie-Therese, put pressure on that shoulder. I'm going to start with the side." If any organs were hit, that would be more deadly than the shoulder. I cut away part of Remy's shirt. Some of the fragments had just grazed her, some had gone straight through, but several pieces were lodged inside. "Hold Remy down, Paul. One arm across the hips, good—careful of that other shoulder. Keep her from moving too much." I began to remove the shrapnel, Dr. Warren making sure I didn't miss a piece. "How was Remy hit? You were with Montgomery, right?"

"Yes. We made it past the first two barricades without being fired on. Soldiers defended the third, but they were drunk and fled after they fired a cannon packed with grapeshot. One piece struck General Montgomery in the neck. He was dead before he hit the ground. Several others were killed, and Remy was among the injured."

"Montgomery's dead?" Colonel Arnold demanded, struggling to sit up.

"Lie down, sir!" Dr. Senter commanded. Several nuns attempted to push Colonel Arnold down, but he held them off. Where he found the strength with his leg in that condition, I didn't know. Maybe he was Achilles reborn, just with a different weakness the enemy hadn't discovered yet.

"Yes, sir," Paul said. "Montgomery is dead."

"Did the rest continue on? Meet up with my men?" Colonel Arnold asked.

I fished out the last fragment of grapeshot from Remy's side and began cleaning the whole area.

"No," Paul said. "We retreated."

Colonel Arnold's head thumped back against the table. "Then it's over."

Chapter Thirty
January 1-3, 1776

Sister Marie-Therese closed Remy's side, and I moved to her shoulder, which was much simpler, even with the chunk of lead lodged beneath her broken collarbone. Paul held her still until the lead was out and collarbone set. For a large man, his hands and strength were surprisingly gentle. When I gave him the nod, he eased his hold and took Remy's hand. She was mostly unconscious, but her face relaxed as soon as Paul's hand was around hers.

Colonel Arnold had passed out and lay still and silent as death, though his chest rose and fell evenly. If we failed to take Quebec with this battle, I doubted we'd have enough men for a second attack, especially with our top two officers dead and injured. Our attempt to take Canada would be over. Unless our reinforcements arrived before more British.

Those were worries for later. We still had to make it through the rest of this battle.

Another shoulder wound came in, and Dr. Senter took him. I had just finished with Remy when Colonel Arnold roared back to consciousness. "I must send a letter! Who can take dictation?"

"I can, sir," Paul said. He extracted his hand from Remy's, took pen and paper from a sister, and moved his chair to Colonel Arnold's side. "Ready, sir."

"To General Wooster, Montreal," Colonel Arnold began.

I stepped back and took a moment, just a moment, to lean against the wall. But the wounded were still streaming in. I wiped my hands and moved to the next man.

Colonel Arnold's voice came and went as he slipped in and out of consciousness. His pain had to be extreme, but he wouldn't take any more rum and refused the offer of laudanum. Around us, the sisters replaced spent candles. My ghosts hovered at the edges of the room, only Dr. Warren and Kit still trailing me from patient to patient. In one corner, Father de Rigauville gave last rites to a dying Canadian.

A blast of cold air blew Suzannah through the door. "They're coming! The British! Evacuate!"

"The patients can't be moved," Dr. Senter said.

"To arms!" Colonel Arnold cried.

"Colonel," Dr. Senter protested, but Colonel Arnold overrode him. "Any able-bodied man, take a musket and get outside! Defend your compatriots to your final breath! Someone give me my pistols!"

Every soldier who could walk, including Paul and Suzannah, ran outside. Over the protests of Dr. Senter, Mother Marie-Catherine, Father de Rigauville, and the sisters, I gave Colonel Arnold his pistols and turned him to face the door though the movement nearly caused him to fall unconscious once more. Loading my own pistols, I planted myself in front of Remy, praising Dr. Warren's foresight. None of his training would go to waste. My ghosts formed a line in front of me, and those with weapons held them ready. Colonel Arnold nodded to me, and we aimed at the doors. Colonel Arnold's guns only shook a little.

From outside, only the distant blast of cannons. I set one pistol down and wiped my sweaty palm down my bloody apron. Colonel Arnold's pistols trembled more violently, and his breath rasped. Only sheer will kept him upright and alert.

"Don't fire!" Paul called before opening the door. "They've retreated back to Quebec."

Colonel Arnold all but collapsed. Mother Marie-Catherine plucked his pistols away. In a voice slurring toward unconsciousness, Colonel Arnold asked Suzannah, "Captain Morgan?"

Suzannah shook her head. "Captured, sir."

At those words, Colonel Arnold's formidable strength reached its end, and he passed out.

"Suzannah, what about Win? Do you know what happened to my brother?"

"I'm sorry, Whit. I didn't see him. I have to find my husband."

Over the next hours, the men who hadn't been killed or captured returned. Win was not among them, but George entered, clutching his side. I helped him to a seat. "Were you injured?"

"No, just my side. Reopened. Win?"

"I haven't seen him for hours."

"I shouldn't have—ah!"

"Let me see." He tried to push my hand away. "Are we really going to go through this again? No one's paying any attention, and I won't expose anything except the wound."

George wasn't happy about it, but he let me tug his shirt up enough to see his stitches had ripped. I sutured the wound closed once more.

"Stay here this time. That's an order, Private Lee. Besides, this will be the best place to hear news of my brother."

George leaned back in the chair, eyes closing. "Yes, Doctor."

Dr. Senter and I worked through the rest of the day. As I closed the last wound, my ghosts faded, all but Kit. I would rather have had Dr. Warren stay. I found his presence more comforting than Kit's, but Kit had a stronger connection to Win. There still was no news, and I began to fear the worst.

Colonel Arnold's letter to General Wooster had gone out as soon as it was finished, and we hoped the general would arrive with reinforcements soon. We had enough men to continue the siege, but only until the ice on the St. Lawrence broke up.

Remy woke toward evening. I had finally convinced Paul and Dr. Senter to get some sleep, but I sat by Remy's side. She tried to move and gasped.

"Easy, Rem. You were wounded, remember?"

"I remember dark and snow. A cannon. General Montgomery?"

I shook my head. General Montgomery's ghost had yet to make an appearance, but I was certain he would arrive sooner or later.

"Paul?" Remy asked.

"He's the one who brought you in. Don't you remember? He's fine. Sleeping." Colonel Arnold was still unconscious, and the sisters already knew Remy's secret. Even so, I lowered my voice. "Paul knows, Rem. He knows you're a woman. Said he's known for a while."

Remy closed her eyes and took several breaths. When she opened her eyes, they were full of trepidation. "And?"

I grinned. "He sat beside you all night."

For a moment, she stared at me, then she laughed. "Ow, ow." She pressed her hand against her side. But then she giggled again, and I couldn't help but join her.

It was the only high point for quite some time.

Colonel Arnold contracted a fever and slipped in and out of consciousness for several days. Dr. Senter wanted to amputate his foot, but I wouldn't let him. I spent the next two days doing all I could to bring the fever down and keep his leg free from infection. On the morning of January 3, the fever broke. Colonel Arnold wanted to get up, but Dr. Senter and I convinced him to remain abed. Hours later, Captain Return Meigs, who had been captured with Captain Morgan, arrived on parole to collect the personal effects of the captured men. Kit drifted beside me as I approached.

"Captain, my brother, Win. Winborn Endicott. Is he among the captured?"

George, who had yet to leave the hospital, joined us.

"He is," Captain Meigs said.

Some of the tension I'd been carrying for the last two days dissipated. The same relief flitted across George's face before he turned away. Kit disappeared as if he had only been waiting to hear Win was alive. My fear, however, surged back. Win had just recovered his health. Prison conditions were sure to be damp. If he fell ill again—

"Captain Meigs," Colonel Arnold called. "What happened after I was wounded?"

Captain Meigs described how Captain Morgan and his men had been trapped between two groups of Regulars. "Captain Morgan fought to the last. A man asked for his surrender, and Morgan shot him dead. He then fought until there was no choice but surrender or die. If every man fought like him, we would have taken the city. Captain Dearborn was also captured, and Captain Lamb was both captured and badly wounded. I'm told he lost his left eye. By best count, nearly four hundred of us are now held prisoner."

Silence blanketed the room. Four hundred. Plus those dead or wounded. If General Wooster didn't arrive soon, we would have no choice but to retreat to Montreal, for we'd never withstand an attack from the British.

"Thank you, Captain," Colonel Arnold said although his voice was heavy with defeat. "Tell the men to keep their spirits up."

"I will, Colonel."

George slumped down in a chair, face in his hands. I crouched in front of him. "He's alive, George. We'll get him back. Why don't you get some sleep?"

He raised his head, eyes bleak as he stared into nowhere. "For the first time, I—" George straightened slowly, mask dropping back over his face. "Sleep is a good idea. Is there a bed for me, Doctor?"

"George, you don't have to—" I was going to say, *shut me out,* but the way his jaw was clenched, eyes blank, he wasn't going to listen to anything I had to say. "Of course."

I gave him the bed at the end of the ward away from the others. As I made my way back down the aisle, Colonel Arnold called me over. "Dr. Endicott, will you take dictation?"

"Happy to, sir." I settled into the chair at Colonel Arnold's side. "Ready, sir."

"The first letter will be to General Wooster, since he has yet to reply, and you will make a copy to send to General Washington." He paused and looked around. All the other wounded were asleep; only Sister Marie-Marguerite on ward duty was awake. Even so, Colonel Arnold lowered his voice. "I heard what your brother said the night he brought me in. Miss Endicott."

Chapter Thirty-One
January 3-14, 1776

I thought I had prepared myself for discovery. But with those two words—*Miss Endicott*—the world around me shattered. I had none of the joy Remy had displayed. Instead, an overwhelming feeling of powerlessness swept over me. I hadn't felt like that since I'd knelt by Kit as he bled to death in the snow. I had sworn never to feel powerless again, but when Colonel Arnold said my name, all my knowledge, all my training didn't matter anymore.

It was over.

"Well, I was right about that. Couldn't be sure what was real and what was a fevered dream. Did Dr. Warren know when he recommended you to me?"

There was no point in trying to deny the truth. My voice clawed through the thickness in my throat. "Yes, sir, he knew. I'd been working with him since I was ten. I only donned men's clothes to leave Boston. So I could tend the wounded."

Colonel Arnold nodded. "You're a more-than-capable doctor, Endicott. There's no doubt about that. But you are a woman."

I closed my eyes and swallowed back my tears, my disappointment.

"However."

My breath stopped. I didn't dare hope, not until he said the words.

"However, Dr. Warren trusted you, and I cannot believe his trust was misplaced. And, like Mrs. Warner and Mrs. Grier, you have earned your place among us. Besides, as you well know, we can't spare a doctor just now."

"You mean I can stay?"

"As long as you continue to dress and act like a man. Your secret will be safe with me, Dr. Endicott."

I met Colonel Arnold's steely gray eyes and saw sincerity. Of all the officers to discover my secret, Colonel Arnold was probably my best option. Colonel Easton and Major Brown would expose me for their own gain, but Colonel Arnold knew when to compromise, where to look the other way. As he had with Jemima and Suzannah. I still had my reservations. I hadn't forgotten the goods in Menut's Tavern or his single-mindedness at the expense of others. But under him, I could continue to serve. "Thank you, sir. You won't regret it."

"I'd better not. Now, the letter: General Wooster, I hope you received my instance of December 31. Our circumstances are, I fear, more dire than I first believed."

I set pen to paper, determined to show Colonel Arnold he hadn't made a mistake.

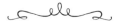

I slept for twelve straight hours, not waking for the prayer bells, nightmares, or knocks on my door. When I finally woke, my body felt like lead, and I was monstrously hungry. I was certain I could have rolled over and slept for another twelve hours, but I had patients to tend.

Remy was well enough to leave bed a few days later, her arm in a sling as her collarbone healed. When Paul wasn't on duty, he was at her side. I waited for her to tell me what I already knew. I'd read enough Shakespeare to know when the woman disguised as a man found her true love, it was time for her to leave disguises behind and return to the real world.

I was in the apothecary cutting and grinding cinchona bark—Colonel Arnold's malaria was flaring again in addition to his wounded leg—when Remy entered. I kept my concentration on my work. The silence stretched, but I ignored the tension of expectation.

"Whit," Remy began.

"When are you leaving?" The words sounded harsher than I'd meant, but I didn't want her to go. I'd been alone until she'd arrived at Fort Ti, and I didn't want to feel that way again.

"Of course you know. If they'll let me, I'll stay until April, when extended enlistments are up. Then, we'll go to Paul's home near Albany and marry."

I stopped chopping. "So, you're staying?"

"For now. We can't abandon our posts."

"And your doctor would not approve you for travel yet." I smiled, and she returned it. "Have you told Colonel Arnold?"

"I was hoping you'd come with me."

"Of course. What kind of friend would I be if I didn't?"

Colonel Arnold was still abed, though he was chafing to be up and about. He listened with growing disbelief and shook his head when Remy finished. "How many of you are there?"

Remy glanced anxiously at me, but I waved aside her worries. Colonel Arnold continued, "I won't send you away. You've fought and bled for our cause. To dismiss you in disgrace would dishonor your service. Besides, we can't lose another man, or woman."

"Thank you, sir."

"However, if you're going to continue spending time with that other young private, change those trousers for skirts."

Remy blushed and ducked her head. "Yes, sir."

Word arrived from the Continental Congress that Colonel Arnold had been promoted to brigadier general. We also learned reinforcements would be slow in coming. In Albany, General Schuyler funneled men to Fort Ti and all points north as quickly as he could, but winter slowed everything.

We fell again into the monotonous pattern of a siege. Patrols were set, and batteries were built to lob shot and shell at and over Quebec's walls. Not everyone was content to follow General Arnold's orders, though, and one of the most recalcitrant was Major Brown. I was checking General Arnold's leg when he ordered Major Brown to bring in six siege mortars left at St. Roch in the aftermath of the failed attack on Quebec.

"Colonel," Major Brown said.

"I'm sorry?"

"It's Colonel Brown. General Montgomery promoted me back in November."

"That order was rescinded after you were caught looting a private residence," General Arnold said.

Major Brown threw a venomous look at me. "Should have known not to trust you when you arrived at Fort Ti on the heels of a self-serving Connecticut man. No better than a mercenary, selling your loyalty to whatever officer comes along."

I flinched but didn't allow myself to back away. General Arnold pushed himself up. "Collect the mortars, Major Brown."

"I am a colonel! That was the rank promised me by General Montgomery, and it is the only title I will answer to."

Exhausted, General Arnold lay back. "I don't have time for this, Major Brown. Retrieve the mortars, and if you insist on the promotion, write to Congress. It's their purview." Major Brown left in a huff, and General Arnold turned questioning eyes on me. "What did you do to earn the major's wrath?"

"I was the one who stopped him from looting in Montreal."

"Ah, a grudge, then. I doubt he'll let go of it anytime soon, since profit and honor are concerned. He's not going to follow orders, is he?"

"I doubt it, sir."

"God help us if others follow his lead."

The only other officer as disaffected as Major Brown was Colonel Easton, and since the two had been hand in glove since before Fort Ti, I didn't think either would ever be won to General Arnold's side. They would, however, bear watching. Already, I had heard grumbles from some of my fellow Massachusetts men about the comfort General Arnold lived in. Brown and Easton wouldn't hesitate to fan the flames of discontent if it harmed Arnold and helped them.

Two nights later, I was walking back to the hospital from the New York encampment after dinner with Paul and Remy. I wore both my pistols. I hadn't gone out at night unarmed since I had been attacked and possessed in Cambridge.

I had just left the last houses of St. Roch behind and was alone on the Plains of Abraham. The waning moon was bright above, throwing my shadow long over the crust of glittering snow. My boots crunched through to the older snow beneath. Breath glistened in clouds from my lips, and the cold ached in my lungs, but it was a beautiful night, stars scattered across the black like embers, no blood or death to be seen or heard, and the only scent on the wind that of deep winter's sleep.

I closed my eyes and drew in a long breath until my throat, tongue, and teeth burned with the reviving cold.

Jemima stood in front of me, an expression of panic widening her eyes and her hands waving me back.

I gasped, the cold air searing through me. Coughing, I pulled my scarf over mouth and nose to warm the air, so I could get my breath back. I glared at Jemima. "Why are you here? There's no battle, no death!"

"Dr. Endicott!" Jacatacqua came up behind me. "I thought I was the only one who liked late night walks in this weather." She was bundled up in one of the British coats from Montreal, scarf, mittens, and hat. "Were you talking to someone?"

"No, just . . ." I glanced once more at Jemima, who was still waving me back. "Just venting my frustration."

"Night can be good for that. I can leave you to it."

"No." I didn't want to be left alone with Jemima's ghost. I was tired of the ghosts' cryptic appearances and messages I couldn't understand. I just wanted them to leave me alone. "I'd rather walk with you. If we go along the river, we can stop at the nuns' bakery. There are always the makings for coffee and tea."

"Sounds perfect."

I hadn't spent much time with Jacatacqua and wasn't sure what to say, but she seemed content to walk in silence. After being surrounded with the noise of men all day, the comfortable silence between us was a relief.

Jemima, however, was persistent, refusing to let me ignore her as she gesticulated toward the hospital and bakery, her frustration growing. When I continued walking, Jemima gave a silent scream and plunged her hands into my chest.

The cold, the maelstrom of sound and memory, the loss of control. Jacatacqua looked concerned. "Dr. Endicott? Whitley, what's wrong?"

In my head, Jemima's myriad whispers coalesced into a single voice, hissing urgently, "Brown. Easton. Danger."

Her gestures suddenly made sense. Brown and Easton were lying in wait, ready to exact revenge of some kind. Brown for my interfering with his promotion, and Easton had perhaps been holding a grudge since Fort Ti.

As if she sensed my understanding, Jemima rushed out of me, and my head exploded with the echo of Jemima's death. The pain sent me to my knees, the taste of gunpowder thick on my tongue. I felt how every bone had broken, how her eardrums had ruptured, how the muscles had torn when the cannonball struck.

"Whitley!" Jacatacqua caught me.

"Ambush," I slurred, words clawing out my cannonball-destroyed throat. "Danger."

And I knew no more.

When I woke, I lay on a rug not thick enough to disguise the hardness of the floor beneath. A fire burned in the fireplace beside me, and blankets, warm and heavy as lead, weighed me down. My head pounded, the bones throbbing along imaginary fracture lines, my mouth dry as gunpowder.

"There's tea." Just turning my head toward Jacatacqua's voice took monumental effort. She sat in a nearby rocking chair in a room I didn't recognize—a bedroom with whitewashed walls and morning light streaming in two windows.

I heaved myself to sitting, the wall mercifully close enough to lean against. "Where?" I croaked. "How long?"

"Only since last night. We're in the nearest house I could find. I didn't want to bring you to the hospital after your warning. Lucky for you, British coats make for good sleds, and you don't weigh near as much as you should. But dragging you here was still warm work."

My hand trembled as I reached for the mug of tea. "You shouldn't be doing such things. The baby."

"Is still months away. I've seen women do much more the day before they gave birth. Would you rather I left you in the snow?"

"No." I tested the steaming tea. Mint. It didn't mix well with the gunpowder taste Jemima had left behind, but the ache of my head eased a little as I drank. "Thank you."

Jacatacqua inclined her head. "You must explain how you knew there was danger ahead and what happened to make you freeze and collapse."

I slowly sipped my tea, trying to come up with a plausible answer, but with my head throbbing, I was in no condition to create a believable lie. Setting aside the empty mug, I asked, "Do you believe in ghosts?"

"The spirits of those who came before? Of course." Her answer was so simple and straightforward. She smiled at my stunned expression. "There are spirits everywhere around us. The spirits of our ancestors inhabit the land where they lived. We call on them often for wisdom and guidance."

"My people believe ghosts are tied to evil and witchcraft."

She shook her head, an amused and pitying smile tilting her lips. "Is that what happened? A spirit entered you?"

Jacatacqua didn't think me mad or in league with the devil. My mind tried to wrap itself around this simple fact. She might be the one person in this entire army I could tell without fear of reprisals. She cocked her head, waiting for my answer.

I told her everything.

Jacatacqua made more tea while I spoke, and when I finished, she said, "So, you don't know why they haunt you, and you don't know how to free yourself or them. Would you like to?"

"To know? Yes, but how? When they aren't possessing me, they can't speak, and when they're in my head, it's hard for me to speak to them."

"I can help you."

That was how, three nights later, we came to be sitting on the floor of my room at the hospital, the door locked because I couldn't risk Mother Marie-Catherine discovering us. If she caught us channeling spirits, we might find ourselves being exorcised or bound to the stake. Still, my room was the safest place for what we were about to try.

A wide, shallow bowl sat between us. Seven candles burned around us, and we both had blankets wrapped around our shoulders to ward off the chill. Jacatacqua emptied a pouch of herbs and curls of bark into the bowl. "Sage, tobacco, cedar, and mugwort. Herbs to calm the mind, bring clarity, and strengthen our connection to the spirits. Now, close your eyes and call out to them. Reach for answers."

As I closed my eyes, she burned the herbs, and their sweet, smoky scents filled the small room. I felt foolish trying, as Jacatacqua had told me, to call to the spirits with my spirit's voice. I had never called to them before; they had just appeared or disappeared according to whims or rules of their own. Still, I did as she instructed.

I need answers. I want to know. Please.

When I opened my eyes, Dr. Warren sat beside me.

"Is there a spirit present?" Jacatacqua asked.

"Yes, it's Dr. Warren." Of course it would be him. I had thought it would be Kit since he had been with me longest, but I should have known that if I called for help, Dr. Warren would be the one to answer.

And yet, I didn't want it to be him, because for this to work, he had to possess me, and then I would learn firsthand how he had died.

"Invite him in," Jacatacqua said.

It was too late to turn back. I had chosen my course, and I had to keep to it. I extended a hand to Dr. Warren. "Will you please help me find answers?"

His eyes met mine, pale reminders of the steady blue-gray they had been in life, asking again as they had so long ago when he had first offered me an apprenticeship, *Are you certain this is what you want?*

"Yes," I whispered.

He raised his own hand and set his palm against mine.

As I absorbed his spirit, the cold didn't feel as intense, and the storm that surrounded my inner self was not as strong. I could even parse out images from his memories: Miss Scollay's smile, his children's laughter. Jacatacqua's herbs were certainly having an effect.

"Dr. Warren?" Jacatacqua asked. "Are you there?"

"Yes." The quiet assurance of his voice rolled out of my mouth. A voice I thought I'd never hear again. Had I been able to cry, tears would have been streaming down my face.

"Whitley seeks answers. Will you help her?"

"I have always sought to aid Dr. Endicott, and death has not changed that. I will give what answers I can, but there are secrets even the dead may not divulge."

"Very well. Why do you, and other spirits, haunt Dr. Endicott?"

"The answer is threefold. The manner of her birth is the first. Death touched her that day, allowing any whom death has claimed to be seen by her."

So Win had been right. The cord around my neck. I must have been dead, even if just for a moment, before Midwife Rowe brought me back to life. My debt to her, it seemed, was even greater than I had thought.

"You said the reasons were threefold," Jacatacqua said. "What are the other two?"

"While any spirit may reveal themselves to Dr. Endicott, we who are bound to her had a connection with her before death. It is this connection that allows us to possess her while she remains conscious of our presence. If we were to possess anyone else, they would have no awareness of us. However, this," he lifted my hands, gesturing to my body and his spirit within, "is as dangerous for us as for her. Although we are called to be with Dr. Endicott during times of need and danger and when death is near, at other times we are free to wander to those other places and people on earth that are imprinted on our spirits. Finally, binding us to Dr. Endicott is her deep empathy for us, her feelings of guilt and responsibility for our deaths. She should n—"

His voice choked off, and I felt the strain in his spirit as he tried to say more, images and whispers whipping around my inner self.

The aromas of sage, cedar, and tobacco intensified as Jacatacqua sprinkled another handful of the herbs into the smoking bowl. Dr. Warren's spirit relaxed, and the winds around me calmed.

"I am permitted to say no more of how we are bound to Dr. Endicott."

If I'd understood what Dr. Warren was saying, the only way to stop accumulating ghosts was to stop caring about the people around me, about the men and women I treated. Impossible.

"You said possession of Whitley is dangerous for you," Jacatacqua said. "How? And if it is dangerous, why possess her?"

"We must protect her, and sometimes to protect her, we must possess her. Our spiritual remains are tied to her life. If she were to die before freeing us from this bond, we would be consigned forever to a place in between. This, too, is the danger of possessing her. Possession weakens us, drains us. After we possess Dr. Endicott, it takes us weeks to recover. But if we possess her too many times, we become forever unsettled, unable to move on to our eternal rest but also forbidden this mortal world, trapped forever between the rest we crave and the life we lost."

"How many times is too many?"

"Three is the limit."

Horror swept me. How could I be responsible for the fates of all their spirits, their souls? I pushed against the bonds of memory holding me, desperate to free myself from this terrible responsibility.

Compassion wrapped around me, and I felt Dr. Warren's understanding and sympathy. When he spoke again, the words were for me. "I'm sorry, Whitley. If I could lift this burden from you, I would."

"How can she free you? Free herself?"

Dr. Warren shook my head. "I am forbidden from answering. Death holds secrets mortals must discover for themselves."

"But there is a way?" Jacatacqua pushed.

"Yes. I have lingered too long in Dr. Endicott's body, and I do not wish to cause her more pain. Whitley." His focus turned inward, love surrounding me. "I am so very proud of you."

He released me, and the memory of a musket ball smashed through my skull just below my left eye.

The pain of Dr. Warren's death vibrated through me as Jacatacqua helped me into bed, but the herbs perfuming the air must have helped because I didn't vomit or pass out though I felt queasy and there was still the bitter bite of opium and sour wine in my mouth. So, it wasn't the pain or fear that brought tears to my eyes, but the knowledge I held. I knew how Dr. Warren had died.

Chapter Thirty-Two
January 15 – February 1776

Over the next few days, I contemplated all I'd learned from Dr. Warren. It was a relief to know that while I might see many ghosts, only a few were truly bound to me and could possess me. Why the others allowed me to see them, I wasn't quite sure—maybe it was simply because I could see them or they wanted to be remembered or maybe because, as Dr Warren had said, I cared.

And that was the problem: my empathy. For as long as I felt for those I treated, as long as I felt responsible when they died, I would continue acquiring new ghosts. I hadn't been raised to ignore the pain and needs of others, and Dr. Warren had taught me compassion alongside medicine. I couldn't stop caring, and I didn't want to be a doctor who had no concern for those I treated. The only answer was to set us all free, but I had no idea how. When Jedediah had possessed me, he had asked if I paid my debts. The debt I owed them must be part of it, but I was no closer to a solution.

There was, however, a problem I could solve: the problem of Major Brown and Colonel Easton. I doubted they would give up after one attempt, so the day after my possession, I sought out General Arnold, who had returned to Menut's Tavern.

"They were going to ambush you?" General Arnold asked.

"Yes, sir. It was only through luck that I avoided it."

"Can't have men like that hanging about camp, especially since you are not the only one against whom they bear a grudge. Leave it with me, Dr. Endicott." By the end of the next day, Brown and Easton had been assigned foraging and scouting duties, and I breathed easier.

Jacatacqua returned to the hospital with a gift: two pouches of herbs. "These are the same as we used the other night. Wear one around your neck, keep another in your pocket. Though they are more effective when they burn, when worn they should lessen some of the negative effects of possession."

"Thank you, Jacatacqua, for this and your help both nights."

"You are most welcome. If you need my aid again, you have only to ask."

The British were content to remain behind Quebec's walls, so injuries from combat were few, but the threat I had feared since last summer took hold.

Smallpox.

Whether the soldiers had caught it while coming up the Kennebec from locals, or new arrivals had brought it with them, in the aftermath of the battle, smallpox tore through what remained of our army.

"We need to inoculate," I told Dr. Senter. "It'll lessen the death toll and shorten recovery time."

"I agree. You've inoculated before?"

"Yes. Dr. Warren believed strongly in the benefits of inoculation, and I've seen them firsthand. My entire family was inoculated when I was four." It had been Dr. Warren himself who had performed our inoculations. That epidemic had been his first test as a doctor. Though his ghost had not yet returned, I could feel his presence, and for a moment, I was again in Castle William, sitting on Da's lap watching with fascination as Dr. Warren calmly and surely cut into our arms and, through the magic of medicine, protected us from disease.

Dr. Senter's voice roused me from my memories. "What course would you suggest?"

"We bring the men in company by company and wait a week between each company we inoculate."

"A week? Isn't that risky?"

"It is, but if we don't wait between companies, we'll have no one left to defend us should the British attack."

"A good point. I'll follow your lead, Dr. Endicott."

The sisters crossed themselves and stayed out of our way when the first company arrived.

I opened one of the pustules on a sick man and scraped out some of the puss, coating small lengths of string with it. Then, I made an incision on the forearm of the first soldier. I lifted the string, and he jerked his arm back. "You're going to put that in me?"

"Yes. We've found if we put a little of the illness in you, you have a milder form of the disease, and then you don't get smallpox again."

"It always works? I won't die?"

"It . . . almost always works." He drew further back at my hesitation, and I hurried to add, "Your chances of surviving are much better if I do this than if I don't. May I continue?"

The soldier wavered a moment longer before nodding. I inserted the string in the cut, set lint over the top, and bandaged the wound. "Next!"

"Dr. Endicott! Dr. Senter! What are you doing?" General Arnold demanded as he limped into the hospital. He should still have been abed, but he refused. He also refused to use a cane. He'd be lucky if his leg healed properly.

"We're inoculating the troops. Against smallpox."

"You're purposely infecting healthy men?"

I set my instruments down. "They'll be ill soon anyway, sir. If we inoculate, their reaction is less severe, and most patients recover. And they can't catch the disease again."

"And if they don't recover? How am I to replace dead men? Men willingly killed by my own doctors!"

"Sir," Dr. Senter said, "the chances of death from inoculation are far less than when the disease is contracted naturally."

"And who is supposed to stand guard while these men are ill? No, doctors, there will be no more inoculations. Isolate the men who are ill and those you've already infected, and the disease will cease to spread."

"But, General—"

"That's an order, *Doctor* Endicott. Remember at whose pleasure you serve."

He didn't need to say more. I didn't think he would expose me. He had given his word after all, but I couldn't risk it. These men could not afford my dismissal. If we didn't inoculate, our army would need every doctor we could muster.

"Yes, sir. No more inoculations," I said through clenched teeth.

"Then get these men back on duty."

The soldiers followed General Arnold out. Huffing with frustration, Dr. Senter began cleaning up. Helpless anger held me frozen. There were people I cared about in this army, and I could not stand by and do nothing while smallpox killed them. General Arnold wouldn't prevent me from protecting them.

I scooped up my lancet, bandages, and a handful of string. Dr. Senter frowned. "What are you doing? Where are you going?"

"It's better you don't know. If General Arnold asks, you can claim ignorance." I left before he could argue, pulling my scarf tighter as the February wind clawed at me.

After the battle, the regiments had been left in shambles, and the soldiers had been reorganized. George had been absorbed into what was left of Colonel Bedel's Rangers, Suzannah and Joseph remained in Arnold's regiment, and Remy and Paul were encamped with what remained of the New York troops. I waited until I had gathered all five before I explained what I planned to do.

"Inoculation?" George said. "Isn't that dangerous?"

"Far less dangerous than remaining in this camp without. The epidemic among our troops is only going to worsen until the disease has no fresh victims to attack. And with new reinforcements expected . . ."

I left my sentence unfinished and let them draw their own conclusions. Paul and Remy gripped each other's hands. She wore skirts instead of trousers, but it was impossible to think of her as anyone but Remy. "We'll do it," she said.

"As will we," Suzannah said. "What about Jacatacqua?"

"It's too dangerous for the baby. George?"

After a pause, George said, "Very well."

"Good. Meet me at the quarantine house within the next hour. Come separately."

The quarantine house consisted of a farmhouse, a barn, and an ever-growing sea of tents. I checked on the men and women who lay ill, not that I could do much for them but give them water or drape another blanket over them. I found five empty mattresses in the barn and grouped them together. I feared to know the fate of their former occupants. A few of my ghosts drifted among the ill, death drawing them to me once more. I wished Dr. Warren were beside me with reassurances that I was making the right decision.

George was the first to arrive. His eyes jumped from one pustule-covered body to the next. "Doctor, can you promise me no one will see—"

"No one will see anything, George. Just your forearm. Listen, the way smallpox is spreading, you'll end up in this barn before long anyway. This way will be much safer. Both Win and I survived it. You will, too. You've trusted me this far, George. Trust me now."

George took a deep breath and expelled it before nodding. I settled him on a mattress, and quickly collected pus from a nearby man. George flinched when I made the incision but said nothing until I was finished. "That's it?"

"Simple as that. Keep your arm covered just in case General Arnold comes through." I doubted he would, but George didn't need to be punished for my disobedience. "You'll have mild symptoms, and you should be fully recovered within two weeks."

I repeated the process for Remy, Paul, Suzannah, and Joseph. Once they were as comfortable as I could make them, I promised I would return daily. Dr. Senter said nothing when I returned to the hospital nor when I disappeared for an hour or so each day.

If rumors were to be believed, I was not the only one breaking orders. Soldiers were self-inoculating, trying to insert the pus under their fingernails. I wanted to offer my aid, but I felt General Arnold's eyes on me far too often as it was. I could not risk more.

To my relief, my friends progressed nicely. Both George and Remy developed slightly higher and longer-lasting fevers, and I wondered if it had anything to do with the wounds they had received. They all developed a few pustules but not nearly as many as they would have had they contracted the disease naturally. By the end of two weeks, they had recovered, and I breathed a little easier. My friends were out of danger, but our army was not, and I wondered how much worse the epidemic would grow before we were allowed to put an end to it.

Chapter Thirty-Three
March 5-16, 1776

On the anniversary of the Bloody Massacre, a letter arrived from Win.

Quebec
28 February 1776

Dear Whit,

We have been given the chance to write home, but I don't want to distress Ma. I trust you to inform the rest of the family what has befallen me if you have not written them already.

We are being relatively well treated. Food is passable and clothing adequate. I am also among friends: John Joseph Henry, George Morison, and Eleazer Oswald keep me good company. Although I miss George Lee's friendship, I'm glad he's not here with us. I have developed a cough, due, I think, both to our battle in the snowstorm and to chill, damp conditions in which we were first kept. Do not worry, it is only a cough. We have been moved to better quarters, and we are being treated by one of the doctors here. I promise to be well soon.

We hope to be exchanged or let out on parole this spring or summer, though that depends on the siege ending, so perhaps that is not something I should wish for. Unless, of course, it ends with Quebec's surrender.

I hope you are well and able to write soon.

Your brother,
Win

I reread the section about Win being ill. I knew he was lying, downplaying the severity of his illness. It was what he always did—partly because he didn't want us to worry, and partly because he didn't want to be confined to his bed. He might say it was only a cough, but he hadn't fully recovered from the illness he'd contracted on the way up the Kennebec. He could already have pleurisy or the beginnings of pneumonia.

My fingers trembled as I folded the letter. I wasn't going to wait until the next one arrived to find out Win's fate. I swept my instruments into a satchel. Next, I went to the apothecary. Mother Marie-Catherine went wide-eyed when she saw me. "Dr. Endicott, what has happened?"

I took anything I might need to treat Win's cough. "I received a letter from my brother. He's ill. I must go to him."

Mother Marie-Catherine watched me for a moment before she left. I double-checked my satchel. It was almost too heavy to carry, but I would manage. I only had to reach Portia, then she could carry me to Quebec.

I exited the hospital and strode straight into Remy and George.

"What are you doing here?" I asked. Remy glanced over her shoulder at a puffing Mother Marie-Catherine. I glowered at the nun.

"Where do you think you're going?" Remy asked. I shook my head and tried to pass, but she and George gripped my arms.

"Let go! I'm going to the city. Win's ill. I have to see him."

George's hold loosened, but Remy's didn't. "You're not even dressed for the cold. It isn't spring yet. Come back inside and—"

"Portia's quick. I'll be in Quebec soon enough." I pulled away, but they blocked my path again.

"Let us at least send for General Arnold," George said. "Arrange for a flag of truce—"

"Because they were so respectful of our last truce flags? No, we don't have time for negotiation. I'll surrender myself."

"Whit, you can't!"

"I will not sit here while Win slowly succumbs to illness. I will not let that happen! I would think you, Remy, more than anyone, would understand!"

She flinched, and I pushed between them and toward the stables. Moments later, George fell in at my side. "The least I can do is come with you."

I didn't slow. George had mostly avoided me since Win's capture. Even during his quarantine, he had said little. I couldn't blame him. I knew how similar Win and I appeared, even more than usual at the moment since I was passing as male. I glanced at George, wondering why he'd answered Mother Marie-Catherine's call. His face was almost as worn and fatigued as it had been during his quarantine, and I could have sworn he'd lost weight in the week since I'd last seen him. Rations had been cut again due to lack of supplies, so perhaps his weight loss wasn't unusual.

"In his letter, Win said he was glad you weren't a prisoner. He'll be upset to see me, but he'll be very upset to see us both."

"I recall a time not long ago when Win didn't do as I'd asked. He doesn't get to be the only stubborn one."

I couldn't argue with that, and though I didn't want to admit it, I was glad George was at my side. "Well, then, I won't stop you from coming with me."

"Thank you. What ails him?"

"A cough. Or so he says. He's never truthful about how ill he is. If he's even admitting it, I fear it's more than just a cough."

George said nothing, only continued with me.

At the stables, Portia whickered a greeting. I scratched her chin. "How'd you like to take us on a ride, girl? Find you a proper stall and some oats maybe, hmm?" I eyed the saddle. "She can carry us both, but I don't know how that would work with the saddle—"

"It'll be easier bareback. We'll just use the reins, and you can sit behind me. It's a short enough ride. Lead her out, and we can mount outside."

"If you're sure."

"I spent most of my childhood on horseback. I can get us to Quebec."

I led Portia outside, but before we could mount, another horse slid to a stop in front of us, spraying old, gray snow in our faces and making Portia prance. I wiped the slush from my eyes and found General Arnold glaring down at us.

"You shouldn't be riding yet, General," I said, the doctor in me overriding the sister for a moment. "Your leg—"

"Is fine. You shouldn't be heading toward Quebec, Doctor."

"My brother—"

"Is ill, I know. Your friend told me. I have received assurances from Governor Carleton that our men will be properly cared for. If you ride into that city now, you're only giving the British another prisoner. Two if Private Lee insists on going with you. You will not free your brother, and you'll be abandoning your patients. Lives for which you are responsible."

"Some of my patients won't listen to my advice." I glared at him. "And my brother—"

"Is one man, Dr. Endicott. You must not let the importance of a single man blind you. I believe your brother would tell you the same."

I refused to agree. One man, if it was the right man, could make all the difference. I crossed my arms and stared past General Arnold to Quebec.

The general leaned forward. "Don't make me arrest you and confine you to quarters, Dr. Endicott. Private Lee, be ready to take the doctor into custody."

"I'm going to Quebec, sir, and nothing will stop me."

"Private Lee, seize the doctor."

George hesitated, eyes flicking from the general to me to Quebec. General Arnold's jaw tightened. "Private Lee, you are a soldier in the Army of the United Colonies, and I have just given you an order. If you wish to remain a soldier under my command, you will follow that order. Now."

George's own jaw ticking, he didn't move. He wasn't going to arrest the sister of the man he loved, and he was going to risk his position in the army for me. This was true loyalty. No wonder Win had fallen for him. Win would never forgive me if my actions made George a prisoner, and I couldn't let George sacrifice himself for me. "Fine. I promise I won't go to Quebec."

"Good. I think you'd best return to the hospital, Doctor, and I'm sure there's somewhere you are supposed to be, Private."

General Arnold waited while I stabled Portia, promising her a ride later, and watched us as we returned to the encampment, those steel-gray eyes piercing my back. George shifted his shoulders, and I knew he felt them, too.

"*Do* you have somewhere you're supposed to be?" I asked when we had almost reached the hospital.

"In my quarters, playing Brag with a few others. I was winning before Mother Marie-Catherine fetched me."

"I'm sorry I took you away from that." I smiled at George, but he was as stony-faced as ever. I rubbed my palm. "Look, I'm sure Win will be fine. He might underreact when it comes to his health, but I, well, I tend to overreact." When he said nothing, I went on. "You're welcome to come in for tea unless you really want to get back to that card game."

"Thank you, no. I won't inflict myself on you any longer."

"What do you mean *inflict*?" I snatched his sleeve before he could disappear. "George, you're not a wound or . . . or a tax Win has forced on me. You're welcome to stay. I'd like you to stay."

He looked down at my hand, but I didn't want to let go until I was certain he wasn't going to run. "You haven't invited me in before. Since the battle, you only sought me out to inoculate me."

"I didn't know if you'd want me to. I know I look like Win, and that must be hard."

He humphed, not meeting my eyes. "There are differences. Small ones, but they're there. When you're nervous, you rub your palm, but Win tugs at his earlobe. There are other things, too. A look in your eyes, how you smile."

I was impressed. No one outside our family had ever been able to pick out the minute differences between Win and myself. "Well, then. You have no reason to leave. Come in for tea. You can read Win's letter."

George tugged out of my hold. He didn't leave, but he crossed his arms, shoulders hunched up to his ears. "You don't have to pretend to be my friend. I don't need—"

"Pretend? Why would you think I'm pretending?"

George set his jaw. Huffing in frustration, I pulled on his arm, but he wouldn't move. I used my Ma glare. "We are going to have this conversation now, either right here where any passing nun can hear or in my room. Your choice."

He let me tow him to my room, where I closed the door firmly and leaned against it so he couldn't run away. "Explain. Why would you think I'm pretending to be your friend?"

"For your brother's sake. That's why you didn't say anything when you patched me up in December. That's why you inoculated me. You know what I am, so of course you pretend. Well, Win isn't here now, and I don't need your pity."

His words shocked me. Did he really think so little of himself and of me? Did he truly believe no one could like him for his own sake?

"Look at me, George." He wouldn't, so I gripped his chin, his rough stubble scraping against my fingers, and forced him to face me. I waited until his eyes flicked to mine before I went on. "I do know what you are." He braced against my next words. "You're exactly what my brother is. A good man."

He made a sound halfway between a laugh and a sob but all disbelief and shook me away. "Win is your family. We make exceptions for family."

"Like your family made an exception for you?"

George didn't answer, only clenched his teeth and avoided my eyes.

I threw up my hands. "I'm not making an exception for Win or you or anyone, and I'm not pretending. I never have been. Believe me, the only thing I'm pretending to be right now is a man. Do I want to help you because you're important to Win? Yes. But I've also helped you because I want us to be friends. I want to be *your* friend, George, because you are a man anyone would be lucky to call a friend."

The hope and disbelief on his face made me want to hug him, to reassure him that he was worthy of friends. But I stepped back instead. He wasn't ready for that.

George shook his head. "I've never had a friend who knows who I really am."

"Well, you'd better get used to it. I'm just as stubborn as my brother, so I'm not going anywhere."

The smallest smile curved George's lips. "Maybe I'll stay, then. Just for a little while."

The drumming of "The Troop" called us to the parade ground. I had heard rumors over the last few days, but I hadn't wanted to believe them. General Arnold and what officers we had, Lieutenant Burr among them, had been involved in a court-martial. After the first rumors went around, I'd gone to Jacatacqua.

"Is it true what they're saying? About the men being court-martialed?"

"They were found together at dawn. That's all Aaron would tell me."

The late winter slush squelched under my boots, and the bitter wind reached its fingers inside my coat as I made my way to the empty, flat Plains of Abraham south of St. Jean that served as our parade ground. Dread tightening my stomach, I searched for George, but it was hard to distinguish one bundled-up soldier from the next even when they were organized into regiments, for no uniforms were visible under the winter coats. Thankfully, George still wore his round rifleman's hat, the side of the brim pinned up, revealing his red-gold hair. He said nothing as I joined him, but he didn't send me away either.

Since my failed attempt to reach Quebec a week and a half ago, George had visited several times. He hadn't opened up at all, his mask firmly in place and formality a wall between us. Mostly we'd sat in companionable silence, George with his eyes closed while I wrote letters or read one of the few English books the nuns had or that I was able to borrow from General Arnold. To my surprise, Mother Marie-Catherine hadn't tried to stop him from visiting.

"You have healed his body, ma fille, but his soul is a long way from whole. He needs the peace of this place even if he does not know it. His trust in you will only aid the process."

I wasn't sure he trusted me, not yet, but given enough time, I hoped he would.

What was about to happen, however, might destroy his ability to trust completely. I glanced at him. He had to have heard the rumors—the entire army had been buzzing with them—but his face gave nothing away. His only sign of tension was how tightly his jaw was clenched. My trepidation grew, and I rubbed the scars on my palm.

The drums and fifes fell silent, and a contingent moved to the center of the field. Two men, stripped of uniforms and weapons, stood between guards. An officer stepped in front of them, paper in hand. General Arnold stood behind him.

The officer cleared his throat and read, "On this day, March 16, 1776, Lieutenant John Malcolm and Private Michael Boyd are to be dismissed from the army for the crime of sodomy. They are dismissed with infamy. General Benedict Arnold approves the sentence and, with abhorrence and detestation of such an infamous crime, orders John Malcolm and Michael Boyd drummed out of camp never to return."

The guards stepped back, and the drums and fifes took up "The Rogue's March." Malcolm and Boyd started forward, heads high. From the ranks, snow, rocks, and rotten vegetables flew. Insults quickly followed. George sucked in an almost inaudible breath. I looked to General Arnold to put a stop to it, but his mouth was set and his eyes as cold gray as the sky.

How could he not stop the cruelty? It wasn't as though Malcolm and Boyd had hurt anyone or stolen anything or given information to the British. Yes, they had broken the law, but what business was it of Congress, General Arnold, or anyone else who they shared a tent or bed with?

It couldn't have taken more than ten minutes for Malcolm and Boyd to get clear of our lines, but I measured each step, noted the degrees by which their heads and shoulders bowed under the onslaught of refuse and insults. I wanted to turn away in shame, but I forced myself to bear witness to each moment. I almost searched the crowd for Remy, but I was afraid of what I might see on her face. Next to me, George flinched as each missile found its mark. I yearned to reassure him, to take his hand, but that would have been foolish with the whole army watching.

After an eternity, it was over, and the drums and fifes beat the dismissal.

"Come to the hospital," I said to George. "We need a drink."

He gave no sign he heard, but he followed me back to my room, where I left him while I fetched tea and rum. When I returned, George sat on the floor, hunched against my bed, shaking with silent sobs, eyes squeezed shut, and fist shoved between his teeth.

My first impulse was to wrap him in my arms like I would one of my brothers, but I held back. My second thought was to retreat and return when George had collected himself. That would be easier. We could both pretend this had never happened, but avoidance wouldn't do any good. Besides, I hadn't invited him to my room to abandon him to his grief and hurt. I remembered what he had said the night he'd been injured—*I'm used to being on my own*. Well, he wasn't alone anymore. I shut the door and poured him rum and myself a mug of tea. I sat beside him, near but not too near, and set his mug between us.

George's tears slowed, trickled to a stop, leaving him with rasping, shuddering breaths.

With Win, I wouldn't have needed words. We would have linked pinkies, our closeness comforting the other. But the way George sat—arms wrapped tight about himself, body tucked as small as he could make it—warned that touching him would be a mistake. The weight of the silence was unbearable, but to ask how he was would be daft and *sorry* seemed inadequate, so I said the first thing that came to mind that had given me relief. "At least they weren't whipped."

Snake-quick, George lashed out. "Oh yes, at least they weren't whipped because that's the worst thing that could happen to them!"

The fangs of his anger and fear sank into me, the venom of his words burning, and I shrank back from the hurt and rage in his eyes.

"It wasn't like they were just humiliated in front of men they'd fought beside, *bled* with. Told by their commanding officer, a man they were willing to die for, that he abhors and detests them! That he would rather have two fewer soldiers when he can't afford to lose one, when he'll let women serve, instead of having them in his army."

I had recognized the injustice of what had happened, but I hadn't understood the depth of it. General Arnold knew both Remy and I were women. We, too, should have been drummed out, disgraced for a gender and limitations we hadn't chosen. But instead, Remy had simply been told to change into skirts, and I had been allowed to keep pretending. Suzannah and Jemima had never even been asked to pretend.

"You know what I remember about my whipping? What I fear others will know if they see my scars?" I held very still and very silent. Since that December night, George had said very little about his past, and nothing about what his father had done to him. I hadn't thought he would ever speak of it again. "I remember my father's words. 'You're no son of mine, no son and no man. It would have been better had you died at birth. Better that than the loathsome, damned creature you are.'" He took a shaking breath, wiping angrily at his eyes. "Those men now know the entire army hates them. But at least they weren't whipped." The bitterness of his words was like a slap across my face. He downed his rum in a single swallow.

"George, I'm sorry. I didn't mean to . . . I'm sorry." I refilled his mug, tea this time. He didn't drink but twisted it around in his hands.

"That could have been Win and me." His voice was ragged with old pain and an incessant fear. "'Abhorrence and detestation,'" he repeated in a whisper. His hands stilled. His whole body stilled. His eyes flared with something unreadable—fear? realization?—and his emotionless mask fell into place once more. He turned on me, voice still a little unsteady. "Why don't you feel the same, Doctor? Why don't you abhor and detest us?"

"I'm sure I told you."

"No, you told me you loved your brother. But you haven't told me why you accept us. So, why?"

George's question hung in the air, and I poured more tea to give myself time to gather my thoughts. I'd never needed to explain to Win because he knew me, trusted me. But George didn't. I had to tell him everything.

"I didn't always understand or accept this part of Win." I stared down into my tea, unable to look at George. I'd hardly ever admitted this to myself, and saying it aloud was harder than I'd thought it would be.

"Win said you'd always supported him."

"I didn't tell Win I knew his secret until three years after I found out. I needed time to—I was confused, scared. When I realized Win was—" I had no words to describe what Win was, beyond insults. If there was such language, it was in no books I'd read. "When I realized Win is the way he is, I was smitten with Henry Knox, and I discovered Win liked him, too. Until that moment, I thought I knew Win better than anyone. Looking into his face was like looking into a mirror. And then from one moment to the next, something I'd been sure of my whole life, like Win's eye color or hair color, changed before my eyes. I didn't know how to feel or what to do or anything."

"Fear, confusion. Multiply your feelings by about a thousand, and you might come close to how Win and I felt, still feel every day."

I well-remembered the stomach-churning confusion, the sleepless nights as I'd tried to think of a way to talk to Win, the guilt when I hadn't. "I'm sorry you ever felt like that, George."

My words were inadequate, but George nodded. "You said you were afraid. What did you have to be afraid of?"

"Not for myself, for Win. Every reverend I'd ever heard made it clear my brother, my other half, the person I love and know better than anyone, was damned. And then there were the mobs in Boston. All it took was one word or a pointed finger, and the mob would turn on whoever they were aimed at. There was plenty to be afraid of."

"How did you overcome it? Your confusion and fear? How did you get here?"

"Well, Win didn't suddenly transform into the terror described in the newspapers and sermons. He was still the same: he couldn't sit still for more than two minutes, he still snapped replies with his quick wit, he was still closer to me than anyone in the world. But he liked men. I mean, he always had, I just hadn't known it. Had his hair or eye color changed, I still would have loved him, accepted him, supported him. This wasn't any different."

"Not different? You can't choose eye or hair color."

"And I believe Win, you, and anyone else, can't choose who you love. Knowing the consequences awaiting any man caught, who would make such a choice?"

George's expression tightened. His experience only reinforced my belief; he would not have chosen a life that led to him being beaten nearly to death and forced to flee his home. How or who we loved wasn't something we could choose.

"It took me about two years to come to those conclusions. In those two years, I searched for answers everywhere—in novels and plays, philosophy, science, religion, newspapers, and the bodies we dissected. I couldn't ask anyone because I couldn't risk putting Win in danger, and I didn't have the courage to talk to Win. Finally, I realized that what I believed couldn't come from without. It had to come from within. I knew Win in my very soul and knew he wouldn't choose something evil, something that would damn him. I had to trust what I knew, no matter what the world said. In the end, I asked myself how love could be wrong, and the only answer I had was that it can't. Love can't be wrong."

"Love can't be wrong," George repeated as if testing the idea. "The army would disagree with you."

"Well, the army is wrong."

George smiled a little, leaning his head back against the bed, his posture relaxing at last. The strain between us had eased, and I sipped my tea, but I couldn't banish what we'd witnessed from my mind. "Where do you think they'll go—Malcolm and Boyd?"

"As far away as they can. They won't stay anywhere near the army that rejected them so thoroughly."

"But you're staying, fighting for General Arnold. Why?"

"For Win. And Captains Morgan and Dearborn, John Joseph, and all the rest who were captured. If we stop fighting, they're as good as dead, for the British will never release prisoners of a failed rebellion. That's why I'll still fight for General Arnold, despite what he sanctioned today. This is bigger than one man. The world itself needs to change. And if I want a better world, a world where I have the freedom to love Win, I have to fight for it."

"You shouldn't have to."

"Neither should you. As the best doctor in camp, you shouldn't have to hide who you are. But when has this world ever given anyone what they deserve without exacting a price?"

George understood. He understood debts and owing and the burden of repayment. Since we'd met, I had hoped he'd become a friend, for Win's sake if nothing else. But I hadn't hoped for someone who might understand me or who I might understand in turn. I poured us each a measure of rum and raised my glass. "To a better world and those who fight for it."

"And to a time when we'll no longer have to."

Chapter Thirty-Four
March 17 – April 12, 1776

March trundled on with wind, snow, rain, and sun by turns, as March is wont to do. With each rainy or sunny day, we watched the ice on the St. Lawrence. As soon as it broke up, ships from England would arrive with troops for Canada's defense. I had never prayed for continued cold and snow before, but I did so then.

Prayers for our own reinforcements remained largely unanswered. General Wooster arrived from Montreal on April 1 to take charge, but he brought only a small relief force—not nearly enough to attempt a second assault on Quebec. Although both Generals Wooster and Arnold were from New Haven, Connecticut, they agreed on almost nothing. Just after the fighting had begun in Lexington and Concord, Arnold had rallied his foot guards and demanded powder from the New Haven powder house. Wooster, who had been Arnold's superior, had refused to give him the keys, only relenting after Arnold had threatened to break down the door. Clearly, General Wooster, once again the superior officer, still held this against General Arnold. The only thing they did agree on was that we needed more men and ready money. Both were out of cash; paper Continentals were worthless; General Arnold's scheme to sell the Loyalist goods had come to nothing; and his credit would extend no further.

Because of our lack of specie, food was hard to come by, and very little in the way of foodstuffs arrived from General Schuyler. The Canadians were not willing to sell to us for Continental script, and after four months, there was nothing left to hunt or gather. Rations were cut further, and we all cut new notches in our belts.

April 2 dawned sunny and warm, the first truly warm day we'd had, and we cautiously removed our winter coats, hoping we wouldn't need them again. I squelched down the muddy track to St. Roch, reveling in the feel of sun on my face. I was to examine the men of Remy's regiment for signs of smallpox. They were due to return home when their extended enlistments expired later in the month, and I was loath to send infected men home to spread the disease further.

The regiment had a house on the outskirts of St. Roch, though I preferred to conduct my examinations outside where the light and air were better. I had my fingers on a man's glands when shouting and gunfire echoed from behind Quebec's walls.

"What on earth?" We all paused, and when the sounds rose again, the men grabbed their muskets. I found myself beside Remy and Paul. Renewed shouting arose. I could have sworn I heard "Capture them!" yelled between bursts of gunfire.

"Prison break!" shouted General Arnold as he burst from Menut's Tavern and ran for his horse. "To arms and attack!"

Part of me wanted to stop him. I knew he shouldn't ride into battle with that leg, but the other part of me admired how well his leg had recovered. It had been just over three months since the injury.

General Arnold's horse reared. Though he hauled on the reins, he was unable to bring the horse back down. Unbalanced, the horse lost its footing in the slick mud and fell directly onto General Arnold's newly healed leg.

"General!" I hesitated. I hadn't spoken to him since the drumming out, trying to reconcile the leader I had started to admire with the man who had allowed two men to be humiliated. Dr. Warren's ghost appeared at the general's side, the first time I'd seen his ghost since Jacatacqua and I had sought answers from him. The look he gave me was a silent reprimand.

"Every human being deserves our care," he'd once told me when I asked how he could treat Tories who disparaged him in public but sought his help in private. "It doesn't matter a man's politics or what he's done. If he's injured or ill, he is our responsibility."

It didn't matter what he'd done, General Arnold needed my aid.

By the time we reached him, the horse had pulled itself up, but General Arnold lay moaning in the mud, white-faced, his jaw clenched and sweat beading his brow. I knelt at his side. "Don't move, General."

There was no blood, which was good, but when I pressed my fingers against his shin, he jerked, making a sound that was part groan, part moan, and part curse. Dr. Warren frowned, shaking his head. I probed as gently as I could. The bones had refractured.

"General, we need to move you to the hospital. Paul and you two there, I need you."

I gasped as General Arnold grabbed my arm. "Wait! The prison break! If we don't aid our men—"

Hoofbeats heralded General Wooster's arrival. Below his oversized gray periwig, he already wore his customary sneer, which didn't bode well for General Arnold. George jogged up just behind him.

"It's a false alarm, Arnold," General Wooster said. "Just Carleton trying to lure us, lure *you,* into attacking."

"How can you be certain?" General Arnold demanded, hand tightening around my arm, my bones protesting.

"Unlike you, I make proper use of my Rangers. Private Lee here can confirm."

General Arnold swung his steely eyes to George, who nodded. "From our position, we could see over the walls. There's no prison break."

My heart fell a little.

General Wooster's sneer transformed into a disdainful and mocking look of pity. "Always acting before you think, Arnold. I doubt this is the last time your rash behavior and brash personality will lead you to injury and humiliation." He waved his hand dismissively at us. "Take the general to the hospital."

"Carefully," I said before General Arnold could argue. The men lifted the general slowly, but he still sank his teeth into his lip when he came off the ground.

Dr. Senter was out when we arrived. I sent a sister to find him, but I wasn't going to wait. True to form, General Arnold refused any rum or laudanum. I set the bones quickly in hopes of causing less pain.

"You must stay off it, sir. You must remain abed for at least a week, perhaps a few days longer."

"I'll get a second opinion on that." That rankled even though I knew he would have said the same to any doctor, male or female.

When Dr. Senter examined the leg, he told General Arnold not to move from bed for ten days.

"I prefer Dr. Endicott's diagnosis. A week, wasn't it? A week and not a day longer."

When General Wooster visited the next day, he radiated smugness under his pompous periwig. "Dr. Senter tells me you are to remain immobile for at least the next week. You are no longer effective at your post."

General Arnold struggled into a sitting position. I took hold of his shoulder to prevent him from rising further.

"I can still serve."

"Not in the field," said Wooster.

"I am not an invalid!"

General Wooster looked pointedly at General Arnold's leg.

"General Arnold will be back in the field in a week, sir," I said. I wasn't quite sure why I was defending him or advocating for him to leave his bed. The goods he'd claimed, the drumming out . . . Shouldn't we have more upstanding officers? But many of the officers I'd met—General Wooster, Colonel Allen, Major Brown—gave me no hope for such. It occurred to me then that I had been waiting for a perfect officer to lead us. A Henry V. But Shakespeare had given even that heroic general-king faults.

There would be no paragon of virtue coming to lead our cause.

I looked down at General Arnold, his fury at inaction and at General Wooster's implications. Despite setbacks and injuries, he was still fighting. We might not be given a better officer to lead us.

"And the next time the same leg is injured?" General Wooster asked. "Besides, we might not have a week for him to recover. If we're ready to attack before then, I cannot be short an officer. I need my officers in the field, and I need them now."

I bit back my question: With what men was he planning to attack Quebec?

"I will not retreat, sir," General Arnold said. "I will not leave Canada. Not until there is no hope of victory. I will . . . I will take charge of Montreal."

General Wooster considered for a moment before agreeing. "As soon as you can sit a horse, Montreal is yours."

"Thank you, sir." General Arnold saluted. Without returning the salute, General Wooster left. General Arnold, face growing redder with each passing moment, held the salute until long after General Wooster was gone.

"Sir, please, won't you lie back down?"

Muscle twitching in his jaw, General Arnold did as I asked. "If it'll get me out of this bed and on the way to Montreal sooner, I'll take some of that opium. This constant pain is unbearable."

Surprised that he would admit any sort of weakness, I gave him a dose and left another on his bedside table before going about my other duties.

"Dr. Endicott."

"Yes, sir?"

"When I leave for Montreal, I would like you to accompany me. I will need a doctor, and I want one I can trust."

"You want one who said you can leave bed three days sooner."

General Arnold smiled. "Perhaps that is a contributing factor, but you have also proven your loyalty and good sense. Will you come?"

My first thought was it was because I was a woman. He wished to keep an eye on me in case I proved incapable where a man would succeed. But then, if Wooster found me out, I doubted he'd be half as accepting. General Arnold had not only allowed me to keep practicing, but he had protected me from Brown and Easton. If I went with him to Montreal, I'd be further out of their reach. My next thought was for our patients, but most suffered from smallpox. All we could do was make them comfortable and wait for them to recover or succumb. My last thought was of Win, but there was nothing I could do for him either, and being this close to him and helpless was a slow torture. Then there were Dr. Warren's last orders: stay with Arnold.

"Of course I'll come, General."

It didn't take me long to pack my few belongings, even with the extra clothes I had inherited from Win's things. I wore his spare trousers and hunting shirt, my own clothing having been consigned to rags with my first black coat.

It took me far longer to make my farewells. Dr. Senter and I discussed the few patients I'd be leaving behind and how to treat those ill from smallpox. April's warmer weather and the melting snow meant mud and flooding, which put our quarantine area in danger of being swamped. I promised to continue trying to persuade General Arnold to allow us to inoculate if Dr. Senter did the same with General Wooster.

"We'll have an easier time convincing the ice to remain on the St. Lawrence," Dr. Senter joked, but neither of us found much humor in the thought.

I assured Jacatacqua the nuns would deliver her baby when the time came and thanked her again for her help. She pressed several more sachets of spirit herbs into my hands. "Good luck, Whitley, in finding your solution."

Suzannah was harder to leave. Though I was not as close to her as I had been to Jemima, with each farewell I was realizing that, once again, I would be a woman alone among men.

"Good luck, Whitley." Suzannah hugged me tightly. "Stay safe."

"You, too."

"I'll be fine. We're to leave soon since our enlistments are up. It's home to Pennsylvania in a few days."

"If I ever find myself in Pennsylvania, I'll visit."

It was difficult to pin down George since, as a Ranger, he was sent out to scout and forage, but I caught him one evening just outside St. Roch when he was returning from upriver.

"You're leaving?" His voice was full of disbelief, and an expression too fleeting to catch passed over his face.

"Someone has to keep General Arnold out of trouble. So you have to promise me you won't get yourself injured or killed."

"I'll do my best, Doctor." He had schooled his face once more, a mask of cold light and sharp shadows in the deepening dark. He cleared his throat. "I shall miss your company and your friendship."

"You still have my friendship, George. I'm just farther away. We'll see each other again."

"Sooner than later if the British have anything to say about it. The ice is breaking up."

Fear spiked through me, and I grasped George's hand. "Then you be extra careful, George Lee."

He stared at my hand, holding his, and I let go. He dropped his hand to his side, fingers flaring out before tightening into a fist. "I will. Good night, Doctor."

"Good night, George." Watching him walk alone into the falling night, I couldn't help but think I had failed him somehow or was failing him by leaving him alone once more. I could only hope he believed everything I'd told him and that I'd see him again soon.

I told Remy the next morning. I found her washing clothes outside her regiment's house.

"Who thought you'd be leaving first? Though in a few days, Paul and I will head south."

"Stop in Montreal on your way."

Remy threw her soapy arms around me.

"Remy! Someone will see!"

"I'm in skirts, Whit. Women hug. And if I can't hug the doctor who saved my life, who can I hug?"

I straightened my waistcoat and jacket. "And what will Paul think?"

Remy laughed. "You think I haven't already told him you're a woman?"

"What?"

Remy's smile faded. "I told Paul."

"That wasn't your secret to tell." Panic spiked through me. All it would take was one incautious word, and I would be dismissed.

"He was already suspicious because you'd been helping me since Fort Ti." Remy lay her hand on my arm. "Paul can keep a secret, Whit."

"I'm sure he can." I tried to calm myself, but so many people knew who I really was, it was hardly a secret anymore. "It's just, too many people know who I am. Maybe it's a good thing we're all splitting up."

"Those of us who know would never put you in danger, Whitley. You can trust us."

"I know." And I did, and I trusted Remy and Paul, but the more people who knew, the less control of my future I had.

"I'm sorry, Whit. I should have asked you first."

I shook away the anxiety she had raised in me. "It's all right. If he saw through your disguise, he was bound to see through mine."

She hugged me again. "Be safe."

I squeezed her tightly, trying to imprint the feel and sight of her on my memory. Who knew when I would see her again? "You, too, Rem."

She kissed my cheek. "When this is over, come visit us in Albany."

The afternoon before General Arnold and I were to leave, I took tea with Mother Marie-Catherine. "So, ma fille, you are leaving us."

"I am. I never thought I'd say this, but I'll miss this place. I'll miss you."

"Oh, ma fille." She covered my hand with hers. "You have done good work here, but now you are needed elsewhere."

"I know, but I wanted to say thank you. I wasn't very kind when we first arrived, and I was wrong to fear you just because you worship differently. It is the same God we believe in after all."

"It is, ma fille."

"We couldn't have made it through the battle or the winter without you. I will always remember the peace and aid I found here, Mother. Merci."

"De rien, ma fille. I hope—"

"Help! Someone help!"

The shouts came from the hospital.

Sergeant Joseph Grier stood in the middle of the surgery surrounded by my ghosts, wild-eyed, Suzannah in his arms. Her head lolled back, and her middle was covered in blood.

"Suzannah's been shot! Help her!"

"Lay her here," I ordered. Jemima followed to the table, hovering by Suzannah's head.

Suzannah moaned. Sergeant Grier gripped one of her hands, but her other hand flapped against my arm. "Whitley. Whit."

"It's all right, Suzannah." I pulled open her shirt and stopped. She was gut shot.

The ball had entered through her lower back, tearing a hole nearly two inches wide just below her ribs. The soft lead of the ball had flattened upon striking her, and as the misshapen ball had torn through her organs, it had reduced them to a pulpy mess. Ribs shattered beyond repair, fragments of clothing twisted among the wreckage.

"Do something, Doctor! Save her!"

I shook my head, helpless tears clouding my eyes. "I'm sorry, there's—"

Before I could finish, Jemima grabbed my head with both hands, the familiar rush of cold paralyzing me. Instead of whispers of conversations past and mercurial memories assaulting me, howls of grief reverberated through my mind.

This was her second possession. One more and—I fought to speak, to make my inner voice heard over the tempest of her grief. "Jemima—"

But she was beyond hearing me. I felt her do what Kit, Jedediah, and Dr. Warren hadn't. Her fingers rifled through my brain, and I saw my own memories flicker by: Da smiling proudly as I first used a saw, Win's face when I told him I knew his secret, Dr. Warren's hands on mine as I examined my first patient. Jemima pulled my medical knowledge to the fore and, holding out my hand, demanded, "Needle and thread! Now!"

"Dr. Endicott," Mother Marie-Catherine began, but Jemima cut her off. "I'm not losing her, dammit! Get me a needle and thread!"

Mother Marie-Catherine took me by the shoulders, dragged me back from the table. "Dr. Endicott, there is nothing more you can do for her but cause her more pain."

"But she can't—she's supposed to go home!" In her anguish, Jemima's voice sounded like neither hers nor mine. "She's supposed to live!"

Mother Marie-Catherine's face was heavy with sorrow as she set a hand against my cheek. "It is a different home she is being called to now, ma fille."

"No!" My eyes blurred with tears I couldn't control. Jemima jerked me away from Mother Marie-Catherine and threw us to Suzannah's side. Sergeant Grier was whispering to his wife, pleading with her. Blood pumped from her wounds, ran down her sides, pooled on the table, dripped to the floor. Jemima's fingers were still in my memories, and suddenly we were back in Boston on a cold, February night, kneeling in bloodstained snow, Kit's pale face growing paler, and me helpless with my bloodstained hands.

"Why don't you do something?" Jemima screamed at Dr. Warren, Kit, and Jedediah, who stood around the table. She swung my glare to the living—the nuns, Dr. Senter. "Do something!"

Even if I'd known how to calm her, stop her, I wouldn't have. I wanted to rage at the war that kept taking friends from me as much as she did. But if she didn't stop soon, the living witnesses to her grief would start to think me mad. Jemima screamed incoherently, her impotent rage ripping up my throat. My eyes fell back to Suzannah, her slowly paling face.

With a wordless sob of rage, Jemima grabbed a sheet and pressed it against Suzannah's stomach. If we could just stop the bleeding.

Suzannah breathed out, her body falling still, a stillness from which there was no recovering. Sergeant Grier's head dropped to the table, shoulders shaking with sobs.

If ghosts had hearts, Jemima's broke then. Her sorrow cleaved through me, leaving both my inner self and my physical body gasping. Tears already flowing, Jemima flung us through the hospital and out the back door. We fell to my hands and knees, the muddy ground squishing between my fingers, like so much cold blood.

"You failed," Jemima rasped. "How could you? After I helped you, *saved* you, how could you fail her?"

My inner voice was drowned under the torrent of her grief. But even if it hadn't been, how could I have explained there was nothing that could have saved Suzannah? Sometimes doctors were just as helpless as everyone else.

Jemima ripped herself from me, and the cannonball that had killed her tore through me once more. I scrabbled at my neck for the pouch of herbs, but I wasn't fast enough and retched up the tea from earlier. Between heaves, I pressed the pouch to my nose, breathing deep and banishing the black spots of unconsciousness dancing before my eyes. Wearing the herbs clearly wasn't enough; I had to be able to breathe them in if they were to have any effect.

The weight of failure and guilt, unavoidable as Suzannah's death might have been, pressed me deeper into the mud. I sank my teeth into my lip to keep from screaming while my body shook, and tears soaked my face and collar. Suzannah was gone. Another debt laid to my account. What if I never earned the life I had stolen from death?

"Dr. Endicott."

Why couldn't they have given me more time? Didn't they know I was grieving? But as Jemima had once said, war was no place for grief. I spat the gunpowder taste Jemima had left from my mouth, tucked the pouch away, wiped my eyes and nose on my sleeve, and blinked up at General Arnold, who, for once, was using his cane.

"You should still be in bed," I managed.

"You said a week. It's been more than that. And I'm taking the opium and using the bloody cane, but I suppose nothing is ever enough for you doctors."

I knew he wanted me to laugh or at least smile, but I couldn't even dredge up a fake smile, not with Jemima's grief and my own still roiling through me. Not when, ten yards in front of me, the muddy ground had been broken for a mass grave. Soon, all those whose bodies had been kept in the winter storage chamber would be interred in this ground. Suzannah would join them.

"She shouldn't have died."

"That's war," General Arnold said. I was ready to snarl at him for his harsh words, but his face was lined with the same heaviness and despair I felt. "When war is waged, people die. That is an inescapable fact. I need a doctor who won't fall apart when a life is lost."

"It's Suzannah." I had to justify the scene Jemima and I had made. "She was supposed to go home and . . . Her death just seems so senseless."

"So we must give meaning to her death, to every death and sacrifice. We must ensure we are victorious, so their deaths will not have been in vain. That's why we keep fighting even when it seems impossible that we could succeed. None of those who have given their lives would want us to give in now, and those of us still fighting and risking our lives do so knowing if we fall, others will carry on the fight. Will you carry on with us?"

I knew what my answer had to be, what Dr. Warren expected of me. Besides, I had come too far to turn back now. Like George had said, if we wanted a better world, we had to be willing to fight for it. "I will."

"Then these are the last tears I will see from you. We leave at first light."

So soon. No time to mourn or grieve when there was still an enemy to face. I stared at the grave before me. Death was done taking from me. Tears still drying on my cheeks, I stood, wiped the mud from my hands, and faced General Arnold. No more tears would fall. Death would not have that satisfaction. "I'm ready, sir. Lead and I'll follow."

Chapter Thirty-Five
April 12 – May 6, 1776

We arrived in Montreal amid a thick fog, which transformed the once-familiar streets into a foreign landscape. Buildings loomed around us, hollow now that many of the residents had fled, and the streets were as empty as our stomachs. I took up residence in the same apothecary I'd used in the autumn, but what stores had been left then were long gone. I had only the instruments I'd brought with me and whatever I could scrounge, for there wasn't money for food or arms, let alone medical supplies.

I wrote immediately to General Schuyler and Dr. Stringer, pleading for medicines. I carried the letter to Château Ramezay, General Arnold's headquarters. The door to his office wasn't quite closed, and the voices trickling out made me pause before I knocked.

"How much specie do we have, Major Franks?" General Arnold asked.

"Not even £300, and a good portion of that is my own money," Major David Franks, one of General Arnold's new aides, replied. He was Jewish, the first Jewish person I'd ever met, and I was glad that my months living among the nuns had taught me to be more open-minded when it came to religion, for he was one of the most intelligent people I'd ever met. Behind his glasses, he had two different-colored eyes, one brown and one greenish-blue. "This is the last of my own money. I'll try my credit. I can try yours as well, but word will have travelled from Quebec how overextended you are."

A sigh. "And how I'll ever pay it all back, I don't know. Unless Congress sends money and wages."

"Perhaps the commissioners General Schuyler mentioned in his most recent letter will bring money from Congress."

"And perhaps the St. Lawrence will reverse its flow and drag the British back to England." Another exhale. "Try your credit, Major, but the money is to be used only for food or gunpowder."

"Eavesdropping, Doctor?"

I started. Captain James Wilkinson, the second of General Arnold's aides, stood behind me, smirking. There was something snakelike about him, perhaps his narrow eyes or how often he licked his lips. I liked him far less than Major Franks.

"Just didn't want to interrupt, Captain."

He snorted and reached around me to knock.

"Yes?" came General Arnold's gruff and annoyed voice.

Captain Wilkinson pushed the door open. "The doctor was skulking in the corridor, sir."

"Not skulking, sir. I didn't want to interrupt. I have a request for supplies, as we have no medicines, and illness is rampant."

"I am well aware of what illness is doing to our troops." General Arnold took my letter and held up another. "You should be receiving some help soon, Doctor. General Schuyler writes a general hospital has been ordered for Canada, so more surgeons and supplies should be on their way."

"A general hospital?" With what money would we build and maintain a hospital? What about the threat of British reinforcements? Surely they would arrive any day, and we didn't have the strength to repel them.

"I know," General Arnold said, as if he could read my mind. "Let us hope our aid does not arrive too late. I shall send on your request, Doctor."

"Thank you, sir." I hoped these Congressional commissioners Major Franks had mentioned brought answers.

They arrived April 29, just when our situation was becoming truly desperate, and we weren't sure how we were going to continue to feed the army. But at least one of the commissioners, we were sure, would have a solution.

At seventy years of age, Dr. Benjamin Franklin was accompanied by Samuel Chase, Charles Carroll, and Carroll's cousin, who was a Catholic priest.

Upon their arrival, I joined the remaining population of Montreal in trying to catch a glimpse of the world-famous man. The cannons fired a military salute as the boat docked, and I wondered if General Arnold begrudged the waste of gunpowder. Everyone cheered and waved as the commissioners entered the city. I caught a glimpse of a balding head and a glint of glasses but no more. The commissioners continued down the Rue Notre-Dame to the Château Ramezay, cheered all the way.

I was not important enough to be included in the festivities at the château, for which I was mostly glad, though I regretted missing what was certain to be a fine meal, probably the last one in Canada. With more men arriving daily and no food arriving with them, rations were barely enough to take the edge from our hunger. I remembered the young officer who had negotiated the surrender of Fort St-Jean. I hoped we could keep the same good humor when our rations were cut again, and the enemy was at our gates.

There was a knock on my door the next morning. I was expecting General Arnold, thinking he'd finally pushed his still-healing leg too far or was in need of more opium. But it wasn't. I blinked, sure I was seeing things. Balding, well bellied, glasses perched on the end of his nose, Dr. Benjamin Franklin stood on my stoop leaning heavily on a cane.

"Dr. Franklin! How can I help you?"

"General Arnold said if I was seeking a doctor, you were the one to see." Though he had not lived in Boston for many years, he still had a Boston flavor to his speech, which had me swallowing back a sudden swoop of homesickness. He studied me from head to toe. Clearly, a young man in a hunting shirt, patched trousers, and much-mended boots was not what he had expected. "You are Dr. Endicott, yes? He said you were young."

"I am Dr. Endicott. Please, come in." I showed him to a chair, noting his gait and how he winced with each step. Gout. As he settled himself, grimacing even more, I prepared and poured tea. He inspected it critically. "Nothing stronger?"

"Not if you wish for the swelling and pain in your legs to decrease."

"I'm seventy years old, Doctor, and have trekked an ungodly number of miles to this desolate place. I should think I've earned the right to drink what I wish."

"Not while you're with me. Especially since I have nothing stronger and no money to buy it with."

He humphed and sipped his tea. "A doctor should not diagnose until he is asked."

"A man should not seek out a doctor unless he wants a diagnosis."

Dr. Franklin chuckled. "Well said." He held up his tea. "Anything else you would recommend?"

"Avoid rich food, wines, port, and get lots of rest. Keep your legs up."

"I was afraid you'd say that. The food will be easy here, but resting, that will not be possible." He sipped again, made a face, and set the cup aside.

"There is one other matter you can help me with. I have erupted in a large number of boils which make traveling more than a little uncomfortable."

Dr. Franklin situated himself on the table while I fetched my lancet. I opened each boil and drained it. Then I dug out the dead tissue, washed the boils with turpentine, and bandaged them. It was not a comfortable process, and Dr. Franklin was not as stoic as General Arnold. He hissed and swore creatively at each lancing and turpentine application. When I finished, he looked at the chair with longing, but sitting would not be comfortable for a while.

"Is there anything Congress can do for you, Doctor?"

"More food, men, supplies, another doctor or two, and as much specie as can be had."

"I was hoping you had more realistic needs."

"You've already spoken to General Arnold, then."

"Early this morning. He laid out the situation very starkly, very matter of fact. The man is certainly no politician."

I laughed at the thought of General Arnold as a politician, but my levity was short-lived. "I know our situation is dire. We won't be able to hold Canada, will we?"

Dr. Franklin's expression was grim. "Rumors have reached us that at least a dozen Royal Navy ships have entered the St. Lawrence. The Canadians will not join us, and it's impossible to transfer enough men to Canada to counter the British force."

"Yet we stay?"

"We must hold them in Canada for as long as we are able, then hold Lake Champlain after that. If the British take the lake and sweep down the Hudson, our cause is lost."

It was a sobering thought. So much rested on our men. Our very ill men.

"There is one thing Congress could do for me, sir."

"And that is?"

"Order General Arnold to allow me to inoculate our men against smallpox."

"I don't know if I have the authority to make that decision without a vote by all of Congress, and by the time that happens—well, just ask Mr. Adams how his suit for independency is coming. I can, however, speak to General Arnold and try to convince him inoculation is in our best interest."

"Thank you, sir. Please, return daily so I can reapply the turpentine and change the bandages."

Dr. Franklin eyed the bottle of turpentine with resignation but agreed.

That afternoon, General Arnold came to see me.

"How's the leg, sir?"

He waved away my question. "Begin your smallpox inoculations, Dr. Endicott. We can't lose any more men to this damned disease."

"Thank you, sir! I will begin immediately." I wrote Dr. Senter with the good news, but our inoculations were too little, too late.

Our new commanding officer, General John Thomas, a tardy replacement for General Montgomery, arrived in Canada the next day, May 1, and was in Montreal by midafternoon. To say he was unhappy to find me inoculating our troops was far too mild.

"What are you doing? Who ordered this?"

"General Arnold, Dr. Franklin, and myself. Men have been succumbing at an unsupportable rate."

"What am I to do with ill men? You will cease inoculations immediately, Dr. Endicott. I will be having words with General Arnold about this."

"But if we don't inoculate—"

"You will cease inoculations, Doctor, and that is an order! Any man found inoculating himself or another will be shot on sight! Is that clear?"

I almost asked what he would do if a woman gave the inoculations, but I refrained. Instead, I gritted my teeth. "Perfectly clear, sir."

Over the next few days, several companies arrived, bringing their doctors with them. The 4th Pennsylvania was led by Colonel Anthony Wayne, who seemed just as determined and battle-smart as General Arnold, and with them was Dr. Samuel Kennedy. Colonel Arthur St. Clair brought the 3rd Pennsylvania and their surgeon, Dr. Rogers. Dr. Merrick arrived with a regiment from Massachusetts, Dr. Lewis Beebe with Colonel Enoch Poor, and Dr. Stephen McCrea with another New York regiment. I was glad to see more doctors, but they pushed straight on to Quebec.

Another unit that gave General Arnold hope was the rest of Colonel Bedel's regiment of Rangers, led by the gruff, rough, thirty-nine-year-old Lieutenant Benjamin Whitcomb. He reminded me a little of Captain Morgan, and I felt a fresh pang of loss and worry for Win and all the men still held prisoner behind Quebec's walls.

But the extra men, much like the inoculations, were too little, too late. On May 6, three frigates loaded with British troops anchored at Quebec, and our retreat began.

Chapter Thirty-Six
May 6 – June 18, 1776

General Arnold summoned me to Château Ramezay, where the general, his aides, and George waited.

"George! What are you doing here?"

"Ships, Dr. Endicott," General Arnold cut in. "Ships have reached Quebec."

It took me a moment to follow what he was saying. "British reinforcements? How many?"

"Too many. Generals Thomas, Wooster, and Thompson have already begun our retreat." Then, to his aides, "Is Lieutenant Whitcomb still in Montreal?"

"I believe so, sir," Major Franks said, adjusting his glasses. "And the rest of Colonel Bedel's regiment as well."

"Captain Wilkinson, find me Colonel Bedel and Lieutenant Whitcomb. Private Lee, I want you to go back toward Quebec and keep me apprised of the British movements. You know the countryside well; do not get captured. Dr. Endicott, prepare the wounded and ill to evacuate to St-Jean and then Île aux Noix. Start sending them on as soon as you can."

I almost groaned at the thought of returning to the Isle of Noise. General Arnold had never been there, so he couldn't know what an unsuitable location it was, but he dismissed us before I could say a thing. In the corridor, I stopped George. "Remy and Paul?"

"Left over a week ago."

A small mercy. They would be safe, but George was headed right back into danger. "George—"

"I'll be careful." For a moment it looked like he might say more, but he only added, "You be careful, too, Doctor."

While George returned east, General Arnold sent Colonel Bedel's regiment to Fort Cedars, but Lieutenant Whitcomb was sent south, first to Fort St-Jean, then Fort Ti, then to meet General Schuyler.

Though worry for George hung in the back of my mind, I couldn't spare him more than a thought and prayer before sleep. Men were still falling ill, and those too ill to move needed care. I had no medicines, no blankets, no beds for them. The barracks were soon overcrowded with the ill, and the growing heat as summer approached did nothing to improve conditions. My ghosts watched with pity, and I was just as helpless as they were.

Not only did the ill need care, but they needed to be evacuated—a daunting task, for there was no way to keep them comfortable on the journey and too few doctors to aid me. When more ill men arrived from Quebec, I was relieved that Doctors Kennedy and Merrick were with them. Both were experienced doctors and looked with dismay at the rows of ill.

"The two of you will travel with as many of the sick as can be moved to Île aux Noix," I told them.

"We paused at that isle on our way north," Dr. Merrick said, brows pulled low. "Do they truly intend to keep ill men there?"

It was good to hear straightforward Massachusetts common sense again. Unfortunately, the army was no place for such. "I'm afraid so. If they'll allow it, send the men on to Fort Ti as soon as possible. Here are my notes on the isle from this fall. Hopefully, they help."

Amidst all this, troops from Quebec arrived in disarray, having retreated with nothing more than they could carry. With the barracks full of ill men, the effective men camped wherever they could throughout the town. It reminded me of Cambridge the previous spring, and I wondered how Da and Lem were faring.

"Dr. Endicott!" Dr. Senter wove through the soldier-crowded streets to the barracks door, his journal peeping out of his pocket and a wagon trailing him.

"Dr. Senter! Good to see you."

"Are these all the ill?"

"No. Many have already been sent on to St-Jean or maybe even Île aux Noix by now under the care of Doctors Kennedy and Merrick. As soon as the wagons return, I'll send more, but there are some who cannot be moved without risking death."

Dr. Senter was silent for a moment, eyes traveling over the sick. "Those too ill to move under their own power had to be left behind at Quebec."

"What?"

"We had to choose—to move them and sentence them to almost certain death or leave them behind to the mercies of the British. Which was the lesser evil?" Guilt imbued his every word.

Horrified, I stared at the sea of men before me. How soon would I be forced to make the same choice? There were over a hundred ill men in the barracks, closer to two hundred, and moving many of them would prove fatal. A little flutter of panic started in my chest, but I crushed it. I had promised General Arnold strength, and these men needed me to be strong, too. As did Dr. Senter. I set a hand on his shoulder, and he took a shaky breath. He said, "I pray the British treat them well. Their fate is out of our hands now. We have a more pressing problem."

He led me back outside to the wagon, and I stared in disbelief at the man lying there.

General Arnold stormed up the street. "Where the hell is General Thomas?"

"Here, sir." Dr. Senter and I stepped aside for General Arnold, who took in the sight of General Thomas lying in the wagon bed with just as much disbelief as I had.

General Thomas attempted a smile, but a shiver drove it away. "I'll do what I can from my sick bed, but you should write General Schuyler in case I don't recover."

When he spoke, the beginnings of a rash were visible on his tongue. He was only in the early stages of smallpox, but already there was nothing we could do.

General Arnold motioned Dr. Senter and me a few steps away. "What are his chances of survival, Doctors?"

Dr. Senter and I exchanged a look. Dr. Senter said, "It's almost impossible to say. In these conditions, not good."

"And even if he does recover, the disease will take at least two weeks to run its course, and he will be much weakened after. Write General Schuyler."

"Damn it all to hell," General Arnold said. Casting one more look at General Thomas, he walked slowly back up the street, more Atlas than Achilles, with the weight of our entire enterprise on his shoulders.

We moved General Thomas inside and began making the rounds with tea. Having someone else to share the workload was a relief, but the relief was short-lived.

A council was called the next morning. With General Thomas ill, General

Wooster took charge once more, sweating beneath his wig and the pressure of expectation.

"We need to make a stand," he declared, and General Thompson thumped the table in agreement.

To my surprise, General Arnold disagreed. "We don't have enough men to risk in battle. Too many of our troops are ill. We should pull back to Fort Ti and prepare to defend the lake."

"Leave Canada?" General Wooster sneered. "Without even attempting a defense? By all reports, the British force behind us doesn't have overwhelming numbers."

"All reports?" General Arnold said. "I thought you made proper use of your Rangers, General. My scout reported the British far outnumber us, perhaps by as many as four to one, especially when you consider half our men are ill!"

The scout had to be George, and relief flooded through me. He was alive and still free.

"More of our men are arriving daily from Fort Ti and points south," General Wooster pointed out.

"And we have nothing to feed them!" General Arnold exploded. "In my last letter to General Schuyler, I told him to hold any more troops at Fort Ti because they'll starve if they're sent here!"

"Enough!" snapped General Wooster, his periwig slipping sideways. "You are outnumbered, Arnold. We will make a stand at Trois-Riviéres. General Thompson, you will command. Take Colonel Wayne's and Colonel St. Clair's regiments with you. Dismissed."

I had not been asked for troop reports, but neither had I been told to accompany the expedition to Trois-Riviéres. I wondered why General Wooster had invited me to the council unless he had intended for me to go and General Arnold had distracted him.

I hurried out before he could belatedly assign me to the attacking force. I had no desire to be present at what was certain to be a doomed effort. If George was in town, I wanted to see him before General Arnold sent him off again. I caught the general at the door. Before I could ask about his scout, he flung the door open, startling George, who stood on the other side.

"George!" I cried.

But he hardly glanced at me. "Sir, the Cedars has fallen, and the garrison, the rest of Bedel's regiment, were captured."

"And General Wooster has just ordered more of our men to die or be captured at Trois-Riviéres. Canada is lost or soon will be." For a moment only, resignation bowed General Arnold's shoulders. Then he straightened, determination blazing from his eyes. "We must take what steps we can to save our army."

Rations were cut and cut again. I replaced my belt with rope because it was easier to keep adjusting. Although my bindings were no longer hiding much of anything, I continued to wear them. I would take no risks.

General Thomas worsened, and on June 2, he died. That same day, the remaining commissioners—Dr. Franklin had left three weeks ago—fled from St-Jean. I sent Dr. Senter to St-Jean with the ill men who could still be moved.

"Don't wait too long to join us, Dr. Endicott." He clasped his ink-stained fingers around mine.

"I'll leave when General Arnold does."

"Are you sure that's wise?" George asked after Dr. Senter left. "You don't think he'll wait too long?"

"He won't allow himself to be captured." If nothing else, I was confident of that.

Amid the chaos, a delegation of thirteen Oneida Indians arrived. It was, I learned, due to their influence that the Kahnawake had remained neutral, so we owed them much. However, General Arnold had no time to show them around, so the task fell to Major Franks. The Oneida were an impressive sight. Their clothing was a mix of hand-sewn skins and English dress, and contrary to my expectations, they were dressed soberly, no warpaint or bare skin. They carried both muskets and bows and arrows, and like our Rangers, tomahawks and knives hung at their hips. I had the opportunity to meet them when Major Franks brought them to the hospital. The major adjusted his glasses, peering at me with his variegated gaze. "Dr. Endicott, the Oneida are curious to see how your medicine works."

"Right now, it isn't working well at all," I said, blocking the entrance to the hospital. "I cannot let you inside unless you have all had smallpox."

The Indians all took a step back, fear in their eyes. Clearly, they knew the dangers of the disease. "You have no cure for this?" one asked.

"No. None of our medicines work, and I would not see you who have done much for us with the Kahnawake fall victim to such a cruel disease."

They looked pleased at my concern for them and, thanking me, followed Major Franks away. They didn't stay in Montreal long, and they had departed by the time our new commanding general, John Sullivan, arrived on June 5. He had no idea of our situation and too much false confidence. George, stationed at Château Ramezay, said General Sullivan and General Arnold argued as often as they met.

They didn't have long to argue.

Well after dark on June 8, I retired to my apothecary and stripped down to my shirt and trousers. Spending all day in the steamy barracks had left me achy, miserable, and itchy. I pressed a cool washcloth to my throat, red with heat rash, and couldn't wait to remove my bindings.

Before I could, the noise of countless feet and voices rose in the streets. Groaning, I retied my cravat and pulled on the rest of my layers. The night was cooling quickly, and a glance up told me it would remain dry, a blessing.

The source of the noise was easily discovered: the remainder of the men who'd been sent to Trois-Riviéres had returned, exhausted and mud-covered, led by Colonels Wayne and St. Clair.

"Doctor!" Colonel Wayne called out. "We have wounded!"

I didn't want to bring them to the barracks. There'd be no sense in exposing them to illness. Instead, I led them to the public storehouse, evicting the soldiers who had claimed the space. I sent one man for the generals and had others gather all the candles and lanterns that could be found. Two more brought me a table, and rolling up my sleeves, I began my work.

Only when Generals Sullivan and Arnold arrived did the story of the battle come out.

"It was a disaster," Colonel St. Clair said. His chestnut hair was darkened with sweat and mud, and his blue eyes flashed with anger. The right corner of his mouth naturally turned down, making him appear even more irate. "Our guide led us straight into a swamp. General Thompson was captured; the retreat was chaos. We have men spread from here to Trois-Riviéres."

"We're vastly outnumbered," Colonel Wayne added. He was round-faced, sharp-nosed, and carried an energy his compact form couldn't contain. "There were twenty-five ships on the river—twenty-five! And who knows how many troops on the ground. Canada is lost. We must retreat."

General Arnold stabbed a finger at General Sullivan. "The might of the British army is coming, sir. Give the order to retreat!"

General Sullivan hesitated before finally nodding. "But only as far as St-Jean. We have no orders to abandon Canada altogether."

General Arnold's jaw tightened with displeasure, and Colonels St. Clair and Wayne openly exchanged disbelieving glances. I was certain, however, General Arnold could bully General Sullivan into retreating further when the time came.

General Arnold began spitting orders. "This will be an ordered retreat! We will take everything useful. Those are General Schuyler's orders. But there shall be no looting of personal property. Make sure your men know this. Everything is to be properly labeled and sent on to Colonel Moses Hazen at Chambly. I shall see to this personally. Dr. Endicott, get the ill and wounded out of here."

"Sir, some are too ill to travel."

General Arnold pinched the bridge of his nose. "Then we'll have to leave them behind."

The words rang in my ears like the tolling of a bell. I was glad I had sent Dr. Senter on. He had already been forced to abandon men once and shouldn't have to do so again.

It was the hardest thing I'd ever done, choosing who would stay and who would travel on. Even once I had chosen and the men were loaded into wagons, George had to pull me away from the barracks door.

"Standing here won't change anything. You've done all you can, Doctor."

"I'm abandoning them. What if the British—"

"Don't." George's voice was tight. "If they have no mercy for the ill, what will that mean for their prisoners? We must have faith."

He was right. I had to believe they would be cared for. I had to.

"I—" George cleared his throat and tried again. "I don't think I appreciated until this moment what you did when you inoculated me. Everything you've done for me." He swallowed hard, throat bobbing. His blue eyes met mine. "Thank you, Whit."

He'd never called me Whit before, not even Whitley. I wanted to celebrate, throw my arms around him, kiss his cheek, but I remembered his reaction when I'd taken his hand. Blinking rapidly, I smiled. "You're family, George. No thanks are necessary."

George and part of Colonel Wayne's 4th Pennsylvania regiment acted as guards for our wagons of ill men. As soon as the ill were unloaded at St-Jean, the wagons were sent back to Montreal for the goods General Arnold was taking from the city: woolens and silks; tin and nails; flour, molasses, and rum. Everything was carefully and clearly labeled and sent to Colonel Moses Hazen at Fort Chambly with specific instructions to guard and store the goods carefully until they could be moved to St-Jean. Like the goods in St. Roch, these were not taken from supporters, but from empty houses or merchants with promises of repayment. General Arnold kept a meticulous list of who was owed what.

We left at the head of the last column of retreating Americans. The men in the last wagon said they had seen the British entering the city when they were only a couple miles away.

But when we reached Chambly, it was clear Colonel Hazen hadn't followed General Arnold's orders at all, for we found the goods in a heap and much depleted by plundering. General Arnold reprimanded Hazen but could take no more time to sort out the mess. The British weren't far behind us.

The goods were loaded onto the *Royal Savage* and a few bateaux captured with St-Jean in the autumn, and sent immediately on to Fort Ti. The sick and wounded were slowly shuttled to Île aux Noix, but General Sullivan would not hear of moving the rest of the army. As our troops prepared defenses, the rest of the doctors went on to Île aux Noix. I remained behind in case of wounded and to keep an eye on General Arnold's leg. He was still taking opium to control the pain, and I worried the drug would mask any warning signs so that by the time he came to me, it would be too late.

But his leg held and, to compound miracles, he convinced General Sullivan to make a full retreat to Île aux Noix. St-Jean was stripped, and the process of transferring the army to the island began. Our eyes constantly turned north, expecting at any moment to see Governor Carleton's troops cresting the horizon or coming down the river.

June 18 dawned sunny and dry. Our campaign had been beset by cold and wet weather almost since the moment we touched Canadian soil, yet as we stood on the banks of the Richelieu River loading the last of the bateaux to retreat to Île aux Noix, the sun shone brightly.

The last of our men loaded the munitions into the flat-bottomed bateau, then dropped to the deck, too exhausted by our retreat and the lack of food to stand for a minute more. I remained mounted on Portia beside General Arnold. I wasn't sure how well my own legs would support me, and it would do the ill men no good to see their doctor collapse. I peered down river to where Île aux Noix awaited us, where George and Major Franks and the rest of our weary army were already encamped. General Arnold had volunteered to take the rear guard and, not wanting to risk abandoning any more ill men, I had decided to remain with him.

The general, however, was not looking ahead but behind.

I couldn't help but remember our arrival here nearly a year ago when we had captured the *Betsy* and much-needed medical supplies. We'd had so much hope then, led by the intrepid Arnold—hope of not only holding Fort Ti but of bringing Canada into our struggle as well.

"Where did we go wrong?" General Arnold murmured. "What could we have done differently?"

I was no military strategist, but I thought it was easy to see the path of our mistakes. We should have started the campaign earlier in the year, for it had taken us far too long to reach Quebec, leaving us little choice but to stage a desperate attack, which had cost us a general and over four hundred of our men. Our treatment of the Canadians, as I had witnessed in Montreal, had done us no favors either. We'd had too few men, supplies, and arms. The list of all the ways this campaign had gone wrong could have filled a book. It was a miracle we had lasted so long.

General Arnold certainly knew this, but he shook his head. "It should have so easily been ours."

If there was anyone who shouldn't blame himself for how this had fallen out, it was General Arnold. "You did all you could, sir. No man could have asked more of you."

"But could I have asked more of myself?"

What more could he have given? He'd sacrificed his own wealth and health, sustaining a serious injury, and had continued to fight. Any other man would have said he had done more than enough and would have returned home to the comfort of his family, but not General Arnold. And where many men would have been looking back in despair, determination glinted in General Arnold's battle-forged gaze.

Captain Wilkinson rode up, his tongue nervously wetting his lips. "Sir, the British are only a few miles away. We must depart."

General Arnold stared at the horizon, unmoving. Captain Wilkinson's horse danced under him. Portia shifted and snorted. I patted her neck. "Calm, girl. We'll go soon."

"Sir?" Captain Wilkinson said, licking his lips again, eyes darting back toward Fort Chambly and the approaching British.

A haze blurred the horizon.

Not a haze. Dust raised by the British.

General Arnold stared at the oncoming enemy, jaw set and a hand on his pistol.

"Sir," I said. "We must retreat. To fight now would make a good ending for one of Shakespeare's plays but would do our cause little good. There will still be battles to fight in the days ahead, and you will be needed."

"Worthy of Shakespeare, eh?" General Arnold almost smiled, hand dropping from his pistol. "We'll have to make that ending a reality another day, then."

He finally turned away from the British to our overloaded bateau, crowded with prone men, packs, and the last of our gunpowder.

"The horses won't fit," he declared. "And we will not leave them for the enemy to use."

Dismounting and drawing his pistol, he shot his horse square between the eyes before either of us could speak. Captain Wilkinson and I exchanged a shocked glance. General Arnold's face remained expressionless, but a muscle in his jaw twitched. Then my shock turned to horror as General Arnold held out his pistol to me.

I slid from my saddle, hand trailing along Portia's neck. She had carried me faithfully through the cannon barrages at Fort St-Jean, through the bitter winter, and through our hurried retreat. She was more a friend and comfort than transportation. She pressed her nose into my shoulder, and I scratched between her ears.

With my other hand, I drew my own pistol. Dr. Warren had given me the pistols as we prepared to leave Boston the morning this war began. "To defend your patients, should the need arise," he'd told me. "I know you will use them well."

Use it well. I couldn't use it to shoot Portia. She was loyal and healthy, and her warm, earthy-smelling head was pressed trustingly against me.

"I can't do it," I said, stepping back, slowly petting Portia for the last time. "I'm still a doctor, sir, and I can do no harm."

"Then I will do it for you. We will not leave her for the British to profit from." General Arnold gave me a moment to turn away. I clenched my teeth, trying to block my mind. But I couldn't block out the sound of the shot echoing over the river and lodging in my heart. My eyes filled, but I blinked the tears back. I had promised General Arnold I was done with weeping. Still, I couldn't bring myself to turn around to see what had become of my poor horse.

"'O sweet Portia,'" I whispered. "Adieu."

"Wilkinson," General Arnold said.

"Sir—"

"Either you shoot the horse, or I shoot it for you."

I drew three measured breaths before the report of a third shot cracked the air.

"Into the boat, men."

I stepped aboard, careful not to catch the fingers of any half-conscious man under my boots. Only after I was seated did I dare look back ashore. My eyes skipped over Portia and the other two horses, not taking in more than a blur of red and brown. One more reminder that this campaign had cost us far more than we had gained.

My gaze gravitated to General Arnold, the only American soldier still on Canadian soil. But for the grief in his eyes, grief echoed in my own heart, there was no sign he was leaving in defeat. Back straight and gait steady, he stepped into the boat, reached back with his right foot, and pushed us off.

I studied General Arnold's profile, proud and unflinching, as we sailed away from Canada. He faced forward to the Richelieu and Lake Champlain beyond, his eyes no longer dwelling on the failure we left behind but instead on what lay ahead. I hadn't been sure of him at first, but as I studied him, I knew he was worthy of the trust Dr. Warren had placed in him. He had his faults, but his valor and his determination to succeed could not be matched. He took risks where others would stand down, saw possibility where others saw only obstacles, and time and again, he had shown he would do whatever was necessary to further our cause. If Dr.

Warren could not fight with us, I was glad General Arnold held the fate of our cause in this northern outpost in his hands.

Because Canada had fallen, and the British were coming.

Historical Note

Any work of historical fiction is a product of two time periods: the one it is about and the one in which it is written. Inevitably, the beliefs, morals, and values of the modern age shade the thoughts, actions, and words of the characters in this book. The facts, however, are as close as I can make them to reality, and most of the people mentioned were real people. Having said that, there are times when the historical truth must be altered, stretched, or shifted to fit the confines of a fictional story. So, allow me a few notes and corrections.

Female Physicians—During the 1700s, there would have been no female doctors in what would become the United States. Women would have worked as midwives. In fact, doctors practicing obstetrics was a fairly new development in the practice of medicine (one which Dr. Warren was taught and did practice). During the war, women would have taken on some nursing duties, but there was no organized system of nursing either on or off the battlefield. That would not develop until the American Civil War.

The first female to receive a medical degree in the United States was Elizabeth Blackwell, who obtained her degree from Geneva Medical College in 1849. Earlier, there was the remote possibility of a woman earning a degree in Europe. Laura Bassi received a doctorate in science in 1732 from the University of Bologna, Italy, and became the first female professor, and Dorothea Erxleben received her medical degree from the University of Halle, Germany, in 1754.

Age—It may seem that Whitley is too young to be working. However, at this time, children would have been working in the house from a young age, especially if they were not in school, and there is evidence that starting a career or apprenticeship early was not unheard of. Benjamin Franklin began working for his father when he was taken out of school at the age of ten, and then he was apprenticed to his brother at age twelve. Two of the British generals who served in the French and Indian War—General James Wolfe and General James Abercromby—began their military careers at ages thirteen and eleven, respectively.

Dr. Joseph Warren—Dr. Warren's role in the years preceding the American Revolution and that fateful spring of 1775 has largely been ignored or unknown until quite recently, with credit for events during those early years going to men like Samuel Adams and Paul Revere. However, Dr. Warren's impact and legacy are undeniable, and it is impossible to know how much greater that impact would have been had he lived beyond the Battle of Bunker Hill.

Because of his large practice and crammed schedule, Dr. Warren often had two apprentices, but never did he have a female apprentice, and there is no likelihood that he would have taken one on. Likewise, there is no evidence (at least that I am aware of) that he and Miss Scollay lived together before he sent her and his children out of Boston in the spring of 1775. She had the sole care of his children during the early years of the war and suffered great financial difficulties but was later involved in a custody dispute over the children with Dr. Warren's mother and brother. In this book, and the books to follow, I have set Dr. Warren's house on Hanover Street. In fact, between 1761 and 1775, Dr. Warren owned or rented four different properties within Boston. The house used in this series, the Green House, was the property Dr. Warren rented from 1770–72, which coincides with when Whitley began her apprenticeship.

Dr. Warren fought on June 17, 1775 only six days after his thirty-fourth birthday, in what has come to be known as the Battle of Bunker Hill (though it was fought on Breed's Hill, hence the confusion of terms when Whitley receives word of the battle). He had indeed been suffering from one of his chronic headaches and had not had proper sleep for several days. Against the advice and pleading of friends, Dr. Warren joined the battle. He had narrowly escaped death at Menotomy (as is mentioned in this novel) and probably was not in a condition to fight. He was dressed as described in this novel, and his official commission as general had not yet come through. As the retreat began, Dr. Warren, though wounded, made sure he was last, fighting to cover the retreat of the other soldiers. In the last minutes of battle, Dr. Warren was struck under the left eye by a musket ball, an immediately fatal shot. There was confusion on the Patriot side as to his fate for several days, but the British knew immediately whom they had killed, and, at battle's end, they mutilated his body and buried him in a shallow mass grave atop Breed's Hill.

Dr. Warren left behind a medical legacy in his apprentices, many of whom (like David Townsend and William Eustis) became important not only in Massachusetts medicine but government. His brother John was also one of his apprentices. John's descendants became some of the first doctors in Massachusetts and have continued to practice medicine from the 1700s to the present day. Dr. Warren also left behind a military legacy through his younger daughter Mary's descendants. A Warren descendant has served in every major war in United States history. His legacy also includes his writings, including the Suffolk Resolves, and orations and letters. Several of his direct quotes (like Mrs. Adams's recitation in Chapter Two and the "who would waste a coward thought" line) are used in this novel.

Christopher Seider and the Boston Massacre—It is widely believed that Christopher (Kit) Seider's death on February 22, 1770, and the following funeral, which was turned into a propaganda event by the Patriot side, helped lead to the Boston Massacre (or Bloody Massacre as it was then known). On March 2, 1770, a brawl between soldiers and Bostonians broke out at a rope walk (rope-making), and already-high tensions rose higher. Over the next few days, there were fights between soldiers and Bostonians across the town. On March 5, 1770, the Boston Massacre occurred, and five men, Crispus Attucks, Samuel Gray, James Caldwell, Samuel Maverick, and Patrick Carr, eventually died as a result. In the following years, the anniversary of the Bloody Massacre was honored with an oration from a notable Patriot of Boston, and twice, in 1772 and 1775, Dr. Joseph Warren was asked to be the speaker.

Samuel Gore, mentioned in the opening of this novel, was actually nineteen years old when he was wounded on February 22, 1770.

Benedict Arnold—Benedict Arnold had genuine respect for Dr. Warren, and though they only knew each other for a few days, they developed a strong and deep friendship. Arnold's relationship with Ethan Allen was as fractious as his relationship with Warren was cordial. It was Allen's account of the capture of Fort Ticonderoga that got out first and was widely believed, and it was not an account that cast Arnold in a good light. Allen did hand over command of the fort and lake to Arnold, as is depicted, and Arnold was removed from command himself at the same time he learned of his wife's death. Her death left him a single parent of three young boys. Their care fell to Arnold's sister, Hannah, when he returned to duty.

Although not detailed in this novel because Whitley does not experience it, Benedict Arnold's march up the Kennebec River was a heroic feat. The maps Arnold had were purposely misleading, turning what he thought would take a couple weeks into a two-month slog through uncharted rivers, swamps, and mountains. The troops who completed the march under Arnold were dedicated to him, body and soul.

In this novel, General Arnold is depicted as having looted in St. Roch. There is no evidence of this, but, as is seen later in his career, Arnold did enjoy the comforts of life and felt he deserved them. He was later accused of looting Montreal, which led to a court-martial in the summer of 1776.

Arnold's injury at the Battle of Quebec was miraculous in that it was not worse. Had the musket ball shattered the bones, it is very possible Arnold would have lost his leg. His injury paired with General Montgomery's death put an end to any hope of victory at Quebec.

Names of Groups and Armies—Roughly two political groups existed in the years leading up to the American Revolution: the Tories and the Whigs. These political groups began in England (during the English Civil War and the Glorious Revolution of the 1600s) and carried over to the colonies. In the most basic terms, Tories were more supportive of the king and Parliament, and in the colonies, many Tories became what we think of today as Loyalists—those who supported the British in the war. On the opposite side, the Whig party grew with the Puritan movement and was less supportive of the king and Parliament. In the colonies, many Whigs became Patriots, supporting the American cause for independence. Of course, members of both political parties also remained neutral during the war.

At the outset of the American Revolution, the colonists would have referred to the British soldiers as Regulars, Redcoats, Lobsterbacks, or Bloodybacks if they were being insulting, as the colonists were British citizens and considered themselves to be British. Through Whitley's thoughts, I try to show the changing views and use of *British* vs. *Regulars*. The army would not have been referred to as *the British Army*, at least at the outset of the war. They would have been called Parliament's Army or the Ministerial Army.

The American side is more confusing. The army began as a conglomeration of separate militias, and militias continued to serve alongside the Continental Army throughout the war. The army started out as the Army of the United Colonies and slowly changed to the Army of the United States and the Continental Army.

Homosexuality—By the time of the American Revolution, every colony (or soon-to-be state) had anti-sodomy laws, making it both dangerous and illegal to be a homosexual. While there were some safe spaces for those of the LGBTQIA+ community and an underground culture, most public opinion and practices were anti-homosexual, especially if people were caught in sexual acts. While there seemed to be harsher punishments for those of lower classes, it was dangerous to be an active member of the LGBTQIA+ community no matter which colony/state you lived in or your social standing.

Lieutenant Frederick Gotthold Enslin was the first soldier court-martialed and subsequently drummed out of the Middle Department of the Continental Army for "attempting to commit sodomy." On March 15, 1778, he was paraded before the army, his coat turned inside out, and he was drummed out of camp with the order never to return. This was the basis for this novel's fictional drumming out of John Malcolm and Michael Boyd.

Women in the Continental Army—Although Whitley and Remy/Rebekah are fictional, Suzannah, Jemima, and Jacatacqua were real women who served during the Canadian campaign. Throughout the American Revolution, other women such as Sybil Ludington, Anna Maria Lane, Deborah Samson, and Lydia Darragh were soldiers, spies, and suppliers of water and ammunition during battles. Women also made saltpeter, sewed clothing, and ran homes and businesses away from the battlelines.

Medical Practices of the 1700s—There were few ready-made medicines at the time, and each doctor, apothecary, midwife, and many housewives had their own recipe book of medicines. Opium was used for many ailments. Both laudanum and Dover's powder were both made using opium.

Broken bones were a much more serious injury than they are today, and most compound fractures would have resulted in amputation. Arnold's fears of losing his leg at Quebec were well founded.

Smallpox was the greatest threat to the health of American soldiers during the American Revolution. The process of inoculation was as it is described in this novel, and despite having been around for years (Reverend Cotton Mather was a proponent in the 1720s), inoculation was still seen as radical. While inoculation could have made all the difference to the Canadian campaign, it was not allowed until it was far too late. Mass inoculation did not start until General Washington ordered it during the winter encampment at Valley Forge in 1777.

Retreat from Canada—The retreat from Canada was much more chaotic and confusing than what I laid out. Not only did who was in charge change at least four times in three months, but none of the leaders agreed or got along, and smallpox, hunger, desertion, and shortages continued to plague the army. General Arnold was also much more active in those last weeks, not sitting safe in Montreal.

Acknowledgements

"Let me give humble thanks for all at once."
Queen Margaret, *Henry VI, Part III:* act 3, scene 3

Thank you first to the team at Beaver's Pond Press, especially to my project manager, Alicia Ester, for your guidance in getting this book from my computer screen and into readers' hands. You have taken what could have been an overwhelming process and made it smooth and easy to navigate—thank you for a great introduction to the publishing world.

I could not have produced this book without my amazing editor, Kerry Stapley. I am so thankful to work with an editor who shares my excitement for and belief in Whitley's story, and has done so from the very beginning. Thank you for your prompting and questions, which helped me fill the gaps I couldn't quite see and bring Whitley's world to life.

A great deal of thanks is due to the VCFA community, those magical writers and illustrators, who made sure I knew I, too, was a writer—a real one—and who helped me grow and flourish. To my advisors—Shelley Tanaka, Sharon Darrow, Amanda Jenkins, and Susan Fletcher—what I learned from you was invaluable and continues to influence my writing daily. To my Craftographers: thank you for all the late-night conversations, craft talk, and laughter. I could not have asked for better classmates and fellow writers to journey with.

Gratitude is also owed to those who help preserve history so that we might not only learn it, but read it, hear it, and experience it. I want to especially thank the staff and reenactors at Fort Ticonderoga. Thank you for your work in preserving this fort and bringing it to life every day. Your dedication, demonstrations, and willingness to answer very specific and random questions helped shape my Fort Ti and its inhabitants.

To my local library, the Worthington branch of Nobles County Library: thank you to the staff—past and present—who provide such great services for our community, and who have provided me with not only countless books but a comfortable writing space.

To my family—immediate and extended—thank you. Curtis, I don't know how many versions of this novel you read, but thank you for each reading and the insights you offered. And thank you so much for designing and illustrating the amazing cover! Tyler, thank you for the sticker design and creating the maps—they are perfect. Mom and Dad—thank you for making reading, writing, and theater priorities as we grew up and for nourishing a love of stories in all of us. Thank you also for your support from my first efforts in crayon and construction paper until now. Thank you for reading, editing, and being travel companions.

To all of my friends who have cheered for, supported, and asked after me and my writing—thank you. Becca, if you hadn't been teaching *Johnny Tremain* when I started teaching at Worthington, I never would have deep-dived into the American Revolution, and this book would not be. Thank you also for listening to my writing woes and joys and reading/editing for me. Linda, thank you for all your support; nothing is more stimulating on a Saturday morning than conversations about ghosts on the Speech bus. Carrie and Kia, thank you for your support and enthusiasm. I always know I can count on you for a quick chapter read, an opinion, and a good book discussion.

Sources and Further Reading/ Listening/Watching

This is not a comprehensive list of books or other resources I used in the writing of this novel (see next section), but if you are interested in learning more, these would be my top recommendations.

NONFICTION BOOKS

Anderson, Mark R. *The Battle for the Fourteenth Colony: America's War of Liberation in Canada 1774–1776*. Lebanon, NH: University Press of New England, 2013.

Di Spigna, Christian. *Founding Martyr: The Life and Death of Dr. Joseph Warren, the American Revolution's Lost Hero*. New York: Broadway Books, 2018.

Ellis, Joseph J. *The Cause: The American Revolution and its Discontents, 1773–1783*. New York: Liveright Publishing Corporation, 2021.

Philbrick, Nathaniel. *Bunker Hill: A City, A Siege, A Revolution*. New York: Viking, 2013.

Waldvogel, K.M. *Spies, Soldiers, Couriers, & Saboteurs: Women of the American Revolution*. Waukesha, WI: Orange Hat Publishing, 2019.

DIGITAL BOOKS

Henry, John Joseph. *An accurate and interesting account of the hardships and sufferings of that band of heros, who traversed the wilderness in the campaign against Quebec in 1775*. Lancaster, PA: William Greer, 1812. https://archive.org/details/accurateinterest00henr.

Senter, Isaac. *The journal of Isaac Senter, physician and surgeon to the troops detached from the American Army encamped at Cambridge, Mass., on a secret expedition against Quebec, under the command of Col. Benedict Arnold, in September 1775.* Tarrytown, NY: Abbatt, 1915. https://archive.org/details/journalisaacsenter00sentrich.

PODCASTS

Liz Covart, *Ben Franklin's World*, produced by Colonial Williamsburg Innovation Studios, https://benfranklinsworld.com.
This podcast covers a wide variety of topics on Colonial and Early America with a new guest speaker for each episode.

Mike Duncan, *Revolutions*, produced by Mike Duncan.
This podcast covers revolutions throughout history (beginning with the English Civil War). The American Revolution is covered in season two.

Michael Troy, *American Revolution Podcast*, produced by Michael Troy, http://blog.amrevpodcast.com.
This podcast is a step-by-step, chronological, in-depth journey through the American Revolution and has an accompanying blog with maps and links.

WEBSITES

American Battlefield Trust. 2024: https://www.battlefields.org.
This website contains descriptions of battles, maps, and biographies of important figures. They also work to preserve battlefields of the American Revolution and Civil War.

Founders Online. National Archives. https://founders.archives.gov.
This website contains the digitized correspondence of seven Founding Fathers.

Journal of the American Revolution. 2024: https://allthingsliberty.com.
A website dedicated to researching the American Revolution, with articles by numerous contributors on a wide variety of topics; they also run a podcast.

Forman, Samuel A. Dr. Joseph Warren on the Web. http://www.drjosephwarren.com.
This website contains digitized copies of Dr. Warren's letters and Boston Massacre Orations, among other information.

LECTURES, VIDEOS, AND SHOWS/MOVIES

American Revolution Institute of the Society of the Cincinnati. 2024. https://www.americanrevolutioninstitute.org.
This institute and museum holds frequent in-person talks on various subjects of the American Revolution and digitizes many of them, so the lectures/presentations are available on their website.

Revolutionary Spaces. 2024: https://revolutionaryspaces.org.
A merger between the Bostonian Society and the Old South Association brings Old South Meeting House and the Old State House together. In their online experience, they frequently hold panel discussions on various topics related to the American Revolution, which can be found on their website.

Sources Used

Forbes, Esther. *Johnny Tremain*. Evanston, IL: McDougal Littell Inc, 1997.

Longfellow, Henry Wadsworth. "Haunted Houses." Poets.org. American Academy of Poets. https://poets.org/poem/haunted-houses.

Randall, Willard Sterne. *Benedict Arnold: Patriot and Traitor*. New York: Barnes & Noble, Inc., 1990. p. 189.

Shakespeare, William. "The Tragedy of Hamlet, Prince of Denmark." In *The Riverside Shakespeare, Second Edition: The Complete Works*, p. 1183–1245. Edited by G. Blakemore Evans. Boston: Houghton Mifflin Company, 1997.

Shakespeare, William. "The First Part of Henry the Fourth." In *The Riverside Shakespeare, Second Edition: The Complete Works*, p. 884–927. Edited by G. Blakemore Evans. Boston: Houghton Mifflin Company, 1997.

Shakespeare, William. "The Third Part of Henry the Sixth." In *The Riverside Shakespeare, Second Edition: The Complete Works*, p. 711–747. Edited by G. Blakemore Evans. Boston: Houghton Mifflin Company, 1997.

Shakespeare, William. "The Merchant of Venice." In *The Riverside Shakespeare, Second Edition: The Complete Works*, p. 284–319. Edited by G. Blakemore Evans. Boston: Houghton Mifflin Company, 1997.

Shakespeare, William. "A Midsummer Night's Dream." In *The Riverside Shakespeare, Second Edition: The Complete Works*, p. 251–283. Edited by G. Blakemore Evans. Boston: Houghton Mifflin Company, 1997.

Warren, Joseph. "Warren's 1775 Boston Massacre Oration in Full Text: Our Country Is In Danger but Not To Be Despaired Of." Dr. Joseph Warren on the Web. Samuel A. Forman. http://www.drjosephwarren.com/2015/03/warren's-1775-boston-massacre-oration-in-full-text-our-country-is-in-danger-but-not-to-be-despaired-of/.

Warren, Joseph. "When Liberty is the Prize, Who Would Shun the Warefare?" Dr. Joseph Warren on the Web. Samuel A. Forman. http://www.drjosephwarren.com/2014/11/when-liberty-is-the-prize-who-would-shun-the-warfare/.